Other People's Houses

LORE SEGAL

The New Press
New York

For my Mother, Franzi

Published in the United States by The New Press, New York
Distributed by W. W. Norton & Company, Inc.,
500 Fifth Avenue, New York, NY 10110

Previously published in hardcover by Harcourt Brace Jovanovich in 1963. A paperback edition was published by Plume Books in 1973.

Most of the contents of this book appeared originally in *The New Yorker*, in somewhat different form. A portion of Chapter Three appeared in *Commentary* under the title "Games à la Mode, 1938."

LC 63-13508
ISBN 1-56584-143-3

Established in 1990 as a major alternative to the large, commercial publishing houses, The New Press is the first full-scale nonprofit American book publisher outside of the university presses. The Press is operated editorially in the public interest, rather than for private gain; it is committed to publishing in innovative ways works of educational, cultural, and community value that, despite their intellectual merits, might not normally be "commercially" viable. The New Press's editorial offices are located at the City University of New York.

PRINTED IN THE UNITED STATES OF AMERICA

94 95 96 97   9 8 7 6 5 4 3 2 1

CONTENTS

Preface ix

Part 1

Part 2

Preface

I did my first writing—I mean writing that understood itself to be *writing*—when I was ten years old. I was one of five-hundred Jewish refugee children housed in Dover Court Camp on England's east coast. We were waiting to be distributed among English foster families.

Before I left Vienna, my father had stood me between his knees and said that I must ask the English people to get my parents out of Austria— also my grandparents, also my aunt, and my twin cousins. I said that I would.

I was being sent on an experimental children's transport to test whether the Nazis would allow a trainful of Jewish children to cross the border. My mother has since told me that she had urged my staying, our living or dying together. My father had determined that I must get to safety, and that I would save them. My mother says that after they came home from the railroad station my father went to bed and lay ramrod stiff for two days.

That winter of 1938 was one of the coldest in English memory. I sat in my coat and gloves and wrote a letter. It was a tearjerker full of symbolisms—sunsets, dawns, and the rose in the snow outside the window, "a survivor," I wrote, "wearing a cap of snow askew on its bowed head." The letter made its way to the refugee committee, which found my parents a job and got them the sponsors and visas to emigrate to England, proving that bad literature makes things happen. On my eleventh birthday, in March 1939, my parents visited me in Liverpool, where I was living with my first foster parents. They went on to the south of England, and their job as "a married couple," that is, a cook and a butler.

My letter had another effect: I had become, without knowing it, a writer. I remember walking around that cold camp, in love with my own words, rehearsing over and over my purple sunsets, thrilling to that clever frozen rose.

I did my second piece of writing later that same year. It frustrated my foster parents (in the book I call them the "Levines") and all their visitors, that a refugee from Hitler didn't understand Yiddish however loudly they spoke it. It frustrated me that no one seemed to understand what might, at that very moment, be happening to my parents. I bought one of those school books with a purple cover and a white label with a red border in which English school children do their homework, and I filled its thirty-six pages with my Hitler stories. It was the novelist's impulse not to explain or persuade but to force the reader's vision: See what I saw, feel what it felt like. It was also my first experience of the writer's grief that what happened on the paper was not what I had intended. As poor J. Alfred Prufrock puts it, "That's not it at all. That is not what I meant, at all." So I added several sunsets. Ruth, the youngest of the Levine daughters and my particular friend, got someone to translate it into English. It made Mrs. Levine cry. I sat and watched her.

1940 and wartime. My father, along with all male German speakers over the age of sixteen, was taken away and interned on the Isle of Man. My mother and I moved from what had been designated a "protected area," and was out of bounds to "enemy aliens." I was twelve. When my mother and I arrived in the ancient market town of Guildford, I was throwing up. Between bouts I lay on a bed in a narrow room at the head of a steep stair, and my mother read me *David Copperfield*. Right then the concept *writer* burst upon me. *This* was what I was going to do. It did not occur to me that I'd been doing it since I was ten.

I came to New York in 1951 and took a class in "creative writing" at the New School. I couldn't think of anything to write *about*. The Holocaust experience, it seemed to me, was already public knowledge; I had read about it in the papers and seen it in the newsreels at the movies. It was at a party that somebody asked me a question to which my answer was an account of the children's transport that had brought me to England. It was my first experience of the silence of a roomful of people listening. I listened to the silence. I understood that I had a story to tell.

I am at pains to draw no facile conclusions—and all conclusions seem facile to me. If I want to trace the present from the occurrences of the past I must do it in the manner of the novelist. I posit myself as protagonist in the autobiographical action. Who emerges?

A tough enough old bird, of the species *survivor,* naturalized not in North America so much as in Manhattan, on Riverside Drive. Leaving home and parents gave strength at a cost. I remember knowing I should be crying like the little girl in the train across from me, but I kept thinking, "Wow! I'm off to England"—a survival trick with a price tag. Cut yourself off, at ten years, from feelings that can't otherwise be mastered, and it takes decades to become reattached. My father died in 1945, but the tears did not come until 1968, when David, my American husband, insisted I owed myself a return to my childhood. I cried the whole week in Vienna, and all over the Austrian Alps.

Finally, I'll posit two oddities that, I think, attach to the survivor: an inappropriate anxiety, together with an inappropriate happiness. The former tends to keep me out of the movies. I've sat next to American friends and felt them cozy themselves into that communal darkness for the pleasure of suspense—a suspense I experience as disagreeable. Is it because history tells me that the barrel of the gun into which the fellow on the screen is staring *will* go off in his face? It did go off. We were there.

And what makes my mother distrust the monthly statement from her bank? She goes down, lines up at the counter, and tells the bank officer that there must be a mistake. He calls up her account on the computer and the account is correct. My mother comes home and says, "It's a mistake. I *can't* have this much money." My mother can't accommodate the happiness of having what we need.

Lore Segal
New York
March 1994

The "Carter Bayoux" of my book once told me a story out of his childhood. When he had finished, I said, "I knew just where your autobiography stopped and fiction began."

He said, "Then you knew more than I."

Part 1

CHAPTER ONE

Vienna: A Liberal Education

"Did you read this, Igo?" my Uncle Paul asked at dinner in the autumn of 1937. "Another speech and Hitler can put Austria in his pocket. I know the university; it's ninety per cent Nazi."

"A lot of Socialist propaganda," said my father.

My mother's brother Paul, who lived with us in Vienna and was twenty-six, a medical student, and generally avant-garde in his thinking, liked taking extreme positions in order to prick my father, who was forty-two and an accountant, to his predictable platitudes.

"You're talking about a handful of lunatics," said my father.

"We Jews are a remarkable people," Paul said. "Our neighbor tells us he's getting his gun out for us, and we sit watching him polish and load it and train it at our heads and we say, 'He doesn't really mean us.'"

"So what should we do? Go and hide in the cellar every time some raving lunatic in Germany makes a speech?"

"We should pack our rucksacks and get out of this country, that's what we should do," Paul said.

"And go to the jungle, I suppose, and live off coconuts. According to your brother, Franzi," my father said to my mother, "every time a raving lunatic in Germany makes a speech, we should go and live off coconuts in the jungle."

"Is it going to be war?" I asked my mother, aside. I had a sick feeling in my stomach. I knew about the First World War. I had

3

a recurring nightmare about my mother and me sitting in a cellar with tennis rackets, repelling the bullets that kept coming in through a horizontal slit of window.

"No, no, no. Nothing like that," my mother said.

I tried to imagine some calamity but did not know how. My mother was ringing the bell for Poldi, the maid, to bring coffee. I decided there must not, there could not, be anything so horrible that we would have to pack and leave everything. I stopped listening to the grownups.

On the eighth of the following March, I had my tenth birthday. On the twelfth, Hitler took Austria and my mother called Tante Trude a cow.

Tante Trude, a cousin of my father's, and her husband, Hans, were having dinner with us and had arrived with the news that Chancellor Schuschnigg had abdicated in favor of Hitler. When Paul called a friend, the editor of a Socialist paper, for confirmation, he was told, "Not yet." We ate with the radio on, and suddenly the music was interrupted for a short speech by Schuschnigg, which ended with the words: "And now I say good-by to my faithful friends and compatriots and wish them all a bearable future." Then they played the Austrian national anthem for the last time: *"Sei gesegnet ohne Ende, Österreich, mein Vaterland."*

"They're playing it slower than usual," Tante Trude said. "Franzi, don't you think they are playing it slower than usual?"

"They're probably using the record they always used," my mother said.

"How can you say so, Franzi, and you a musician. Listen, Hansi! Igo! Don't you agree with me, they are playing it slower than usual?"

"Trude, you are a silly cow," my mother said. "Don't you understand what has happened to us?"

"What has happened?" I asked.

"Hans, our coats," Tante Trude said. "You heard what she called me, and in front of the child."

Everyone was standing up. "Trude, I apologize," my mother said. "We're all nervous tonight." But Tante Trude was already walking out of our front door.

Very early the next morning, my parents took me downstairs and we stood in a long line of people outside the bank at the corner; the bank did not open. All around us in the street were young men in strange, brand-new uniforms, saluting each other with right arms stretched forward. It was a clear, sunny March morning. Bright new flags were flying, but my parents hurried me back home.

By May, Poldi, the maid, had to leave our Jewish employ. My father was given a month's notice at the bank where he had worked as chief accountant for twelve years. A week later, an S.S. sergeant commandeered our ugly, tall, lightless flat and all its furnishings, including my mother's Blüthner piano. My father, who had to remain in the city until the end of the month, went to stay with Kari and Gerti Gold, good friends of my parents, who offered him the use of their now empty maid's room. My mother and I went to the country to live with my favorite grandparents, and I had the happiest summer of my life.

My grandparents lived in a big village near the Czechoslovak border, some twenty kilometers from Vienna. I used to think the village was called Fischamend after the great bronze "fish on the end" of the medieval tower that stood on the central square, cater-corner from my grandfather's shop, but now I rather think it took its name from its geographical location at the point where the River "Fischer ends" in the Danube.

Our house was huge, old, and rambling, with thick walls. The ground floor was taken up by my grandfather's dry-goods store. The first week, I amused myself by messing with the rolls of fabric on the shelves in the storeroom behind the shop, where my grandmother made dirndl dresses and aprons for sale, until she told me to run along and see my grandfather.

Out in the shop, I danced on the counter until my grandfather got down the box full of ribboned medals and picture post cards *"vom Grossen Krieg"* (from the Great War) as a treat for me. There were pictures of men in peaked caps and mustaches, and ladies looking over their rosy shoulders out of oval clouds, but I preferred the drawers full of shoelaces, buttons, hairbrushes, and catgut for violin strings. One day I found a violin behind the boxes of gum boots, but the whole summer's searching never turned up the bow.

My grandfather told me to run along out to the yard, and he lent me his young salesgirl, Mitzi, who was standing idle, to play with. Mitzi and I would sit on the sunlit outhouse roof, sucking the little sour grapes from the huge vine that grew and twisted like a thick, tough snake along three walls of the square yard and was too ancient to ripen its fruit. We talked for hours, or, rather, I talked. I told Mitzi my life plans. I was going to look like her when I grew up; Mitzi was fifteen. She had fair hair, a fine country color, and a pretty, petulant mouth. Mitzi was my only friend in Fischamend until Paul got thrown out of the university.

My Uncle Paul was the hero of my childhood, a role in which he by no means recognizes himself. He says he remembers himself as shy, except in his own set, with a tendency to fall over his own feet, but precocious. He says he was one of those clever kids who have a mission to enlighten their benighted parents and expose the foolishness and knavery of all the world. Paul punished his anti-Semitic teachers by failing his examinations, so that when the Nazis dismissed Jewish students from the Vienna university, he was still one semester short of his medical degree.

Paul was a slim young man with a rich head of hair. Old ladies embarrassed him by commenting on his immense violet-blue eyes. What a pity, they said, they were hidden behind glasses. He carried his long, witty nose with an air of melancholy.

It was Paul, not my father, who had been the man in my life: Our affair, dating from my birth and based on a mutual enthusiasm, was an entirely happy one. In the evening, before my light was put out, this Paul, who hobnobbed by day with his glamorous friends, artists and revolutionaries all, sat by my bedside and initiated me into what was going on in politics, science, and poetry. For light entertainment, he would sing the four-footed German student songs, accompanying himself passably on his guitar and taking, every once in a while, a lip-smacking draught from an imaginary stein of beer.

Or we talked about me: Paul encouraged me in drawing and

painting, for which he said I, unlike himself, had an interesting talent. He was a fair audience for the impressionistic dances encouraged at my dancing school, though, after some hours, he might thank me and tell me he had had enough and wished to be left alone to get on with his studies. If I persisted, he slapped me roundly and looked into my face with such frank and genuine irritation that I went away, unprotesting, to find my father and tease him for a while, but there was not the same satisfaction in it.

The only treachery my uncle had ever perpetrated upon me was a bicycle tour he took the summer before Hitler, into the Austrian Tyrol and across the Alps into Italy. He went with his own friends. I was not invited.

Hitler put an end to that. There was no gadding about after Paul arrived at Fischamend late in May, sneaking into the yard by the back door and up the back stairs to the east wing of the house, in which my mother and I were staying. His right ear was gashed and bleeding freely. My mother sat him down in a chair and sent me for water and bandages, with instructions not to let my grandmother catch wind of anything, but when I returned from my errand, my grandmother had arrived on the scene and was tying up my uncle's face, toothache fashion, saying quietly and bitterly, "Yóu and your clever friends never did have any sense—getting into street fights with the Nazis!" Paul patted his mother's hand and grinned at me across the room.

After this incident, I understood that Paul was going to stay indefinitely.

Now Paul's friends came out to Fischamend from Vienna to visit. Liesel came to spend a weekend. Liesel had been Paul's girl for years. She was beautiful and witty, and even my grandmother approved. She was blonder than Mitzi, and more delightful to talk to, because she would talk back to me and we had conversations. I sat on her lap while she and Paul sat in the yard at a card table with paper and pencils. They were writing a fairy story for me. The heroine was called Princess Vaselina. The hero was a pretentious commoner named Shampoo von Rubinstein, and as they wrote they laughed and laughed.

When Liesel left, my grandmother said it was Paul's own fault. She said that if he and his friends had not spent their time playing at socialism and walking round the picture galleries, he could at least be a doctor now. I did not like him to be scolded, and I went to sit on his lap, but he said that my grandmother had a point there, and he looked quite depressed.

The next visitor was Paul's friend Dolf. According to my grandmother, he had had the most baleful influence on Paul's career. Dolf was a poet. I thought he was splendid. He was extraordinarily tall and seemed to be embarrassed about it; he had a way of scratching the top of his head that stood his shock of black hair up in a cone and made him look even taller. He was so tall that when he sat down in a chair he folded like one of our folding beds. Paul made him write a poem in my autograph book. He wrote:

> Dear child,
> We are followed from our cradle and first cry
> Until the grave, by hate and lie.
> From our cradle till our last rest,
> Attends us other men's distress.
> Be true and help.
> You'll come to understand—
> But of yourself, I hope, and not at Life's hard hand.

He illustrated it with a facetious drawing of my uncle, in angel garb, hovering over my bed. The picture pained me; I felt it spoiled the noble tone of my book. This is the only notice Dolf ever took of me. His indifference excited me. I danced interminable impressionistic dances for him. I learned to stand on my head—an accomplishment of which I am still capable and proud, though it has never worked for me any better than it did then. When Paul and Dolf went for a walk by the Danube, they took me along. Each young man held one hand. Their talk of pictures and books bounced from one to the other above my head; like a watcher's at a tennis tournament, my eyes, if not my understanding, followed it.

On the outhouse roof next morning, I told Mitzi the new plan for my life: I was going to be a student at the university; I would walk with young and clever men by riverbanks, talking of painting and poetry; I would take bicycle tours in the summer. Mitzi had never a word to say against it.

When Dolf left Fischamend, Paul and I saw him off at the little railway station. Paul gave Dolf a book as a good-by present, and Dolf gave Paul a book. When the books were unwrapped, each turned out to be *The Little Flowers of St. Francis.*

The next day my father arrived, late in the evening, after the shop was closed. We were sitting upstairs in the corner room. I remember Paul was in the armchair with a book; my grandmother was laying out a game of solitaire. They were watching me do a new dance I had invented and laughing at the silly song my mother was playing. As I came waltzing around, I saw my father in the doorway, so tall he had to duck his head. I thought, That's the end of all the fun, and was horror-struck to be thinking so. My father was making the mock-sentimental face he always put on when he found my mother at the piano. He turned his eyes up and said, "La-la, la-la, la-laaaa. Very pretty."

"Igo! I didn't see you come in." My mother closed the keyboard and stood up. "Sit down. What is happening in Vienna?"

My father told us that Tante Trude and Onkel Hans were leaving for England. They had money abroad. He said there were lines outside the foreign consulates. Everyone was panicking because of the anti-Jewish articles in *Der Stürmer.*

Then my mother took me off to bed.

Next day at lunch, which we ate in the storeroom behind the shop so that my grandfather could keep his eye on the door, my father told me to take my elbows off the table. (The three lessons I recall my father contributing to my early discipline were that one must not slouch at table by leaning on an elbow, that one must never eat sausage without a piece of bread to go with it, and that one must always wash one's hands after playing with an animal.)

My father then turned to my grandfather and proposed his plan of sinking his considerable severance pay into my grandfather's business and becoming my grandfather's partner.

"Ja so," said my grandfather and scratched his little Hitler-type

mustache, the only distinctive feature on his little person. He said, "That way we could pay off arrears in good order and put the shop on its feet."

My grandmother had put down her fork and sat looking from her son-in-law to her husband, with her handsome black eyes opened to their large fullness. "You are going to put the shop on its feet, Joszi, so it can walk right out of your hands into the pockets of the Nazis!" my grandmother said in a thick Hungarian accent. She and my grandfather had both come to Vienna as children. My grandmother had mastered German perfectly, but she imitated my grandfather's accent and odd grammar so cleverly that he smiled. Paul and my mother laughed. My father put on his mock-amused face. He turned up the corners of his lips and said, "Ha-ha, ha-ha, ha-haaaa. Very funny."

My mother stopped laughing and said, "Igo, please . . ."

"Maybe you haven't looked outside today," my grandmother said. Overnight, there had appeared in the street, outside the entrance of the shop, letters tall as a man, painted in white on the macadam: KAUFT NICHT BEIM JUDEN ("Don't buy from the Jews").

"The local boys," my father said.

"Franzi, your husband is almost as silly as mine," said my grandmother.

"Please! Mutti . . ." my mother said.

"Franzi, your mother knows almost as much about everything as your brother Paul," said my father.

My mother had begun to cry. My mother always cried when my grandmother and my father were being rude to one another, though it had happened, throughout my childhood, whenever they met.

The other way my father had of making my mother unhappy was by getting ill, which he always did when I least expected it and always, it seemed to me, when there was some excitement my mother and I had planned, a birthday party or a Christmas visit to Fischamend. My mother would meet me at the door as I came home from school and say, "Now *you* must be my friend, Lorle; they have taken Daddy away to the hospital." And we would go down into the blue dusk and bitter-cold street and take a tram across Vienna to see my father, laid out flat in a white hospital bed without even a pillow, his pale, peaked nose pointing at the white ceiling.

"When is he going to come home?" I would ask my mother, seeing her pale, shrunken face, in which her eyes looked large out of all proportion. Her lips seemed a dark pink, with a rough surface as if they were sore.

"I don't know, darling."

"Is it because of the kidney again?"

"Nobody knows what it is this time. The doctors are testing for an ulcer. Lorle, I have a favor to ask: Will you be a real friend and not ask me anything for the next twenty minutes? By then this migraine will be better, and we will talk again. All right?"

"All right. What time is it now?"

"You can talk to Lore as you would to a grownup," my mother told my grandmother. Sometimes my mother talked to me about my father. I was flattered, but I did not like to listen, and I cannot remember what she told me.

And always my father would get better again and come home. It seemed strange to see him upright again, wearing his navy-blue business suit. My mother would cook him special diets and fetch him his bicarbonate of soda, and on Sundays he and I would take our morning walks. "Don't fill her up with ice cream before lunch," my mother would call after us.

And my father always bought me an ice cream and said when we went home we would make a joke with Mutti. The joke was our ringing the bell and having my mother find us standing outside the door with our hands before our chests like squirrels, trembling in mock terror, which meant we had been bad again and I had had an ice cream.

The Sunday after my father came out to Fischamend, I said I would rather stay in and read a book or draw with crayons, but my mother said the fresh air was good for me, and my father said he would tell me a story.

The trouble with my father's stories was that they were all one interminable Kipling story about the fight that Rikki-tikki-tavi, the mongoose, had with a snake. My father's voice droned above my head. I walked beside him, telling myself my own delicious, mildly sexy stories. The air was just the temperature of my bare legs and arms, so that I could not tell where I ended and the world began. I remember, now, that the water meadows along the Danube are so thickly grown with pink-tipped daisies and yellow buttercups that you can't help walking on them; they form a carpet underfoot. The mosquitos had ripened and raged that year. There were some local children skipping flat pebbles across the water, and my father sat down on the crest of the bank and told me to go and play with them.

I remember to this day the pressure of my father's hand on the precise spot on my back, three inches to the right of my spine, where he used to push me to go and play. The fact was, I always longed to play with other children but never knew how. This time I had walked forward and stopped, and stood rubbing the back of my left hand to and fro across my temple, watching the group by the river. The biggest, a man-sized boy, turned and threw a little pebble. I thought it was a game and felt pleased; all the children were coming toward me up the bank. Then I saw that they had filled their mouths with Danube water, and I turned and ran, but they spat it down the back of my dress and called me "Jew." I howled all the way home, walking beside my father, I don't know whether from shock and fright or because of the obscene wetness that glued the stuff of my dress to my skin.

"That's that Willi Weber's young brother Karl," said my grandmother. "He is the leader of the Hitler Youth Brigade."

"The bastard!" said my Uncle Paul. "And I always linked his paragraphs for him! Teacher Berthold had a thing one year about linking consecutive ideas, and Willi Weber never could connect anything."

"Yes!" said my grandmother. "If you'd spent more time on your own work instead of writing everybody else's essays, you might be married to Liesel now and on your way out of the country."

Paul looked sad. He had had a letter from Liesel that morning to say that she was going to be married and she and her husband were leaving for Paraguay. Paul said, "Willi used to do my drawing exercises. It wasn't a bad setup we had there."

The next day, my grandmother happened to meet Willi in front of the shop, and she said, "You owe us twenty-five schillings for your winter coat and galoshes. Can I send Mitzi over in the morning to collect?"

But when she came into the store and boasted of what she had done, my grandfather said, "You know they had the rot in their potatoes. They can't pay."

The following morning, the front of our house had "Jew" and dirty words written in red paint all over it. The bloody color was still wet and dripping down the stone when my grandfather went out to take the shutters down. He washed it off—the letters disappeared slowly but the color blotched the wall—and that's as far as it went that time; neither we nor they had yet realized the possibilities.

In late August came the first of the war scares. We had got into the habit of drawing the curtains in the sitting room at six o'clock every evening and gathering around the radio to catch the British news broadcasts. I don't know if the weather clouded over or if the grim mood of the adults created in my mind the distinct memory of yellowish-gray clouds standing for days over the low roofs of the village houses.

One day, the first German regiment moved in. By noon, the square outside our windows was black with tanks, armored cars, radio trucks. Our yard was requisitioned for the paymaster's headquarters. The soldiers borrowed one of our kitchen chairs and the card table on which Paul and Liesel had written the story of Vaselina.

Two helmeted guards stood on either side of the table while the German soldiers in their gray-green uniforms filed past to collect their money. I sat in the passageway that led from the storeroom into the yard, watching. I had the cat on my lap. My father leaned out and told me to wash my hands. My mother said for me to go and play upstairs or the soldiers might see me. What bothered me was not that they might see me, but that in fact they did not, and I got hold of the cat and turned its ears inside out and tied my skipping rope around its neck until it yowled.

The paymaster looked around. "Well now," he said. "Now, you don't want to do that to the poor pussy."

"Pardon?" I said politely. Though I had heard very well what he said, I wanted to hear him say *"Kätzchen"* again—the unfamiliar harsh-sounding diminutive of "cat," so different from the tenderly comic sound of the Austrian *"Katzerl."* The animal meanwhile was choking. The paymaster rose and came over, saying, *"Armes kleines Kätzchen"* ("Poor little kitten"), and untied it. He asked me if I knew how to skip rope, and I said yes. He ordered one of the helmeted guards to hold the other end of the rope. The line of soldiers stood at ease against the vine-covered walls. I skipped and recited:

> *"Auf der blauen Donau*
> *Schwimmt ein Krokodil . . ."*

This was about the time that Neville Chamberlain paid his visit to Hitler in Munich.

I opened my eyes in the night because a voice below my window was saying, "SQ calling XW, SQ calling XW, move east twenty kilometers on Route 46, over," or some such gibberish. Startled out of sleep, I sat straight up in my bed in the darkness. The words seemed so pregnant with meaning that I tried to hold them against the forgetfulness already overtaking them as an engine started up and raced away down the street. There was a great cranking up of heavy engines, and a rolling of truck after truck, and an earth-cracking, wall-wrenching rumble of tons of iron tank on iron caterpillar chain through the narrow streets. It worried me that the vehicles moving away from the square threw the light of their headlamps across my ceiling not in the direction in which they were going but in an opposite direction, and before I tucked myself back to sleep I promised myself to try to remember to mention it to Paul.

It was autumn, which brought with it a new school term and an apparently insoluble problem.

After the Annexation, the Austrian schools had been ordered to segregate Jewish children. The city of Vienna had made the switch in simple stages. On the morning following Annexation, immediately after prayers, the teacher had announced that instead of poetry we would have an hour of handicrafts and would take down the pro-Austrian, anti-German posters that, in the enthusiasm and heated blood of the past month, we had been made to paste and pin around the schoolroom walls. "Teacher," said a little girl called Greterl, "can I have this one I cut the paper leaves for to take home? It says 'Red-White-Red to the death.' " "No, you cannot, you stupid idiot!" said our teacher, who had always been a mild, good-natured woman, and she tore the pretty poster in two and stuffed it into the rubbish sack with which each classroom had been provided that very morning. Filled with paper sentiments, it was bound, with all possible haste, for the incinerators. By the end of the week, the desks in our room had been rearranged so that the half-dozen Jewish children in the class could sit together in the rear, with two empty rows between us and the Aryans in front. A question of some worriment soon developed among the six of us in the back, and I was chosen to carry it to the teacher: What were we to do about the "Heil Hitler!" which was from now on to greet the entrance of the teacher and begin class prayers? After some discussion, it was settled between us that just as in the past the Jewish children had remained silent during the "Our Father," so now we would not need to articulate the words of the salute or raise our right arms, though we should stand up as a matter of respect. I think both the teacher and I had a sense of satisfaction at having, in the general confusion, dealt neatly with a pretty problem. Within a week, all the Jewish children in our school were assigned to a separate classroom. We knew very well

that no teacher wanted to teach Jewish classes. We heard them arguing passionately. I remember the teacher who came into our classroom the first morning of the new system. She was a soft-faced,
stout young woman, and her eyes were red. We stood up to greet
her with the awe of children in the presence of a grownup who
has been crying. She told us to get out our readers and to read
to ourselves. We scrabbled for our books in our desks. We opened
them. We watched the new teacher walk over to the closed window
and lean her elbows on the sill. Her shoulders were visibly shaking.
Soon her weeping turned from a suppressed whisper into loud,
tearing sobs, while thirty children sat in petrified silence. The following week, the school had been cleared of Aryans, and Jewish
children and teachers had been brought in to make ours the Jewish
school for the district.

In Fischamend, the problem was not so easily handled. There
was a single village school, and a single Jewish pupil, and that was
I. The school was the one to which my mother and Paul had gone
as children, when my grandparents first moved from Vienna to
the country. They had been the only Jewish pupils and had met
the problem head on; when Willi Weber called Paul a dirty Jew
and hit him, my mother, who is seven years Paul's senior, hit Willi
Weber, and so a working balance had been achieved. My mother
says that she always got on pleasantly after that, except when they
played a game called the old bird-seller game in the schoolyard
and she had to be the Jew merchant. It made her cry. Who wanted
to be an old Jew all the time, when everybody else might be a
bird of his own choosing?

Now segregation had become the law. We were at an impasse
out of which came a most delightful solution. My uncle went to see
his embarrassed old schoolfellows, who were now the local party
leaders, and suggested that he had the academic background to
act as my official tutor. My father would teach me mathematics,
my mother the piano. Paul would be responsible for the rest.

This arrangement, I suspect, killed any tendency I might have
had toward disciplined scholarship, for it left me with the impression that knowledge comes in ravishments of the mind. The history

of Luther gave me a poke in the ribs. I suddenly understood that events happened one after another, stretching away behind me from where I stood, and forward from when I would be no longer standing there. I remember the stunning brilliance of this revelation; if the content seems a little thin now, that is sometimes the way with visions. We looked at pictures and Paul kept a step ahead of me, asking my mind to perform more than it could. He made me look at Michelangelo's Adam lying on a hill in the beginning of the world, and asked me what I saw. I said Adam had no clothes on. Paul said that's right, and what else did I see. I said God was dressed in a cloth and carried by angels. Paul said yes, but why was God's arm stretched down to Adam and how was Adam's arm lifted up? He said for me to look at the picture some more, and again tomorrow if I could not tell today, and to look very quietly—but instead my mind screamed with frustration and rage. It is eerie to see nothing where another person sees something, and even eerier trying to remember how it was to see nothing after one has seen it. I came across the picture years later and saw the Adam, the weight of the earth still in him, raising his immense shoulders at the crooking of the single finger of the life-giver, and I wondered and could not properly recall what it was I had not seen that autumn in Fischamend. And we read poems. One day it was Heine, who, Paul said, was a Jew, and the next day it was Christian Morgenstern, who, he said, was not, and here was a poem about a worm, called "The Worm's Confession." Listen:

> Inside a shell
> A worm does dwell,
> A worm of rarest sort,
> Who, whisperingly,
> Only to me,
> Opened his little heart. . . .

That was the day they held the Hitler rally outside the open window. The squadrons of White Shirts and Brown Shirts, with their drums and music, approached through the arch at the base of the Fischamend tower and drew up in very straight lines across the square. Flags flew. Presently a loud-speaker blared out a Hitler speech reporting on his latest visit to the Duce, in Rome. When Hitler started on the Jews, my mother drew the curtains close, though it was midmorning and the day was stifling hot. But I had caught sight of my own friend Mitzi, and I cried excitedly, "Mummy, look, there's Mitzi! She's carrying a flag!" I was leaning out between the curtains to wave when Paul grabbed my arm so harshly I roared—and there, for a minute, Hitler and I yelled contrapuntally across the peopled, listening summer square until I was rushed into the back part of the house.

That evening, Mitzi came to the upstairs, living portion of the house, on the pretext of bringing a message to my grandfather, and found us gathered around the radio. Within the hour, Willi Weber knocked at the door.

"Hello, Willi," said my Uncle Paul.

"Hello, Paul," said Willi.

"Well, Willi," said Paul, "what do you want from us?"

Willi said he had come to borrow our radio for use at party headquarters.

"Help yourself, Willi," said Paul. "I know you will."

Downstairs, some men were calling for my grandfather. A large truck had been backed up to the shop door, and when they had emptied the shop, my grandfather signed a form that said he was happy to contribute his share to the support of the Winter Help Fund of the parish of Fischamend.

"So what?" said my grandmother when he came upstairs and told us what had happened. "You've been supporting the place for twenty years, giving everything away on credit!"

"Pst!" said my father, who happened to be facing the south windows and saw the heads appearing above the sill. We looked around. There were heads in the two west windows, also. Beneath the second-story windows, a narrow corrugated-iron ledge jutted out over the lower floor like a little roof. Ladders had been put against the ledge, and boys and girls from the village, still in their uniforms, had climbed up and were sitting in our windows. They stayed all night. Now and then, one of the boys would swing his legs over the sill and step into the room with us. There were some books they didn't approve of, and possessions they did, and they carried everything portable away.

The next day, the shop remained closed. The family sat around the dining-room table. I remember sitting under the table, playing with their shoelaces and listening: It was clear that we must leave Fischamend, but we had nowhere to go. The villagers stood in the street, throwing stones against the upstairs windows until they were all smashed, and, around dusk, the S.S. boys came and took the three men to the police station next door. My mother and grandmother waited in the room where I slept, leaning out of the empty window frame. My bed was pushed against the inside wall and barricaded with a mattress. All night, even while I slept, it seems to me that I heard the two women's voices speaking softly in the darkness.

At some point, I was awake, and knew that the men were back. I don't know how I know that my father had been slapped and that his glasses had been knocked off and broken. I have a vivid and quite false memory of this brutality, as if I had been a witness.

The lights were on in all the house, and there was much walking and opening and shutting of doors and drawers. I was still half asleep, in the chilly predawn, when my mother dressed me.

She said we were catching the early train to Vienna and I was going to stay with my cousin Erwin until they could find some place for all of us to live together again.

We left the house through the yard door. I touched the stones of the walls with my hands, thinking, This is the last time I shall see you! I tested for the appropriate emotion: It seemed wrong of me to be feeling nothing so much as excitement at going to stay with Erwin.

(It was, in fact, the last time any of us saw Fischamend. Twenty years later, in New York, Paul was to receive a letter from a Vienna lawyer who said he represented Mrs. Mitzi K., the former Mitzi ————. Mrs. K. was interested in buying the Fischamend house, which had been restored to our ownership after the end of the war. Mrs. K. wanted to reopen the shop. If my uncle would agree to have the accumulated taxes due on the property since September, 1938, as well as the cost of essential repairs such as the removal of the east wing, which had been wrecked by Allied bombardment, deducted from the price offered by Mrs. K., less the lawyer's own fee, the 4,690.77 Austrian schillings that remained would be transmitted to the United States. This letter threw Paul into such a passion, I was astonished at him. A general helpless exasperation and the desire to be quit of the past made him finally close with the offer. A year later, he received the equivalent of eight hundred dollars, which he divided with my mother; Mitzi is mistress of her house and shop.)

By nightfall, we had all been stowed away with friends and relatives—Jewish apartments, in those days, were infinitely expandable, to take in the newly homeless. Paul stayed with Dolf, who lived with his mother and his sister Suse; my grandparents moved in with my grandmother's oldest sister, Ibolya. The maid's room at the Golds', where my father had stayed, was now to accommodate both him and my mother, but first my parents took me along to Erwin's.

Erwin's father made them come in and sit down, while Erwin and I danced in the foyer. We were both only children; we were going to have a ball, but Tante Gusti, whose corset shop had been confiscated by the Nazis that morning, was nervous and put her hands to her head. Erwin's father told us to settle down, and Erwin, without that one extra hop I always gave in the face of prohibition, stood still with his eyes on his father. I was impressed. I never quite believed that this Onkel Eugen could really be a cousin of my father's; he seemed so different—slim, athletically built, elegantly dressed, and full of ideas. He asked my father what he had done about emigrating, and my father said he was going to the American Consulate tomorrow, to put our names on the quota, but Onkel Eugen said the quota for Austrian nationals was filled till 1950. My father said there were Hans and Trude in England, and Kari and Gerti Gold thought they might get into Panama, and if they did, they would see if they could get a visa for us. Onkel

Eugen said he was in contact with some business associates in Paris, and he thought something was moving there.

I have been told that people who are hungry can talk of nothing but food. In 1938, in Vienna, Jews talked endlessly about ways of getting out of the country. Erwin and I got bored. We slipped away into his room and played house. ("I'll say, 'Let's go inside,' then you have to say, 'I don't want to,' then I have to cry. Then you have to say . . .")

The next day I went to the Jewish school with Erwin. The men went out mornings, as punctually as they had once left for business, to make the rounds of the consulates. One day when I was off from school, I went with my father. He met a friend and stopped to talk. The friend said he had heard something was doing in the Swiss Consulate and he was going over to put his name on the list. I had caught sight of one of those small flat boxes that had recently been attached to houses at street corners, where, behind chicken wire, pages of the newspaper *Der Stürmer* were fixed open for the public to read. Yesterday, I had heard Tante Gusti say to Onkel Eugen that there was an exposé this week of the private lives of well-known Viennese Jews, and that the grocer's wife had said to her, "But Frau Löwy, I didn't know all those famous people were Jews!" The grownups had laughed so hard and so long that I thought it must be one of those loaded jokes. I inched over and looked through the chicken wire. There was a picture of an old man with monstrous lips, and another of a very fat woman standing with her feet planted grossly wide apart, but I had no time to make anything of it before my father came and hustled me away. "Where are we going?" I said, embarrassed to have been caught peeping.

"To the Swiss Consulate," he said. "To put our names on a list."

By the time we arrived at the Swiss Consulate, the waiting line reached into the street. A woman in the front said that she had a chance of going to Hong Kong the day after tomorrow, but if there was any chance of Switzerland coming through she might wait the week, and six voices behind her said at once, "What do you want to wait for?" and told stories of So-and-So and what had happened to him because he waited a day too long.

When not sitting in the waiting rooms of consulates and embassies, everybody was going to the classes that had sprung up all over the city. Jewish professionals were scurrying to learn hand skills, to feed themselves and their families in countries whose languages they would not know. My father, who had originated the accounting system of the bank for which he worked, learned machine knitting and leatherwork. The sad little purses and wallets he made turned up in our luggage for years. My mother learned large-quantity cooking. She took a course in massage, too, with Paul, and when they came to see me at Erwin's they practiced on me.

On November 10th, a Jew named Grünspan assassinated a minor Nazi official on a diplomatic mission to Paris. When the news reached Vienna in the afternoon, school was dismissed. We were told to go home by the back roads. Erwin's parents sat beside the radio all afternoon. Toward evening, the doorbell rang, and outside stood an elderly neighbor from across the hall, and his wife, and an immense mahogany sideboard, which they were being made to move into our flat. A couple of uniformed Nazis stood along the banisters. They said to get on with the sideboard, there was more coming. In the course of that night, they forced the five Jewish families in the apartment house to move themselves and their households into our seven-room, fifth-floor apartment. The rooms soon had the grotesque look of usual objects in unusual positions: chairs stacked high on wardrobes, a table upside down on the bed with china, books, and lamps between its legs. The wife of the elderly neighbor sat on a chair crying, in a thin voice, without intermission. The Nazis became playful. They had discovered the main switch and kept turning the lights off, sometimes for as long as half an hour, then off and on, and off and on. Into the middle of this walked Tante Gusti's brother, hoping to hide out because his own apartment was being raided, but he was intercepted by the guard at the entrance and taken away. Tante Gusti stood in the doorway and wept. All night, the heavy baroque furniture bumped on the stairs, and squeaked over the tiles of the hall. I sat down and howled for my mother.

In the weeks that followed, Erwin's apartment, with the five families milling around, looked like a slum. Onkel Eugen's bed was kept open, and he jumped into it whenever the doorbell rang. Erwin and I were told that if anyone asked us, Onkel Eugen had influenza and a high fever, but we saw him walking around all day in his striped silk pajamas. In the evening he sat and played chess with Erwin. He said Erwin was going to be a great champion.

One day Erwin's parents began to pack. They were going to France. My mother came and packed my bags. Erwin and I promised we would never play the house game with anybody else. Erwin said he was going to build an airplane and come to see me.

(In 1946, when I was in London and Erwin was in Paris, we did correspond briefly, but lost touch again after he and Tante Gusti left for Brazil. A year ago, I met Tante Gusti, who was visiting a sister in New York. She told me a strange story. She said they had lived well in Paris, not at all like refugees, because of Eugen's business connections. Then the French interned all German-speaking men. She got permission for herself and Erwin to visit Onkel Eugen in camp. They found him in shirt sleeves, sitting at a long table with hundreds of prisoners. He looked healthy, but thin, and he was unshaven. Erwin held his mother's hands. Tante Gusti said his hands were icy cold and he never mentioned the visit afterward. There grew up such a tabu on this subject between mother and son that Tante Gusti never knew if Erwin understood when the French handed the camps over to the advancing Germans and the Jewish inmates were sent to Auschwitz. The boy's callousness grieved and estranged her. After the end of the war, she discovered in his wallet a newsprint photograph of one of those skeleton survivors of concentration camps—two huge eyes in a hairless, toothy skull—that might, with a stretch of the imagination, be thought to have resembled Onkel Eugen. Erwin was carrying it from one to another of the agencies, looking for his dead father among the first confused lists of survivors.)

After the departure of Erwin and his parents, I remember two

rooms in a back street where I lived with my parents, and there
Paul and my grandparents came to see us.

"Now Paul wants to go to Palestine. Paul as a farmer—can you
imagine?" my grandmother said. "He can't even walk into a
room without all the lamps falling over. If you had attended to
your studies, you would be a doctor now. Or if you had taken
languages, like that Professor Glazer always said . . ."

"A Nazi even in those days," Paul said.

"He used to say, 'Frau Steiner, your Paul has a real talent for
languages. . . .' "

"I didn't think the world needed another linguist," Paul said.
"What it needs, of course, is more aging medical students."

My grandmother laid back her head and laughed beautifully.

"Maybe I'll become a famous farmer," Paul said. He put his
hand out and drew me to his chair. "I went to the Jüdische Kultus
Gemeinde [Jewish Congregation] this morning to put my name
down to go to one of their new training farms. By the way, did
you know they had an incendiary bomb in the temple during the
night. It was still smoking. They paid twelve of us to stay behind
and clear out the debris."

"Congratulations," my grandmother said. "At the age of twenty-
seven, Paul earns his first money on a wrecking team. What did
they give you?"

Paul hesitated. "Three schillings."

"What? What?" cried my grandmother. "And I suppose you
lost it?"

"There was a kid there," Paul said, "a red-nosed, sniveling sort
of kid, very young, and he said even if he got a visa to Palestine
he didn't have a suitcase."

My grandmother looked at Paul with her handsome black eyes
that were always on the verge of anger. "And you gave him your
three schillings?"

"Mutti, one can't make money off the destruction of the temple
by the Nazis."

"You can't make money off the Nazis? Why can't you? They

can take away your parents' shop and your brother-in-law's job. . . ."

"But Muttilein, that's what I mean."

"Marry," said my grandmother. "Find yourself a wife to look after you. I can't any more," and my grandmother started to cry.

Paul went and sat on the arm of her chair and stroked her hair. "Mutti, I would start looking tomorrow, but just figure the odds against my happening to want to marry the very woman who happens to want to marry me."

But this time my grandmother would not laugh. She turned her face from him and dismissed him with a flick of her hand.

Early in December there was a rumor about an experimental children's transport being sent to England. My father took me to the Jewish Congregation, which had moved its headquarters to the empty temple. What looked like thousands of children and parents were moving around the floor of the burned-out shell of the hall and standing in a queue around the gallery where, on the high holidays, the women had sat in their hats and black dresses. But my father took me around by the offices and asked to see Great-Aunt Ibolya's youngest son's fiancée, who worked for the organization, and that was how my name got put down one hundred and fifty-second on the list.

In the streetcar going home, my father held my hand. He said, "So you will be going to England."

I said, "All by myself?" and I remember clearly the sensation, as if my insides had been suddenly scooped away. At the same time I felt that this "going to England" had a brave sound.

"Not all by yourself!" my father said. "There will be six hundred other children."

"When am I going?" I asked.

"Thursday," said my father. "The day after tomorrow."

Then I felt the icy chill just below my chest where my insides had been.

CHAPTER TWO

The Children's Transport

The children were due to assemble at nine in the evening on Thursday, December 10, 1938.

"She can take my best crocodile belt," said my father, wanting to give me something.

"Igo! She can't use your belt! And we've been asked to pack as little as possible. The children have to carry their own luggage. Pick up the suitcase," she said to me. "Can you lift it?"

I lifted the suitcase against my leg and leaned my weight against it. "I can carry it," I said.

"I have to pack her enough food to last till they get to England," my mother said. "How can I pack enough food to keep two days?" Her face was red. All that day my mother's face looked dark and hot, as if she had a fever, but she moved about as on any ordinary day and her voice sounded ordinary; she even joked. She said we were going to pretend it was the first day of the month. Before my father had lost his job, the first of the month had been payday and the day I was allowed to choose my own fanciful supper, against a promise that there would be no fussing about food during the rest of the month. But today my appetite had no imagination. I said I didn't want anything. "I don't mean for now. I mean to take with you," said my mother. She was wanting me to need something that she could give me. I searched around in my mind, wanting to oblige her. *"Knackwurst?"* I said, though I could not at the moment remember exactly what kind of sausage that was.

"Not without bread," said my father.

"Knackwurst," said my mother. "You like that? I'll go down this minute and get you one." But at that moment the doorbell rang.

All day the room was full of people coming to say good-by, friends of the family, and aunts and uncles and cousins. Everyone brought me bonbons, candied fruit, dates, sour sweets, and chocolates we called cat's tongues, and homemade cookies, and *Sacher Torte*. Even my Tante Grete came, though she was angry with my parents because I had been sneaked onto the transport and her twins were to be left behind.

My father tried to explain. "This is just an experimental transport, don't you see. They don't even know if they can get across the German border, and Lore only got on because Karl's fiancée happens to work on the Committee and did us a favor. I could hardly ask her for more."

"Naturally. How could you be expected to ask for help to save someone else's children?" Tante Grete said. She had a long and bitter face. "But maybe Lore can ask people once she gets to England. She can tell about her cousins Ilse and Erica, who had to stay behind in Vienna while she got away. Maybe she can find a sponsor for them."

My father said, "I've given her a list of names to write to when she gets to England. There are some cousins of Franzi's who've lived in America for years who might sponsor us. She's going to write to them, aren't you? And there are Eugen and Gusti in Paris, who have business connections, and in London Hans and Trude . . ."

"Whom I called a cow," my mother said.

"There's a family in London who might be related to us, though they spell their name G-R-O-S-S-M-A-N-N and ours is G-R-O-S-Z-M-A-N-N. And there is the Jewish Refugee Committee there. You'll write to them, won't you?"

I stood in the center of my circle of relatives, nodding solemnly. I said I would write letters to everybody and I would tell the *Engländer* about everything that was happening and would get sponsors for my parents and my grandparents and for everybody.

"Well, well," my aunt said. "She can certainly talk, can't she!" and she got up. She embraced me and kissed me and, despite being mad at me, she wept bitterly.

(I met Erica in 1946 in London, where she had a job as a nurse-maid to an English family. She told me that Ilse had got to Palestine illegally and was in a *kibbutz*. They had both tried to get a sponsor for their mother, but Tante Grete had been arrested in her hallway early in 1940 and sent to Poland.)

When Tante Grete left the apartment, it was after seven and my nervous father said we should be going, but my mother cried out; she had forgotten to get the *Knackwurst*. "I'm going to run down," she said, and already she had flung her coat about her, but my father blocked her way.

"Are you an idiot? Do you want her to miss her train?"

"She wants a *Knackwurst!*" my mother cried.

"Do you know what time it is? Suppose you get arrested while you're out!"

I had never before seen my parents standing shouting into each other's faces. I kept saying, "I don't really want any *Knackwurst*," but they took no notice of me.

"She likes *Knackwurst*." My mother wept. She skipped around my large, slow-moving father, and she ran out through the door.

My father still ignored me. He stood by the window. He went to the bathroom. He opened the hall door and looked out. He checked his watch.

My mother came back with her triumphant, beaming, sad red face. Nothing had happened—no one had even seen her. She had got a whole sausage and had made the man give her an extra paper bag. She called me to come and look where she was put-ting it in my rucksack, between my sandwiches and the cake.

"Let's go, for God's sake," said my father.

We went over the Stefanie Bridge on foot. I walked between my parents. Each held a hand. My father talked to my mother about going to the Chinese Consulate in the morning.

"Daddy," I said. "Daddy, look!"

My mother was saying to my father, "Grete mentioned some-thing about getting into Holland."

I tugged at my mother's hand. "Look at the moon," I insisted. There was a white moon shivering in the black water of the Danube underneath us, along with a thousand pretty lights from the bridge.

My father said, "Holland is too close, but I'll go and see, if there's time. I'll do the Chinese Consulate first thing."

They kept talking to each other over my head. I was hurt. They were making plans for a tomorrow in which I would have no part. Already they seemed to be getting on very well without me and I was angry. I withdrew my hands and walked by myself.

We got into a tram. Across the aisle there was another little Jewish girl with a rucksack and a suitcase, sitting between her parents. I tried to catch her eye in order to flirt up a new friend for myself, but she took no notice of me. She was crying. I said to my mother, "I'm not crying like that little girl."

My mother said, "No, you are being very good, very brave. I'm proud how good you are being."

But I had misgivings; I rather thought I ought to be crying, too.

The assembly point was a huge empty lot behind the railway station in the outskirts of Vienna. I looked among the hundreds of children milling in the darkness for the girl who had cried in the tram, but I never saw her again, or perhaps did not recognize her. Along a wire fence, members of the Committee stood holding long poles bearing placards; flashlights lit the numbers painted on them. Someone came over to me and checked my papers and made me stand with the group of children collecting around the placard that read "150–199." He hung a cardboard label with the number 152 strung on a shoelace around my neck, and tied corresponding numbers to my suitcase and rucksack.

I remember that I clowned and talked a good deal. I remember feeling, This is me going to England. My parents stood with the other parents, on the right, at the edge of the darkness. I have no clear recollection of my father's being there—perhaps his head was too high and out of the circle of the lights. I do remember his greatcoat standing next to my mother's black pony fur, but every time I looked toward them it was my mother's tiny face, crumpled and feverish inside her fox collar, that I saw smiling steadily toward me.

We were arranged in a long column four deep, according to numbers. The rucksack was strapped on my back. There was a confusion of kissing parents—my father bending down, my mother's face burning against mine. Before I could get a proper grip on my suitcase, the line set in motion so that the suitcase kept slipping from my hand and bumping against my legs. Panic-stricken, I looked to the right, but my mother was there, walking beside me. She took the suitcase, keeping at my side, and she was smiling so that it seemed a gay thing, like a joke we were having together. Someone from the Committee, checking the line, took the suitcase from my mother, checked it with the number around my neck, and gave it to me to carry. "Go on, move," the children behind me said. We were passing through great doors. I looked to my right; my mother's face was nowhere to be seen. I dragged and shoved the heavy suitcase across the station floor and bumped it down a flight of stairs and along a platform where the train stood waiting.

There was a young woman in charge inside our carriage. She was slight and soft-spoken. She walked the corridors outside the compartments and put her head in and told us to settle down. We asked her when we were going to leave. She said, "Very soon. Why don't you all try to go to sleep? It's past eleven." Still the train stood in the station. I saw Onkel Karl's fiancée on the platform, looking in the window. I remember standing on my head for her. She smiled upside down and mouthed something. I wiggled my toes.

It was after midnight when the train left the station. There was only room enough for four of the eight girls in the compartment to stretch out on the seats. I was the smallest one. I remember that I had the place by the window and I kept trying to bend my neck into the corner and at the same time shield my eyes with an arm, a hand, or in the crook of an elbow against the electric bulb in the corridor, which burned through my closed lids. The chattering of the children subsided little by little until there was no sound except the noise of the train. I have no notion that I went to sleep, except that I was awakened by a flashlight shining into my face. In its light, behind it and lit like a negative, was a girl's face. She said it was time for someone else to lie down in my place. And before I had altogether picked my stiff limbs out of my corner, this other person was creeping into it. The girl who had wakened me was pretty. She said I could sit with her on her suitcase. I liked her awfully. I copied the way she sat with her elbows braced on her knees, her chin cupped in her hands, quite still. I thought, This is me, awake, watching the children sleeping. I watched the black outside the window turn a queer, beautiful blue that faded into gray and presently lightened to a dead white. The bulbs in the corridor still burned a foolish orange. The sleepers humped shoulders to hide their faces from the light. In the next compartment someone was whispering. Someone let out a laugh and was quickly shushed. A girl in my compartment sat straight up, stared for a moment, and seemed to go back to sleep, except that her eyes stayed open.

The girl on the suitcase asked me if I wanted to go to the lavatory and wash my face. I wandered down the corridor, peering into every compartment door to see people sleeping. In the lavatory there was a glass sphere over the washbowl. If you turned it upside down, green liquid soap squirted out. If you stepped on the pedal that flushed the toilet, a hole opened and you could look through it at the ground tearing away underneath. I played until the knocking at the door became so violently impatient I had to let the others in.

By the time I got back to my compartment, everyone was up. Everyone was talking. The children were eating breakfast out of their paper bags. I didn't feel like *Knackwurst* for breakfast and it was too much trouble to eat a sandwich, so I had candied pear and three cat's tongues and a piece of *Sacher Torte*. A big girl said we had left Austria during the night and were actually in Germany. I looked out, wanting to hate, but there was nothing out the window but cows and fields. I said maybe we were still in Austria.

It was important to me, because I was collecting countries. Born in Austria, I had vacationed in Hungary and visited relatives in Czechoslovakia, which was three countries I had been in, and Germany would make four. The big girls said it was so Germany, and it puzzled me.

As the morning advanced, the noise swelled. Everyone seemed to be jumping. In the next compartment, a tall, vivacious girl had organized a game. I went in and found a place to sit, but I couldn't understand the rules, so after a bit I organized the small girl sitting beside me into playing ticktacktoe on the outside of her paper food bag. Just as we were getting interested, the morning was over and we had to go to our own compartments to eat lunch. I made her promise faithfully that she would stay right there and play with me after lunch, but I never went back to find her.

The train had become deadly hot. A trance fell. We ate silently. I had bitten into the sausage and found I couldn't bear the taste, and I thought I would eat it for supper. The sandwiches had become too dry to eat, so I had some dates and cat's tongues and a piece of cake and then I sat and sucked some candy. I noticed again the noise of the train, which had been quite drowned out in the commotion of the morning, and I fell asleep.

I woke in the late afternoon. I blamed myself for having slept all kinds of sights away. Now I would stay awake and watch. I concentrated on the little girl sitting opposite me. She held a suitcase on her lap. Her snub-nosed profile was outlined against the gray of the window. I kept my eyes on her for such a long time that her face looked as if I had known it forever. She would not talk with me, and I went back to sleep.

I looked for the little girl when I awoke, but I couldn't tell which one she was. I studied all the children in the compartment. None held a suitcase on her lap. The lights in the compartment had been put on and the window was black again. I went back to sleep.

I started up as the train rode into a station and stopped. The big girl said this was the border and now the Nazis would decide what to do with us. She told us to sit as quiet as we could. There was much walking about outside. We saw uniforms under the lights on the platform. They entered the train in front. I held myself so still that my head vibrated on my neck and my knees cramped. Half an hour, an hour. We knew when they were in our carriage, which seemed to settle under their added weight. They were coming toward us down the corridor, stopping at each compartment door. Then one of them stood in our doorway. His uniform had many buttons. We saw the young woman who was in charge of our carriage behind his shoulder. The Nazi signed to one of the children to come with him, and she followed him out. The young woman turned back to tell us not to worry—they were taking one child from each carriage to check papers and look for contraband.

When the little girl returned, she sat down in her place and we all stared at her. We did not ask her what had happened, and she never told us. The carriage rocked; the Nazis had got off. Doors slammed. The train moved. Someone shouted, "We're out!" Then everyone was pressing into the corridor. Everyone was shouting and laughing. I was laughing. The doors between carriages opened and children came spilling in. Where there had been only girls there was suddenly a boy—two—three boys. Dozens of boys. They pulled hats out of the recesses of their clothing, like conjurers, and the hats unfolded and set on their heads were seen to be the hats of forbidden Scout uniforms. The boys turned back the lapels of their jackets and there were rows of badges—the Zionist blue-and-white, Scout buttons, the *Kruckenkreuz* of Austria—and it was such a gay thing and it was so loud and warm I wished I had a badge or a button to turn out. I wished I knew the songs that they were singing and I sang them anyway. "Wah, wah, la la," I sang. Someone squeezed my head; I held someone around the waist and someone held me; we were singing.

The train stopped in a few minutes; we were in Holland. The station was brightly lit and full of people. They handed us paper cups of hot tea through the windows, red polished apples, chocolate bars, and candy—and that was my supper. When the train started up once more, a hundred children from our transport who were staying in Holland (the advancing German Occupation was to

trap them there within two years) stood ranged on the platform—
the smallest, who were four years old, in front, the big ones in the
back. They were waving. We waved, standing at the open windows,
and all along the train we shouted "God bless Queen Wilhelmina"
in chorus.

Inside the train the party went on, but I could not stay awake.
Someone shook me. "We're getting off soon," they said. I heard
them, but I could not wake up. Someone strapped my rucksack
onto my back again and put the suitcase in my hand. I was lifted
down from the train and stood on my feet in the cold black night,
shivering. I remember thinking that now I was in Holland, which
made five countries, but it was too dark to see it and I wondered
if it would count.

Inside the ship, I lay between white sheets in a narrow bed, wide
awake. I had a neat cabin to myself. I had folded my dress and
stockings with fanatical tidiness and brushed my teeth to appease
my absent mother. A big Negro steward came in with a steaming
cup, which he placed in a metal ring attached to the bedside table.
I said, "Is that coffee for me?," to let him know that I spoke
English. He said, "It's tea." I said, "Brown tea?" He said, "English
tea has milk in it." I searched in my mind quickly for something
more to say to keep him with me. I asked him if he thought I was
going to get seasick. He said no, the thing to do was to lie down
and go to sleep at once and wake up on the other side of the Channel in the morning. And then he put the light out and said, "Remember now, you sleep now."

When I was alone, I sat up and prayed God to keep me from
getting seasick and my parents from getting arrested, and I lay
down and woke next morning on the English side of the Channel,
with the boat in dock. For years I wondered if I could count having been on the ocean, since it had all taken place in my own
absence.

We waited all morning to be processed. We waited in the large,
overheated crimson smoking room. It had little tables and chairs
so heavy that they wouldn't budge, however hard we tried to
rock them. For breakfast we finished what was in our lunch bags.

I had to throw my sandwiches in the wastepaper basket—they were so dry they curled—but when I came to the *Knackwurst,* which was beginning to have a strange smell about it, I remembered my grandmother always said that there was always time to throw things out. I put the sausage back in the bag.

Newspapermen had come aboard. All morning they walked among us flashing bulbs, taking pictures. I tried to attract their attention. I played with my lunch bag: "Little Refugee Looking for Crumbs." Not one of them noticed. I tried looking homesick, eyes raised ceilingward as if I were dreaming. They paid no attention. I jumped happily; I tried looking asleep with my head on the table. I forgot about them. I was bored. We fidgeted and waited.

My number was called late in the morning. I was taken to a room with a long table. Half a dozen English ladies sat around it, with stacks of paper before them. One of the papers had my name on it. It even had my photograph pinned to it. I was pleased. I enjoyed being handed from one lady to the next. They asked me questions. They smiled tenderly at me and said I was finished and could go.

I stood in the corridor and wondered where. The boat seemed almost deserted. I walked up some stairs and through a door and finally came out into the open air onto a damp deck. There was a huge sky so low it reached down to the ground in a drizzle as fine as mist. A wide wooden plank stretched between the boat and the wharf. There was no one around to tell me what to do, so I walked up the plank.

I stood on land that I presumed was England; the ground felt ordinary under my feet, and wet. A workman was piling logs. I stood and watched him. I don't know if it was a man or woman who came and took my hand and led me into a shed so huge and vaulted it dwarfed the three or four children who were at the other end and swallowed the sound of their walking. I was told to find my luggage. I walked among the rows of baggage; the floor was covered with it from end to end. It seemed utterly improbable that I should come across my own things. After a while, I sat down on the nearest suitcase and cried.

Some grownup came and took my hand, and led me to my

belongings (following the numbers until we came to 152), and showed me the way to the waiting room. It was full of children and very warm. The photographers were there taking pictures. I pulled my suitcase a little away from the wall and sat on it, looking dreamy. I think I fell asleep.

It seems to me that then and for weeks to come I was in a state of excitement and at the same time constantly sleepy. Scenery and faces shift; we were always waiting. At the wharf we waited for hours. There was another railway carriage, a new station, other platforms where we stood in columns four deep, photographers taking pictures. At the end of the day, we arrived at Dovercourt. There was a fleet of double-decker buses waiting to take us from the station to a workers' summer camp where we would stay while the Committee looked for foster homes. I began to take notice again. I had never seen double-decker buses before. This at last must be something English. I remember asking if I might ride on top. I sat on top and in front, and was the first to see, through the dull gray winter dusk, the camp, like a neat miniature town on the edge of the ocean. I remember wishing, as we drove in, for some glow of sunset, some drama to mark our arrival.

The buses drew up in front of a huge structure of glass and iron, and we all got out. Inside, it was big and hollow, like a railway terminal. We sat with our baggage at long trestle tables, while a small man with an enormous bald brow stood on a wooden stage, out in front, and talked through a megaphone. He explained that he was the camp leader. He called us by number, divided us into groups of four—three small children, and one older one to be our counselor—and told us to go and leave our things in the cottage assigned to us and come right back to have our supper.

The camp consisted of a couple of hundred identical one-room wooden cottages built along straight intersecting paths. To the right, at the bottom of every path, we could see the flat black ocean stretching toward the horizon over which we had come. Back of us was England.

Our little cottage had little curtained windows that gave onto a miniature veranda. We thought it was sweet.. We squealed, choosing our beds. The counselor, a thin girl of fourteen or fifteen, held her nose and asked what the horrid smell in here was. "Whew!" said all the little girls. "What a horrible smell! What can it be?"

I knew it was my sausage, and was badly frightened. Like a pickpocket whose escape has been cut off, I mingled with the crowd. I held my nose, looked ostentatiously in corners, and helped curse the dirty, idiotic, disgusting person who was responsible for stinking up the place. It felt so good to be mad at someone I almost forgot it was me we were yelling at.

"All right, everybody!" said the counselor. "Let's go, then."

I told her I didn't feel very well and did not want any supper. I would stay in the cottage and go to bed. As soon as the others were gone, I fetched the brown paper bag out of my rucksack and looked the cottage over for some place, some corner where a sausage could be hidden so as not to smell. I kept thinking that I would presently find such a special niche for it. Meanwhile it was cold in the unheated cottage. I took off my shoes and got under the blanket. I laid my head back against the chilly little pillow. I got up again. I thought of starting a letter to ask someone to be a sponsor for my parents, but instead I went and knelt at the bottom of the bed with my elbows on the window sill and looked out. In the direction of the assembly hall the sky glowed with light. I wished I had gone along with the others. I was thinking of putting my shoes back on and going to look for my roommates, when I heard them coming along the path and I remembered my sausage. Now it seemed that what I needed was a long stretch of time to take care of it—and here were feet already on the veranda steps. The door opened. I was lying between the sheets, breathing hard, having just in time skidded the *Knackwurst* into the corner under my bed.

The children did not let me forget it. The counselor, who slept next to me, said "Someone must have made in her bed!" I hummed a song to show I did not feel myself meant in the least, and one of the little girls asked me if I had a stomach-ache, to be making such a horrible noise. The counselor giggled. Finally, they went to sleep.

During the night the temperature dropped; the memorable, bitter winter of 1938 had set in on England's east coast. By morning, the water in the sink in our cottage was a solid block of ice. The tap merely sputtered. We could not wash our faces, and we set out guiltlessly for breakfast with unbrushed teeth and our mothers not even betrayed.

Outside, the vicious cold wind from the ocean knocked the breath out of us. We bucked it with lowered heads. The hall had been constructed for summer use. At our first breakfast, we watched the snow that had seeped between the glass squares of the roof and the iron framework fall in delicate drifts through the indoor air. It sugared our hair and shoulders and settled briefly on the hot porridge, salt kippers, and other wrong, strange foods. It was rumored that one of the girls had had her toes frozen off. We were fascinated. It seemed right that the weather should be as unnatural as our circumstances. (As long as we stayed in that camp, we slept in our stockings and mittens and we wore our coats and caps all day.)

My mind during that first breakfast was on my sausage. I had to do away with the sausage without doing away with it. It was difficult to focus on the problem; I kept forgetting to think about it, yet, all the time, the place where the sausage lay on the floor against the wall, under the bed, remained the center of my guilt, a sore spot in my mind.

I ate in nervous haste. I meant to get to the cottage before the others came back, but when the meal was done we all had to sit and listen to the camp leader make announcements through his megaphone. He told us the camp regulations—that the ocean front was out of bounds, that we were to write letters to our parents, that we must stay in hall because some English ladies from the Committee were coming to choose children to go and live with families in different parts of England. We were going to learn to dance the *hora,* he said, for the ladies.

The trestle tables had been cleared away. There was some ragged singing going on. "Dance!" said the camp leader to a small circle of children he had collected in the center of the hall. He bobbed at the knees encouragingly. His eye roved the hall. He went trotting from one group of children to another. "Come on, everybody! Let's show the English people how we can dance!" No one moved. The camp leader wiped his brow. He took off his jacket and rolled up the sleeves of his shirt. His arms were covered with a perfect sleeve of hair. I was rooting for him. I would have gone myself, but I didn't know how the dance went and I wasn't sure if he meant me when he said "everybody."

I went and stood with some children watching workmen install two extra stoves. They were big black stoves with fat black L-shaped chimneys that carried the smoke out through the roof. When the stoves were lit, they created rings of intense heat in which we stood all morning jostling for places, for the warmth made no inroad on the general chill.

The camp leader had found some of the older children who knew how to do the *hora*. They danced in a ring, their arms around each other's shoulders. I looked for the camp leader and saw him standing with a group of ladies in fur coats. He had put his jacket back on. He was bowing and bobbing his head to the ladies. He walked them all around the hall. They stopped and talked to some of the children. I stalked the party with my eyes. I would ask them about getting a sponsor for my parents and the twins. They were moving toward me. I felt flushed; it came to me that I did not know the words to say to them. A cloud of confusion blocked the ladies from my sight, though I knew when they were in front of me and when they had passed. I saw them going out to inspect the kitchens. The camp leader held the door for them.

Before I knew what I had decided, I was walking out of the hall into the freezing air, going around the outside of the building toward the kitchens. It had stopped snowing. A door opened and a man in a long white apron came out with a steaming bucket, which he emptied into a trash can. He was whistling the tune of the *hora*. He waved to me and went back in and shut the door. The trash can went on steaming.

For a moment there, I saw what to do with my sausage. The

idea of throwing into the trash can what my mother had gone especially to buy me, because I had lied that I wanted it, brought on such a fierce pain in my chest where I had always understood my heart to be that I stood still in surprise. I was shocked that I could be hurting so. I started walking toward the cottage, weeping with pain and outrage at the pain. I had a clear notion of myself crying, in my thickly padded coat and mittens that were attached to one another by a ribbon threaded through the sleeves and across the back. And my hair was light brown and obstinately curled. No wonder the photographers had not taken my picture. I noticed that I had stopped hurting. I suspected that I was some-how not crying properly, was perhaps only pretending, and I stopped, except for the sobbing, which went on for a while.

When I came to the cottage, I walked around to the back, having decided that I would bury the sausage. I found a piece of wood and scraped away the top layer of snow, but, underneath, the earth was frozen and unyielding. I scraped and hacked at it with my heel. Tufts of muddy iced grass came loose. I stood look-ing around me. The wind had dropped and the air froze silently. And then I saw something; I saw where, in the middle of a semi-circle of snow that must in summer have been a flower bed in a grassplot behind the cottage, there grew a tall, meager rosebush with a single bright-red rosebud wearing a clump of freshly fallen snow, like a cap askew. This struck me profoundly. I was a symbolist in those days, and roses and the like were just my speed. It excited me. I would write it in a letter to Onkel Hans and Tante Trude in London, saying that the Jews in Austria were like roses left over in the winter of the Nazi Occupation. I would write that they were dying of the cold. How beautifully it all fell into place! How true and sad! They would say, "And she is only ten years old!" I ran around the cottage and up the veranda steps. I emp-tied my rucksack onto the blanket, looking for pen, paper, and my father's list of addresses with a rapidity that matched the rate at which my metaphor was growing and branching. I wanted to be writing. I was going to say, "If good people like you don't pluck the roses quickly, the Nazis will come and cut them down." I hopped onto the edge of the bed, and, hampered by coat and gloves, with freezing ears, plunged with a kind of greedy glee into my writing.

The counselor's thin face appeared behind the cold glass of the window. She opened the door and came in. Everyone was sitting down to lunch, she said, and they had sent her to look for me. I recognized the authentic voice of the exasperated grownup. I wanted to get her to like me. I kept chatting. I walked to the dining hall beside her, telling how I was writing to some people in London who were going to get a visa for my parents. I watched out of the corner of my eye to see if she was impressed. Her face was blue and her eyes little and wind-reddened. Her mouth was set in a grin; I could not tell if it was against the cold or if she was laughing at me. I wouldn't talk to her ever again.

To my surprise, she began to talk to me. She said people were saying that there were new persecutions going on in Vienna, that all food shops were closed to Jews, that Jews weren't allowed to go into the streets day or night and were being fetched out of their apartments and taken away in cartloads. She said she was frightened because of her mother. I told her not to worry; there were so many Jews, they probably wouldn't even get to her mother.

After lunch, the camp leader addressed us through the megaphone. He said he had heard the rumors about new pogroms in Vienna, that he had no official word and we were not to believe them or worry ourselves. Now we would observe one minute's silence and pray for our dear ones left behind. There was a shuffling, a scraping of five hundred chairs as we got to our feet, followed by such a thunderous silence that a little dog belonging to one of the kitchen staff could not bear it and set up a long, terrified howl. The faces of the children opposite me struggled to retain a decent solemnity, but laughter spread through the hall. I felt my face smiling and laughter coming from my own throat, and was horrified because I knew that the sin of my gaiety would be visited on my parents in the very disaster that I should have been this instant praying away.

I borrowed a pencil and sat down on a bench against the wall and wrote a letter home. It was a letter in code, to pass the censor. I wrote, "Here are some *questions* that you must answer *immediately*. What did you have for dinner today? Did you have a nice walk this morning? Are you still living at the same address? Do you understand these *questions?* PLEASE ANSWER AT ONCE." I wished there were someone to show my letter to—not a child but a grownup, who would appreciate it.

The camp leader was still on the stage, talking to some people. I went straight up to him and I said, "How long does a letter to Vienna take, please?" He said it took about two days. I said that I was writing to my parents to find out if they were all right. He said that was fine. His eyes were looking sharply over my head at a new bunch of ladies in fur coats standing just inside the door, and though I knew very well that he was waiting for me to move on so that he could go to them, I still said, "I wrote a letter in code." "That's good," he said. "Just a minute, now." And then he turned me, not ungently, out of his path. I watched his back striding away, bowing and bobbing to the ladies. I thought, He doesn't even know my name, and I walked away myself, but my shoulder felt for hours the pressure of his hand.

I went back to the bench by the wall and sat. Outside, the dusk of an English winter day, which starts imperceptibly almost immediately after lunch, was settling over the camp, and it looked cold. I sat with my mittened hands inside my pockets, sinking every moment more deeply into my coat. My head kept nagging me to go and write another sponsor letter; it might be this letter I might be writing this instant that would save my parents. The lights came on in the hall, but still I sat. I tried to frighten myself into activity by imagining that the Nazis had come to the flat to arrest my father, but I didn't believe it. I tried to imagine my father and mother put into carts, but found I did not really care. Alarmed, I tried imagining my mother taken away and dead; I imagined myself dead and buried in the ground, but still I couldn't care anything about it. My body felt, for the first time in days, wonderfully warm inside my coat, while my eyes sportively attached themselves at random to a child and followed her across the hall to join the *hora* dancers, and watched their clever feet doing the steps. The music had become familiar, and I sang it in my head.

There was a lady in a fur coat walking up to where I sat, and she spoke to me. She said, "Would you like to come and dance with the other children?" I said, "No," because it did not seem possible that I could get up out of my coat. "Come along," the lady said. "Come and dance." I said, "I don't know how," looking straight before me into the black of her dress where her fur coat flapped open. I thought, If she asks me a third time I will go. The lady said, "You can learn," but still it seemed to me she had not asked me in such a way that I could get up and go, and I waited for her to ask me the right way. The lady turned and walked off. I sat all afternoon waiting for her to come back.

In the evening there was an entertainment. We sat in rows. The camp leader got up on the stage and taught us to sing songs in English: "Ten Green Bottles," "Rule Britannia," and "Boomps-a-Daisy." Then he introduced a muscle man. The muscle man threw off his cape and he had nothing on underneath except a little pair of plum-colored satin trunks. He looked bare and pink standing all by himself on the stage, but he didn't seem to feel the cold. He flexed his biceps for us. He could flap his diaphragm left side and right side separately, and wiggle each toe in turn. His head was small and perfectly round, like a walnut. Afterward, the camp leader went up to thank him. He said the muscle man was sorry that he could not speak German but that he had come all the way from London to entertain us. The muscle man stood smiling with great sweetness, but I knew he didn't even know that I was there.

At the end of the entertainment, the camp leader announced that we were to remain in hall after breakfast tomorrow to welcome the Mayor, who was coming to welcome us. The ceremony would be broadcast by the B.B.C. He asked for a show of hands from the children who spoke English. They were to be introduced to the Mayor. I raised my hand, stunned by the opportunity opening before me. I could tell the Mayor about the rose in the snow; I would ask him to be a sponsor for my parents. In bed that night, I asked the counselor how to say "growing" in English, but she didn't know. She told us that a new transport of Jewish children from Germany was expected in camp. I understood from her that this was to be regarded as a calamity, because German Jews talked like Germans and thought they knew everything better than everybody else and would ruin the whole camp. I was surprised. At home I had learned that it was the Polish Jews who always thought they knew everything and were noisy and pushy in public and ruined everything for the *real,* the Austrian, Jews. I asked our counselor how to say "plucking," as in "plucking flowers," in English, but she said how should she know?

That night I lay for hours in a waking nightmare. The more I worked on my speech for the Mayor, the fewer English words I seemed to know; the less I felt like speaking to him, the more I saw that I must speak or it would be my fault if my parents did not escape. I must have fallen asleep, for I woke in a thumping panic from a dream that a crowd of people had discovered my sausage. When I had calmed a little, I leaned out into the dark and felt under the bed. There was the paper bag. I brought it out and stealthily squeezed it well down into my rucksack, and I thought the crackling and rustling of the paper must be echoing from one end to the other of the sleeping camp.

All the next morning we stood in rows waiting for the Mayor. He sent a message that he was going to be delayed. I had given up the preparation of my speech. I imagined that once I was face to face with the Mayor the words would roll from my tongue. I shifted my weight from one foot to the other and yawned. I had a fantasy: I was saying my sentences about the rose to the Mayor. His look was full of wonder. He asked me my name. He invited me to come and live with him in his house.

At some point, I happened to look toward the stage, and there were some men standing with the camp leader. They were talking. I wondered if one of them might be the Mayor. Maybe it was the gray-haired man in the raincoat. He had a cold in the head and kept blowing his nose and clapping the camp leader on the shoulder every time the camp leader clapped him on the shoulder. Or maybe it was the other man, holding a microphone and trailing a long wire. The camp leader was talking into the microphone, and then the man with the cold talked in English. I could not concentrate on what he was saying. There was a long queue of children filing past. I wondered what they were doing; they couldn't be the English-speaking children being introduced to the Mayor, because if they were I would be among them. I could not understand what was happening, and I lost interest. Afterward, they were gone and I was sitting down again on the bench by the wall, and I was never sure that there was such a person as a Mayor.

There seems to be only a certain amount of room in my memory. I cannot keep the subsequent days separate in my mind or remember how many there were. There was some attempt to keep us occupied. I remember English lessons going on in various corners of the hall. I remember a drawing competition that I either won or thought I ought to have won—I don't recall which. The *hora* tune had become a hit. We hummed it while we dressed in the morning and the children walking by outside would be whistling it, too. There was always some group dancing, keeping warm in the hall. I think I might have been a week in that camp, perhaps a little more.

One evening the youngest of my roommates and I were sent to go to bed and found four large boys in our cottage. They were heaving our belongings over the veranda railing into the snow. The little girl and I watched, holding the spokes, our eyes on a level with the big boys' feet. They wore long wool socks and short pants, and, in between, their knees were knobbly. I thought they were lovely. I admired the energetic, devil-may-care way they told us the cottage was theirs and we should go and find out where we belonged. Then they went in and shut the door. "That's those Germans," said the little girl and began to cry, but I felt suddenly extraordinarily happy to think of the boys inside the familiar walls of our cottage; I had a sense of the camp and the cottages full of boys and girls—Austrians, Germans, and even Poles—and I hated the little girl beside me who had sat down on her suitcase and was howling dismally. She was intefering with my loving everybody.

I don't know how long we sat outside the cottage. Eventually, some person came walking by and found us sitting on our suitcases in the snow. The little girl was still wailing in a bored sort of way. This person asked us what had happened and was quite upset and took us along to the office, and the muddle was discovered. It seemed that we were part of the original Austrian transport slated to be moved to another camp, but not until the next day. And so it turned out that the Germans really had ruined everything. The little girl and I were put into a narrow room with bunk beds for the night. We cursed the Germans with heated indignation and excited ourselves. We talked far into the night. We told each other things and we became quite intimate.

About the second camp I remember only that it was not a proper camp like our first camp. The assembly hall was made of brick; the cottages, instead of being wooden, were made of stucco. It was all wrong and strange, and before the newness of it could pass away I moved again.

One evening I was sitting by one of the stoves, writing a letter to my parents, when two English ladies came up to me. One of them carried a pad of paper, and she said, "How about this one?," and the other lady said, "All right." They smiled at me. They asked my name and age and I told them. They said I spoke English very nicely. I beamed. They asked me if I was Orthodox. I said yes. They were pleased. They said then would I like to come and live with a lovely Orthodox family in Liverpool. I said yes enthusiastically, and we all three beamed at one another. I asked the ladies if they would find a sponsor for my parents, and watched them exchange glances. One lady patted my head and said we would see. I said and could they get a sponsor for my grandparents and for my cousins Erica and Ilse, who had not been able to come on the children's transport like me. The ladies' smiles became strained. They said we would talk about it later.

I finished my letter to my parents, saying that I was going to go and live with this lovely Orthodox family in Liverpool and would they please write and tell me what did "Orthodox" mean.

There were cars waiting early the next morning to take twenty little girls to the railway station. All day we traveled north. All day it snowed. I was trying to write a sponsor letter in my head about the little bushes outside stooped like old peasants under the heavy shawl of snow, but I couldn't tie them in with Jews and Nazis. I had a nervous notion that while I looked out one side of the train the interesting things were happening on the other side, so I kept running between the compartment and the corridor, to look out there. After a while, the older girls clucked their tongues and said couldn't I sit still for just one minute, and I said I had to go out, and did, and I didn't dare to come back. I looked out of the corridor window until I was tired, and then I went along to the lavatory and messed with the soap. When I judged I had been away a reasonable time, I came back. I stopped stock-still in the doorway of my compartment. My rucksack stood on my seat; the brown paper bag had been taken out and torn open, and my guilty sausage lay exposed to the light. It was ugly and shrivelled, with one end nibbled off. The thing had lost the fierce and aggressive stench of active decay and had about it now the suffocating smell of mold; it thickened the air of the compartment. One of the English ladies was standing looking at it, her nose crinkled. The seven children were sitting looking at me, and I died there on the spot, drowned in shame. The waters closed over my head and through the thumping and roaring in my ears I heard one of the little girls say, "And it isn't even kosher." The English lady said, "You can throw it away in the station when we change trains." Dead and drowned under their eyes, I walked to my seat. I packed up the sausage; I took the rucksack off the seat and sat down. After a while, I noticed that the other girls were no longer staring at me and that the lady, when she looked in to see how we were doing, smiled pleasantly. But still I had not the courage to get out of my seat, though now I really needed to go to the bathroom.

In the station there was a large trash can and I dropped my sausage in. I stood and roared with grief. Through my noise and my tears I saw the foolish children standing around, and heard one of the English ladies saying, "Come on, now. Are you all right?" They both looked upset and frightened. "Will you be all right?" they asked.

CHAPTER THREE

Liverpool: Mrs. Levine's House

We arrived in Liverpool in the early evening. There were people from the Committee waiting with cars to take us to a great house.

I remember that all the doors stood open. Lights were on in all the rooms and hallways, and many people were walking everywhere. Our rucksacks and suitcases stood on the landing. Some ladies took off our coats and caps and gloves and piled them on the beds. Someone asked me if I wanted to go to the bathroom, and though I did, quite badly by now, I wondered how I was going to find my way back, and I didn't even know where it was. It seemed too complicated. I said I didn't need to go.

In a big room, a long table with a white cloth was laid as if for a party. On the far side of the room was a fire burning in a square hole in the wall. I went and stood in front of it. A tall gentleman stood looking at me. I told him I had never seen a fire in a wall before and that in Vienna we had stoves. He said how nicely I spoke English, and we chatted until a lady from the Committee came to show me to my seat. It seemed it was the first day of Chanukah. Candles were lit. Everyone stood still and sang a song I did not know. Then all the children sat around the table. We had cakes and little plates with colored jelly such as I had never seen before. If you poked it with a finger, it went on wobbling for a while.

A Committee lady going about with a list of names came to stand behind me with another lady. The Committee lady said, "Here's a nice little girl."

I turned, eager to charm. An enormous, prickly-looking fur coat rose sheer above me. An old woman looked at me with a sour expression from behind her glasses. She frightened me. She had a small, gray, untidy face with a lot of hat and hair and spectacle about it. I had imagined that the family who would choose me would be very special, very beautiful people. I signaled to the lady with the list that I wanted to go with somebody else, but she didn't see, because she was attending to the woman in the fur coat, who said, "How old is she? See, we wanted to have one about ten years old—you know, old enough to do for herself but not too old to learn nice ways."

I watched them talking together over my head, and I kept thinking that if I listened harder I would know what they were saying, but always it seemed that my mind wandered, and when I remembered to listen I couldn't tell if I had to go with this person. I wasn't even sure if they were still talking about me, so I said in desperation, out loud, "I'm not ten. I'm half past ten. I'm nearly eleven."

They looked surprised. The old woman in the fur coat grinned shyly at me and I felt better. She asked me where my things were and took my hand and we went and found my coat in the bedroom. There was a young man who carried my luggage out of the house to one of the cars in the snow in the street. He got into the driver's seat. The old woman made me get in behind with her. I remember that as the car started up I looked back through the rear window in a panic moment to see if I could see one of the Committee ladies. I wondered if they knew I was being taken away. And if my parents would find out where I was. But I could not frighten myself for long. My childhood had not prepared me to expect harm from grownups. I think I rather felt I had a way with them, and as soon as we were settled in the car I started to tell the old woman how I had studied English at school, and privately as well, and that I always got A's in my reports. In the half dark of the back seat, I could not tell if this stolid, fur-wrapped person beside me was properly impressed. I said, "And I can figure-skate and dance on my toes." She said something to the young man in front that I could not make out. I was too sleepy to think up more

English conversation; I decided to leave it all till later and I let my eyes close.

I was set on my feet in the dark and shivering cold and I closed my eyes, wanting only to go back to sleep, but they walked me up the garden path toward an open door lit from inside. There were people, and in the background I saw a maid in a black dress and white cap and apron looking at me over their heads. Someone took off my coat again. An old man with glasses sat on the far side of another fireplace. He drew a little low footstool from under his chair for me to sit on, in front of the fire, next to a large Alsatian dog, whose name, they said, was Barry. A maid in uniform brought a cup of tea like the tea on the boat, with milk in it, and I hated the taste. I said it was too hot to drink and that I wanted to go to sleep, but they said I must have a bath first and called a maid. They said her name was Annie. They told me she would give me a bath, but I was ashamed—I said at home I always bathed myself. They took me upstairs into a bathroom and let the water run and went out and shut the door, and I was so sleepy I thought I would stand and pretend, but then it seemed easier to get into the water.

I think it was one of the several daughters of the house who took me up another flight of stairs to my room. I know there was a maid peering at me through the banisters, and when I was in bed, just before the lights went out, I thought I saw a white-capped head stuck around the door. This made five maids. I was impressed. We had never had more than one maid at a time. Then I went back to sleep.

There was a maid in the full daylight to which I awoke. She stood just inside the door, looking at me and saying, "Taimtarais." I looked back at her without raising my head from the pillow. She stood very straight, heels together, toes turned out. Her arms hung neatly by her sides. She wore a bright-blue linen dress, and over it a white apron so long that it hung below the hemline of her dress. She was a big, firmly fleshed girl, with black hair and bright round cheeks. Her nose was incredibly uptilted.

I said, "Pardon?," not having understood what she had said, and she said again, "It's taimtarais," and went out the door.

I wondered if I should get up. I lay looking around the big, light, chilly room. Someone had brought up my suitcase and rucksack and set them on the chest of drawers. They looked oddly familiar in their strange new surroundings. Presently I got out of bed and dressed. I wondered if I was supposed to go downstairs. I thought I might look silly just to turn up down there among all those people I didn't know, so I took my writing pad and pen with me. I would go in and I would say, "I have to write a letter to my mother," and they would say to each other, "See what a good child. She loves her parents."

When I came out onto the landing, my heart was pounding. There was a door opposite. It stood slightly ajar. I could see, reflected in its own mirror, the top of a neat dressing table. There were photographs stuck all round the mirror, and on the table were a brush-and-comb set, and a pincushion in the shape of a heart. I held my breath. I gave the door a little push. I saw the corner of a bed with a green satin counterpane and wanted to look further in, but the quiet in the house frightened me and I backed away. I wondered where all the people might be and peered over the banisters to the floor below. I saw a green carpet and a number of doors, but they were all shut. I think I got the notion then that the five maids in uniform were inside the rooms, cleaning. Slowly I made my way down to the floor with the green carpet and then down the next flight to the ground floor. I thought I heard voices behind a door and tried to look through its frosted-glass inset. I could make out nothing, but my silhouette must have appeared upon it, because a voice inside said, "Come along. Come along in."

I came into a warm, pleasant kitchen-living room with a big table in the middle and a fire burning briskly in a fireplace. The dog, Barry, lay with his paws on the brass fender, and a fat lady sat by the window, sewing. She said, "Come in. Sit down. Annie will bring your breakfast."

I said, "I have to write to my parents where I am."

"Well, you can have your breakfast first."

The maid in the blue linen dress came in with a boiled egg for me, and tea and toast. She pushed in my chair and buttered my bread. Miserably, I watched her pour milk into my tea. I looked up at her. Her nose had such an upward sweep that from where I sat I could see way into the black caverns of her round little nostrils. It occurred to me that she was winking at me, but I wasn't sure and I kept my eyes on my food and ate it, peering around me now and then. I expected every moment that the doors upstairs would open and release all the people. Everything was quiet. The fire crackled. The fat lady sewed. The dog was scratching, drumming with his hind leg on the fender. The maid was clattering pans in the scullery, and when I was finished she came and fetched away my dishes.

I sat at the table happily writing a letter. I wrote how last night we were taken to a house and there was an ugly old woman who had chosen me and how I had not wanted to go with her. It had been like a slave market. I thought that was pretty clever. I wrote, "The people I am going to live with are very rich. They have five maids. There is a fat lady here sewing. She said I should call her Auntie Essie, but I'm not going to. She doesn't look like an auntie to me. She is very fat." It amused and excited me to be writing to my mother about this person who was sitting there within touching distance. I felt a rush of blood to my head; it had come to me in a flash that this was the identical old woman in the fur coat—and yet it wasn't, either. This lady had on a loose cotton dress. She was quite different. But she was elderly, too, and large, and she wore glasses. Perhaps it was the same one, and yet perhaps it was not. I kept looking surreptitiously across at her. She raised her head. Quickly and guiltily, I bent mine over my letter. I wrote that I had found the chocolate my mother had hidden for me in the bottom of my suitcase. Then I said I loved them, in block capitals, and that it was *very* important to write me what was the meaning of the word "Taimtarais."

When my letter was sealed and addressed, Mrs. Levine gave me a stamp and told me to find Annie and she would post it for me.

Annie was in the drawing room, in the front of the house, lighting the fire. The flames were rushing with a fierce hiss upward into the chimney. I sat down on the little footstool and watched. I wanted to cry. I cradled my head in my hands and planted my elbows on my knees and let homesickness overcome me as one might draw up a blanket to cover one's head. I never knew when the maid left the room or how the day passed. Once, I came to as if with the wearing off of a drug that left me sober and sorrowless in a strange room; I looked curiously about me.

There was an old man sitting on the far side of the fireplace. His little eyes blinked incessantly behind his thick glasses, and he was watching me across the quiet of the room. I recognized him immediately; he was the same old man who had pulled out this footstool for me last night. I had a notion that he had been sitting there ever since, watching me gently and patiently, with the fire crackling between us. He was curling his finger for me to come to him. I got up and stood beside him. I could see his little wrinkled left eye from the side, and a second time through the lens, magnified and yet as from a tremendous distance behind the sevenfold rings and more of the thick glass. He was tickling a silver sixpence out of his purse. When he gave it to me, he put his finger to his lips and winked at me to signify secrecy. I nodded conspiratorially. I had to laugh—and that frightened me. I sat down quickly, wanting to lose myself again in grief.

In the course of that day, I developed a technique: I found that if I sat curled into myself on the low stool facing the fire, and stared into the heart of flame until my eyes stung and my chest was full of a rich, dark ache, I could at will fill up my head with tears and bring them to the point of weeping and arrest them there so that they neither flowed nor receded. Though I knew when, toward evening, the house filled up again with people and that they were in the room whispering about me, I would not turn, so as not to disturb the delicate balance of my tears.

I must have been a great trial to the Levines in that first week.

"Have some tea," Mrs. Levine would say. "Annie, go and bring her a nice hot cup of tea. It'll make you feel better."

I shook my head. I said I didn't like tea.

"She doesn't like tea," Mrs. Levine said. "Here, how about going for a walk. Eh? The fresh air will do you good." She smiled encouragingly into my face. "You want to go for a nice run in the park with Auntie Essie? "

I said I didn't feel like going for a walk. It was cold, I said.

"I know what she wants," Mrs. Levine said, looking up at Annie. "She wants somebody to play with. I'll go and call that Mrs. Rosen that got the other little refugee and she can come over and play. Wouldn't that be nice?" she said to me. "Wouldn't you like a nice little girl to play with?"

I said no, I felt perfectly cheerful and I didn't feel like playing with any children, and I was trying to think of something grown-up to say to Mrs. Levine to keep her there talking to me. "How long please does a letter take from Vienna to England?"

"Two or three days," said Mrs. Levine, with her smile frozen on her face. She sighed, and, groaning, she rose from her knees. She was too fat and old to have conversations with me while I sat under the dining-room table refusing to come out. "That's the third time since breakfast she asked me that," Mrs. Levine said and looked at me from the distance of her full height. I think it frightened her that the refugee she had brought into her house to protect from persecution was talking back to her and watching her out of melancholic and conscious eyes—I caught the look she looked over my head at Annie with a turning outward of her hands and a turning down of the right corner of her mouth.

The next afternoon I stood at the window and saw the thin, angular, tall woman leading a small fat child up the path toward the front door. The little girl had red hair and a white rabbit's-wool hat tied under the chin. She carried a red patent-leather pocketbook.

Mrs. Levine walked into the hall to let them in and I came to the drawing-room door and watched in some excitement. The child stood perfectly still and allowed herself to be peeled out of her thick little coat, switching the pocketbook to the right hand while the left was being slipped out of the coat sleeve and un-gloved and back to the left to get the right glove off.

Then Mrs. Levine called me to take my visitor into the dining room to play and Annie would bring our tea.

The little girl stood in front of the fire holding her pocketbook, looking straight before her. She was an exceedingly plain child and I knew that I could boss her. I started on that exchange of essential information which in later life lies hidden under our first urbanities:

"What's your name?" I asked.

"Helene Rubichek." She didn't ask me mine so I told her what it was and asked her how old she was.

"Seven."

I said that I was ten years old. I told her that my father was in a bank and asked her what hers did. She said her father had had a newspaper but he didn't do anything now. I said mine didn't work in the bank any more either, and because it felt so easy to be saying things in German for the first time in a week I went on to tell her about my mother who played the piano and my grandparents who had a house. I said, "I know a game. Let's guess which of our parents will come sooner, yours or mine."

"Mine are coming next month," she said.

"I bet mine come sooner than yours," I said, and then I asked her what she had in her pocketbook, but Helene put her head on one side so that her cheek came to lie like a fat pouch on her shoulder and wouldn't answer.

"Anyway," I said, "let's play," because I remembered the game Erwin and I had played together and wanted to be playing. "Let's play house. Do you want to?"

"Yes," said Helene.

"All right," I said, "I know where we can play." I took her by the hand and led her to the dining-room table in the middle of the room and made her get under it and crawled in after. We squatted together. "Now they can't even see us," I said, looking in delight around this pretty, compact little world under the table roof, hedged in by a complex of chair legs. "Now we have to be comfortable," I said. "Are you comfortable?"

"Yes," said Helene.

"All right, let's play. I'll be the mother. You be the child. You have to cry and I'll make you feel better. Put your pocketbook down so you can be comfortable." Helene put her head on one side and looked straight before her. "Never mind then," I said, "go on," and I bobbed up and down in my excitement because I knew precisely what it was I wanted her to be doing so that I could do what I wanted to do. "Cry!" But Helene sat growing fatter and more stolid every moment. I thought it was because she wasn't properly comfortable, holding the pocketbook, and I said, "Put it down over there."

Helene said, "No."

"You can have it back as soon as we've finished playing. Please," I wheedled. "I'll take it for you, come on," and I put my hand out to take it, but Helene had gripped her pocketbook with surprising strength. "Come on," I said, tugging at it, "please!" But as I looked into her face I saw that it had broken up, changed out of all recognition, and become perfectly red. The cheeks had closed up over both eyes. I knew what was happening. Helene really was crying. A round black hole appeared where her mouth had been and out of it came a hideous roaring.

The door opened. Mrs. Levine and Mrs. Rosen came running. I came out from under the table protesting that I had only wanted Helene to be comfortable. Mrs. Rosen had hold of Helene's wrist and was pulling out the rest of her, cramped in a fat little ball, yelling monotonously. "Come on now," she kept saying, "do stop crying, will you? Do stop."

Mrs. Levine said to me, "What do you want to pick a fight for with the little girl when she comes to visit? You have to be a little hostess, don't you?"

"But I said 'please,' " I explained while Mrs. Rosen over my head said to Mrs. Levine, "She never did that before. For goodness' sake stop, can't you? At home she never even opens her mouth. She gives me the creeps. I tell my husband if it wasn't for her parents coming in a month I wouldn't know what to do with her, she makes me so nervous. My husband laughs at me. He says she'll come around. He always wanted children. He comes home at night and he brings her toys and that little pocketbook and he jokes and laughs, but it's me that's left alone with her all day and all she ever does is stand around and I don't know what she wants or if she understands what I say to her and I get so nervous." I was watching in fascination the way Mrs. Rosen's left cheek kept jumping independently of the rest of her.

Now Mrs. Levine had begun to talk about me and I listened with that hungry silence which one renders to conversations of which oneself is the subject. "This one talks all right," Mrs. Levine was saying, "don't you?" and she patted my head. "When I tell her to come out from the table and be happy with us, she says she's happier down there. She's got an answer for everything." Mrs. Levine bent down to little Helene, whose noise was becoming exhausted and mechanical. "We'll have some nice tea, eh? And cake. Go call Annie," she said to me.

Annie came with the tray and she spread the cloth and poured our tea and heaped little Helene's plate with cake while I watched in an agony of impatience. I was dying to get back under the table, ridden by the sharp and clear desire to have Helene sitting beside me in our miniature house in an orgy of coziness, but Helene kept stuffing her fat face, with leisurely solemnity. Her pocketbook lay beside her plate. When she was finished Annie gave her another slice and then Mrs. Rosen came in bringing Helene's coat and said it was time to go.

"Say good-by to the little girl," Mrs. Levine said at the front door.

"Good-by," I said, and then in German I called after her, "Are you coming again?" but Mrs. Rosen was leading her away down the path as if it were something at once fragile and not very appetizing that she had there by the hand, and Helene never turned around.

I asked Mrs. Levine if Helene could come again and she said, "You funny kid, first you pick a fight and then you want her to

come back!" But she said Helene could come back. I asked when.
Mrs. Levine said maybe she could come again next Saturday.

Then it happened; starting hot between my legs, it ran down
my stockings, and I knew that I was wetting myself. I saw Mrs.
Levine looking at my feet where a wet spot was forming on the
hall carpet, but I thought, "Maybe she isn't looking at me. Maybe
she is looking at the dog, scratching at the front door." I said,
"Look at Barry at the front door. He knows somebody is coming."
Mrs. Levine raised one corner of her mouth. She said, "You
better run up to the bathroom now. Annie! Come here and bring
a cloth," and as I was going up the stairs I heard her say to her
daughter Sarah, who had come in the front door, what I did not
make out at the time though my ears retained the sounds intact,
and when I was in my room that night, lying in bed, I remembered
and understood that what she had said was, "I told you they don't
bring up children over there the way we do here in England," and
Sarah had said, "Oh Ma, what do you know about what they do
'over there'—or about bringing up children, either!"

I explained it to myself. Mrs. Levine could not have understood
when I told her how I always got A's in my report; I must tell her
that I was always first in my class. I would say to her the bit about
the slave market. I would write the very next day to my father
and ask him how to say it in English. I lay in bed thinking up
clever things to say to Mrs. Levine. I imagined sentimental situations in which to say them, calling her "Auntie Essie," but when
I came downstairs the next morning, Mrs. Levine was sitting with
her head bent over her sewing, and I found I could not say "Auntie
Essie"; it sounded silly in daylight and face to face. But neither
could I call her "Mrs. Levine," because she had told me to say
"Auntie Essie." I watched and waited for her to raise her head
from her work before I addressed her, and poor Mrs. Levine,
happening to look up, meaning to poke the fire, was startled to
find herself under this close scrutiny. "What are you staring at me
for, for goodness' sake!" she cried out. Immediately she recol-
lected herself, though flustered still. "Why don't you read a book or
go for a walk? Take her for a run in the park," she said to Annie,

who had a way of appearing on the scene whenever there was anything going on. "Come on, now," she said rather desperately to me. "You don't want to cry—I didn't mean to shout at you. Now, come on, will you?"

It occurred to me to say, "In Vienna, Jews aren't allowed to go in the park."

The effect was instantaneous and marvelous. Mrs. Levine bent down and took me in her arms, but not before I had seen her face flush and her eyes fill with tears, and I knew they were for me. I was immensely impressed. I held myself very stiff against her unfamiliar and solid bosom; I felt restless in that embrace and began politely to extricate myself. I said I had to go and write a letter to ask my father something.

But all day I was grieved because Mrs. Levine had taken me in her arms and I had not liked it. I kept trying to think up ways in English to avoid the direct address, so that I could have conversation with her, but I never could think of one when I needed it. And now I didn't dare look at her in case I caught her eye and she might think I was staring. My nervousness around her increased, until by evening whenever Mrs. Levine came into a room I must get up and walk out of it. I am sure that I wounded her deeply. "All right," she said, "you'd better go up to bed now," and just then I wet myself again.

I used to pray to God not to let it happen any more. I remember, I made deals with fate. I said, "If I walk all the way upstairs as far as my door without opening my eyes, I won't wet myself again," but as the days passed, it kept happening more and more often.

Meanwhile, Saturday morning, I had my first letter from my parents. It had been addressed to Dovercourt camp, readdressed to the other camp and came to me via the Liverpool Refugee Committee.

When Helene came in the afternoon I could hardly wait to take her into the dining room and shut the door. I said, "I know a game. Let's get under the table."

Helene said, "No."

"All right. We can play it out here. It's a guessing game. You have to guess in how many days you will get a letter from your parents. First you guess and then I guess my letter, and the one who guesses too early has lost. Go on. You guess."

Helene looked straight before her. "Go on," I said, "guess how many days."

Helene said, "Three."

"All right," I said, "you guess three days. Now it's my turn, I have to figure." I figured that the letter I had taken to the corner post box in the morning would take two or three days to reach Vienna, say four to be on the safe side, and they would answer the next day or the day after, say another four days, that makes eight, and then four days back, twelve, add two more days to make sure, that's fourteen. "I guess fourteen days. Now let's get under the table." But Helene would not, and cried, and Mrs. Levine ran in to scold me and Annie brought our tea, and after that Mrs. Rosen took Helene home.

But on the following Monday the twenty refugee children who had been distributed among the families of Liverpool were taken to the Hebrew day school, and after that I saw Helene every day.

On Thursday I came in glory. I said that I had had a letter, which made it five days, and I had guessed fourteen days, so I had won by nine.

Next day at break, in the schoolyard, Helene said that she had won too and she had had a letter. "You didn't win," I said. "I won. Because you said three days and your letter took six so you lost by three days, see?" Helene did not see. She looked straight before her. "Let's do it again," I said. "I sent a letter today and I have to figure." This time I figured so well that I made it twenty-one days. "Twenty-one days," I said happily. "Now it's your turn. You guess."

"Two days," said Helene. In all the weeks we played, she never did catch on.

A delightful thing had meanwhile developed. I had written my parents about my friend Helene Rubichek and how her parents were coming to England. My parents knew Anton Rubichek by name as a journalist and got in touch with him and arranged to send me a present, a box of sweets perhaps, a surprise. More wonderful yet, my parents were going to visit Helene's parents on Saturday at the very time Helene would be visiting me. This intrigued me: I wanted Helene to describe to me the room in which they would be having their coffee, to give me an idea how the furniture was arranged, so that I could the better think of them sitting there, but Helene wasn't at all good at giving anybody any ideas and I made up my own picture. The next letter from home destroyed this picture: It seemed my parents had never sat in that room at all. It was explained in an enclosed note, sealed and addressed to Mrs. Levine, who read it to her daughters. They were very excited, and then Mrs. Levine called Mrs. Rosen on the telephone and they talked a long time. I got a new picture of my parents standing outside Helene's parents' apartment door, which had been locked and taped and sealed off with an official seal. The neighbors said the Rubicheks had been taken away that morning.

This troubled me deeply: I practiced imagining what my parents were doing, and where, at the very instant that I was thinking of them and then trying to imagine that they were really doing something entirely different in quite another place. It made me giddy, and I went to Mrs. Levine and told her my stomach felt sick. She gave me some medicine and I vomited, and then I felt better. I sat down and wrote a letter home.

I posted it the next morning on my way to school. During break I found Helene and said, "This time I guess thirty days."

Helene said, "I'm not playing any more."

"Yes you are," I said, appalled because I could not face the weeks ahead unless they were divided into periods of which I could see the end, with a letter to wait for, like the piece of chocolate that my mother had always put in the middle of the plate, underneath so many spoonfuls of rice pudding. "Don't you like to play?" I said quickly, for Helene was laying her cheek on her shoulder. "I'll show you how to win. Guess twenty days and then you won't expect a letter and suddenly it will come as a surprise, you see?"

But Helene said, "I won't get any more letters."

"Yes, you might," I said, but I knew that Helene had turned obstinate past recall.

At the house after school, I had begun to write my autobiography, to let the English know, as I had promised my father, what had happened to us under Hitler. But when I came to write it down, I felt a certain flatness. The events needed to be picked up, deepened, darkened. I described with gusto the "horror-night" of Schuschnigg's abdication—not mentioning how unsolemnly rude my mother had been to Tante Trude. I wrote how, the next morning, "the red flags waved like evil ghosts in the wind and I stood still and held my hands in horror before my eyes, having already an inkling of the charm of the darling Germans." (*"Die lieblichen Deutschen"* were the words I had heard my mother use.) I wrote, "The sun shone in the cloudless blue. Was it for us it shone or for our enemies? Or was it only for the happy people in distant lands who would surely come to our aid?" I showed it to Sarah.

Sarah must have been fifteen years old at the time. By far the most intelligent, spirited, and imaginative of her family, she was the Elizabeth Bennet of the Levines. She was constantly irritated with everyone, trying to bully her father into asserting himself, her mother into being better informed, her five sisters into greater awareness and elegance. To me, she was the touchstone of everything English. My book became our common project. She encouraged me to finish it, and she was going to help me translate it and publish it. Together, we would expose Adolf Hitler to the world.

In bed at night, I dreamed about Sarah, but in the daytime I sought out the comfortable sanctuary of Annie's kitchen. I liked to watch her trip busily about, like the good sister in the fairy tale my father had taken me to see in the children's theater. She looked so tidy in her linen dress and long apron. Her eyes were lowered demurely, but her little round nostrils stared outrageously. There was a game I played: I would stalk her around the kitchen, trying to maneuver myself into positions from which I could get a good look into the inside of Annie's nose.

Annie never made me finish up my cups of nauseating tea

with milk, or told me to cheer up and *do* something, like Mrs. Levine; she never corrected my Viennese table manners or pulled me up when I used a German word instead of the English one I didn't know, like Sarah. Mostly, Annie was not particularly listening to me, and this gave me a certain freedom in talking with her.

I would say, "Annie, do you like Mrs. Levine?"

And Annie would say, "Yes. Mrs. Levine is a very nice lady."

I said, "I like her. I didn't like her in the beginning, but now I do." And I would discuss with Annie my impressions of the daughters of the house and ask Annie which one she thought was the prettiest. I said I thought Sarah was beautiful. I liked her the best—the others continued to confuse me. I knew that there were six. It took me weeks to figure out which of them lived in which of the rooms on the second floor, and which of them were married and only came to visit. I did not dare to talk to any of them, because their names and faces were interchangeable. Then I would say, "And Uncle Reuben, he is nice," surprised to come across him in my mind, just as I was always surprised to come into a room and find him in it. This house full of women was inclined to forget Uncle Reuben except at mealtimes, to feed, or at times when his eyes were bad, to fuss over. But whenever I did recall his existence, I liked him. "He is kind," I said. "He gives me sixpence every Sunday. I like him very much."

Annie said yes, Mr. Levine was a very nice man. I liked talking things over with Annie. And if Annie winked her eye and made me laugh and I wet myself, I would say brazenly, almost carelessly, "Annie, look what that silly Barry did." Annie would say, "That dog, he's getting just terrible," and she would get a cloth and wipe up the pool.

One day the dog must have had a cold in his insides, because he really did make a pool. I watched him do it, and I was so pleased that I cried, "Hey, Annie, guess what? The dog made a pool. Look, behind the settee in the sitting room."

Annie said, "Miss Sarah, there goes that dog again. You see what I told you, he's getting worse and worse."

Sarah said, "Barry, come here at once." She took hold of his collar and said, "Lore, was it Barry who made that pool?" and looked me straight in the eyes.

"Right behind the settee; nobody could even have got in there except Barry," I said, with all my heart because it was the truth.

"Well, then," Sarah said, "don't you think he should be taught not to do it? He's been living in our house long enough, don't you think, Lore? Maybe he needs to be punished. Hand me his lead."

I stood and watched her spank the dog—not very hard or very long, but he laid down his front legs and raised his head, gave three high-pitched howls, and fled into the kitchen.

Later I heard the visitors in the sitting room. I didn't know if I was supposed to go in. Barry was alone in the kitchen, and I didn't want to go in there, so I went up the stairs looking for Annie.

There was no one on the green-carpeted landing. All the doors were shut and blind. I stood listening, and I wondered about those five maids in their caps and aprons. I never had seen any of them again or ever stopped expecting to. (It must have occurred to me at some point that there never had been any maid but my own Annie, but mystification had become a habit of mind. Only now, with this writing down, is it obvious how Annie's curiosity had taken five separate peeks at the little refugee that first night; only now does Auntie Essie finally merge with the ugly old woman in fur; now I understand the word "taimtarais," which Annie said every morning when she came to wake me and which my father never did find in any dictionary.)

Annie's dustpan and broom leaned outside my room on the top floor. Annie was inside, but she wasn't cleaning. She was standing at my dressing table eating my chocolate. I heard the small rustle of her finger poking choosily into the box of sweets my mother had hidden in my suitcase for me—saw with my own eyes how Annie lifted one out and put it into her mouth. I dared not breathe in case Annie should turn around and know that I had seen her. With a beating heart, I backed away, wondering how I should ever face her again, or what I would say to her when we met. I crept down the stairs.

From the drawing room came the happy squealing of a little

child. I opened the door and walked self-consciously in. One of the married daughters had brought her small son to visit. The baby was running around in circles. Mrs. Levine said, "This is little Lore. Look who's come to play with you, Lore. This is our Bobby," and she caught hold of the child and she squeezed him and hugged him and said that she would like to eat him up.

"Oh, Ma!" said Sarah. "You spoil him." Mrs. Levine said, "Say hello to the little girl. Go and shake hands." But the child escaped from his grandmother's grasp and slipped past his mother and his Aunt Sarah and continued his crazy circling, making airplane noises the while, and wouldn't stop to look at me.

Little Bobby had a pair of those peculiar ghetto eyes—as if a whole history of huckstering and dreaming were gathered in the baby's deep eyes. His cheeks were soft and round. I thought he was the most beautiful child I had ever seen. I yearned toward him.

So did his grandfather. Uncle Reuben kept curling his beckoning finger and holding out a silver shilling, which the little boy caught from him like a relay runner snatching the baton, not staying to see his grandfather wink and put a conspiratorial finger to his lips. Bobby's mother said, "Now say thank you to your grandfather and come here at once. Come when I tell you. I'll put your shilling in my purse for you, or you'll lose it. Take his hand," she said to me, "and bring him here."

I put my hand out gladly, but the baby ducked and yelled and ran. I ran after him a little way, but I felt foolish and stopped. I thought, He's only little. I don't run around like that any more. I meant to stand there watching him smilingly, the way grownups watch children, but I did not know how. I rubbed the back of my hand to and fro against my temple in an agony of self-consciousness. I wished I had my little footstool to curl up on, but it was on the other side of the fireplace and it was impossible to think of walking so far with them watching me.

Now they had begun to talk about me. "That's all she ever does," Mrs. Levine was saying to her married daughter. "Write letters home or she just sits around. I tell her she should occupy herself.

She's got to try and be happy with us here. But she doesn't even try."

"Leave her alone, Ma," Sarah said.

"But I am," I said. "I am happy."

"So why do you sit around all day just moping?" Mrs. Levine said, looking at me through her spectacles.

"I'm not moping," I said. The truth was that I never exactly understood the word "moping." After the first days, I had lost my capacity to cry whenever I felt like it, and now I didn't even feel like it any more. Often when I giggled with Annie in the kitchen, I would stop in horror, knowing I must be heartless: I had been enjoying myself; it was hours since I had even remembered my parents. I used to go and look in the mirror to see what Mrs. Levine saw in me.

"You are so moping," she said.

Little Bobby, who could not brook divided attention, crept between his grandmother's knees and pushed his shilling into her chin, saying, "Look what I got, Grandma! Grand-maaa!"

"I'm not moping," I said. "I just like sitting by the fire."

"Always an answer," Mrs. Levine said. "I never saw such a child for arguing. And you think I can get her to go out for some fresh air?"

"Look, Grandma!" little Bobby said. "Look what I can do!" And he tipped his head back and laid the shilling on his forehead.

"My little *Bubele!*" cried Mrs. Levine. She squeezed his face between her hands and kissed him on the mouth.

"I will go," I said very loud. "I will go for a walk."

"You want to go now?" Mrs. Levine said. "Will you go with Annie?"

I blushed furiously, thinking of Annie and the chocolate, but I was committed to saying yes. I was almost glad I was going for a walk with Annie. I wanted to be angry with her.

I decided not to talk to Annie. We walked through the park gates. I knew that Annie was bad. I removed my hand from hers in a gesture of disassociation. I looked up from time to time with horror and awe at this Annie who had stolen my chocolate, but she was walking very straight, her nose pointing upward. I started kicking little stones; Annie let me. My freed hand kept getting in the way. I put it in my pocket, but it felt as if it didn't belong there and I took it out again. Presently I held it up for Annie, and she took it and swung it as we walked. I helped her swing it higher.

"You know," I said and looked up expectantly, "where I come from Jews aren't allowed to go into the parks?"

"Aren't they, now," Annie said. We walked on.

"You know what! You know what I'm going to do with my money? I'm saving it for when my parents come here."

Annie said, "How much you got?"

"Three shillings. Uncle Reuben gives me sixpence every Sunday. He gives Bobby a whole shilling, and he doesn't even say thank you," I said in a mean voice. "He's spoiled," I said, for the anger that was working in my chest and had bounced off Annie now found its mark. "All he can do is run around and make noises. He's just a baby, isn't he, Annie! I bet he doesn't even know what to do with all that money."

"Oh, well," said Annie comfortably, "there's always something you can do with money."

That very night, Annie knocked at my bedroom door. She was all dressed up in a navy-blue uniform with a red collar and red-ribboned bonnet, and she looked very smart and strange, almost like somebody I didn't know at all. She said could she come in, and did, and stood just inside my door.

I was proud to have her in my room in her uniform. "Where are you going in that?" I asked, making conversation.

"It's my Salvation Army day. We got a meeting," Annie said. "We have a band and hymn singing. We sing hymns and sacred songs and we have this collection to give food to the poor people and bring them the Word of the Lord."

I listened intelligently. Annie had never spoken such a long sentence to me before. I was flattered. She was even coming over and sitting down on the edge of my bed.

"Today I don't know if I'm going, because I don't have any

money to put in the collection. So I don't know if I'm going." Annie looked down at her immaculate black shoes and gave them a
dusting with her black-gloved hand.

I noticed absently that her stockings were black, too. There
was a brand-new thought working in my mind. It was so tremendous it made me dizzy. I blushed. I said, "If you like, I can lend
you some money."

"Oh, no," Annie said. "No, that I never would. I wouldn't
borrow money from you, though you are a darling child, that you
are, and I'll pay you back every penny come payday—half a
crown if you can spare it."

I was shocked at the largeness of the sum, for though I valued
friendship above money, I had an attachment to the silver coins
that had accumulated over the weeks. I counted five of the six
into Annie's upturned palm and watched her take out her black
purse and drop them in and clap it shut.

Then Annie asked me if I would like to come into her room. I
blushed again, because Annie was taking so much account of me,
and because I wanted so very badly to go into her room I said no,
and immediately regretted it, especially after Annie had gone and
her footsteps sounded away down the stairs.

It was, I think, on the following afternoon that I came downstairs and found Mrs. Levine sitting by the window just where
she had sat the first morning, and she was sewing a blue dress for
me. I remembered with a shock of remorse how I had not liked her
and how I had written about her to my mother. I suddenly liked
her enormously. I was glad that she was old and ugly so that I
could love her forever, even if nobody else did, and was casting
about in my mind for something to say to her so that I could
address her as "Auntie Essie," but she spoke first.

"Is that you, Lore? Come here. I want you." She had not raised
her head and I could tell by her voice that there was something
the matter. I looked around and I was glad that Annie was there,
busying herself in the far corner of the dusky room. "I have to
speak with you," Mrs. Levine said. "I hear that you are going

around telling people we don't give you enough pocket money. I was very upset. I think that's very ungrateful of you."

"I didn't," I said, but without conviction; I was trying to recall to whom I had said such a thing. "I never," I said.

Mrs. Levine said, "I was quite upset. We do everything for you, and when I hear you are saying Uncle Reuben gives Bobby more money than he gives you I get very upset. And criticizing everybody—how my grandson is spoiled, and this one you like, and that one you don't like. You don't do that when you live in other people's houses."

I felt the blood pounding in my head—confused because she was accusing me of thoughts I did not recognize, and not accusing me of thoughts for which I had long felt guilty. I wanted to go away and think this out, but I knew I must stand and let Mrs. Levine scold me as long as she felt like it.

Her hand that was guiding the needle trembled. "It's not that I expect gratitude," she said. "But you might at least say 'thank you, Auntie Essie' when you see me sitting here sewing a dress for you, but you never notice what people do for you."

"I do," I said. "I do notice." But a small sulky voice inside me said, "If she doesn't know I love her, I'm not going to tell her."

Mrs. Levine had not done with me yet. She was thoroughly worked up and she said excitedly, "And how often have I asked you to call me 'Auntie Essie,' but you never even remember—though you always say 'Uncle Reuben' to him, and then you go around telling people he doesn't give you enough pocket money and I'm sure he gives you as much as he can afford." Mrs. Levine was silent, sewing agitatedly on my dress.

I stood trembling. I looked toward Annie. I thought that any moment she would speak up and tell Mrs. Levine that there had been a mistake, and explain everything, but Annie seemed still to be dusting the same shelf, and her back was to me.

I ran out and up to my room and threw myself on the bed meaning to cry and cry, but I managed only a few dry sobs. I was thinking how that little Bobby really did get twice as much money as I. It surprised me that I had not thought of it before. It made

me angry. I decided that I would not go downstairs for supper,
nor to breakfast the next day, nor ever again. I would stay in my
room and starve. I tried to cry some more, but I did not particularly
feel like crying. I wondered if there was something the matter with
me. I began to dream a dream—I imagined that I was weeping
bitterly and that Sarah came into my room and saw me so and
softly begged me to tell her why, and I could not speak because
of the tears in my throat. My heart ached deliciously, imagining
how Sarah wept for me.

I lifted my head from the pillow, listening to footsteps coming
upstairs. Perhaps Mrs. Levine was coming to look for me. I held
my breath, but they had stopped on the floor below. A door opened
and shut. I heard the bathroom chain pulled and then somebody
went back down. That was the front doorbell now—Uncle Reuben
coming from his shop, or Sarah. Soon everybody would be home.
They would sit around the table without me.

I thought of writing a letter to my mother, but I didn't move
from the bed. There was too much now that I could not tell her;
it had shocked me profoundly to realize that everybody did not
love me, and I knew if my mother were to find out that there were
people who did not think me perfectly good and charming she
could not bear it. The room had become dark and it was chilly. I
was getting bored. I thought how Annie would have to come up to
my floor when she went to bed. Maybe I would call her. Maybe
she would come in. I thought, If she invites me again to come into
her room, I will go. I wondered how long it would be before Annie
came upstairs.

After a bit, I walked out onto the landing and sat on the top
step. Presently I went down to the floor with the green carpet and
hung around there, and then I went all the way down to the ground
floor. Everybody would be home by now. I could hear them talking in the living room, but I didn't know if I should go in. I
wondered if Mrs. Levine was telling them all those things about
me. I stood outside the door trying to hear what they were saying,
but my figure limned itself on the frosted glass and Mrs. Levine

called out, "All right, then, so come in. You don't have to listen
behind the door."

I came in with my head on fire. Mrs. Levine was biting off her
basting thread. She asked Annie if we had time to try on before
supper, and though I kept waiting for the catastrophe Mrs. Levine
only said, "So, you want to have that little Helene over to play
with you?"

I said no, I wasn't playing with Helene any more, but I had a
new friend at school, called Renate. Mrs. Levine said to ask her
to come to tea on Saturday.

Renate was two months older than I. She had tight black hair
and wore glasses, and she was as smart as I was. After I taught her
the game about guessing about letters, she only lost once, and she
had come up with such fantastic and imaginative mishaps to de-
lay her mail that she spurred me to ever greater stretches of un-
likelihood. If she made her letters travel the long way around
the world, I must send mine via the moon, and so the thing got
out of hand and wasn't any fun any more. But Renate thought of
a new game. We had to guess when our parents would come. I
said, "I guess two years." Renate guessed five years. I said, "All
right, mine is six years," but she said that didn't count because I
had had my turn. I said I didn't care. I knew a secret. She said,
what. I told her how I had heard Mrs. Levine tell her eldest
daughter that Mrs. Rosen didn't know what she was going to do
with Helene now that her parents were dead.

"Oh," said Renate, "then Helene is an orphan." And so Renate
and I stood having our secrets together. I asked her if she would
like to be best friends with me, instead of Helene, and she said
she would.

But I kept looking curiously at Helene who was an orphan.
She stood by herself in the middle of the schoolyard looking
before her. She still wore her little thick coat and her rabbit's-wool
hat tied under the chin. One would never have guessed from looking at her that her parents were dead. I tried imagining that my

parents were dead, but whenever I tried thinking about my father I would see him spread-eagled high above the ground comically wriggling his arms and legs, trying to get down from the thing like a telegraph pole on which he was trussed up. I wondered if that might mean that he was dead and tried to imagine him climbing down but could not crystallize this idea in my mind's eye and so I removed it from him and focused it on my mother, but whoops, there she went, too, right up on the pole, and I knew that she could not come down until I had removed my thought from her. For the rest of the week I was continually at work to stop myself from thinking of my parents so that they could keep their feet on the earth. Mrs. Levine worried about me: She would see me suddenly shake my head or change chairs or dive under the table and would say, "For goodness' sake, can't you sit still a minute? I never saw such a child for fidgeting."

Renate came on Saturday. I took her into the dining room and we played house. We sat under the table and pulled the dining-room chairs to hedge us in closely all around. Renate said that she wanted to be the mother and I must be the child, which wasn't the way I had imagined it, and she kept bossing me instead of my bossing her and she talked too quick and moved too suddenly and everything was quite wrong again, so that I wished with all my heart that it were Helene I had with me again, docile, under the table.

In the months that followed, Renate and I became very good friends. We had different games, and in the end it was I who won by a year and a half. A conspiracy between the grownups to save me the pain of waiting and possible disappointment had kept me in ignorance of my parents' being expected in Liverpool on my very birthday.

One Tuesday in March, I was called out of class into the study of the headmaster. Mrs. Levine was there, and they both looked very kindly at me. Mrs. Levine said for me to get my coat. There was a surprise waiting for me at home.

"My parents have come!" I said.

"Well!" said Mrs. Levine, "so! Aren't you excited, you funny child?"

"Yes, I am. I'm excited," I said, but I was busy noticing the way my chest was emptying, my head clearing, and my shoulders being freed of some huge weight that must, since I now felt it being rolled away, have been there all this time without my knowing it. Just as when the passing of nausea or the unknotting of a cramp leaves the body with a new awareness of itself, I stood sensuously at ease, breathing in and out.

Mrs. Levine was saying to the headmaster, "You never know with children. All she ever does is mope around the house and write letters home, and now she isn't even pleased."

"I am *so* pleased," I said and began to jump up and down, though what I wanted most was to be still, to taste the intense sweetness of my relief. But it would never do to have Mrs. Levine think I was not pleased and excited, and I had to jump up and down in the taxi all the way back to the house.

And in the two easy chairs, in front of the sitting-room fire, sat my mother and my father, and I hugged them and smiled and I grinned and I hugged them again and I made them come upstairs to show them my room, and I showed them off to my new English family, and I showed off my new familiarities to my parents, and then the children arrived for my birthday party, bringing gifts. Crackers exploded. There were paper hats, and little cakes and jellies to eat. I bobbed and leaped and ran and chatted, and all the time I knew that, incredibly, my mother was in the room with me. Her eyes, huge and dilated with the suppressed tears of her exhaustion and the shock of her relief, followed me around the room like the eyes of a lover.

Afterward the neighbors came in to have a look at the little refugee's parents. The women talked Yiddish to my mother. She smiled and tried to tell them in her stunted school English that she did not understand Yiddish, but they did not believe her and talked louder. She applied to my father, who was the linguist of the family, but he looked merely stunned. I try to recall his presence during the visit to the Levines, and see him sitting in the same armchair, rising when my mother rose, speaking only to echo what she said. Whenever I went over to kiss him, his face would break up and he wept.

In the evening, after everyone was gone, my mother opened the suitcase. She had brought some of my things from home, including my doll, Gerda, who had had a hole poked through her forehead where the customs people at the German border had looked for contraband. There was a box of sweets packed especially for the little friend Helene Rubichek.

"Oh, her," I said. "She isn't even at school any more."

"No," Mrs. Levine added, "that Mrs. Rosen couldn't keep her. She's in another home now."

"Where is she?" I asked, momentarily frowning at the glimpse I caught of little Helene stuck on the telegraph pole wriggling helplessly between heaven and earth.

"I don't just remember," Mrs. Levine said, "but I think they put her in another town."

And so I put Helene out of my mind.

My parents stayed at the Levines' for three days, and the fourth morning they left to go to their first English job in a household in the south of England. Mr. Levine was taking them to the station. They stood in the hallway by the front door. They had their coats on. "Come on down and say good-by nicely to your father and mother," said fat Mrs. Levine, but I sat on a step halfway up the stairs. I didn't know what to do with myself. I had one arm twisted around the banister, and I waved and wiggled my head.

I remained in Liverpool until the summer. It seems to me that after my parents came to England life at the Levines' was less emotionally strenuous; I remember less about it.

Annie never remembered the half crown that I had lent her. I used to study her. From the free and easy way that she talked and laughed with me, I could tell she had forgotten that she owed me two shillings and sixpence. I was too shy to remind her, but I never quit thinking that some day she would remember and give me back my money. This expectation became attached to Annie like an attribute, like the playful angle of her nose and the warm grip with which she used to swing my hand when we went walking in the park together. I always liked Annie.

I went on loving Mrs. Levine when she wasn't looking. There was no hope now of our coming together. The phrases that she spoke to me and the tone in which I answered had become ritual. Now, seeing me sit idly by the fire, she would often say, "Don't you even want to go and write a letter to your parents?" And I would say, "No, I don't feel like writing."

Mrs. Levine said, "My goodness, I never saw such a child for sitting around doing nothing."

"I'm not doing nothing," I said. "I'm watching the fire."

"And always an answer to everything," Mrs. Levine said, and Sarah said, "Knock it off, Ma. Leave her alone."

I used to keep thoughts of Sarah in abeyance till I went to bed, and then I imagined such situations, such things for her to say to me, such profundities for me to answer, that I excited myself and I couldn't fall asleep. There developed a serial story, which I carried with me through the years, from one foster family to the next. New characters were added, but the protagonist remained a pale, tragic-eyed girl. Her hair was long and sad and she wept much. She suffered. She kept herself to herself. I regretted my daytime self, which was always wanting to be where everyone else was, though I never did learn to come into a room without stopping outside to hear if they were talking about me, to gather myself together, invent some little local excuse, or think up some bright thing to say, as if it might look foolish for me to just open a door and walk in.

"Illford": The Married Couple

When I was an adolescent, Tante Trude and Onkel Hans showed me the letter about the snow-capped rose which I had written them from Dovercourt camp. I was embarrassed for them because they had been taken in by my propaganda. They had sent this letter around among the refugee committees and had moved the family called Willoughby to sponsor my parents on a married-couple visa. ("Married couple" was the technical designation for a husband-and-wife team of cook and butler. Domestic visas were the only working visas readily available to foreigners at a time when England needed to replenish its diminishing servant class. There was an anecdote, widely circulated at the time, about the young lady of wealthy Viennese stock who came downstairs on her first morning in the house of the English people she believed to be her saviors, at half past ten o'clock, wearing a blue crêpe-de-Chine dressing gown with tassel, looking for her breakfast.)

From the letters my mother wrote me to Liverpool, and the stories she has told since, I have an idea of my parents' life those first months in England. They traveled a day's journey south. Mr. Willoughby fetched them from the Mellbridge station and drove them to Illford Village, in Kent. It was toward the end of the day. The sky is immense in that part of the country. The round hills of the downs rise softly and nobly. The little bridle paths and the hedges that divide a field from its neighbor trace, lovingly as a Cézanne pencil, the large contours, the little surprises of their curves. Very old clumps of elms stand here and there. The car went along the back country roads. My mother looked through the bare hazelnut hedges on either side of the road, and she was moved by this free and charming land where she had come to live. Mr. Willoughby drove through a wide, open gate up a gravel drive toward a handsome, gentle white house, and around it, and set my parents down at the back door.

Mrs. Willoughby was in the kitchen to meet them with a most kind welcome. They must be tired, she said, and would want to rest. She told my father to bring the bags, and led them along a flag-stone passage and up two flights of a narrow wooden back stairs that opened into an attic bedroom. The door was missing, Mrs. Willoughby said, but Groszmann could put up a curtain tomorrow. She would find a piece of stuff, but meanwhile they should just rest and not think of doing any work today, unless Mrs. Grosz-mann would want to come down later and Mrs. Willoughby could just show her which was the kitchen china and which were the cups for Mrs. Willoughby's early-morning tea, which she liked brought up to her on a tray at seven—but not to worry about anything, just unpack and make themselves at home. My mother said she would come down with Mrs. Willoughby right away.

In the kitchen, my mother looked over Mrs. Willoughby's shoulder into china cupboards and broom closets, at the sinks in the scullery, and the food-filled shelves of the pantry. Mrs. Willoughby said maybe Mrs. Groszmann was hungry and would like a little supper? She would set out an egg for her and Groszmann on the kitchen table. Now, since they were here, Mrs. Willoughby might as well show my mother around the front of the house. They went along the flagstone passage again and through a green baize-covered door into a carpeted hall. Here, Mrs. Willoughby said, was the library. My mother said what a lovely room and there was something she wanted to ask—maybe Mrs. Willoughby could ad-vise her what to read to quickly improve her English. Did Mrs. Willoughby have *The Forsyte Saga,* which my mother knew very well in German, and that would help her read it in English? Did Mrs. Willoughby like Galsworthy? Mrs. Willoughby said she didn't know, but my mother could see, later, if there was a copy, and she could borrow it so long as she brought it back when she was finished. "And this is our drawing room." "Ah," my mother cried, "a piano! It is a Bechstein, no?" and she told Mrs. Willoughby that she had had a Blüthner, which the Nazis had taken, and that she had studied music at the Vienna Academy.

"Oh, really?" said Mrs. Willoughby. "In that case you must come in and play sometime when everyone is out."

My mother was dissatisfied. She wanted to let the Englishwoman know that she, too, had once been comfortably circumstanced, had had a well-appointed flat and a *Herrenzimmer*. "My husband," my mother said to Mrs. Willoughby, "was accountant—like your husband, isn't it?"

"Was he?" said Mrs. Willoughby. "Mr. Willoughby, you know, is a civil servant."

"Mr. Groszmann," countered my mother, "was in a bank. Main —what do you call it?—*chef* accountant."

"Chief accountant?" suggested Mrs. Willoughby.

"Chief accountant," said my mother, "and he—how do you say?—*organiziert?*"

"Organized?" said Mrs. Willoughby.

"Yes. Organized all the system of accountants."

"Ah?" said Mrs. Willoughby. Then she gave my mother a paper she had written out to hang on the back of the kitchen door, showing a list of the rooms and on which day each must be turned out, to help my mother organize her work. My mother thanked her earnestly. She had no system of her own, she said, but she would do her very best for Mrs. Willoughby. She thanked Mrs. Willoughby for visa and employment. She asked Mrs. Willoughby to have patience with her.

My parents had been engaged to work at Illford House for one pound a week between them. To be more precise, my mother was engaged to work for one pound a week, with the stipulation that my father could live in the house and receive food in return for his services as butler and handyman. Like all English servants, they were to have Thursday afternoon, and every other Sunday afternoon, off.

In bed that first evening, my father said out of the darkness, "Franzi . . . ? I was thinking. Do you remember that passage behind the kitchen we used for the maid's room?" My mother says she felt very close to him at that moment because she, too, had been trying to remember what sort of mattress poor Poldi had slept on. She says there was a trick to lying on the Willoughbys' mattresses. You had to push the lumps of kapok to either side and make a valley between them and then lie still.

My mother was downstairs by six o'clock the next morning, nervous and eager to start. She stood in Mrs. Willoughby's great empty kitchen, wondering what to do first. The house was silent. My mother tried to imagine what Poldi at home would do first thing in the morning. She had a single vivid image of Poldi with a long-handled broom—Poldi sweeping. My mother began to open closet doors looking for the broom cupboard, and suddenly she remembered about the early-morning tea. She tried to recall where around the kitchen she had seen a tray. While she hunted, she kept wondering if she was actually supposed to carry it in to Mrs. Willoughby. Would she find Mr. and Mrs. Willoughby lying in bed together? It then came to my mother with a shock that if she was to make tea, water would have to be heated, and that she must light the coal stove. It was already six-thirty. From that moment on, for many years to come, my mother was never again at a loss to find things she was supposed to do.

I had a letter from my mother telling me about that first funny morning. My mother arrived with the tray at exactly seven. Mrs. Willoughby drank her tea, told my mother that they would have scrambled eggs for breakfast, and turned on her side next to Mr. Willoughby, who had not even waked up. My mother hoped my father would know what "scrambled" meant, but he did not. While he went into the library to look for a dictionary, my mother rushed upstairs to unpack her books to find *Mrs. Beeton's English Cookery*. Breakfast was late, but Mrs. Willoughby had been nice about it.

Everybody, my mother wrote, was very good to them. Mr. Willoughby was most polite. He had asked questions about Vienna. He was an accountant for the government and went to London every morning after breakfast. Besides him and Mrs. Willoughby, there were two daughters. Miss Elizabeth, the elder, worked in a museum in London and she caught the early train to town. My mother brought her tea to the schoolroom upstairs and Miss Elizabeth toasted bread on a small oil stove. My mother wrote that the smell of toast and tea and oil in the sleeping house, with the dark still outside the windows, was very special and nice. She said that Miss Elizabeth was very nice and spoke gently, though she never said much. The younger daughter was called Joanne. She stayed at home with her mother. She had a pony called Picket. There was a son, Stephen, but he was away at school.

My mother said that she had spoken to Mrs. Willoughby about a sponsor to bring my grandparents to England. She said Mrs. Willoughby often reminded her of her own mother, which was odd because Mrs. Willoughby looked quite different, very thin, with very blue eyes. She had told Mrs. Willoughby about me, and this morning Mrs. Willoughby had said I could come and spend two weeks of the summer holidays with my parents. As soon as my father came down from resting, she would have him write to the Levines about it, but for me not to seem too anxious to get away.

My mother said now she must stop writing and start dinner. She was going to make an *Apfelstrudel* for a surprise. She said she wished she could make me one. She said she loved me and that she and my father lived for the day when they could have me with them.

My father's career as a butler lasted three days. His first job in the morning was to do the front hall, but my mother says that after she had dusted the dining room and lit the fire and set the table for breakfast, she would sneak around after him and wipe away the excess polish he had left on the red tiles. The evening my father served his first dinner, he stayed so long in the dining room that my mother came to the door to see what had happened to him. Mr.

and Mrs. Willoughby were sitting at the head and foot of the table, with their daughters on either side. Their four heads were turned toward my father, who stood with a napkin over his arm holding a tureen of cabbage. Mrs. Willoughby was saying, "Now try it again, will you, Groszmann, from the left side." My father looked as if he had stopped listening some while ago. My mother crept back into the kitchen and wept bitterly out of pity for him, he looked so ridiculous.

Two days later, when guests were expected to dinner, my mother asked Mrs. Willoughby if she might do the waiting at table. She thought she could learn pretty quickly. Mrs. Willoughby was discouraged by my father's lack of progress, but she hesitated. "I don't see how you can come into the dining room in your kitchen apron."

My mother ran upstairs, got out her good afternoon dress, a classic black wool that she had had made the winter before Hitler. "Why," said Mrs. Willoughby, "but you look very nice! I'll go and find you a cap and apron and, yes, I think that will do very nicely."

"This is our Mrs. Groszmann," Mrs. Willoughby said to her dinner guests. "She comes from Vienna." The guests nodded pleasantly to my mother, who smiled and set the soup down in front of each, neatly, from the left, and so she did very well and everyone was pleased.

My father was demoted from butlering to gardening, about which he knew even less. He had a city man's tenderness toward things that grow, and he pottered at his own pace in the kitchen garden among the vegetables.

During those first weeks, my mother developed a small pocket of resistance. One evening Mrs. Willoughby noticed that she was not wearing her white cap and apron. My mother said she had forgotten, and when she brought the second course she had put them on. Next day she had forgotten again. Mrs. Willoughby looked at her but said nothing. After that my mother served in her good black dress and the matter was not mentioned again.

My mother had something else on her mind. It took her a few

days to translate it into English. One morning as she stood before Mrs. Willoughby, who was sitting at the dining-room table after breakfast writing out the day's menu, my mother spoke up. She asked Mrs. Willoughby if it would be possible, since she herself was addressed as "Mrs." Groszmann, for my father to be called "Mr." Mrs Willoughby looked up with her blue, blue eyes and thought a moment. She said that she didn't know how they could do that. She said that the cook was always "Mrs." and that the man-servant was called by just his last name, and she didn't see how they could very well change.

My mother, shocked by this refusal of her direct appeal, looked through the window, where, under the sweet, harsh light of the April morning, Mr. Willoughby and my father walked among the flower beds. She watched their backs side by side. Mr. Willoughby was wearing his black town suit and bowler, ready for his train. My father was two heads taller. Despite his stoop, she thought he looked very well in his tweed knickerbockers. The men were bending to inspect the row of young hyacinths at the end of the path. They turned, and my mother saw that my father was wearing his green gardener's pinafore.

On weekdays, when Mrs. Willoughby and Miss Joanne were alone, they took their lunch on trays in the drawing room, and after my mother had cleared up and washed the kitchen, the hour and a half till teatime was her own. My mother tells me that all morning she would plan what she might do with it. She wanted to write to me; she wanted to write to her parents, and she must get a letter off to the Committee in London to find a sponsor for them; she wanted to take a bath; she wanted to walk in the fresh air; she wanted to study her English, for she found herself too exhausted at night after cooking, serving, and clearing up from dinner; she needed to sleep an hour, but my father had gone to lie down upstairs and what she needed above all was to be alone. She sat at the kitchen table, aware of her leisure slipping away. She kept looking at the clock, calculating how much time she still had before preparing the tea tray. One afternoon, the door opened and

Miss Joanne came through the kitchen, trailing grass and hay from the stables. She dropped a dirty blouse into the scullery sink and went out again, leaving both doors open. This caused a draft where my mother sat, and my mother got up and slammed the door behind the girl. Then she was sorry. She remembered how she had disliked the ill-natured maids in her mother's house, who fussed over their clean floors. She remembered that she owed these people her life. She went to the sink and washed Miss Joanne's blouse and starched it; then, angry at herself for this servile act, she went to the china closet, took out Mrs. Willoughby's best Minton, and made herself some powerful Viennese coffee. She tasted the delicate fluted china between her lips, half afraid that Mrs. Willoughby might come in and catch her, half wishing that she would. My mother wanted to make herself known to the other woman.

It was becoming increasingly clear to my mother that there was much Mrs. Willoughby did not know. "Why didn't you embark in Austria and come direct?" she asked my mother one day. "Why did you come such an awkward way around?" My father, who had just entered the kitchen, stared in astonishment. "Do you know we had to wait eleven weeks for you and Groszmann?" said Mrs. Willoughby.

My mother tried to tell Mrs. Willoughby some of the things that were happening to Jews in Austria and Germany.

"Tch, tch, isn't that incredible?" Mrs. Willoughby said. "Quite, quite incredible." And her eyes began to wander. Mrs. Willoughby would rather not know what she was being told, and besides, my mother's conversation, in which Mrs. Willoughby had to be active, supplying the missing words, must have been tiring.

My mother had another weapon; she is a great believer in laughter. She laughs readily and with abandon until she looks as if she has been crying. She had always been the comedienne of the family, and her routine of funny faces and gestures had caused the uncles and cousins to say that Franzi's talents were being wasted. She is a true punster and takes equal delight in her cleverest and most terrible wordplays. These she now wanted to share with Mrs.

Willoughby by translating them into English. When Mrs. Willoughby looked puzzled, my mother explained them painfully. Mrs. Willoughby would look tired.

One day Mrs. Willoughby told my mother she thought it would be nice for her to meet some English people. My mother was surprised and gratified. Mrs. Willoughby said she had invited the vicar's cook to take her tea with my mother and father on their next Sunday off.

It was a very wet afternoon. Mrs. MacGuire arrived at the back door on the dot of four. She was a stout, decent-looking middle-aged woman, dressed all in black. She let my father take her coat and galoshes but kept her hat on while my mother gave her tea at the kitchen table. She spoke with a heavy Irish brogue; my parents recognized only an occasional word of her conversation. My mother had baked a Viennese cake for her, which she understood Mrs. MacGuire to say was far too rich. Mrs. MacGuire asked for a piece of paper and pencil, so that she might write down for my mother how to make a good plain sponge. At five o'clock, Mrs. MacGuire put on her coat and galoshes and went home.

After that, my parents always went out of the house on their free afternoons.

On a morning late in May, my mother fell down the stairs. She was overworked and sleeping badly, and she came through the curtain onto the landing at the head of the back stairs and went headlong with a tremendous clatter. Mr. Willoughby came rushing from the front of the house to the second-floor landing and ran down after her, but by that time my mother had picked herself up and was sitting on a step resting her head on her arms. She heard Mr. Willoughby's trembling voice say, "What happened?" My mother raised her head. Mr. Willoughby, in his pajamas, had turned his avenging eyes up to where my father stood, petrified, at the head of the stairs, looking down. "Tell me the truth!" cried Mr. Willoughby. "Was it a fight?"

My mother explained that the fall had been an accident. She has told me how, through the dizziness and nausea, she wanted to

stop talking, as if it were too much trouble—as if it were too late
—to explain anything.

And so the Willoughbys had put my parents in their place; the
refugees belonged to the class of people who eat in the kitchen,
sleep on cheap mattresses, and throw their wives down the stairs
in an argument—which goes to show that people have, after all,
an innate sense of justice and cannot with equanimity be served
by their fellows when these too closely resemble themselves.

My parents were meanwhile adjusting their image of their mas-
ters. "She has no sense of humor," said my mother. "She doesn't
know any geography," said my father, "and the naïve questions
that he asks me about the Nazis!" "They don't know how to
eat," said my mother. "Do you remember the time I made them
an *Apfelstrudel* and they asked for custard to put over it?" "They
don't understand," said my parents, and so they put the English
in *their* place.

But my mother had a difficulty; she liked Mrs. Willoughby. She
liked to see her on her way into the garden, wearing her blue-
green wool kerchief that made her eyes more astonishingly blue,
and there was about this thin, trim lady a quiet toughness, a presence, a capability in the firm, easy way she handled the reins of
her household that was new to my mother and that she admired.

Even Mrs. Willoughby's obtuseness was incorruptible. She came
into the kitchen on a Sunday when it was raining too hard for my
parents to leave the house and said, "Oh, Mrs. Groszmann! Since
you are here, maybe you wouldn't mind bringing in our tea?"

My mother minded it very much. She acquiesced in silent outrage. At the door, Mrs. Willoughby turned back. "But first why
don't you come up and get the linens to make up your little girl's
bed," she said. "It's this Thursday she's coming, isn't it?"

My mother followed Mrs. Willoughby to the linen closet, vow-
ing never to think an ungrateful thought about any English person
again. "Not these," said the lady, laying some folded sheets in my
mother's arms. "These are our good sheets, and you don't want to
get her used to this kind of thing. Set them down on the tallboy."

With my mother's help, Mrs. Willoughby emptied the linen closet
till she came to a pile of rust-stained sheets in the back. "There,"
Mrs. Willoughby said, "and you and Groszmann had better take
the morning off, too, and go up to London to fetch the little girl."

"How good you are," said my mother, close to tears.

"Then do you think you could catch the 5:15 down from Waterloo and be back in time to get our dinner? We can just have something quick, don't you know. Maybe cold meat and a nice green
salad and a tomato aspic that you can prepare in the morning, before you leave?"

On Thursday morning, my parents fetched me from Paddington
Station. We had lunch at the station restaurant and spent a gay
afternoon window-shopping. We met Tante Trude and Onkel
Hans, who took us to coffee and music at a Lyons Corner House,
and we caught the 5:15 and were in Illford a little after six.

I walked into the kitchen and looked curiously around. It was
big and had a red-brick floor. It was papered with bright-green
wallpaper. A fire was burning in the black stove.

My mother laid a cloth on the kitchen table and brought out the
Continental breads and *Knackwurst* she had got in London. She
cut and spread colorful open-faced sandwiches and urged me to
eat. "Eat," said my father, "go on," and they both sat and watched
me until a rasping buzz sounded through the quiet kitchen. I followed my mother's eye to the wall above the door. There was a
box with a glass front, showing three rows of three round holes.
Each hole had a small red tongue. Under the holes it said:

FRONT BEDR.	SOUTH BEDR.	EAST BEDR.
WEST BEDR.	GUEST R.	SCHOOLR.
DINING R.	DRAWING R.	LIBRARY

The drawing-room tongue was waggling frantically.

My mother got up, called me to her, quickly pulled a comb
through my hair, and straightened the collar of my cotton frock.
"That's Mrs. Willoughby, and I want you to look nice. Remember
to thank her for letting you come and stay with us."

We walked along the stone floor of the back passage, through the baize door, which closed noiselessly behind us. The front hall was carpeted and hushed. A door stood open. Inside the drawing room was a profound order, a still, sweet light. A thin lady in a flowered dress sat in a deep armchair. The lady said, "Mrs. Groszmann, there's a bit of a chill in the air. I thought I might have a little fire."

"I'll light it at once," said my mother. "Mrs. Willoughby, this is my Lore."

"How do you do," said the lady. I saw the blue eyes my mother had written about. The room was full of flowers. The patterned-damask chairs stood on delicate bowlegs on soft, patterned carpet.

I said, "Very well, thank you."

My mother had bent to put a match to the sticks in the fireplace. The polished wood of the mantel reddened with the jumping flames.

I said, "I came by myself all the way from Liverpool. Except the guard of the luggage van was supposed to look after me."

"Isn't that nice," said Mrs. Willoughby. She told my mother that Miss Elizabeth was staying in town, so there would be only three for dinner.

I looked at my mother and said, "Thank you for having me."

Mrs. Willoughby said, "I'm very glad you could come."

Back in the kitchen, my mother cleared the table and said, "Now, before we do anything else you better sit down and write to the Levines."

"Can I tomorrow?"

"Right this moment," said my mother. "You don't want them to think that as soon as you are with your parents you forget all *they* have done for you. You don't want to be ungrateful."

I was not ungrateful. At times I had felt a good deal. (There had been the first Friday night, during the unfamiliar Orthodox lighting of the ritual candles, when I had been struck with the oddness of my being there at all. It seemed wonderful to me that these Levines should have taken my strange, uncomfortable self into their inmost house. I was moved to tears, which exasperated Mrs. Levine, who kept asking me what was the matter *now,* and I couldn't tell her.) But this evening I was moved by other things. "Can I go out and see the chickens?" I asked.

"As soon as you have finished your letter," said my mother.

I squirmed and sighed and complained that I didn't know what to put in the letter, and wrote and blotted and wept to have to do it over. And so passed the first evening.

Next morning, I breakfasted with my father at the kitchen table while my mother cleared the dining room and washed the dishes and collected her brooms, dustpan, and polish. My father invited me to come with him to feed the chickens, but I chose to go with my mother, who was going to "do" the drawing room. I liked the front part of the house.

We were alone in the drawing room. I went and stood in the bow window that looked over the lawn through the row of damson trees at the rounded hills beyond. A great bowl of roses stood on a small inlaid table. I knelt to see my green-and-golden image elongated and monstrous-nosed in the copper bowl. "Don't touch the flowers," said my mother from the hearth, where she was kneeling to clean out the ashes. I tiptoed away across the carpet and stuck my face among the sweet peas and saw them and myself mirrored, pastel-colored and pretty, in the high polish of the piano top. "Leave the piano alone," said my mother, who was dusting the mantelpiece. I sat in Mrs. Willoughby's armchair, feeling my fingers across the patterned silk and scrolled wood, with my feet in the air so that my mother could vacuum underneath me. I dreamed I was Mrs. Willoughby's youngest daughter. "Can I buzz the servants' bell?" I asked. My mother said I certainly could not and why didn't I go into the garden to find my father, but I said I wanted to come upstairs with her.

Upstairs, I stood by Mr. and Mrs. Willoughby's bedroom window and watched my father down below walking through the gate into the field. He was mobbed by chickens. The hysterical brown birds flapped so thickly about his feet that he had to pick his steps carefully, holding the bucket aloft and shooing them gently with his other hand.

"There he is," I said to my mother, who was making up the bed.

"Who?"

"Daddy."

My mother came and looked, and she smiled.

I said, "Why doesn't *he* ever get up when the bell rings?"

My mother said, "Because I always do . . . because I know what they want. Lorle! You and I must have a talk." I felt her looking at me, but I didn't want to talk. I knew whose side I was on.

"I want you to know that I don't mind working. I like to move about and to work; I do really. And Daddy is not a strong man."

"He's not ill now," I said.

"Not so as to have to go away to the hospital, but he is not strong. He never feels completely well, and he's always afraid of getting ill again."

I said, "There's Mrs. Willoughby in her straw hat," but now my mother could not stop.

"I keep wondering if I'm doing wrong to take all the responsibility away from him, but I did let him do everything in order to get you on that children's transport. It was he who went to the Committee and the consulate and the emigration office and did everything, and I thought he seemed stronger than he'd been in years. Even after you had all gone inside the station and they wouldn't let us in, he wouldn't leave till the early morning, when they told us the train had left. But then we got home and he collapsed, you see, and it was too much for him. And then I start taking over, and when he gets better it still seems easier and quicker for me to do things. I get in the habit, and I may be doing him a great wrong."

I watched Mrs. Willoughby with her basket and gardening shears walking among the rose beds.

"Do you think I am wrong telling you all this—but you will be gone soon, and then I will have no one to talk to again, and you are my friend, aren't you?"

I said, "Yes. Can I go upstairs now and read a book?"

"Lore," said my mother, "try and spend a little time with your father. He loves you very much."

But I did not want to hear about my father's love, which so outweighed my light return.

"Ask him to tell you a story."

"Later," I said.

"Yes," said my mother. "You go up now and read. I'll call you down for lunch."

From the attic window I watched my father walking after Mrs. Willoughby, who had called him to put down his bucket and bring the basket full of cut roses and the gardening shears into the house behind her. I felt sorry for him because I did not like him enough. I thought it must be lonely for him outside the friendship that bound my mother and me. I practiced feeling how it would be never to feel completely well. I thought of the day I had vomited in Mrs. Levine's house and tried to remember the sensation and then imagined it going on all day and the day after. Was *that* how my father went around feeling? I watched, that summer morning, and created a knowledge of my father's walking—circumspectly, his lips slightly parted and his eyes straight before him, concentrating every nerve to avoid a jolt in his own movements or a sudden change in direction, as if he were guarding some fragile moment of well-being against a return of his nausea.

My father and Mrs. Willoughby disappeared under the veranda roof below me. I promised myself to be loving to my father in the afternoon and to ask him to tell me a story, but by lunchtime he had succumbed to an attack of weakness so profound it operated like a paralysis and he dragged himself up the stairs to bed.

My mother and I were left alone in the sunny kitchen. She was whistling, clearing the table, carrying dishes in to the scullery sink. The scullery was full of sunlight. The taps flashed silver. The steam rose over the sinks like a bright mist in which my mother stood, and the Viennese song she whistled sounded incomparably sweet and gay. I could tell that she really did not mind working.

Afterward, we sat at the table dreaming together; one day we would all be living together again in an apartment of our own. And then my father came back down; he was feeling better. Mrs. Willoughby rang for tea, and after that my mother started dinner.

Sunday was our Sunday off. My father wanted to show me Mellbridge, half an hour's bus ride away. By the time the three of us,
in our Viennese best, came down the stairs, it had begun to drizzle.

"And it's a twenty-five-minute walk to the main road, where the
bus stops," said my mother. "What do you think?"

My father stood waiting for my mother to reach a decision
and answer herself.

"We have plenty of time to catch the 3:10, so we can take it
easy," my mother said.

We felt ourselves in luck that we had only a minute to wait for
the bus and that the rain began to pour hard as soon as we were
settled. We almost expected it to clear the moment we were to be
set down at the bus stop in the center of town; however, it did not.
The cinemas were closed on Sundays, my mother said, but we
would walk up the High Street and see if there were any cafés where
we might get a hot cup of coffee. The streets were deserted. It
poured heavily and steadily. "All the English people are staying
at home," I said.

There was a little teashop open, just off the High Street. It was
pretty inside. The tables had clean white cloths. A fire burned in
the grate. It was quite empty. The waitress wore a black dress and
white cap and apron. My mother smiled at her, but she looked
sour and long-faced. They did not serve coffee, so we had an English tea of tea and scones and marmalade. We spoke English loudly
while the waitress was near, but when she had walked away we
whispered in German. The waitress was looking genteelly into
space.

My mother kept looking at her. "I think maybe she is not allowed to sit down while there are guests, do you think?" my mother
said. We called for our check and got back into our damp coats
and left.

"Let's stop in this doorway and think what to do. The next bus
back is not till 5:40." My mother asked my father if his feet were
wet. He said he couldn't tell. I said that I could tell mine were wet.
"And there's the walk at the other end," said my mother. "I suppose a taxi would cost pounds. I know what we can do now. Let's

start walking back to the bus stop. There's a waiting place there and it's covered, and we can sit down. We can play twenty questions. Are you tired, Igo?" she asked my father, who was walking along with his back very bent and his feet dragging so that he kept almost tripping himself. He said he thought he was rather tired. "Well," said my mother, "it won't be long. You see, we are already here."

"Where?" my father and I said, looking around us.

"Why, right 'here,'" said my mother. "And soon we'll be 'there.'" She made little jokes all the way and kept looking at my father. I could tell that she was frightened.

Back at Illford House we went upstairs to our room. It was damp, and we got under the blankets. My father fell asleep almost at once. My mother and I pretended this was all fun. We whispered together—next year perhaps I might move to the south of England and be near my parents and we could spend all the free afternoons together. We wondered if there was a likelihood of finding another home for me as good as the one I had with the Levines in Liverpool.

Miss Joanne opened the curtains at the door. "Oh," she said, "I didn't know there was anyone here," and she stepped into the room and walked on through into the attic storeroom beyond. My father wakened and sat up. She stayed in the storeroom, scrabbling around, for half an hour. A couple of times she came through, carrying boxes. I watched her narrowly. I could not tell if she had even noticed me.

On Monday came a letter from the Levines. It seemed that Uncle Reuben might be having to have another of his eye operations. Mrs. Levine was very upset and feeling very poorly with a pain in her side, but she was happy, she said, that I was having such a happy time with my parents.

My mother made me write by return mail, with a special message to poor Uncle Reuben. "Don't mention anything about your leaving them," she said. "We can't bother them at such a time."

Another letter came at the end of the week. The crisis with Uncle Reuben's eyes had passed for the moment, but a cousin of Mrs. Levine's was down with something very damaging, and Mrs.

Levine, despite the pain in her side, went almost every day to nurse her. If my parents would like to have me stay with them longer, this would be all right with Mrs. Levine. Mrs. Levine was sure my parents must be very unhappy to have me living almost the other end of England. The Levines would always think of me with the greatest affection.

Now it came to us that I was not to return to Liverpool and that when my visit at Illford House ended on Thursday I had nowhere to live. My father began to cry. My mother took Mrs. Levine's letter in to Mrs. Willoughby. Mrs. Willoughby called the vicar, who gave her the address of a church ladies' committee in Mellbridge for the assistance of refugees from Europe. The next day the chairman of the committee called; she had found a home for me with a nice family called Hooper, in Mellbridge—if my parents did not mind my living with Christians. My parents did not mind. We kept saying wasn't it lucky and just what we had hoped for; everything was turning out for the best.

On Thursday my parents took me to my new foster family.

The Hoopers lived in an orange brick street of identical semi-detached houses with narrow alleys between them leading to the back doors. In front of each half house there was a square yard of grass surrounded by a neat privet hedge, with a little iron gate and a tidy flagstone path leading to three white steps and up to the front door. The Hoopers' front door, during the time I lived there, was never used except that first Thursday afternoon, for my parents and me.

Mrs. Hooper opened to us. She was a large, soft woman with fine black eyes. She must have been thirty-five or -six, a few years older than my mother. Mrs. Hooper's upper lip was shrunken because of her missing teeth. "Hello," she said. "How do you do. I'm very glad t-t-t-t-t . . ." Time stood suspended. We waited on the front steps watching Mrs. Hooper's tongue twist against her palate, her whole face working. ". . . t-to meet you." We followed her into the little front parlor, which had the chill air of a room that is not lived in. It had the bluest wallpaper I had ever seen. Mrs. Hooper made my mother and father sit on the matching settee and armchair. She herself perched on the piano stool, smiling shyly and trying to wrap her left hand into a corner of her apron. I looked all around. In the narrow bow of the window stood a closed writing desk with an ornately framed enlarged snapshot of two little girls in white dresses screwing up their eyes against the sun.

My mother was looking yearningly at the piano. It was an upright, and had a lace scarf on top and a china vase with crêpe-paper roses. My mother asked Mrs. Hooper if she played the piano. Mrs. Hooper said as a girl she used to, and asked my mother if she could play. My mother said she hadn't played for a year, since the Nazis took her Blüthner away. My mother stood up and touched the keys and played a major chord and a broken minor chord.

"Oh," said Mrs. Hooper. "Oh, you play ever so beautiful." She made my mother sit down at the piano. "You're from Vienna, aren't you. Can you play a waltz?"

My mother shook her head. "Not very well."

"Or can you play some Chopin. You know, the one that goes 'Tra la la, t-t-tra lalalala t-t-t-t-tra la la la . . .' "

My mother played the "Polonaise in A Major" for Mrs. Hooper. The piano tinkled like an old barroom piano, and Mrs. Hooper cried. She said the music wasn't half beautiful.

The dog barked. Footsteps came up the alley. Mrs. Hooper said that would be Gwenda, and presently a girl came in and stood in the doorway. She had a clever, delicate, undernourished face and wore the ugly black pleated tunic and white blouse of the English schoolgirl. She studied me across the room. I looked steadily back.

Mrs. Hooper and my mother made up the conversation between them. My mother was thanking Mrs. Hooper for giving me a home. Mrs. Hooper kept saying she was sorry Mr. Hooper would not be back in time to meet my mother and father. And then the dog barked again. Gwenda looked at her mother and said, "Albert." Doors in the back were fiercely banged, the parlor door was thrown open, and in it stood for the space of a second a blond fellow with a spotty face. I thought he was a man. He must have been seventeen or eighteen. He stared at the strangers in the room and backed out and shut the door.

Mrs. Hooper excused herself and went out, and presently she came back and said to Gwenda, "You go out and talk to him." She said to us, "You'll have to excuse Albert; he says he's too mucky from work to come in. He's shy, see," she said, "but he's a good boy. He's got ever such a nice job down at the gasworks and he makes good money." She seemed at once to be trying to hear and trying to cover up the fierce whispering and hissing in the back. Gwenda came in rubbing her shoulder.

"What did he do?" Mrs. Hooper asked.

"He didn't do anything," said Gwenda, and she sat down with her chin trembling. Her eyes filled slowly with tears.

"What did he do to you?"

"Nothing, Ma!"

My mother said they must be going to catch the bus back to Illford. She took Mrs. Hooper's hands, and she said she wished her English were better to thank Mrs. Hooper with. Mrs. Hooper said for me to take my parents out the front way. "See, he's washing himself," she said, nodding toward the back of the house.

I said good-by to my parents outside the gate. My father was crying with a tiny whimpering sound; my mother's face had the familiar shrunken look and great sore eyes and lips. My father said he thought he felt ill, and she walked him away. I remember their backs moving off down the road together—the large, heavy, stooping person of my father propelled by my small, plump mother, who had given him her arm and seemed at once to be holding him up and looking lovingly around into his face as if she were holding on to him.

CHAPTER FIVE

"Mellbridge": Albert

I went into my new home and closed the street door and stood in the hall. The door into the living room-kitchen, in the back, stood open and I wondered if I was supposed to go inside. I could see a square table so large it left only a margin for chairs. On one wall was a tall dresser with dishes, and on the opposite side, a grate with a fire. A large yellow dog in the yard was leaping at the window and barking. Gwenda and Mrs. Hooper were both addressing the closed door to the scullery, which doubled as bathroom.

"Come on, Albert!" Mrs. Hooper said. "Rover wants to come in and I got to go."

"Albert," said Gwenda, "come on, open up. Ma's got to get outside to the toilet. Come on, now! Albert?"

"Oh, there you are," said Mrs. Hooper, seeing me in the doorway. "What was your name again?"

"Lore," I said.

"Lorry, eh? Oh. Well, you go on upstairs. Gwenda, take her up, and mind you don't worry Albert's things." She dropped her voice as if she were speaking behind the back of a sick person. "He's upset, see!"

Gwenda was fourteen, three years older than I. "Your ma and dad, they work for a family, don't they?" she said as we walked up the narrow stairs.

"Yes," I said. "But in Vienna my father was chief accountant in a bank and my mother plays the piano. She studied in the Vienna Music Academy. What does your father do?"

"Dad's a stoker on the railway and he belongs to the union."

"Oh," I said. "Does that Albert live here, too?"

"Yes. They adopted him out of the orphanage three years ago. Albert's all right. He's going to marry Dawn. She's my sister."

"How old is she?"

"Sixteen. In there is my ma and my dad's room."

Mr. and Mrs. Hooper's bedroom was in front, over the parlor. Gwenda and Dawn shared the room over the kitchen, and the room over the scullery was for me. My room had a wardrobe in it and a bed. It had linoleum on the floor, and was narrow as a passage. (I remember I had a recurring dream, in those days, of apartments vast as the halls of the Kunsthistorisches Museum in Vienna, and in my dream, rooms seemed continually unfolding before me.) I went to the window and looked out over the yard and the strip of back garden. It was as wide as the half house, with a flagstone path running the thirty-foot length. At the foot of the garden, beyond the privet hedge run wild, I could make out, in the gathering darkness, an open space, a sloping field. "What's that?"

"That's the playing field of the County School," said Gwenda. "That's where all the snooty girls go. They wear green uniforms, the stuck-up things."

"Where do you go?"

"To the Central School, down by the station. Ma says when school starts I'm going to take you."

"Why don't you go to the County School?" I said.

"What, me!" said Gwenda. "With them and their la-di-da talk!"

I didn't say anything then, but I had no doubt in my mind that I was going to go to the stuck-up school and talk la-di-da myself.

Gwenda said, "This used to be Albert's room. He's going to sleep on the settee in the parlor. You can unpack, and I'll take some of his things down."

After she had gone, I started to take dresses out of my suitcase and hang them in the wardrobe, but I was too impatient to finish, what with all that I was probably missing downstairs. I kept hearing the dog bark and footsteps in the alley. Doors opened and shut. Voices and dance music from the wireless came up through the thin floor boards. I took some drawing paper and crayons out of my suitcase and, thus fortified, went down into the kitchen full of people.

The light was on. The wireless was blaring "A Tisket, a Tasket" so loud under the low ceiling that I blinked. A girl at the table was eating tangerine sections out of a tin. She looked a little like Gwenda, except that she had a long chin, and every feature was bigger and thicker. She wore her hair like most girls that year, in two horns, one over each temple, with the back hair falling long and loose, and this she kept swinging away from the boy, Albert, who stood behind her trying to get hold of it. She said, "Tch, oh, *A*LBERT! Hello," she said to me, and stared a little.

"Hello," I said.

Albert was glaring just past my head. He walked around the side of the table by the fire and pulled a chair out and sat leaning so far backward on two legs that we all gasped. Then he put his two feet on the table.

In the open scullery door, a man was unbuttoning his collarless shirt. His face was black with soot and dirt. When he smiled, his teeth showed white, with a little gap between the two front ones, which looked very friendly. I liked him. He seemed to be looking and smiling at me. "How are you?" he said.

"Come on, Gwenda," said Mrs. Hooper. "Hand your dad the towel so he can wash up and I can give him his supper."

"How can I?" said Gwenda. "With Albert in the way." With his head against the mantel and his feet on the table, Albert was straddling the margin.

"You let Albert be," said Mrs. Hooper, "and come around the other side. Dawn, get up and let her through."

"Tch, *oh!*" said Dawn. She got up. She came around the table and lowered the blaring wireless. The relief was blissful. Albert reached over and turned it back up and louder.

Mrs. Hooper was setting a place for Mr. Hooper's supper, and he came in from the scullery with his face scrubbed and his hair flattened down with water and a clean blue-and-white striped shirt with the sleeves rolled up his brown arms. Mrs. Hooper brought him a plate of meat, potatoes, greens, and gravy, and sat down beside him with her arms on the table and watched him eat and told him everything that had happened—how my mother hadn't played half beautiful on the piano, and how Albert would not come in even to say good evening.

"Oh, Albert!" said Dawn. "You are a pill."

Mrs. Hooper said, "Let him be," and Dawn said, "Look, Dad, with his feet all over the tablecloth."

But Mr. Hooper wiped his mouth with his napkin and moved to the armchair between the window and the fireplace and grinned at me before he pulled the paper up between himself and his family.

Albert must have known that he had been a pill. Next evening, he came home from work with a present he said he had bought with his pay money. It was a game with cards and pictures, and Albert explained that it was played like lotto, but Mr. Hooper was having his supper on one side of the table, and I had my drawing things spread out. I was doing a village in perspective, with houses, streets, and cars. I had been drawing this for years, and I could do it pretty well. Gwenda, who was watching, said she wanted to draw, too, and I gave her paper and lent her some crayons.

"You're late," Mrs. Hooper said to Albert.

"Well, I had to go all the way in town, didn't I, to get the game!"

"All right," said Mrs. Hooper. "Go in the scullery and get washed so I can get your supper." But Albert said words under his breath and Mrs. Hooper told him not to swear. Albert found some dance music on the wireless and turned it up so high that the set rattled, and he walked out into the scullery and banged the door. "He's upset," Mrs. Hooper whispered. I was shocked at this violence and afraid that it was somehow my fault, and I kept my head down when Albert came back, with his yellow hair wet and jutting over his low forehead and his face all red from the water, but he sat down across from Gwenda and me and ate his supper like a lamb.

I did another drawing. This one had houses, streets, a church with spire, and even a village square. Gwenda was doing a house with a fence. Dawn stood watching. Albert asked Dawn to come and sit beside him, but she said no, she wanted to draw. I was hurt for Albert. I thought if he had asked me I would have gone to sit beside him. Albert finished his supper, and afterward he came and stood behind Dawn and stroked her hair and bothered her, she said. "Tch, *oh!* Da-ad!" she said. "Tell Albert to let me be. Daaa-ad!"

"Albert, let Dawn be," said Mr. Hooper, from his armchair.

"*I'm* not doing anything. You tell her to let me be."

"Dawn, let Albert be," said Mr. Hooper, and settled back into his newspaper.

I knew that Albert would have liked to be drawing, too, and my heart thumped, but I was too shy and too afraid of him to offer my paper and crayons, and Albert was too shy to ask.

"What's those there supposed to be?" he asked Gwenda, in a mean voice.

"Birds," said Gwenda, "on the roof of the house."

"Birds," said Albert. "Yeah!"

Gwenda said, "Albert is going to play goalie for his team tomorrow, aren't you, Albert?"

"Yeah," said Albert, and then he went and sat down, and he didn't put his feet up.

Except for Mr. Hooper, who had the day off and went early to work on his allotment, where he grew our vegetables, we all went to stand in the drizzling rain to watch Albert lose the soccer game for his team.

"He's ever so good," said Mrs. Hooper. "The ground is slippery for him."

Dawn stayed at the sidelines with her mother, like a young lady, but Gwenda and I kept Albert company behind the goalposts.

Every time the ball came at him he would take off and throw the length of his body straight over the ball, which shot into the goal below him. We suffered for him and we would go and help clean him up. I held Gwenda's handbag while she wiped the mud out of his eyes with her handkerchief. "That was a good try," we would say. "You couldn't have saved that one, never in a million years."

We walked home with Albert between us. "You were ever so good," we all said. Dawn supported him on her arm, looking admiringly round into his face. "That other team," she said, "they didn't know half the time what they were doing."

I saw an opportunity to get into Albert's good graces. "And they were all so big," I said.

"They weren't, either, not all that big," said Dawn. "Albert isn't all that short."

"The ground wasn't half slippery!" Mrs. Hooper said.

But Albert knew that he was too short for goalie, and that he had loused up the play. All afternoon, he kept trying to be funny. Gwenda and I had gone up to my room, and she was standing by the window with her back to the door. A thundering and sharp slapping sound came up the stairs, making her jump, and a huge headless shadow appeared in the doorway, its arms raised. Gwenda turned red and then white, and began to tremble and to cry. I began to cry, too. I don't know why, because I hadn't a moment's doubt that it portended anything worse than Albert with his head stuck inside his back-to-front jacket. My heart never missed a beat to see him standing in my doorway, growling and cracking a leather belt like a whip. I howled to keep Gwenda company. Mrs. Hooper came running up the stairs and said, "Oh, Albert, *now* look what you've done!" and sat down on the edge of my bed and folded Gwenda under one elbow and me under the other and rocked us on her soft bosom. We roared.

Albert backed away, muttering about trying to have a little joke, God damn it.

"And don't you swear in this house!" Mrs. Hooper said. She shepherded us tenderly downstairs, where we paraded our tear-stained faces before Albert. Albert was walking around the scullery. Afterward, he went out and came back with a new card game for everyone to play, but we said we were too upset, for goodness' sake, to play games, and to put that thing away.

I remember the shelf on the bottom right-hand side of the kitchen dresser, where all Albert's games were kept. I had half an expectation that the family would sit down one evening around the table and all play together, but always Mr. Hooper removed to his chair and his paper, and Mrs. Hooper wandered between the kitchen and the scullery, fixing things and worrying. Gwenda and I drew at the table, Dawn quarreled with Albert, and Albert fiddled with the wireless, following the programs of dance music around the dial. Albert's wireless was a real pain to me. Except for one tune that had no lyrics and was called "In an Eighteenth Century Drawing Room." I once waited a whole Thursday afternoon when my parents were visiting to have it come on for my mother to hear. "Don't you like that?" I said. "Listen to this one. Do you like it?"

"Mein Gott!" said my mother. "That's a Mozart piano sonata. In C major. I used to play it! What have they done!"

"Isn't it terrible!" I said, thankful that I had been saved from confessing how pretty, how marvelously orderly and sweet it sounded in my ears.

Albert had come in to take his tea with us; he sat with his shy, sulky eyes lowered, not saying a word so long as my parents were there, but afterward he danced around the table, singing my tune in a facetious falsetto. I removed my eyes from stocky Albert with his hunched shoulders and slightly bowed legs mincing a minuet, to spare him and myself, as one looks away from a person in an embarrassing predicament.

I usually tried to not see Albert. I used to watch Gwenda, who would talk to him and look at the permanent redness about his nostrils and the virulent pink-and-purple eruptions on his adolescent skin without appearing to be revolted. This puzzled me about her.

Once, Albert and I happened to arrive at the front gate simultaneously, and there was nothing for it but to walk up the narrow

alley to the back door together. I kept hard to my side of the
wall to avoid contact with his person, from which, as he moved
beside me, there came a body warmth. All the while, I kept up a
mindless conversation, which, out of my confusion, sounded like
flirtation. "Listen to that dog," I said. "He knows we are coming.
I wonder if he knows it's you and me." Albert said not a word.
There was a moment's confusion over the matter of the back-door
handle, to which each of us had raised a hand, and our eyes
accidentally met. Before I could avert mine, I had seen, with surprise, where I had expected pure hatred—for had I not turned him
out of his bed and room?—a mere surface of blue, an insult. I
walked into the kitchen ahead of him. The house was silent. There
was no one home, and, terrified at finding myself alone in a room
with Albert, I murmured that I had drawers to clean and ran upstairs to my room.

Downstairs, the wireless shouted. I sat on my bed. I dreamed a
daydream: I was looking Albert in the face. I was saying, "Don't
you know that everyone would like you better if you were nicer
and better behaved?" In my dream, Albert was converted and became a good boy and a gentleman, all due to me.

I stayed upstairs till I heard Mr. Hooper come home, and then
I went down to the kitchen. I looked surreptitiously at Mr. Hooper's
eyes. He had brown eyes, not alien, chilly, Christian eyes like Albert. I knew that Mr. Hooper was Christian, too, but not a blue-
eyed Christian. To all intents, Mr. Hooper and Gwenda were
Jewish; I adopted them.

Gwenda I liked awfully. The only quarrel I remember having
with her resulted from our drawing together, and was the occasion
of my first political insight. Gwenda now had her own crayons,
and they were a different combination of colors from mine, so we
figured out a system of exchange: If she borrowed my pink, I would
borrow, say, her sky-blue. However, if my pink, which I never
used, was long and her sky-blue, which was much in demand, was
short, I would also borrow her green, to make up for the difference
in length. The complication arose if she needed her sky-blue back
while I was still using her green, because then she would have

to make amends for the blue with another crayon of equal length, and we forgot which was whose and there were words. I don't know to which one of us was given the revelation that we should pool our resources and each use out of the common property according to need. We got a big box and put all our crayons in it. For the rest of the evening, we went about with our arms around each other. Next day came the counter-revelation: both of us wanted to do our skies at the same time, and there were words. Still, it seems to me that Gwenda and I were tender and decent with each other, and as the weeks went on, we were friends. If one cried, the other cried, too.

Once, on the day before a Sunday visit to my parents, Albert spoiled the village I had done to take to them as a present. It had houses, streets, church spires, a church square, and even people walking in it, and I had left it upside down, wanting the Hoopers to admire it without wanting to seem to want it, so that it was just possibly an accident that Albert took it to use for a shoe wiper. I was momentarily pained at the loss and started to cry. Gwenda came running to see what was the matter, and, on being told, she cried so sincerely that I wondered if the situation were really as sad as all that. That was the day Albert brought home Monopoly.

Toward the end of the summer, Mrs. Hooper took Dawn and Gwenda and me downtown to the Air Raid Precaution headquarters to be fitted for gas masks. We put on the black, ugly masks with their flat snouts; we looked strange and monstrous to each other. For the little children there were Mickey Mouse masks with blue snouts and pink, floppy ears, which didn't fool them. They howled in terror at the close, evil-smelling rubber over their faces. The experience jarred Mrs. Hooper, and on the way home she kept asking me if I thought there was really going to be a war. I said no, there was not; Hitler would never go to war once he realized the Allies meant business. Mrs. Hooper was relieved. I must know—after all, I came from over there.

War was declared on September 3rd; we heard of it over the wireless, and Mrs. Hooper had hysterics and began to tremble and sent Gwenda and me to fetch Mr. Hooper quickly from his allotment down by the river. We ran all the way. "War!" we shouted, coming in sight of Mr. Hooper squatting near the little corrugated-iron tool shed on his length of land, which was striped with rows of tomato plants, carrots, lettuce, and beans. "Mum says you got to come home, it's war!" cried Gwenda, arriving breathless and in terror.

Mr. Hooper straightened up. "Charlie!" he yelled across to a fellow weeding at the far end of the neighboring allotment. "War!"

"Which?" shouted Charlie, putting his hand behind his ear in a pantomime of not having heard.

"WAR!" yelled Mr. Hooper, with his hands cupped into a megaphone before his mouth.

"OH!" Charlie shouted back, and nodded his head in pantomime of having understood and went back to his weeding.

Mr. Hooper sent us home, saying he wanted to get his beans picked before it started raining and he'd be along in a little bit.

But it didn't look to us as if it were going to rain. It was marvelous how the sky continued blue in spite of the war. The sun was high and hot, and we walked back slowly. Albert had got home, and there was dance music coming out of the wireless, as usual. I was comforted. Wartime seemed much like any other time, except that we carried our gas masks in cardboard boxes on a string around the neck wherever we went.

School had begun. Gwenda and I came and went together, though she was two classes ahead of me. On the first morning, we had louse inspection. I presented my head graciously; it must be clear to everyone that this was not meant for me. There was one teacher who taught all subjects, and I remember feeling that she had nothing new to tell me. I turned to reading. I read under the desk all day. I read all evening and in bed at night and brought my book to breakfast. "Whose is this?" Albert would ask, without looking at me and holding the book between forefinger and thumb as if it were some unpleasant object he had found on his chair.

Shortly before the Christmas holidays, a yearly examination was held at the Central School and both Gwenda and I won scholar-

ships to the County School. My parents welcomed this change in
my fortunes with enthusiastic pride—my father cried tears; my
mother went in and told Mrs. Willoughby. The Hoopers reacted
with a different sort of pride. They weren't going to have any kid
of theirs, they said, going to school along with a class of girls she
didn't belong to.

Full of indignation, I commiserated with Gwenda, but, to my
surprise, she shared her parents' view. "Ma and Dawn, they went
to the Central School," said Gwenda.

"But don't you want to go to a better school," I said, "where
they teach Latin and you can go to the university? My Uncle
Paul went to the University of Vienna until the Nazis threw him
out. He was going to be a doctor. I'm going to the university."

"I'm going to get married," said Gwenda. "Dad and Albert
didn't go, and Albert works in the gasworks, and my dad got elected
secretary to the union."

"Do you like Albert?" I asked parenthetically.

"Yes," Gwenda said. "He belongs in our house."

We were sitting together in a hole we had made in the privet
hedge at the bottom of the garden. I looked out over the grounds
of my new school—at the playing fields, the tennis courts, the
trees grouped around the outdoor stage, and the ample building
along the top of the hill. I would not believe that Gwenda could
really feel different from me about things, and I said, "Don't you
think that's nice?" and watched her face with curiosity.

"It's wicked," said Gwenda. "All that for just a few girls."

"But it's nice," I said. "And the girls in their green uniforms,
don't you think they look nice?"

"They're stuck-up," said Gwenda. "I like the girls at the Central
School. They're my friends."

"I'm going to be friends with the girls at the County School,"
I said. Gwenda and I sat close, comparing our snobberies. "What
are you going to be, then, if you don't go to the university?"

"I'm going to take typing in my last year," Gwenda said, "and
I'm going to be a secretary."

"I'm going to be a painter," I said. "And I'm going to travel.

My Uncle Paul used to travel in Italy with his friends before Hitler. I'm going to have lots of friends. Poets, and people like that." Gwenda listened with all her heart; her eyes glowed with enthusiasm while I roamed in my delicious future and picked and chose, like a child let loose in a sweetshop, until Mrs. Hooper yelled to us from the scullery to come and wash our hands and have our suppers.

"So who is going to get your new uniform?" Mrs. Hooper said. "I'm sure I don't know what all they need up at that fancy school."

Next day, I took my gas mask and went to see the lady of the Refugee Committee and told her, and she closed up the office and went shopping with me. She got me the green princesse-style tunic and green beret with the school emblem, and I never knew who paid for it.

"Yah!" said Albert. "Here comes Miss La-di-da."

Albert loathed me. At Christmas, he gave me a game—a small one. For the rest of the family he had bought a collapsible snooker table, with balls and cues and chalk, which he played by himself throughout the holidays.

Christmas Day also happened to be Dawn's seventeenth birthday, and Albert gave her a ring. After tea, he turned on the wireless really loud and stood behind Dawn's chair and drummed out "A Tisket, a Tasket" with a flat palm on each of Dawn's breasts. Mrs. Hooper began to carry the tea dishes into the scullery, and Gwenda left the room. I pretended to be drawing, but I looked in fascination at what Albert's hands dared, and at Dawn, who allowed it. Her hands lay loosely in her lap, the right one cradling the left, which wore the ring. Dawn's eyes stared straight before her with a look of patience.

With the beginning of the new term, I was inducted into the fourth form at the school on the hill, behind the Hoopers' house. "Will you take care of Lore, here? She's new," said the teacher to a girl sitting in the front row. "Katherine will show you around. You sit here, and, Daisy, will you move to the empty desk in the back?"

"Ah, no!" said this Katherine. "Why does Daisy have to go?" She looked at me with a cold and insolent blue eye.

I talked to Katherine. I told her how I had come to the County School on a scholarship. Katherine looked back at Daisy and put her thumb to her nose. I decided she couldn't have meant me, not with me standing there. I said, "I'm from abroad, and when I came to England I went to a Hebrew school, and after the first term I was top of the class."

"Don't you like it in the new school?" my mother asked the next Thursday.

"I do like it," I lied. "I love it." I spoke with enthusiasm about the courts and lawns and trees and a special room for art classes, with easels.

"It always takes a while in a new school to make friends," said my mother.

"I've got plenty of friends," I said, for I could not bear my mother to know that I was the kind of person who didn't have. I had sneaked into Dawn's and Gwenda's room, where there was a small mirror on the wall, to try to understand what people saw when they looked at me. My eyes looked back, critical, anxious, and overeager. My nose had lost its baby roundness and was growing sharp, like my father's. My face was small, made narrower by a mass of high-standing, tight light curls. (My mother wanted me to have my hair cut short, but I would not. I thought once it grew long enough it would also turn black and fine and silky and would fall in a tragic way about my face. Then I would look interesting and sad, and even Albert would feel sorry for me.)

I began to wonder that Gwenda and Mr. Hooper should seem to be fond of me. I watched them. I intercepted their eyes looking at me and tried to imagine myself as I appeared to them—and there I was with my sharp and narrow face. I studied Mrs. Hooper, too, and she puzzled me. Often when she spoke to me, she was looking nervously at Albert—and yet I didn't think she really disliked me.

Early in 1940 a detective called at Illford House to check if my parents were friendly or spying aliens, and a month later my father was called before a tribunal, along with all male "aliens of hostile

origin." Mr. Willoughby went with him and vouched for my father's being friendly and having no explosives, inflammable materials, maps scaled more than one inch to the mile, or vehicles.
Then he drove my father home.

In London the air raids had begun. Mr. Hooper and Albert dug
a shelter in the back yard. I asked Mrs. Hooper if they were
going to bomb us, and she said she was sure she hoped not, but
in the evening I heard her tell Mr. Hooper that they weren't going
to drop bombs. "They never would on us," she said. "Would they,
Fred?" She sat and watched him while he cut up his meat.

"No," said Mr. Hooper. "Not on us. They'll drop them all around
us in a circle. Right, Lorry?"

"Tch, oh, Freddy!" Mrs. Hooper said. "I mean they wouldn't
bomb England once we show them we mean business. We'll send
ours over and show them, and they wouldn't dare."

"You take a load off my mind," said Mr. Hooper.

And so it was clear to me without benefit of doubt that the
grownups knew no more about it than I did, and were as power-
less as I to prevent it, and then I knew that the bombs were certainly going to drop.

It soon turned out that every alien over sixteen, male or female,
was hostile. Specified areas within a certain mileage of the east
and south coasts were designated "protected areas," and my parents had to leave the Willoughbys within twenty-four hours. The
Committee offered a shelter farther inland, in which refugees could
stay while they looked for other jobs, and on the way there my
parents stopped off at the Hoopers'. Soon, my mother said, somehow or other, we would all live together.

It was summer again. The lady from the church committee
brought me a second-hand tennis racket. It felt elegant in my hand.
I left it lying around in the kitchen for everyone to see. Albert
picked it up and it felt powerful in his hand, and he swung it in
the air. "Wheeough!" cried Albert. I think he would have liked
to slug me with it, but instead he began to chase Gwenda around
the table. He had my green beret stuck on his head.

"Hey, that's mine!" I said.

"Wheeoops!" yelled Albert.

"Albert, put that down before somebody gets hurt," said Gwenda, with the table between herself and him.

"Dad!" Dawn cried. "Look what he's doing!"

"Watch it!" said Mrs. Hooper, and the arm she raised to shield herself received the full blow of the descending racket. Mrs. Hooper was suddenly sitting on the floor between the fireplace and the table with such a look of surprise that we all laughed, until we saw the pain in her face. Her arm hung limp and useless out of her sleeve. Gwenda and I began to cry. Mr. Hooper knelt by his wife and took hold of the disabled arm, and despite Mrs. Hooper's screaming he wrenched it back into its socket and raised her to a chair, where Mrs. Hooper sat holding her shoulder and rocking to and fro. Her face was white and tears still pressed out of her eyes, but she could move her arm, she said, and it was all right.

Albert had fled at the sight of what he had done and was walking round and round the scullery with a sulky, scarlet face. "Goddam tennis racket," he said. I went and stood in the door. "You're just like the Germans," I yelled, with my head hot and pounding and my heart bursting in pure relief. "You're a Nazi!" I screamed, not because of what Albert had done to Mrs. Hooper, but because he had kept me in the subjection of fear all these months. Only now his teeth were chattering, and when Gwenda and Dawn kept going out on pretended errands for the poor sufferer, to give Albert baleful looks, I began to wish they would leave him alone.

It seems to me that after that I was less aware of Albert and less affected by his presence.

One day I came back from school and Mrs. Hooper was home alone. She was nervous and kept wrapping her hand into her apron, and her chin was trembling. I made her sit down in Mr. Hooper's armchair by the kitchen window. She told me how a great-aunt of Mr. Hooper's, who lived in an old-persons' home, had got pneumonia and was quite ill. Mrs. Hooper began to cry.

"She'll get better, won't she?" I comforted.

Mrs. Hooper shook her head vigorously. "No, she's ever so ill. You know, with pneumonia at her age. I think I have to nurse her, see, and she may have to come and live here, and we d-d-don't have a b-b-b-b-bed."

I said, "Oh. Well. Maybe she can have my bed?"

Mrs. Hooper was crying so hard I put my arms around her. "Yes, I expect," said Mrs. Hooper.

"Then where will I sleep?"

Mrs. Hooper cried harder.

"You don't have to worry," I said. "I can find somewhere to live," and I rocked Mrs. Hooper on my chest, "and then I can come back, you know, when she's better."

Mrs. Hooper dried her eyes. "Yes," she said. "And maybe anyway it would be better if you lived with some people where their children go to the County School."

I went downtown to tell the committee lady I needed a new home. She looked through the card index and said there was a family called Grimsley who wanted to take a refugee.

I went straight out to see the Grimsleys, who lived in an oyster-pink brick street of identical semidetached houses so new that the street was still unpaved and the front garden was a square yard of churned, dried white mud. Mrs. Grimsley opened the front door, peering with a distracted air over my head for her two boys, who, she said, were playing somewhere out front. She must have been twenty-six or -seven, plump and fair, with a bland, round forehead so furrowed with embarrassment that I made her sit down and questioned her about the house and family. Mrs. Grimsley seemed anxious to please. When I left, she asked me if I thought I would be coming to live with them, and I said, "Yes, all right."

On the weekend, Gwenda helped me move. She put my suitcase on the back of her bicycle, and as we walked, we promised each other that we would be friends forever, and I would come over and visit her. I wrote my parents, who had got a new place in Sussex with a Mrs. Burns-Digby, to give them my new address with the Grimsleys.

I remember, on the first evening Mr. Grimsley brought me home a bag of marbles. Marbles were the rage among the children in the street that season, and after supper, in the kitchen, he taught me how to play. I had beginners' luck and won seven of his marbles from him, including a beautiful crystal miggie with white marbling.

Mr. Grimsley was a very fair, very young man who rode to the factory on his bicycle every morning, leaving Mrs. Grimsley at a loss amidst her brand-new furniture and cheap, shiny fixtures. There were three Grimsley children. Sylvia was eight years old, a simple smiling child with her mother's bland, convex forehead. She went to Central School. Seven-year-old Patrick was a spastic who bumbled about the house with jerking, uncontrolled movements, squinting fiercely. Alan, the handsome, bright, angry five-year-old, kept setting fire to the plastic curtains in the brand-new bathroom. Mrs. Grimsley asked me whatever she should do with him, as we sat in the kitchen over our cups of tea. I said it was the bad habits they picked up in the street. In Vienna, I said, I had never been allowed to play with the street children. Mrs. Grimsley said yes, that was right, but after supper Alan banged his fists on the closed front door, and poor Patrick tried to do it, too, missing the door altogether. Mrs. Grimsley opened it, looking guiltily at me, and said, "Just for a few minutes, before their bedtime."

I knelt on the settee in front of the window with my forehead against the glass, feeling my marbles around inside their bag, watching the children. I remember thinking, If I let go my hands on the windowsill, my head will go through the glass, and I let go my hands and heard the crash and felt the outside breeze about my head, and saw the windowpane like a collar around my neck, and howled. Mr. and Mrs. Grimsley came running, and in the street the children collected to watch Mr. Grimsley carefully break off the jagged glass pointing at my throat and draw me, unhurt, back inside. I said, "You see, my hands slipped on the windowsill. I was leaning like this, you see, when I slipped," and it seemed even to me that that was the only way it could have happened.

In school the girls continued to be beastly to me. In the afternoon I would run across the playing field through the hole in the privet hedge to try and find my old community with Gwenda. I asked her to teach me some swear words, but she looked solemn and said she would not say them out loud. I said, "Why, they're just a bunch of letters," but Gwenda said she would not, not for anything. "Suppose someone said if you don't say some swear words you can't have your birthday party next week—wouldn't you say them?" Gwenda thought about this and then she said no, she would not say them for anything. I said I would; I would say them for nothing—it was just I didn't know any. Gwenda was going to be fifteen, and she was taking shorthand and growing very pretty.

As I was leaving, I saw Albert watching Gwenda and me from behind the window of my old room. Gwenda said he slept there now. I asked her if her father's great-aunt was going to move in. Gwenda said no.

Then I had a desperate letter from my mother. Two policemen had come with a van and taken my father away. Mrs. Burns-Digby had telephoned all around, and it seemed that they were interning all male aliens of hostile origin over sixteen. Mrs. Burns-Digby had found out that the aliens from that part of the country were being held in a transit camp in West Mellbridge, where my mother could not go because it was inside the protected area, and she was worried about my father, who had not been at all well. She begged me to go and see him.

I borrowed Gwenda's bicycle and rode the twenty miles to the nearby town. The address my mother had given in her letter turned out to be an old school building that had been made into a temporary camp. The playgrounds and tennis courts were fenced in with six-foot-high chicken wire, and there were men inside, walking up and down or standing in groups. They all looked as if they might be my uncles or great-uncles, but I could not catch sight of my father. Two soldiers stood guard at the front gate. Their feet, in huge army boots, were planted wide, and there was a good-natured look about their scratchy, blanket-thick khaki uniforms, but they had bayonets mounted on their guns and I didn't know if I was supposed to talk to them. I cycled two or three times around the compound and then headed back to Mellbridge.

It turned out that my mother had been misinformed. My father had been shipped straight north to the Isle of Man, where he met my Uncle Paul, who had come to England the previous year, and many friends and relatives.

About this time Mr. Grimsley's factory amalgamated with a munitions factory in Croydon; when the family moved, I went to live with Mr. Grimsley's father and mother.

The elder Grimsleys lived opposite the railway in an old street of purple brick attached houses. The spanking-white step led through the front door straight into the parlor-living room. The large square table filled the room completely, except for an armchair between it and the fireplace and a dark, heavy sideboard, covered with a lace scarf, on which stood a china dog and a scalloped china bowl that said "Greetings from Blackpool" and was full of pencil stubs, rubber bands, hairpins, and threepenny bits. The wallpaper was bottle green with chartreuse birds of paradise on a hedge of wild rose, and there were many pictures: an oval wedding picture of the Grimsleys, circa 1880; photos of children (including a snapshot of a sailor son squinting his eyes against the sun, in an ornate gilt frame), grandchildren, and pets long dead; landscapes with cows and cottages with hollyhocks; Watts's "Hope," chained to her green ball, riding the green, chilly water; and a life-size girl child in brown velvet with lace collar, her arms around a life-size St. Bernard dog.

In the armchair, quietly amidst this riot of neat objects, his head against a lace antimacassar, sat Mr. Grimsley, a delicate, frail old man who still made his predawn milk round with a little cart and pony.

Out in the scullery-kitchen, which also served as the family bathroom, Mrs. Grimsley, her lovely white hair built up high like the Queen Mother's and her soft, radiant smile showing ill-fitting, cheap false teeth, filled food bowls for the shaggy mongrel, the two tabbies, the parrot left by the sailor son on his last visit, and the canary that belonged to Pearl. Pearl, the skinny, pious, forty-year-old daughter, had thin hair and a pinched nose. She worked on the other side of town as a housemaid, and when she had left Mrs.

Grimsley began to put up the eggs and bacon for the sons who kept coming, clattering down the stairs from the attic where they slept in cots, dormitory style.

The first week after I came, they put in an extra cot for the Cockney evacue called Tony. Tony stole a threepenny bit from the scalloped china bowl from Blackpool and then said he hadn't. I asked him to come into the yard with me. I made him sit beside me on the back fence and talked with him. I said we were both living on the kindness of the Grimsleys. I said Pearl even went every night to sleep at the neighbor's so I could have her room over the kitchen and it would be ungrateful to steal and lie to them. I tried to look deeply into his eyes, but his face was turned away from me. With a sheepish, half-laughing look he jumped off the fence and ran, with his head down, to buck the youngest Grimsley boy, who was coming out of the back door. They fell down together, rolling and laughing on the ground.

The London air raids were becoming serious. Mellbridge lay in the path of both the British heavy bombers leaving on their nightly missions to Germany and the Germans, who flew over two hours later with their different, foreign drone and were followed by searchlights and antiaircraft fire all the way to London and back toward the coast an hour after. In the early dawn, the British planes came home, flying in the same formations in which they had left in the evening. The Grimsley boys, Tony and I, and all the neighbors leaned out of the windows to count the gaps.

The bombs that fell in our area were mainly strays, but my mother was worried and unhappy. She had it on her mind that if something happened it was not even in her power to come to me. But she had had a letter from Kari and Gerti Gold, who were working as cook and butler for a doctor's family in a pleasant town in Surrey. Kari had not even been interned, though he and Gerti had had to register as aliens and had to be home by the eleven o'clock curfew. There was a helpful refugee committee who would surely find a job for my mother and a place for me to live nearby, and the Golds urged my mother to come. My mother gave notice to Mrs. Burns-Digby and sent for me.

I went to say good-by to the Hoopers, who were in an uproar; Albert had been called up and was going into the army. Dawn was in tears. Dawn and Albert had been going to be married, and then decided to wait till he came back from the war. Gwenda said she would walk me to the station.

Albert and I said good-by. Our hands met briefly, but our eyes slid away, for he and I shared, like an obscenity between us, the knowledge that we had hated one another.

CHAPTER SIX

"Allchester": The Alien

On the train to Allchester, my mother said she had brought writing paper and I could start my thank-you letters to everybody back in Mellbridge who had been kind to me—the Hoopers, the Grimsleys, and the committee lady—and I must not forget the Levines in Liverpool. But I felt sick and went into the lavatory at the end of the corridor and vomited away most of the morning.

When we arrived, we went straight to the lodgings that Kari had found for us—a narrow little room at the head of the stairs. My mother made me lie down and sat by me and read me *David Copperfield*. We ate pears out of a paper bag, and it was cozy and nice. We did not know that my father had become so ill the authorities had declared him a friendly alien and given him his release papers, and that he was even then traveling toward Allchester.

My father had only the address where the Golds worked to connect him with us. He arrived at the house late in the evening, as they were preparing to go to bed, and he looked so tired and ill they made him come into the kitchen and gave him a cup of coffee. They wrote on a piece of paper the address where my mother and I were staying. My father got lost in the blackout of the strange town and stopped a policeman to ask the way, and the policeman arrested him for being an alien of hostile origin out on the street after the curfew and took him to the police station, where he entered the offense in my father's alien's registration book—so that subsequently my father was called in for questioning every time he changed his job or address. Then the policeman himself walked my father to our lodgings.

I was asleep in the narrow single bed and did not know until I woke up the following morning that my father was back. My mother later told me that my father had ten shillings left from his railway fare and that she had about ten shillings and one pear left in the paper bag. They sat on the edge of the bed all night and cried together.

In the morning, my mother looked up the number of the Refugee Committee and telephoned. She was told to come right over.

There was a Mrs. Dillon on duty behind the desk. Mrs. Dillon was a small woman in her late forties with gray hair cut short like a little girl's. She wore a navy-blue cotton turban and a blue-flowered print dress. (Blue, she liked to tell people, was her favorite color.) Her eyes were very bright and blue, and one was set higher and deeper in her face than the other. She asked my mother what was the matter with me, I looked so green.

I sat slumped way down in a chair, half listening. My mother told Mrs. Dillon that I had been sick all day yesterday, and Mrs. Dillon closed up the office and drove my mother and me up West Street in the rumble seat of her old Ford. It was a leisurely, sunny street, with colonnaded shops and English people going about their business. Mrs. Dillon nodded and waved to acquaintances. She sang *"Un Bel Di"* in an uneven, cheery soprano. She told us she had studied singing in Italy when she was a girl. She turned off in an uphill direction, where there were great silent houses behind high walls—I could see fruit trees and climbing roses inside the gardens—and past them to the last and grandest of the houses, a Georgian red brick. Beyond, the country opened out.

Mrs. Dillon led us through the gate, on which was the word "Adorato," and around the right of the house into the kitchen garden. A black cocker spaniel came to greet Mrs. Dillon, who embraced and kissed him. She settled my mother and me on chairs under a pear tree in the kitchen garden and went into the house. The garden was shaped like a huge triangle. It was set in the fork of the roads going north to London and east through the town to the sea beyond. Everything looked rich and green. A gardener was weeding among the vegetables. There were rows upon rows of berrybushes—gooseberry, raspberry, and red and black currants—ripening under a great net held up by poles at the corners, like a low room with a roof of net. The net sagged under the weight of an immense black cat that was sleeping in it. We could see a sloping lawn shaded by a walnut tree, and beyond that, on a lower level, past the rock garden and the six poplars, a rose garden at the back of the house, out of which Mrs. Dillon presently came, bringing another lady with her. She said this was her sister, Miss Douglas. This lady looked much neater in the same kind of flowered dress, and thinner and straighter and older and uglier. I was feeling ill again. Miss Douglas said she and her sister would like to have me come and live with them. I could stay right away. My mother went back to the office with Mrs. Dillon. Miss Douglas took me inside, where I very quickly asked for a bathroom to vomit in. And that was how I became a member of that household of women. There were Miss Douglas and Mrs. Dillon and I, and Milly, the maid, in the kitchen with her baby, Lila. The only male creature ever to come into that house was Canon Godfrey, a very tall, beautiful old man in clerical black and a wide-brimmed hat. I would see him at odd times during the week padding noiselessly, with turned-out toes, up the carpeted stair to the upstairs front room, which Miss Douglas had made into a study for him. The gardener was called Bromley, and came daily. He fetched his lunch at the tradesmen's door and took it to eat in the tool shed behind the kitchen garden.

Mrs. Dillon sent my mother to a Scottish family just outside town, who were looking for a cook-housekeeper. My father was harder to place. He stayed in the little room at the head of the stairs—the lodging Kari Gold had found for us—and Mrs. Dillon found him gardening work by the day.

I saw my parents every Thursday, when my mother was off. Sometimes the Golds invited us over to the house where they worked.

Kari was a handsome, gregarious man and Gerti was a most hospitable woman. The kitchen was always full of people. A former newspaperman with whom Kari had worked as a sports reporter on a Vienna daily came down from London. There was a young composer called Hans Frankel and his fiancée, who worked as a nursemaid in the Allchester area, and a Viennese lawyer and his wife, who were also a "married couple." There was a pleasant haze of smoke and the smell of strong coffee that Gerti kept making all the afternoon.

Once the door leading to the front of the house opened, and the doctor's wife stood stock-still to see her kitchen full of relaxed and jabbering foreigners. My eyes met hers in the second before she backed quietly away and closed the door. No one had seen her but me.

The women were sitting around the table talking, telling anecdotes of their preposterous "ladies." They spoke of their lost parents and relatives, from whom they heard nothing beyond the rare twenty-five-word Red Cross form letters. They sat and cried. The men stood talking of politics and discussing the progress of the war.

Some Thursdays we all met again at the club that the Committee organized for the Allchester refugees in the abandoned firehouse downtown. There was a big hall with a wooden floor that looked dusty under the naked electric bulbs hanging from high up on the ceiling. All around the walls were framed photographs of the firemen's football teams from the year 1927 through 1940. Mrs. Dillon stood behind the trestle table set with paper cups and poured tea. Beginners' English classes were held in a small office off the main hall. A lecturer came down from London to give talks on "What Is Expected of the Alien in a Foreign Country." Once, Mrs. Dillon gave a concert of arias and accompanied herself on the piano.

My mother tells me a story that I seem to have chosen to forget, for I want nothing to spoil my infatuation with that formal, gentle town. Its Georgian and Victorian houses stand amidst lawns, birdbaths, rock gardens, flower beds, all enclosed by high rose- and ivy-covered walls. My father worked as assistant gardener in a small park belonging to a Mrs. Lambston. Mrs. Lambston kept a donkey to amuse her children in the school holidays. During the term, the donkey helped pull the manure and take garbage down to the bonfire. My mother says that one day Mrs. Lambston thought the donkey was looking tired and told my father to unharness the poor dear and pull the cart himself. My mother swears that this is what brought on a new hemorrhage that laid him up in the All-chester County Hospital, just back of Adorato.

After my father came out, Mrs. MacKenzie, the lady for whom my mother was working, invited him to stay with them, so that my mother could look after him. The MacKenzies lived in an Elizabethan water mill belonging to the National Trust—Mr. Mac-Kenzie was an architect. On Sundays, when I went out to visit my parents, we all had our dinner in the living room, whose walls, floor, and ceiling were warm-colored unvarnished old wood, at a great, heavy oak trestle table. That was a magnificent table, at which there was room for the four MacKenzie daughters, their school friends, an ancient grandmother, a simple-minded cousin, and, as often as not, some friends of Mr. and Mrs. MacKenzie—architects, writers, and ballet dancers, come to rest up from the nightly shock of the London blitz—and there was room, too, for the refugee cook, and the cook's daughter, and the cook's sick husband.

I was in love with the MacKenzie family, and could have been in a state of happiness those Sundays had it not been for the presence of my father, who was always turning to my mother to have her translate what people were saying to him, and never understood the jokes going around. If the twins, who were fifteen, got the giggles and started my mother off, Mr. MacKenzie, at the head of the table, seeing the three helpless, would pass the plates round the other side, but my father would put on his mock-amused face and say, "Ha-ha, ha-ha, ha-haaa, very funny." I kept my eyes lowered to my plate. My mother stopped laughing and said she must go and look after her dessert in the kitchen.

Mrs. MacKenzie said, "Mr. Groszmann has been in one of those ridiculous internment camps and he has been rather ill, but you're better now, aren't you? I think you're getting your color back."

"What?" said my father, turning to me for a translation and answering in German, "Not much better. All these wooden steps are hard for me, and I think the air out here is too damp to do anybody any good. Tell them."

"He says he is much better, thank you," I said, blushing painfully, "and he thanks you very much for letting him stay in the Mill with my mother."

After a few weeks, my father did get stronger. Mrs. Dillon found him a new little room in Allchester and, when Mrs. Lambston refused to have him back, persuaded Miss Douglas to let him come in three days a week to help Bromley in our garden. One day the following spring, I was coming up the hill from school and saw Mrs. Dillon holding the front door open, waiting for me. She had a handkerchief balled up in her hand. She made me come into the drawing room and sit down on the sofa, and she sat down beside me and patted my hand. She said my father had had a stroke, right at the bottom of the garden, and they had taken him to the County Hospital. "Your mother is with him." Mrs. Dillon kept stroking my hands with her handkerchief. "Poor darling," she said.

"I'm all right," I said, embarrassed by her sympathy, which I did not feel I deserved, for my eyes were dry and my heart beat steadily.

"Such poor, cold hands," murmured Mrs. Dillon. "Come sit closer to the fire and I'll build it up warm and nice for you."

"I always have cold hands," I said.

At night, they had the maid bring me hot chocolate to have before the fire, and Miss Douglas said to Mrs. Dillon, "We'll send him magazines. Mary, don't forget to make up a package of old *Punches* and *Tatlers*."

When they thought I had gone up to bed, Mrs. Dillon told Miss Douglas, who had been out of the house at the time, what had happened. "It seems he had just finished the lawn and was going to put the machine away, poor thing, because when I found him he was lying in the path outside the tool shed and he had lost all control of himself, poor man."

I stopped listening outside the door and went up the stairs to my room. I argued that what Mrs. Dillon had said about my father losing control might not have meant that he had lain in the path in his own excrement, but I could not get rid of this picture in my mind. Often, later, and particularly when I was talking with my father face to face, I would wonder if that was what Mrs. Dillon had meant.

The next day, I went to the hospital straight from school. My mother was waiting for me in the corridor outside the ward, and she smiled, because she was so pleased to see me, though her face was a high red color and her eyes were shining wet. "That terrible hat they make you wear," she said, smoothing my hair under the panama with the school ribbon. "Dr. Adler says Daddy is doing very well. I don't want you to be frightened if he doesn't recognize you, or says anything strange. It's all the medicines he's been getting. I just want you to stay a minute. Oh, and darling, I don't know whether they told you. Daddy's left side is paralyzed, which often happens after a stroke. The doctor says there's a good chance it might disappear completely. Come along. For just a minute."

My mother walked in front of me into the huge hospital ward and around a screen. Gerti and Kari were standing at the foot of the bed in which my big father lay neatly under the hospital blankets. I could see the hump of his feet. My mother walked around to the right side of the bed. She sat down on a chair and leaned her sad, red, smiling face over his pillow. "Here she is, in her terrible school hat," my mother said in her bright, ordinary voice. "Daddy has been asking for you all afternoon."

My father's eyes looked straight up at the ceiling. His face was white and he was frowning, seemingly preoccupied with the struggle to free his right hand from under the blankets. My mother helped him get it out. The hand looked bloodless, white, and soft, as if even the nails were soft. He waggled the fingers impatiently toward the headboard behind his pillow. He said, "Tell her to come out. She should come out from behind there." He seemed to be trying to turn his head to look behind the headboard.

"She's right here. Look. Come forward, where Daddy can see you," my mother said to me.

I stepped up until my face was between his face and the ceiling. His mouth twitched. He began to cry with the right side of his face without the left side moving. When he stopped crying, he was looking right at me, and he said, "If it's Miss Douglas behind there, she should come out."

I looked at my mother in horror. She said, "Come out from behind there, Miss Douglas."

My father relaxed. In a minute, he said in a conversational tone, "Franzi, before I forget, the papers are in a niche behind the stove in the *Herrenzimmer*. The rel . . . rel—papers." He lay frowning in puzzled irritation at the lost word. "The rel . . . the rel— those papers," he said, waggling his impatient fingers.

"The release papers, yes," said my mother. "They are all right."

"They want to see them at the police station," said my father.

"I'll take them."

My father closed his eyes, exhausted.

"Go outside," said my mother, "and wait for me."

As I turned away, I noticed the weight of Kari's hand on my shoulder and knew that it had lain there all the time. When I looked back, I saw my mother tuck my father's hand under the sheet. The right side of my father's face had begun to cry again.

My mother went to see my father every day. She did the Mac-Kenzies' housework in the morning and got their lunch and then took the bus into town and stayed with him till five. Then she took the bus back to cook dinner. Thursdays and every other Sunday, which were her days off, she stayed all evening.

One day, she was massaging his paralyzed left foot and felt a slight curling of the toes. Dr. Adler said it was a good sign. This doctor was Jewish, too, but not a refugee. He was fat and old and had a square, grizzled head. He patted my mother's arm and said she was a good woman and told her to try and take it a little easier. "Have a little holiday for yourself once in a while," he said.

My mother asked me to visit my father in the hospital for those hours she could not be there, and I wondered while I sat beside him that I should be feeling nothing but excruciating boredom. Later, when he was better, it seemed all right to bring a book.

"What are you reading?" my father asked.

"It's homework. In a way."

My father said, "I don't want to stay in the hospital any more. I wish your mother would take me home."

"You know you can't climb the wooden steps at the Mill. You'll have to stay here until you are better."

"I'm not going to get better as long as I have to stay here. The nurses don't understand when I talk to them. I asked your mother to write to your Uncle Paul. He studied medicine in Vienna. Vienna has the best medical school in the world."

"Firstly, Paul never got finished with his studies, and secondly, he is now in the Dominican Republic doing farm work. What would he know that your doctor here doesn't know?"

"These English doctors don't know anything."

"They're good enough to look after a hospitalful of English people," I said, and then bent quickly to kiss the rude words away. My father's skin felt unpleasantly chilly, flaccid under my lips. It seemed wicked in me that I did not like to kiss him and I kissed him again.

He looked for a moment as though he might be going to cry, but he only said, "Look!" and moved the fingers of his left hand lying on top of the blanket ever so slightly.

"There, you see," I said. "You couldn't have done that a few weeks ago, could you?"

"No," said my father. He lay quietly.

I surreptitiously picked up my book.

My father said, "The doctor recommends physical therapy. Paul once took a course in therapy in Vienna."

I said nothing.

My father said, "The doctor didn't even come to see me today."

"Because you're getting better. He doesn't have to come and see you every day."

"So, if I'm better, why can't your mother take me home?"

"Because she will have to give notice to the MacKenzies and find a room for both of you," I said, with my irritation rising again. "She'll have to go to work for both of you, won't she? So you will have to stay here till you can look after yourself."

"You could come and look after me," said my father.

"And what about school?" I had been fourteen in March, which was the legal school-leaving age, and I did not want to think about this.

"After school you could come," he said.

"And what about homework? And what would you do for the rest of the day? Who would get your meals for you?"

"You and your mother could manage if you really wanted."

"Daddy!" I leaned forward and looked into his face, and I was trembling. "Promise me something. Promise you won't tell Mummy that you don't want to stay in the hospital. It will only make her worry more. Will you promise? For me. I mean, there's nothing she can do about it."

"She can take me away," said my father. "Are you going to read again?"

"I'm just looking at my book."

"Are you angry with me?"

"No."

"Franzi!" said my father.

I hid my book.

My mother came smiling between the beds down the long ward, kissed me, and sat on a chair at my father's left side. She massaged his hand, and told us stories. "Did you hear the explosion around nine o'clock last night? Well, it was a stray bomb, and it fell right at the end of the MacKenzies' field—a direct hit on Mr. Mac-Kenzie's vegetable marrow. It broke all the west windows. We spent the morning cleaning up the mess."

"Franzi," said my father, "did you write to Paul?"

"Not yet. I will bring pen and paper tomorrow, and we will write the letter here."

My father avoided my eyes and said, "When are you going to take me out of the hospital?"

"As soon as the doctor says you are well enough. Lore, did you tell your father about the school concert?"

"We are having an end-of-term concert, and I'm going to play the Mozart fantasia."

My father looked at me and said, "You can borrow my best crocodile belt to wear for the concert."

"But it's much too big for me," I said, "and besides, it's a man's belt."

My father had begun to cry. "Look, Franzi," he said. "That's all I can do," and he wiggled his fingers on the blanket.

My mother found a job as cook in Harvey's restaurant. The kitchen was in the basement, and there was a grating in the pavement for a skylight. I would see the steam coming up by the time I walked to school. On the way home, walking with a friend, I would say, "Down there is where my mother works."

My mother fetched my father from the hospital. He was dressed in his good herringbone suit from Vienna. The pants hung like gray elephant skin around his thin legs, and the collar of his shirt stood away all around his neck. His face had the sick no-color of a plant that has sprung up in a cellar. He had shaved, but small islands of white stubble stood on his upper lip and his left cheek. He smiled his embarrassed one-sided smile.

The room my mother had found on the London road, at the far side of town, distressed me. I asked Miss Douglas if I might take some flowers, and she gave me three roses and an iris. They were a great disappointment. They neither raised the ceiling nor pushed out the walls nor cheered up the green linoleum; they were four flowers stuck in a milk bottle in a mean room. "Why, at least, can't we have a teapot?" I asked my mother. "Why do you have to bring the kettle to the table?" "Maybe next time you come I'll see if I can get at my china," said my mother, "but I think it's in that bottom trunk and I don't want to unpack. I don't think the landlady likes us." We came upon this landlady in the hall, and made her jump. She was nervous. She was a tall, skinny working woman, with brown teeth. After two weeks, she told my mother that Mr. Groszmann made her nervous, being so quiet all the time and then all of a sudden there he would be on the stairs, and she had a daughter coming to town in two weeks and would need her room.

My mother came to Adorato to speak to Mrs. Dillon. They had tea in the dining room, but before my mother left, Miss Douglas invited her to sit with us in the drawing room awhile. Mrs. Dillon called my mother "Franzi," and it seemed she had asked my mother to call her "Mary." After my mother left, Mrs. Dillon and Miss Douglas had an argument about this in very low voices.

Soon afterward, Mrs. Dillon bought a house around the corner. It was called Clinton Lodge, a smaller, less elegant version of Adorato. She rented the front bedroom to my mother and father, and the other rooms to other refugees who were having trouble finding places to live, for people did not care to have German-speaking aliens in their houses, in those days. There were Mr. and Mrs. Katz from Munich, who had a brother in the U.S.A. and were waiting for the American quota. There were two elderly women from Berlin, who shared a room. There was a Viennese widow, Mrs. Bauer, whose small son had left by the same children's transport as I but had stayed in Holland. She was waiting for the end of the war. Their bedrooms were piled high with trunks, which contained their total possessions, disguised under tablecloths or hidden under bits of carpeting; the rooms had an air of permanent temporariness.

The seven refugees lived kindly together. German and Austrian accents mingled good-humoredly. Clinton Lodge came to be known around town as an example of strangers living in one house without hostilities, except for my father, who quarreled with everybody. One night, I went over to warm up the supper my mother had prepared for him in the morning, before she went to the restaurant. She was out playing the piano for a Viennese singing teacher. Mrs. Bauer intercepted me in the hallway. "I wish you would get your father out of the kitchen. Mrs. Katz and I want to get our supper and set the table. I've asked him to move, but he pretends he doesn't hear me."

My father was sitting at the kitchen table with his notebook, ink, pencils, and erasers spread around him. The doctor had said he could not do any more gardening, and he was taking a correspondence course in English accounting, writing the answers in his bad grammar, meticulously underlined in red.

"Hello, Mrs. Katz. Hello, Daddy. Come into the drawing room. They need the table out here."

"I need the table, too," said my father.

"Come on, Daddy, I'm taking the dishes inside," I said, in the irritable voice that had become habitual with me when I spoke to him. I wondered how he was going to disentangle the partially paralyzed left leg that was twisted as if it did not belong to him around the chair leg, but I thought, He manages all day when I'm not here, and walked away into the drawing room.

Presently I heard him limping after me down the hall. "I can't eat anything tonight," he said.

"You can at least try, can't you? The doctor says you've got to eat."

"The doctor, the doctor—always the doctor," said my father.

"Why didn't you let them have the table for their supper when they asked you?"

"I have as much right to the table as they have," he said.

"But you have no right to make things harder for Mummy. She works nine hours in the restaurant and three hours playing the piano, to make extra money, and when she comes home she has to listen to complaints and make excuses for you. You never think of her, do you?"

"I think of her. I think of her," said my father, with his head drawn back from my yelling. His vest stood away from his collapsed chest. "I'm not feeling well tonight," he said.

"So don't think about how you feel all the time. Think of all the thousands of people who are being killed every day."

"What's that to me?" said my father.

"Daddy! What would you rather have—your health or the end of the war?"

"The end of the war and my health," said my father, with a faint smile.

"No, but seriously, Daddy! Say someone gave you only one wish: either the war will be over tomorrow and you will be ill for a year or you can be well tomorrow and the war will last another year. Which would you have?"

"I want to be well," said my father. "So, are you angry? Why are you angry?"

"I'm not angry."

"Take this away, please," said my father, looking miserably at the piece of meat loaf speared on his fork.

"Not until you've eaten at least what's on your fork."

My father put the forkful into his mouth, and vomited.

Mr. Katz helped me take my father upstairs, and I helped him to bed. He lay exhausted and smiled embarrassedly with his half face. I sat on the edge of the bed and massaged his left hand. "You're better now, aren't you?"

"Yes. Are you going to stay with me till your mother comes?"

"Of course. Do you think I would leave while you are feeling ill? Show me how you can move your fingers."

My father wiggled his left fingers for me.

"You want to go to sleep?"

"Yes," he said.

"Daddy," I said, "let's not tell Mummy about your being sick. All right?"

"All right."

But when my mother came home, I met her at the door and said, "Daddy vomited. Mr. Katz helped me take him to bed and when I came back Mrs. Katz had cleaned everything up. You don't have to go up. He's asleep now."

"Maybe I will just go up and look at him."

I set supper on the kitchen table for her, and when she came down I said, "Mrs. Bauer and Mrs. Katz wanted to cook their supper, but Daddy wouldn't let them have the table."

"And you had an argument with him about it?"

"How can you even argue with him? Sometimes he doesn't make sense any more. Sometimes I say something to him and what he says isn't an answer to what I said at all. It gets me so angry."

"Darling, he is ill. Imagine you were afraid you were going to throw up any moment while someone stood there arguing with you."

"But I get so angry," I said.

"Well, try not to. He is ill, and you are young and well. Don't argue with him."

"I can't promise."

"Try," said my mother.

"I've put on coffee. Anybody want coffee?" asked my mother when we joined the others in the drawing room. "Katzerl, I hear you helped Lore clean up after Igo. You are very good."

"Oh, well, he was feeling bad tonight, poor man."

"I'm going to put up a little card table so tomorrow he can work upstairs," said my mother.

"All right, all right, don't worry about it. Sit down, will you, and rest yourself. Aren't you tired?"

My mother sat down and stuck both feet out in front of her and let her arms hang down the sides of the chair. She had pulled her hair over her eyes like a rag doll's.

"Franzi!" Mrs. Katz cried. "Franzi, you clown, you look horrible. Stop!"

"You wanted to see how tired I am," said my mother.

"Oh, Mum-my!" I said, and everyone was laughing so that we did not at first hear my father's terrified voice calling "Franzi!" from upstairs.

I ran up with my mother. My father was sitting in his bed, and the upper part of his body heaved as if he were having to drag up each breath from some deep source inside himself. "I can't breathe," he gasped.

"Swing your feet out and you can sit more comfortably." She sat down beside him. "You'll feel better in a minute. You know how these attacks pass."

Between his heavings, my father said, "That doctor says I don't have asthma. You see I do."

"He says it's nervous asthma. Sit quietly and it will pass."

"It's asthma," said my father. "My mother had asthma; I know what asthma is like."

"You see you're already better. A few moments ago you couldn't even speak. You want to lie down?"

"Yes."

But as soon as my mother had helped my father back into bed and covered him, he sat up again and swung his legs over the edge of the bed and gasped in a shocking way. "Open the window," he said.

"But if it's asthma, opening the window won't help," I said.

"Open the window," my mother commanded. She put a blanket over my father's lap, and presently he got better and she helped him back into bed and put a pillow behind him.

He said, "Stay with me."

"But you haven't even had your coffee, Mummy."

"I will later."

"But Daddy is better now."

My mother said, "Darling, didn't you say you had to get back to Miss Douglas's at nine? It's almost half past now."

While I was getting on my coat, my father was saying, "I wish you would write to Paul about my asthma. These English doctors don't understand my case."

"I'll write tomorrow," said my mother.

"You aren't going down again tonight, are you?"

"I'm going to stay right here and go to bed. Look, I'll show you how tired I am." She pulled her hair down over her eyes and stiffened her legs and let her arms hang rag-doll fashion.

When I looked in on my father the next day, Mrs. Bauer was in despair in the kitchen. "He's laid supper on the kitchen table. He laid it at noon today!"

"It's for your mother," said my father when I went upstairs to argue with him. "You said I never think of her, but you see I do."

"But you can't monopolize a kitchen table all afternoon and evening in a house where there are five other people."

"Franzi has as good a right to the table as anybody else," said my father. "Why are you putting your hat on again? Aren't you going to stay with me?"

I had turned toward the wardrobe mirror to fix my hair under my school hat.

"Why are you angry with me?"

I did not answer. In the mirror I saw him coming up close behind me.

"Would you like to have my crocodile belt for your own?"

"Mind!" I said, stepping away from the mirror as if to get a better distance, but it was really to force him to back away, and though I knew that his feet were not quick enough to realign themselves, his failing to move infuriated me so that I turned and put a hand against his chest and pushed him. Astonished, I saw the astonishment on his face as he felt himself keeling over. Falling, it seemed to me, with infinite slowness, he struck the foot of the bed with his shoulder and slid almost gently to the floor. I knelt on the floor. I said, "You fell over." We heard footsteps already on the landing. My mother, who had arrived downstairs in time to hear the thump, came running in. "You probably didn't know he was behind you," she said.

"I didn't," I said.

"And you couldn't step out of the way fast enough, Igo, could you?"

"I couldn't," said my father.

"You think he is well enough to go to work?" my mother asked Dr. Adler when he came to give my father his weekly checkup.

"Well, how do you feel?" the doctor asked my father and patted him on the knee.

My father sat with his shirt open. He lifted his right shoulder and turned his palm out in a questioning gesture. He smiled embarrassedly and looked at my mother.

"He walks better, don't you think?" said my mother.

"He does, he does," said the doctor.

"I just wish he ate more."

"You must eat more," said the doctor to my father. "Eat, eat," and his right hand made motions of putting food into his mouth while he nodded encouragingly.

My father lifted his right shoulder and turned his hand out.

"You be a good fellow," said the doctor, and patted my father's knee. "You've got a wonderful little wife to look after you. And I don't want *you* to get too tired, either," he said to my mother at the door. "Get some rest, now."

"Did you hear what the doctor said? You're supposed to rest," I said to my mother.

"I'm going to," she said. "I'm going to the kitchen right now to have a cup of coffee."

"I'll make it. You sit down. Look at the way you're sitting, as if you're ready to jump up any moment. Only half of you is on the seat."

"That's the only half that's tired," said my mother.

"Oh, Mum-my! Why do you have to play for those singing lessons? Mrs. Dillon says you wouldn't have to pay the one pound ten a month for my schooling. The Committee would pay it."

"But I want to pay it. And I like to play the piano."

"And why did you tell the firewarden you would watch one night for Daddy as well as one night for yourself?"

"Because Daddy can't get up every time the siren goes off and walk around the streets at night."

"But they wouldn't expect him to. You could get a certificate from Dr. Adler."

"Darling, that's not the point. We're refugees. It's important for us not to shirk anything we can do. You see, they even suspend our curfew for the nights we are on duty."

"But the doctor said you are supposed to rest. You're doing too much."

"Darling, would you really like to help me?"

"Yes."

"Then don't nag me. I promise you if I feel I am getting too tired I will stop playing for the singing lessons. All right?"

But I could no more stop nagging my mother than she could stop jumping, and that week Mrs. Bauer had the flu and my mother volunteered to do her fire watching for her. I remember, on the way back to Adorato I cried about it.

I watched my mother in those days the same way I watched my father, imagining their bodies under the skin, rather like the intricate anatomical drawings I remembered from Paul's medical books, only with moving parts, all liable, momentarily, to go wrong. Remembering how in Vienna my father had always fallen ill when I was not expecting it, I kept myself in a state of alarm. I kept expecting calamities as if this would prevent them from happening. While I lay in bed at night, whenever I remembered during the school day, and always on my way over to Clinton Lodge, I invented awful things that might be happening to my father, precisely where, and in every circumstantial detail. In this way I kept up a sort of intimacy with my father's continuous malaise. I can imagine as if it were a memory out of my own life the afternoon he spent in the men's room at the local milk office, afraid to come out in case he had to vomit again. It was his first day there as a file clerk. He told my mother, and my mother must have told me, that by the end of the morning he was feeling very ill. A girl was explaining the filing system to him when he began to retch. He said, "Excuse me," and stumbled among the chairs toward the door of the men's room. The door was locked from inside. My father prayed, Please, don't let me be sick here, knowing the girl's surprised eyes were watching at his back, and then toppled backward as the door opened into his face. "Whoa, there!" said the man coming out, and put a hand up to steady my father, who pushed past him into the lavatory and locked the door and vomited. Afterward, he felt better, though his legs trembled and his body was heaving the way it did when he was going to have an asthma attack, and he quickly pushed up the window. The cold air turned the perspiration icy on the exposed surfaces of his face, neck, and the backs of his hands. He concentrated, as if listening to the complex of violent and terrifying sensations, wondering if he was about to have another stroke. Someone outside rattled the doorknob; rattled again and again, and went away. My father was breathing more quietly. He washed his hands under cold running water, thinking he could go back into the outside office, when he suddenly retched. All afternoon, people came to the door and went away again. At half past five, when everybody had left, my father let himself out and came into the street. He was afraid of collapsing

"There's a taxi," said my mother. "But it's only a block and a half now. Now let's make it as far as Miss Douglas's gate."

My father worked in the milk office for a month. One Sunday morning, while I was dusting in Miss Douglas's drawing room, he had another stroke, in the bathroom at Clinton Lodge, falling against the door, which was locked from the inside—a circumstance I had failed to imagine, and at a moment when I had forgotten to think about him. It was a relief for the next weeks to be able at any moment of the day to think of him safe in a hospital.

One evening, just as my mother had hung up her coat and taken off her shoes and put the kettle on for a cup of coffee, a man rang the front doorbell and asked for her.

He smiled at my mother. "You Mrs. Groszmann? The doctor wants you to come over to the hospital, Ma'am."

"Is my husband very bad?" asked my mother, finding her coat to put around her shoulders.

The man held the door. We hurried alongside. "Lucky you live so near the hospital," he said.

"Yes. Yes, we are lucky," said my mother.

"Cold," said the man. "Only a quarter to nine, and looks like blooming midnight."

A cruel wind blew across the open courtyard between the porter's lodge and the huge hospital doors. It whipped the skirts around our legs. Inside, the elevator was on the ground floor, chained open, and there seemed to be no one in attendance, so we ran up the stairs. The doors of my father's ward were closed. A nurse, who looked hardly older than I, came out.

"Nurse," said my mother, "I'm supposed to see my husband."

"Not now, you can't. It's not visiting time now."

"They sent for me. Where's Sister?"

"Ooh, I don't know *where* she is," said the little nurse, looking up and down the empty corridor. "She'll be along, I expect. I have to go to work in this other ward." She went on her way.

My mother opened the door. The only light came from the

faint blue lamps down the center of the ceiling, but we could make out the hump of my father's knees in his cot. My mother started toward him, but it was a strange man lying in my father's bed. He opened his eyes, saw us, passed his tongue over his lips, and closed his eyes again.

Sister was already walking toward us, with the young nurse coming behind, her hands clapped over her mouth and giggling. "Mrs. Groszmann, your husband has been moved to another ward. I left a message at the porter's lodge. Silly of them."

"How bad is he?" asked my mother.

"Nurse here is going to work in your husband's new ward, so you go along with her."

We followed the nurse through a maze of corridors that led to the older buildings. I remember how her head bobbed up and down before us, and how she drew her hand along the wall and swung around the corners.

There was a strange Sister waiting for us outside this other ward. "Is that Mrs. Groszmann? Mrs. Groszmann, the doctor would like to see you."

"How is my husband?"

"If you'll wait in here, nurse will bring you a chair."

We were shown into a bare little cloakroom. A mufti coat and a Sister's scarlet-lined cloak hung on pegs. On the wall were notices: "Please Turn Out the Lights." "The Hospital Is Not Responsible for Property Left in This Room."

"I wonder what happened to the chair," said my mother.

I went to stand in the doorway, looking out into the blind corridor with its bare electric bulb reflected in brown linoleum and in the shining yellow oil paint of the walls. A door opposite was thrown open, and I saw a kitchen, steam rising over a sink, a nurse sitting on a table swinging her legs. Someone was laughing. The door closed.

There were people coming toward us—the Sister, and a young doctor I did not know. I pulled back into the room. They passed the door and then stopped. They were talking just outside. I could see the doctor's sleeve. The sleeve disappeared, and then the doctor was in the room with us. "All right, you can go in to your husband now," he said.

"How bad is he, Doctor?" my mother asked.

"He had another stroke, and he was calling for you all afternoon. We're surprised he's still alive. He's got a heart like an ox" is what I thought the doctor said, and I looked at him in amazement. I had the impression that he was shouting at my mother. "Dr. Adler left word that you could stay the night. Sister here will make the arrangements, and I'll be on duty. You can call me. Or call Sister. You'll be all right."

My father lay stretched on a bed with his head in a net of tubes and bottles and tanks. His eyes showed slits of the white eyeballs. I wondered if he was dead, but then I saw there was a small, furious pulse beating at the base of his throat.

"Here's a chair," said the Sister, "and you can take one from that bed. I'll be at the desk in the corner, behind the screen, if you need anything. Would you like a nice cup of tea?"

"Yes, Sister, please," said my mother. "You are so kind."

"That's right. You make yourself comfortable. The night always seems long."

"Mummy," I whispered, "what does the doctor mean about Daddy having a heart like an ox?"

"I think he said 'oxheart.' That's a medical word, though I don't just know what it means."

The little nurse who had shown us the way came with a cup of tea for my mother. "I put sugar in, and I never even asked you."

"I don't take it usually, but this will be lovely," my mother said.

"No, you wait. I'll get you another. Always do everything wrong, that's me." She bore the cup away, and that was the last we saw of it.

"What time is it?" I asked.

"Twenty-five minutes to ten. Darling, why don't you go home? You have exams coming."

"And you have to go to work. I'm staying as long as you're staying."

I shifted on the hard chair. The man in the bed next to my father's raised himself on an arm and slapped his pillow. Behind him the great room was full of the impatient movements of bodies looking for relief, and of noises—coughing, snuffling, and a small sound something between a whimper and a laugh. The ward was getting hotter, and the heat and the noise joined into one swelling roar, and I jerked myself out of sleep. "What time is it?"

"Five minutes to ten."

Around midnight, my mother took an envelope out of her purse and began to write on it, smiling to herself.

"What are you writing?"

She passed it to me. It said, "W D Y G H?"

"What?" I asked.

"It says, 'Why don't you go home?' "

"Lend me the pencil." I wrote, "I'm S A L A you're S."

My mother smiled and put the envelope back in her purse. At half past twelve, my father opened his eyes and asked what day of the month it was. My mother called the nurse, and the nurse called the Sister, who brought the young doctor. They took his pulse and touched his cheek and stood around the bed, but he lifted his right hand with the old impatient gesture and brushed them all away. My father had put off dying for that night.

When we came out of the hospital, the streets were turning a weird electric blue. Trees and houses were collecting their bulk and outline. It was very cold. The milkman at the corner was rattling the empties. He touched his cap to us.

I looked at my mother and saw that there were tears running down her face. "Darling, I promise you something," she said. "If Daddy dies, I won't be unhappy any more." Now that she had begun to talk, she began to sob. "I'll cheer up very quickly, I promise. You won't have to worry about me any more. It's just that now he is so poor."

I considered the probability of my father's dying, with terror, because I might have no tears for him and the emptiness of my unnatural heart would be exposed to my mother and proved to myself.

But it seemed my father was not going to die, after all. He began to get better—to sit, to walk again, and to want my mother to take him home.

One day, old Dr. Adler turned up at Clinton Lodge.

"Is my husband worse?" cried my mother. "I only left him an hour ago."

"No, no. Nothing like that. Could I come in? I was just leaving the hospital and wanted to see you a moment. Maybe you would make me a cup of coffee, too? Your husband is doing very nicely and we're going to be sending him to a convalescence home soon. I've been talking to Mrs. Dillon, of the Refugee Committee, and it's being taken care of."

"Ah, how good you all are!" said my mother.

"We were also talking about you, and both Mrs. Dillon and I think that you should take a holiday."

"Maybe when my husband is better—"

"Mrs. Dillon has been in touch with Mr. Harvey, where you work, and they want you to take a week off beginning this Friday."

"Thank you, but I don't think I can afford, right now—"

"Here's the address of a house that belongs to one of the doctors on the hospital staff," said the doctor. "He and his family are going to be away for a week, and they want you to go and stay there. There's a German housekeeper, who will look after you. Here is the bus schedule. I've marked Friday afternoon. . . ."

I visited my mother on Sunday and found her shelling peas. "I thought you were going to rest!" I said.

"I'm resting," said my mother. "Darling, it's very unrestful for me to have to sit doing nothing."

"Why don't you at least sit in the middle of the chair."

"I forgot. But really I'm resting. Didn't I sit in the drawing room this morning, Mrs. Hubert?"

"Yes, after you swept the upstairs and made the beds," said the old housekeeper.

"But I'm feeling much better," said my mother. "Darling, you will go and see Daddy in the convalescence home, won't you?"

"You're not supposed to be thinking about Daddy while you're on your holiday!" I shouted, almost in tears. "Rest!"

When I got home that night, I heard Mrs. Dillon talking on

the telephone in the dining room. "He's quite impossible and they don't think they can keep him. The servants say he's always calling and then he talks to them in German," she was saying. I knew she was talking about my father. "And the other patients are complaining they can't sleep, because he calls for you all night." Then I knew it was my mother she was talking to. I leaned my head against the door and cried.

My mother came back that night and took my father home to Clinton Lodge.

It was 1943. I had turned fifteen. The repeated suspense of my father's relapses and partial recoveries, my mother's helpless exhaustion, along with the nightly German rockets, had become the conditions of our life.

Early in June of 1944, my father was back in the hospital. It was the week of the landing of the Allies on the French beaches. We told him about it, but he did not hear.

Then one night my father died. I had one short, harsh paroxysm of grief, and even afterward I found I was able to produce a creditable pain in my chest by recalling how my father had wanted to amuse me with the story of Rikki-tikki-tavi, and to lend me his crocodile belt on all the important occasions of my life, and how he had wanted to make me a present of it the day I pushed him onto the floor.

My mother and I sat in her room. Mrs. Katz brought our meals on a tray and stayed to talk—about how good my mother had been to my father, and how she had nothing to reproach herself with, and how this must be a comfort to her now.

My mother shook her head and said, "Not so good. Not as good as you all think. You don't know how often I lay in bed, with him right beside me, and my hands like this." My mother interlaced her fingers and pressed them passionately together. "How I would long for him to be allowed to die, for his sake, but not for his sake only. For Lore's and for my sake."

"But that's only natural," Mrs. Katz said. "You didn't want him to suffer."

"Oh, I don't blame myself for that," my mother said. "I will tell you what I can't forgive myself. You remember when he came back from his first day at the milk office, he was so ill he could hardly move his leg? I wanted to take a taxi up the hill to the house, but I kept thinking how silly to take a taxi for just two blocks, and I made him walk."

"It's all over now," said Mrs. Katz, for my mother had begun to cry, her face shrunken and red.

"I could have taken a taxi for him," said my mother. "It wasn't even the money. I was afraid the taxi-driver would think it silly for just two blocks, and our being refugees. I made him walk those blocks uphill because I was afraid of looking silly to the taxi-driver. I'll stop in a minute," said my mother, sobbing out of the depths of her chest. "I promised Lore that if Igo died I would cheer up quickly. And you will see, I will."

One Sunday, about a week after my father's death, I came back to Clinton Lodge and found the fat doctor having a cup of coffee with my mother. "Are you ill?" I asked her.

"Goodness, no. Dr. Adler was so kind as to be worried about me."

"I was just passing the house on my way home from the hospital, and I thought I would look in on your good mother. She was making herself a cup of coffee and I asked her to give me one. As a friend, you know. As a doctor, I should tell you that you have no business taking so much caffeine." He tapped her on the wrist with a forefinger. "I suspect you drink altogether too many cups of coffee, and it's not good for your nerves."

"My nerves *have* been playing me tricks lately," said my mother. "You can't think what incredible mistakes I've been making at the restaurant. Poor Mr. Harvey! Yesterday I put salt in the peas twice, so today I put none in the potatoes. Don't go to Harvey's for lunch tomorrow, because they're serving shepherd's pie made with unsalted potatoes."

"I promise not to come to Harvey's if you will promise some-day to cook me a real Viennese dinner."

"*Wiener Schnitzel*," said my mother. "Any time you like."

In the middle of that week, my mother said, "You'll never guess what I did today. I bought myself a new dress. I left the restaurant half an hour early, went to the bank, took out twenty shillings, and went and bought myself a pink dress."

"How do you mean, pink? A sort of pinkish gray, you mean?"

"Pink," said my mother. "It was the only pretty dress in the shop and I put it on to see how silly I looked, but then I took down the knot in my hair and did it more loosely, like this. Look, you see—there is still a wave, and the pink brings out the red lights. It looked very well on."

I was pretty sure she was kidding me. "So where is it?"

"It's being altered for me. Now I can't even take it back. I told them to go ahead, and I'll have it for the weekend."

That weekend, Dr. Adler came and had *Wiener Schnitzel* with us. My mother wore the pink dress. It was very pink. I watched the doctor to see if he thought it strange, but he was in great spirits and said my mother looked like a girl. Her face had a high color; her eyes were too bright. After dinner, we went into the drawing room and she sat across from the doctor, making jokes and laughing in shrill, harsh bursts in her throat. Later, the doctor asked her to come for a stroll around the block.

On Monday, Mrs. Dillon was waiting for me by the front door of Adorato. She asked me to come in a moment. "Come into the drawing room. Sit here on the sofa." She sat down beside me.

"Has something happened?" I asked in alarm.

"Well, no, I don't think so. Not yet. Guess who came to see me at the refugee office? Mr. Harvey. He's worried about your mother."

"Why is he? Mummy is all right. I haven't seen her laugh so much in years."

"Well, that's what seems to be the trouble. Mr. Harvey says she is a changed person. He says even when things were worst she was always conscientious about her work, and now all of a sudden she doesn't seem to care. He says she keeps making mistakes every day. He told her the restaurant just can't afford to go on like this, and she laughed in his face."

"What's going to happen, then?" I asked. Panic settled familiarly back into my chest.

"He says he doesn't know what to do. Today she forgot to light the oven under the roast and they had to take it off the menu. He says he took her aside to talk to her seriously, but she blew right up in his face. He says he never in his life heard her shouting before. She said why can't she take it easy, like all the other people do all the time. He wants me to talk to her, but I think maybe you should. You can talk to her. You tell her she must be more careful and not make so many mistakes."

My mother was in the kitchen at Clinton Lodge. "Roast chicken and cucumber salad," she said, "and not for Mr. Harvey and his customers but for you and me. Roast potatoes, too. Take off your coat."

"How are you doing in the restaurant?"

"Fine," said my mother.

"Are you still making so many mistakes?"

"What do you mean, mistakes?"

"The way you were telling Dr. Adler?"

"Sit down and eat before everything gets cold. Other people make mistakes," she said. "Everybody does. Mr. Harvey ruined a whole fish dinner once. He told me so himself."

"Maybe you make too many mistakes."

"Did Mr. Harvey say something to you?"

"No. Where would I see Mr. Harvey? He came to see Mrs. Dillon. I mean, it's just that you should be a little more careful, and not make so many mistakes. And he says you're not even sorry. He says you didn't light the fire under the roast today and that the restaurant can't afford to go on like this. Maybe if you stopped drinking so much coffee. Mummy!"

My mother's face was paling and shrinking before my eyes. Her mouth darkened to a red, sore look, with little unevennesses like lines up and down her parted lips. Her eyes increased in size as they filled with tears. She looked into her plate and put down her fork. When Mr. Katz came in with a friendly good evening, my mother got up and went out to the scullery. I heard her clattering the dishes, and in a little while she went upstairs and closed the door.

In the weeks that followed, my mother kept herself to herself.

The sound of a sudden voice could make her cry; we were all afraid to speak to her. She did not entertain the doctor again. She went to work every day. She has told me that those were the hardest weeks she has ever lived through because she had to focus every nerve, every minute of the day, to hold on to herself, because the moment she relaxed she could feel herself altogether scattered.

I watched her strained face surreptitiously. I don't know at what point I realized that the calamity for which I was set was not going to occur. My mother was making jokes and laughing again in her old way, from the chest, and with her head thrown back. She talked to the people who came to visit. Whenever she mentioned my father, which she did readily, I would look around for a book. My mother told everyone the story of how she had made my father walk up the hill instead of taking a taxi. She still tells it to me once in a while, but it is only quite lately that I have told her that the time my father fell on the floor in front of the wardrobe mirror it was because I pushed him with my hand.

CHAPTER SEVEN

"Allchester": Miss Douglas and Mrs. Dillon

One morning not long after I came to live at Adorato, when the two ladies thought I had gone off to school, I was standing in the dim carpeted hall outside the dining-room door listening to Mrs. Dillon gently scolding Miss Douglas for too harshly scolding me. She was saying, "That's never the way to make a Christian out of her."

There had been a certain contest between the Jewish Committee, which saved me from Vienna, and the Church Refugee Committee, which had the care of my bodily needs in England. Each strove for my soul, without much passion.

My early upbringing had been assimilated Austrian: Jewish mainly on the High Holidays. My mother might prepare the Passover table to celebrate the exodus of the Hebrews from Egypt with a rich feast and all the ritual trappings, but she produced the hard-roasted egg (in remembrance of the joyous sacrifices made before the destruction of the Temple) clucking like a hen that had just laid it; my Uncle Paul wore his parsley dipped in salt water (in remembrance of the bitterness of the persecution of the Jews) jauntily in his lapel. During the prayer where we curse the Egyptians—" 'If He had merely brought us forth from Egypt . . . *dayenu* [it would have been sufficient]; if He had merely inflicted justice upon them . . . *dayenu;* if He had merely slain their first-born . . . *dayenu* "—my mother drew an imaginary line under the list of *dayenus* and totted them up.

On Yom Kippur, the Day of Atonement, I sat in the white imitation-marble gallery of the synagogue with my mother and the other women. The men sat downstairs wearing their hats, chanting Hebrew and bobbing their bodies to keep time. Their lips never stopped moving, right fists striking their chests in the ancient gesture of contrition. A Yom Kippur service lasts from sunup to sundown. I fidgeted. I threw my cap into the air, and the *shammes,* the temple orderly, put me out onto the brilliantly sunny street. My grandmother said it was always fair on Yom Kippur, while it rained on Christian holy days.

One sunny day, I got mixed up with a Palm Sunday procession. My parents and I were visiting my grandparents in Fischamend. I happened to be walking past the church just as the procession was coming out of it. At the door, Father Ulrich was passing out the palm branches. He put some in my hand, along with a little colored picture of Jesus holding his gown open to show where his heart was bleeding. I walked with the little girls. They were dressed all in white with garlands in their hair. I held one of the blue ribbons that streamed from the velvet sky carried on four poles over the blue-and-gold Madonna. Her crown and scepter came behind on purple pillows. The altar boys swung censers. The priest joined the end of the procession, singing in Latin out of his holy book. As we came through the arch under the tower into the open square, I saw my family looking down from the corner window of our house. I waved my palm branches in the air. They kept waving to me and gesturing. I did a little dance step for them.

By the time the procession passed my grandparents' house, my mother was standing at the door that led into the yard, and she hauled me inside. (This was in 1937, and Jews were already nervous.) My mother put the palm branches in a vase. As for the holy picture, she said why didn't I take it up to Marie when she came back from church. I had been trying to decide if it was a very beautiful picture or not very nice at all—I took my cues from my mother, in those days, in matters of taste—and I could tell from her

face that this picture was not nice. "I don't even want it, anyway,"
I said.

The maid's room was in the attic. Marie opened the door to me
and I peered inside. It was dark. There was a lilac tablecloth
pinned over the curtains. The room looked different from any other
room in my grandparents' house. It smelled different—of closed
windows and a candle burning under a picture of the Virgin and
Child. Marie made me sit beside her on the bed. I gave her the
picture. She said it was lovely of me; she had a whole boxful, if I
would like to see. She went and fetched an old tin candy box and
spilled the contents onto the bed. There were holy pictures of the
Virgin and the saints and the Child Jesus among the lilies. There
were glossy picture postcards from a certain young man, Marie
said, with red roses and hearts and ribbons, but she said she liked
my picture the best, and she would show me where she was going
to keep it next her heart. She unbuttoned her blouse till I could
see the crevice between her elderly breasts, and pushed the picture
down there. I said I had to go; my mother was waiting downstairs.

Christians were comical people. My grandmother had lots of
stories about them. There was the time handsome young Father
Ulrich had asked his congregation to collect silver foil to be made
into a great ball in aid of the church's Winter Help Fund, and little
Wellisch Greterl had spent the night with the fat, drunken sweet-
shop-owner Kopotski for a bar of chocolate wrapped in foil. The
grownups found this enormously funny. In my grandmother's
stories, the Christians always spoke with peasant accents.

After Hitler had come, while I was staying with Erwin in
Vienna, I used to go to a Miss Henry, a young lady from London,
to learn English. Miss Henry seemed quite intelligent. Her flat, on
the Ringstrasse, looked much like our own. She lived with her
mother, who gave lessons in the sitting room while Miss Henry
gave me mine in the bedroom. The only pictures there were a
black-and-white engraving entitled "Tintern Abbey" and a framed
photograph of a young man in S.S. uniform whom I often saw in
the hall waiting for Miss Henry as I came out from my lesson. I
had asked my father if she was a Christian. My father said yes,

but that English people were Protestants instead of Catholics, like Austrians. Now, when she was giving me dictation, I would peek curiously at this Miss Henry who was not a proper Christian. I tried to catch her off guard, for some sign.

This was my preparation for deciding between Judaism and Christianity—my mother had always said I must make up my own mind—when I left Austria.

When I wrote my parents from the camp that the two English Jewish Committee ladies had asked me if I would like to go and live with a lovely Orthodox family, my father wrote back by return mail, begging me to go quickly to whoever was in charge and tell them I was not Orthodox and should be assigned to a different family. He said "Orthodox" meant being very religious and following laws I knew nothing about, and that I would be doing everything wrong and people would be cross with me, but his letter did not reach me until after I had been settled with the Levines.

They had been taken aback by my ignorance of the Jewish laws. Sarah explained the rules, and by the end of the winter I did her credit. I took easily to being religious. I was a purist. Mrs. Levine had to make me do up my shoes when I came down with the laces dangling, not having wanted to mar the Lord's Shabbos with the work of my hands; I would not accept her offer of ice cream one second before the six hours after lunch when, the law said, milk might mix innocently with the meat in my stomach. One day I came into the scullery and found to my horror that Annie was washing the meat dishes with the milk swab. I hastened to point out her error. She took me by the shoulders with hands very wet from the washing water and shooed me out firmly, saying, "What the eye does not see . . ."

Then, during my year in the south with the Hoopers and the Grimsleys, I lost the broad North Country accent I had picked up in Liverpool, and had become a Socialist, when circumstances made me once more mobile.

My Kentish working-class accent distressed the Allchester ladies, and Miss Douglas took me in hand. In the morning, I walked with her around the dewy garden. I carried the watering can and filled

up the birdbaths. Miss Douglas, in her wide straw hat and gardening gloves, walked with her basket and a pair of scissors and cut
fresh flowers for the drawing room. In the evening, I changed my
shoes and put on the green silk dress Miss Douglas had found at
the church bazaar she had organized. She had put on new buttons
for me. After dinner, I joined the ladies and the cocker spaniel
and the big black cat in the drawing room. (I always took breakfast and lunch with the ladies in the dining room, but dinner was
a grown-up meal, which children took in the nursery or schoolroom; since there was no longer any such apartment at Adorato,
Miss Douglas put my supper on a plate and I had it in Milly's
kitchen.)

If the weather was particularly fine, we would move to the
veranda and I would be sent to fetch Miss Douglas's sewing
basket. The English-summer daylight lasts far into the night hours.
Long after the veranda and the lawn lay in shadow, the sky remained radiant, very high, the color of light. Miss Douglas stopped
hemming the new bib for Milly's baby; Mrs. Dillon rested the
counterpane on which she was embroidering flowers with a hundred
colored strands of silk. "How perfectly lovely!" she cried out.
"What a glorious day!" Miss Douglas lifted her nose into the pale-
gold air and pointed where a rose had blown since our morning
round, where the light caught the two last poplars, where three
birds with golden underbellies, tilting on the wing, showed their
backs in shadow, and then Miss Douglas and Mrs. Dillon took up
their work once more, and, seeing me lolling in a chair, Miss
Douglas would tell me to sit up straight or make me fetch work for
my idle hands lest the Devil find mischief for them to do.

In September, I was sent to the private high school, where I
took, or made, opportunities to tell every new acquaintance that
I was a Jewish refugee and that my mother was a cook and my
father a gardener.

When I saw my mother on Thursdays at the refugee club, she
would ask me if I had written my thank-you letters to my old
foster families yet, and I would say, "No, but I will." The neces-

sity of those letters, I remember, hung like a small but constant shadow over my adolescence. "Tomorrow I will write them," I said. "Stop worrying about everything." But my mother continued to worry about that, as she worried about my father and about my grandparents, and she was working too hard, which worried me so that I began not to look forward to Thursdays.

One morning at breakfast, Miss Douglas told Milly that she might set the porridge on the sideboard. "We will help ourselves. Lore, perhaps you will serve us, like a dear child."

Mrs. Dillon made signs for me to bring the dish around Miss Douglas's left side, and as soon as the door closed behind Milly, Miss Douglas said, "Curious, isn't it, the way they always get their backaches on a Friday. Yesterday was her afternoon off and I never heard anything about a strained back, did you? If she had rested yesterday, instead of gadding about town all afternoon, I suppose she might be fit to do her work this morning."

"But she has only one afternoon a week off," I said, "and there are seven days for work."

"That's neither here nor there," said Miss Douglas. "Duty comes before pleasure."

"What do you mean?" said Mrs. Dillon at the same time. "She has every other Sunday afternoon as well."

"But only afternoons," I said. "And then we leave the supper dishes for her. Maybe Milly is run down—"

"Maybe you had better run off to school," said Miss Douglas.

"Goddam slave driver!" said Milly in the evening. She stood with her palms flattened against the small of her back. Milly was a big, powerful girl, and efficient in a slapdash way. "I'd like to see *her,* just once, put in a useful day's work."

"She does," I said. "Her hands are never idle."

"That's right. She does the flowers every morning."

"And her charities in the afternoon," I said. "She visited her deaf and dumb today even though she was feeling faint, just because it was her day. Anyway, Mrs. Dillon did the cooking and Miss Douglas took the baby off your hands."

"Yeah, and she took the cream off the top of the baby's milk and put it on *her* porridge. If she doesn't stop eating everybody's ration, what with her high blood pressure, she's going to really faint one of these days—phffft! And good riddance. It wasn't even her milk! It was the baby's government milk. And she took the top off your milk, too." Milly pointed to my glass. "What's this supposed to be?" she said, waving my lettuce leaf in the air and rattling my three biscuits on a saucer. "And you know what they're having? Soup, fricasseed chicken, and apple mousse. Stingy old things."

"They're not," I said. "It's just that it's not good for children to have a big meal before going to bed. Miss Douglas says it gives them bad dreams. Besides, if they were stingy, they wouldn't even have me. Miss Douglas brought me the silk dress from the bazaar and Mrs. Dillon pays for my piano lessons. They are not stingy."

"So why are they paying me fifteen shillings a month?"

"And room and board," I said. "Anyway, it's because of the baby, Miss Douglas says. In other places, maids aren't allowed to have their children live in. My mother can't have me."

"You really want to know why she lets me have the baby?" said Milly, sticking her face into mine. "I'll tell you why. She likes to play with her, that's why. Ouch!" She straightened and massaged her back.

"What's wrong with being fond of children?" I said, but I was always in trouble with my arbitrations between the back and the front of the house; I usually knew the kitchen to be in the right, but it was the drawing room that attracted me.

"You go on in," said Milly, "and let me clear the table and wash up the dishes and fill their damn hot-water bottles and turn down their goddam beds, so I can get done. Go on."

But I hung around waiting to see what might be left on the plates from the dining room. I was hungry. The plates came out, but Miss Douglas came out with them and personally put the leftovers away under little nets in the larder.

That evening, I proposed to Miss Douglas that I be allowed to do the housework one day so that Milly could stay in bed and rest, or go out, or do anything she liked for one whole day. I was surprised that Miss Douglas was not as delighted with the notion as I. "Why don't you let her, Hanna?" said Mrs. Dillon. "I could do the cooking." And so Milly was told she could have the whole of next Thursday off, and I overslept and Mrs. Dillon had to get Miss Douglas's early-morning tea, and Miss Douglas herself came up to my little room under the roof to get me out of bed. Downstairs, Mrs. Dillon had lit the kitchen fire, dusted the dining room, and laid breakfast. She put her finger to her lips. I burst into tears and threw myself against her bosom. If Mrs. Dillon did not precisely push me away, she seemed to withdraw into herself, shy at having me cry all over her. I let go and cried standing on my own feet.

"And next time," said Miss Douglas at breakfast, "I hope you will let me run my house and my servants as I see fit." I cried some more, out of a deep grievance against the difficulties of doing good. "Run along now, or you'll be late for school as well."

That was when I listened outside the door and heard Mrs. Dillon tell Miss Douglas that that was not the way to make a Christian out of me. I felt a sudden furious loyalty to myself: *No* one was going to make *any*thing out of me.

When, the next afternoon, we were walking the dog on the Downs, I attacked Mrs. Dillon's Jesus. "Why," I said, "if he came to earth to save everybody, is there a war going on this minute and people being killed and Jews being persecuted?"

" 'God moves in a mysterious way his wonders to perform,' " Mrs. Dillon said.

"If he can perform wonders," I said, "what does he need to send his son to earth for?"

Confusion filled Mrs. Dillon's innocent eyes, but she battled it and was left looking obstinate. "Because," she said. "Anyway, it says in the Bible, 'God so loved the world, that he gave his only begotten Son.' And there is the Holy Ghost, Three Persons in One. It's difficult to explain. I wish my dear husband were alive. He was a vicar, you know. He could explain it all to you. All I know is what Jesus said, 'I am the way, the truth, and the light,' and if you would pray to him he would help you to believe."

"But if I don't believe in him, how can I pray to him to make me believe in him?"

"That child!" I heard Mrs. Dillon say to her sister when I listened outside the drawing-room door that evening. "She'll argue the hind legs off a donkey."

It was my own choice to go to the Christian religious-instruction class in school—because I always got the best marks for my compositions in this subject—and my ladies would often take me along to peripheral church activities. When Miss Douglas went to help decorate the church for Easter, I went along. The back seat of the car was heaped with lilies of the valley, daffodils, and almond blossom from the garden, and pussy willow we had been collecting on our walks. Bromley had brought in pink and blue hyacinths and lilies in pots, which would go to the hospital after the services. The verger unlocked the cupboard where the vases, bowls, and watering cans were kept in the back of the church. Here we met Mrs. Montgomery, who had the pew behind Miss Douglas's pew. The ladies exchanged greetings in decent church voices. Mrs. Montgomery had brought along another refugee child. I had not seen her before, and yet she looked familiar. She was an exceedingly plain girl. She wore glasses and was stout and had breasts and the beginnings of a mustache on her upper lip. Her name was Herta Hirschfeld. She came from Vienna, too, but was older than I.

It was very still in the sunny church, except for the verger shuffling between the pews, dusting the deep old polish of the wood while the two ladies in their hats decorated the windows at the ends of their pews. Herta Hirschfeld and I kept passing each other in the center aisle, carrying watering cans that we filled in the vicar's lavatory, next to his study. I maneuvered to let Herta catch up with me in the back passage. I asked her if she had ever been in Liverpool and she said no.

"There was a girl I used to know called Helene," I said.

Herta said her name was Herta, but my experience henceforward of fat Herta was complicated by having tagged on to it the memory of fat Helene.

"Is that your lady?" I asked.

Herta said yes.

"You don't go to the high school, do you?"

Herta said Mrs. Montgomery sent her to the school where she herself had gone as a girl, in the next town.

"You never come to the refugee club on Thursdays. I go with my mother. My mother is a cook. My father is in the hospital."

Herta said she didn't have her parents in England. I asked her where they were, and she said she didn't know. They had crossed the Austrian frontier into Hungary illegally and she hadn't heard from them since, but she had a brother in Palestine working in a *kibbutz*. She asked me if I was a Zionist. I said I wasn't sure. Herta said, "When the war is over I'm going to Palestine to work in a *kibbutz* with my brother. We are going to help build a Jewish state." I said I didn't think I was a Zionist. I was going to stay and become English.

Canon Godfrey came along the passage with his wide hat and turned-out toes. He recognized me as Miss Douglas's little girl and asked me how I did and said he was pleased to see us working so busily.

I met Herta again the following week. At this time, the Jewish Committee began to send a weekly rabbi down from London to give us religious instruction between trains. We met him Mondays after school in the firemen's hall, which was just across from the railway station, in the office that was used for the refugees' English classes. The rabbi's name was Dr. Lobel. He was a broad-shouldered young man with beautiful olive skin. His cheeks were almost blue under the close-shaved beard. I might have got a crush on him if I hadn't started arguing instead. I asked him if Jesus was a real person.

"There is historical evidence of a person living in that era who claimed to be the son of God."

"How do you know he wasn't?"

"There have been many false prophets throughout history," said

Dr. Lobel. "Sometimes they were charlatans, sometimes self-deluded cranks. For instance, the god kings of ancient—"

"How do you know," interrupted Herta Hirschfeld, "that Jesus wasn't the real son of God?"

Dr. Lobel shifted in his chair. "Judaism teaches us that there is only one God, indivisible," he said, picking up the Hebrew reader for beginners.

"It says in the Bible," I said, "that 'God so loved the world, that he gave his only begotten Son,'" and was surprised at the sudden taste of tears with the sweetness of the words in my mouth.

"If he wasn't the son of God," said Herta, "how could he perform miracles?"

"He healed the deaf and dumb," I said.

"And he walked on the waters of Gennesaret," Herta said.

I watched closely, waiting for the rabbi to pull the water out from under Christ's feet, but the young man had slipped far down into his chair. He looked harassed and bored. "All right, now, that'll do. Take your readers. Page twenty-seven. You're holding it back to front," he said, putting his hand out to turn mine front to back. "Begin here. *'Baruch Hashem . . .'*"

"*'Baruch Hashem,'*" I read. "'Blessed be the Lord God of Israel.'"

Herta and I walked away from class together. "It's silly, actually," I said. "Nobody could walk on water."

"If he were the son of God he could," Herta said.

I was taken aback, for I had assumed we were really on the same side. "I thought you were going to Palestine to build a Jewish state," I said.

"I am."

I was meaning to call her on her divided loyalty, but the sun was going down at the end of West Street and the windows of the shops blazed as if they were on fire inside. The crowd walking against us on the pavement was silhouetted black, each body outlined with a fine halo of light. I turned to Herta. Where I expected to see her eyes behind the glasses were two circles flashing red and gold. I was used in those days to signs and visions, and was not surprised to feel suddenly suspended even as I walked, my self hovering over my right shoulder in an ecstasy of comprehension. I said nothing about it to Herta, but we parted tenderly at the corner, where I turned uphill toward Adorato.

Rabbi Lobel must have reported on the dangerous influences at work on the Allchester refugee children, for the Committee in London decided that we needed the counterinfluence of nice Jewish homes. Both Miss Douglas and Mrs. Montgomery received letters asking them to see that their Jewish wards spent the upcoming Yom Kippur in the synagogue. Arrangements would be made for each to take the holiday meal with a suitable family.

I was assigned to a family called Rosenblatt and told to meet them at the temple. There were not enough Jews in Allchester at that time to have a regular synagogue, but a downtown restaurant had been converted for the High Holiday services. I sat with Mrs. Rosenblatt and her daughter, Sheila, a smug little girl with fat, shiny cheeks, dressed in a pink dress and bonnet, and patent-leather shoes. She wore a gold bracelet, which I thought dreadfully vulgar. "Ma," she kept saying, "I'm bored." She wanted to go to her father and her brother, Neville, who sat on the other side of the aisle, with the men. Her mother said she should sit still and be a good girl, but she fidgeted and wriggled until her shoulders rested on the seat of her chair. "So go on," said Mrs. Rosenblatt. "Go to your father. You want to go with her?" she asked me, but I said no, thank you.

I had seen Herta sitting two rows behind me, like a grownup, absorbed in her prayer book. I opened mine and Mrs. Rosenblatt showed me the place. I tried to follow in English. "Blessed be the Lord God of Israel," I read. It failed to move me. I wanted to pray, but the place was too noisy. The chanting men didn't even keep together. They bobbed and bowed like so many rocking chairs going at different speeds. I was glad Miss Douglas wasn't there to see how Jews carried on in church as if it were their own home. The *shammes*, walking around with his day-old beard, was remonstrating loudly with Sheila, who had got tired of sitting with her father and was trying to get back up the aisle to her mother. Mrs. Rosenblatt and a neighbor were chatting, comparing the headaches they had from fasting. They looked just like the women in the gallery in Vienna where my mother had sat. Their big bosoms were pressed high by corsets under their best black dresses. They wore smart hats. They seemed to be passing the same orange stuck full of cloves like a pincushion, which was supposed to keep one from fainting away, and at certain passages of the service their eyes became hot and dark and they cried wet tears.

I did not want any part of them. It grieved me that I did not love them. It made me feel hard and wicked. I clenched my right hand over my chest and struck it surreptitiously, as I had seen my father do, once for each sin. "God, I'm going home to dinner with Mr. and Mrs. Rosenblatt and I don't even like them." Thump. "Sometimes I can't stand my own mother." Thump. "Some days I even forget to think about my father. God, I listen outside the door to hear what Miss Douglas and Mrs. Dillon are saying about me." Thump. "I steal chicken from the larder and eat it in bed. I love Jesus Christ better than I do you. *Lieber Gott,* take away my sin and make me good."

It seemed that the service was over. The men were folding their prayer shawls and wrapping them away in velvet, gold-encrusted bags. People embraced. Strangers wished one another *"Shalom Aleichem."* Mr. Rosenblatt came and took his wife into his arms and kissed her, and they told me to come along, very kindly.

The following week, when Mrs. Montgomery and Herta called at Adorato, Herta and I compared notes. Herta said her Jewish family had asked her to spend every Saturday with them, but she wasn't going.

"I know," I said. "I'm not going back, either. Mine lived in one of those ugly new apartment buildings."

Milly came out to call us to tea. She had wheeled the trolley into the drawing room and set it before Miss Douglas. It was my duty to carry around the cups.

The beautiful thing about the drawing room was that it mirrored itself, distorted and precise, in the circular convex glass, gilt-framed and eagle-topped, that hung over the mantel. In it, the rich Turkish carpet rose to a gentle mound. At the far side of the room, the bowl of delphiniums, the Hepplewhite table with its delicate square legs, the drop leaf raised against the wall, looked tiny, as if they were at a tremendous distance. Miss Douglas herself, in plum-colored jersey suit and dickey, sitting right below the mirror, appeared banana-shaped, arched into the circular frame; her real voice speaking out of the real room said, "We won't wait for Mrs. Dillon. She runs around all day, poor dear, always doing good. She has her refugee club today."

"No, she doesn't," I said. "That's Thursdays."

"Take Mrs. Montgomery her cup of tea, dear, carefully," said Miss Douglas. Her large, veined old hands presided with authority over cozy, pot, and hot-water jug, the milk, the little sandwiches, and the plate of chocolate biscuits. "Take Mrs. Montgomery the sugar, dear. She has her church, you know, and there are her old people. Herta, a little kumquat jam for you?" Miss Douglas was spreading a generous dab of the jam on her own infinitesimally thin slice of brown Hovis bread and butter. She bent her head with deliberation and delicately licked a speck of the sweet stuff from the knuckle of her little finger. "Did you know that Mrs. Dillon has a house, at the other side of town, that she has turned into a home for old gentlefolk? We feel so sorry for them, poor dears, having been gently brought up, to be poor in their old age. And now she has bought another house for her refugees. Why, there she is now." The cocker spaniel had walked to the door. Even Ado, the cat, had risen, yawned, and was sitting expectantly. Mrs. Dillon had entered the house.

Mrs. Dillon opened the door with a bounce of spirits. She greeted her sister, asked the visitors how they did, said hello to me, kissed the dog, noticed the cat, and sat down smiling and sighing.

"Poor dear," said Miss Douglas, "you must be exhausted. A cup of tea will do you a world of good."

"I spoke to your dear mother on the telephone today," Mrs. Dillon said to me, "and she sends you her love. I was trying to persuade her to come and work for my old folks, but she says your father is so poorly, poor man, she doesn't know what's going to happen, and she doesn't want to bind herself. I was quite sorry. She is such a dear little person, and so reliable."

The ladies then talked about the advantages of hiring refugees, expressed their indignation at people who were prejudiced indiscriminately against German-speaking persons. Miss Douglas said she would hire one immediately to take the place of her girl if it weren't for that dear little baby. "I have her from the Home for Unmarried Mothers, you know, where I do a little charity Tuesdays and Fridays. She is not at all a good servant, but I don't have the heart to get rid of her. It's hard for these girls to get placed. I want you to see our little Lila."

Miss Douglas asked me to ring for Milly, and she asked Milly to take away the trolley and to bring in her baby.

Lila was not an attractive infant. She was cross-eyed and slow. Miss Douglas set her on the rug in front of the fire, and placed her big hand tenderly over the baby's head so that it fit her like a cap.

"Up, up," said Mrs. Dillon to her dog. "Up you come! There. You know you're too big to sit on Mother's lap, don't you? Yes, you do. You know you are. Poor sweet," she said, in an aside to Mrs. Montgomery, "he gets so jealous."

At the time my parents moved to Clinton Lodge, Herta challenged me about it. "So now your parents live in their own place, are you going to live with them?"

I had been worrying about this myself, but I said, "Of course not. You see, my father is not well. And my mother goes to work. Besides, they only have one room."

Herta said, "If I had my parents living in town, I would live with them."

"Well, I visit them," I said.

These visits were not a success, though for my mother's sake the Clinton Lodge refugees put up with me. Among the papers from those years (the letters from my Uncle Paul in the Dominican Republic, the Red Cross letters from Vienna, the ration cards, the

Alien Registration Cards, the receipts for the monthly one pound
ten shillings my mother paid the Committee toward my schooling)
I've come across a tribute written by the house poet to "Franzi on
her Birthday, December, 1942":

> She busily at early morn
> Goes to her work that's never done.
> To cook and bake and scrub and stir;
> A hundred mouths are fed by her.
>
> Comes home at last and nurses Igo
> Makes cakes for Lore to help her grow
> And is amusing gay and bright,
> In our small circle every night.

The poem to me on my fifteenth birthday reads:

> Let us hope she'll grow to be
> Happy in this company
> Neat and friendly, cause no strife,
> But help us lead a peaceful life.

I was not happy in their company. I came to Clinton Lodge like
a native returning home after a lifelong absence. My German was
uncomfortable in my mouth. The manners I had learned from my
parents no longer felt adequate or proper. These people seemed to
me underbred. They laughed too loud. They moved restlessly
around the house. The Germans cleaned and the Austrians cooked.
When I came over on Saturday after lunch, my mother would be
drinking coffee from the tablecloth in the kitchen, instead of tea
from the knee in the drawing room. "Next time," she said. "Today
I'm in a hurry. I'm going to visit Daddy in the hospital."

"What, in that dress?" I said.

"But this is my good dress. I had it made the winter before we
left."

"It's those flaps hanging down from the belt. In England you
don't wear things like that. Maybe if I cut them off—"

"You're not cutting anything off," said my mother.

"Yes, I am."

"No."

"Yes."

My mother was in a hurry and she was tired. "So be quick, then," she said. But even without the flaps my mother did not look like Miss Douglas or Mrs. Dillon or Mrs. Montgomery. It was the distribution of flesh underneath that was wrong.

"Why didn't you go with your mother to visit your father?" asked Mrs. Bauer.

"I can't," I said. "Miss Douglas is having people to tea, and she needs me. Good-by."

But I stopped outside the door and heard Mrs. Katz say, "Poor Franzi. That child is getting as chilly as the rest of the English."

The pain of their disapproval remained with me after I had forgotten the persons who had inflicted it, for by the time I reached the Clinton Lodge gate Mrs. Bauer and Mrs. Katz had dropped away, as the country one has been touring drops behind the horizon into the past. As I ran up the hill and into the sight and presence of Adorato, there occurred a perceptible change. I came, walking more slowly, through the side gate, stepped quietly into the back hall, my jaw reset to speak English, my facial muscles to smile, my bones realigned at the waist, the seat of politeness, and opened the door into the drawing room.

"There you are, dear child. Come and say hello to Canon Godfrey and Mrs. Montgomery. Take Mrs. Montgomery her cup, carefully, and the sugar."

Mrs. Dillon beamed at me out of her sweet blue eyes. "How nicely she carries round the tea," she said to Canon Godfrey, who sat beside her. "Doesn't she? Almost like an English girl."

I watched them all in the round mirror under its eagle. Mrs. Montgomery was telling Miss Douglas that Herta had done very well at school and the headmistress was having her take the scholarship examinations for Cambridge next year. Herta was there, too, sitting upright in her chair, balancing the cup and plate as cleverly as any English lady, but she had grown quite stout, with a high bosom. It exasperated me that she sat just far enough outside the circle around the fire so that her legs up to the knees were reflected in the golden mirror and the rest of her was not.

I asked her to sit on the rug with me, but Miss Douglas suggested that if we had finished our tea we could go and walk in the garden.

That winter afternoon Herta told me she was going to be converted.

"You're not!" I said, incredulous and revolted, assailed out of memory by an alien smell, by the forbidden regions of a housemaid's bosom. "You don't want to be a Christian!"

"Yes, I do."

"Come on! You don't believe all that nonsense about God coming to earth as his own son?"

"It's not nearly such nonsense as our prayer book that does nothing but bless God," Herta said with heat. "The people of Israel this, and the people of Israel that, as if there were nobody else in the world!"

"Yes, and maybe you believe that a virgin can have a baby. Maybe you don't know something."

"Maybe I know more than you!" cried Herta. "Do you know about spiritual impregnation? With God, all things are possible."

"If all things are possible," I shouted, "why does he let wars happen, and concentration camps, and why are your parents lost!"

"That's because you don't understand," said Herta, with her brows very black. "There's something Christ said. 'I am the light.' But I can't explain it to you. It's something I saw once when I was walking the dog on the Downs, in the evening, how light is everything. You wouldn't understand."

"Why wouldn't I?" I said. "You think you are the only person who understands anything. I knew that long before you—the time we walked up West Street."

I looked into Herta's fat face, but there was no fire flashing in Miss Douglas's late-November garden, and I could see Herta's eyes behind her glasses looking very small and pink-rimmed, with such sparse, stiff lashes, I was sorry they weren't prettier.

"Anyway," I said, "are you going to be Church of England?"

Herta said she was going to be High Church.

In the following weeks, I became used to the thought of Herta's becoming a Christian. The busy Christmas season was upon us, and I was helping Miss Douglas do good. I came along on her rounds, visiting her deaf and dumb and blind where they lived. If they were gentlefolk, we brought them handkerchief cases, or sachets that Miss Douglas had been making in the evenings from dried lavender out of the garden. We sat with them and had tea. Miss Douglas would make conversation with sign language into their hands and tell them about me, and I would go and stand near them and shake hands. If they were poor people, Miss Douglas stayed in the car and I went and rang the doorbell and left a parcel of food.

I became very indignant, and was a Socialist again for almost a week. It wasn't fair, I said, that some people should be poor, as well as deaf and dumb, and I gave Miss Douglas an argument.

She was busy setting up the manger on the piano top in the drawing room and asked me to pass her the cotton wool for snow on the roof of the stable. "That's the way things are arranged," she said. "If everyone were well off, what would become of charity? I do hope the snow doesn't catch fire from the candle in the manger. Last year, the piano top was quite badly burnt. It's a good thing we have insurance."

I said, "If everybody were well off, then everybody would be equal. And nobody would have to eat in the kitchen."

Miss Douglas said that would never do. Everything would be turned topsy-turvy. "The way things are arranged," she said, "the lower classes wait on me, or if I am giving a charity party for my poor deaf-and-dumb children I am happy to wait on them, and their mothers, too, but it would never do to sit down together."

"Why wouldn't it?" I said, and Miss Douglas told me to run along and see if I could help Mrs. Dillon.

Mrs. Dillon was never so happy as in this season, when to her year-round activities was added her Nativity play, which she wrote, produced, directed, costumed, and sang in. It was done every year in St. Thomas's, the fine Norman church, so old that it was half sunk into its little graveyard at the bottom of West Street.

The drawing room was full of splendid striped shepherds' robes from Palestine. In the evenings, Miss Douglas sat before the fire sewing angels' gowns out of Indian Head. I helped Mrs. Dillon paste jewels onto the crowns of the Three Kings.

Mrs. Dillon said I could have been one of her angels to kneel around the manger, but she didn't think the Jewish Committee would like it.

I asked her if Herta could be an angel now that she was converted.

"Herta converted?" said Mrs. Dillon. "What ever gave you that idea?"

"Well, she is," I said.

"No, she's not."

"Yes, she is."

"I wish there were just one subject," said Miss Douglas, "on which you would not contradict."

"I don't know what you're talking about," said Mrs. Dillon. "I was talking just yesterday to Mrs. Montgomery, who's going to be my innkeeper's wife, and she was telling me all about the trouble she's been having with Herta, how Herta insists on going to religious instruction in school though she could have been excused because of being Jewish, and then when one of the girls said that the Jews had killed Jesus, Herta went right over and smacked the girl's face."

"What, Herta did?"

"And when she was called to the headmistress, she said that Jesus was not the son of God, and that he was self-deluded, and that the Virgin could not have had a baby, and she was quite rude about it."

"You mean Herta Hirschfeld?"

"Herta Hirschfeld, Herta Hirschfeld. And they called poor Mrs. Montgomery, and when Mrs. Montgomery tried to talk to Herta, Herta said she didn't want to talk about it, and she became quite hysterical, and poor Mrs. Montgomery doesn't know what to do with her."

I saw Herta at Mrs. Dillon's Nativity play, where she sat near the altar, strangely lighted by the lantern behind the manger, half in the shadow of the immense round pillar. She looked odd— bloated and fat, and as if her brows had grown together. I waved to her when I went up front to help Mrs. Dillon with the wings and halos, but Herta was deeply absorbed in her prayer book and did not see me.

In the course of the following year my headmistress took a group of sixth-form girls who were thinking about going to the university on a day's excursion to Oxford, and I fell in love. Oxford seemed everything that I was not: at ease with itself, at one with its own past—upper class, English.

Mrs. Dillon talked to me in the drawing room, sitting beside me on the sofa. She said, now that I was sixteen, didn't I think that at the end of the year I should leave school and get a job.

"But I'm going to try for Oxford," I said. I explained to her about the stacks in the Bodleian, the sunny High and the students in black gowns riding their bicycles to lectures, about paneled halls, bell towers, and the still, green quadrangles with fretted arches, fanned ceilings, and moldering stone faces. "There's something Henry James wrote about 'the ache of antiquity,' " I said, catching myself on the edge of tears.

Mrs. Dillon, in her blue flowered cotton frock, blinking her eyes in anxiety over me, obviously did not understand about beauty and history. She said, "It's just that I was thinking, darling, now that your father has passed on, I mean about your mother having to work in that dreadful restaurant kitchen."

"But Mummy *wants* me to go to college," I said. "And Herta is going. She got her scholarship to Cambridge."

I met Herta on the street and told her about my planning to go to Oxford. Herta, in her tweed suit, which she filled out in a new stout, grown-up way, looked through her spectacles and said, "And you think Oxford will make a Christian out of you?" It seemed her parents had turned up in Hong Kong and she was only waiting for passage to be arranged to join them in Palestine on her brother's *kibbutz*. She said she was very excited.

I think that was the last time I saw Herta, but one day, not long afterward, Mrs. Montgomery came to see Mrs. Dillon at the refugee office. Herta had confessed that she did not want to go to Palestine. She wanted to stay and be baptized into the Church of England. Mrs. Montgomery was disturbed—it seemed unnatural in a girl, she said. After all, they were still her parents.

I was now engrossed in my own plans, cramming for the exams, waiting for the results, and assumed that Herta had gone up to Cambridge. I didn't know until a year later, when I came back to Allchester for the Christmas holidays, that Herta had jumped out of her bedroom window on the third floor into Mrs. Montgomery's garden, and was dead.

I was accepted at Oxford, but for the year following. It had taken me only minutes to understand that my circumstances would not allow me to wait, but it was years before I overcame the pain of having to accept a second-choice university. I remember my sense of having been maimed for life, and I lay it to Miss Douglas and Mrs. Dillon, who wielded their influence for five years, when I was impressionable, trying to bring a new soul into the Church of England, and, instead, turned out a temporary snob and an Anglophile forever.

CHAPTER EIGHT

London: Frocks, Books, and No Men

My college was an all-women affair, a member of the University of London. It was housed in a complex of unassuming modern brick, without beauty, but the afternoon I first walked through the little gate in the black iron railing that set off its grounds from the rest of Regents Park, a sudden mild golden light emerged capriciously, unbelievably, out of the drizzling autumn; the students walking along the paths between the wide lawns, under old plane trees, took off their mackintoshes and shook their hair free from their kerchiefs. I thought, This is me going to college!

The girl who stood next to me in line for registration looked interesting, with her large white face and straight hair drawn severely back. I told her my name was Lore and that I was Jewish. She said she was glad to meet me. Her name was Monique and she was American. I had thought she was English, and I was quite disappointed.

A good proportion of the students lived in the college dormitories, but for economy's sake my mother and I had taken a room together. Outside the window were the scrappy grounds of Primrose Hill. Inside, the brownish, tweedy wallpaper and the heavy, dusty green of the ancient curtains created a khaki drabness—I kept trying to offset it by odd arrangements of the drab furniture—but in the downstairs hall, in front of the table where the lodgers' mail was laid out, I had seen a young man. He wore a scarf showing the colors of Kings College. He looked around at me, but I had

on my unbecoming green blouse and looked away and ran upstairs where I rapidly changed into my white silk blouse, saw it
needed ironing, changed back, combed my hair, wished it were
longer and my nose shorter, wished I didn't wear glasses, and ran
back down. By that time, of course, the young man had gone, but
on the mail table I found the envelope with my scholarship check.

(I look back to the generosity of this scholarship with amazement: It paid my full tuition and "maintenance," inquiring into
neither my status as a foreigner nor my future intentions. I was
asked to send in a semiannual report as to my continued attendance
at the college and a statement of my needs for rent, food, clothing,
books, fares, and miscellaneous items, which were totaled and sent
me in the form of monthly checks.)

It seems to me that I spent my three college years walking
through London, the elegant shopping districts, the picture galleries, the churches and secondhand bookstores. My state of mind
was near euphoria, alternating with a painful sort of desperation
because I had no one with whom to be in love, and over all there
hung a cloud of guilt because of the studying I was not doing. I
loved my lecturers but studied the variety of their performances
instead of the subjects of the lectures. Instead of taking notes, I
doodled loose-leaf books full of faces, dancing figures, elaborate
houses—whole townships. I read, but nothing to its conclusion
and never what had been assigned. In my first term, I decided to
ground my present studies in a comparative survey of world literature of the past. Beginning with the orient, I came across a quote
from the diaries of Lady Murasaki. Writing about her school career, she says: "It was not long before I repented having . . . dis-
tinguished myself, for person after person assured me that even
boys become very unpopular if it is discovered that they are fond
of their books. For a girl, of course, it is worse. . . . I became
careful to conceal the fact . . . with the result that to this day I
am shockingly clumsy with my brush." I closed the book, immensely excited: What my own experience had revealed about
modern middle-class England appeared to have been true in the
court circles of eleventh-century Japan. Lady Murasaki and I were

two women with an unfortunate intellectual tendency. Where she had tried to conceal her books, I had tried to take the curse off mine by reading messily. In the beginning, I had had to work hard to unlearn the disciplined ambition of my early years in the Vienna schools. In my first year at Allchester High School, I had won the prize in penmanship out of sheer habit, but by my Upper-Fourth year I was becoming so clumsy with my pen that my writing was all but illegible, and in the Lower Fifth I was able to boast a "C" in spelling. I was surprised that my classmates did not seem to like me any the better; somewhere I had miscalculated. My best friend, Margaret, a clever, elegant English girl, kept on getting brilliant marks, yet *she* was always first to be chosen on any team.

I had always assumed that when I got to the university I would *really* start to work. I thought that any moment now I would go on reading Lady Murasaki's diary, instead of looking out of the library window to where the trees dipped their dark wet branches into the mist and a big white goose, rising out of the pewter-colored lake, waddled through the iron gate into the college grounds and came up the path toward the library. She started up the steps with a hop and a flap, and came face to face with Dr. Milsom, our professor of Middle English, coming out of the building. Up went the professor's arms, black briefcase flying; out went the goose's white wings. Neck stretched, she turned, half-flying down the steps, and did not stop till she had reached the middle of the wet lawn, where she shook and chatted with herself. The professor, having regained his composure, walked toward the gate, raising his hat to Monique, who came on brilliant red legs like some tropical bird, high-stepping up the college path. (It is hard to convey what a sudden stroke of color can do to an English townscape. I remember, sometime late that year, coming out of the park into Baker Street and seeing, outside the underground station, a cart piled high with peaches. The peddler, his hands deep in his ragged coat pockets, stared at the circle of rush-hour Londoners collected on the wet pavement, staring at the fruit that burned in the greenish October dusk with a light absorbed in some other time and place.)

When I came out of the library, Monique called to me to

wait for her. "Look at them," she said, pointing around the grounds full of women in uniform mackintoshes, flat-heeled walking shoes, and kerchiefs tied under their chins. "Who would have thought English women dress as badly as people always say? Restores your faith in prejudice, doesn't it? In New York," she continued in her attractive husky contralto, "we wear raincoats because it's so British, but *we* keep sending them to the cleaners, whereas now I see they are *supposed* to look filthy."

"That's because the English don't wear mackintoshes to be stylish but to keep dry," I said, "and it never stops raining long enough to have them cleaned."

"There!" said Monique. "There! That's what I mean! Did you really think it would rain continually in England?"

"I didn't have the opportunity to form prejudices," I said. "I came here when I was a child of ten so I'm about fifty per cent English myself."

"Fifty per cent? Ah!" Monique said. "You're one hundred and fifty per cent English. It's just that hundred per cent that will always elude you and me."

In our khaki room, my mother met me with the news that she had found a job. She was going to be housekeeper to an old German gentleman, a Professor Schmeidig.

"Mu-mmy! You said you were going to look for a restaurant job. You *promised* you weren't going back to private service!"

"This is different, Lorle. I'm going to be a sort of companion-housekeeper. The London restaurants don't need any more Viennese cooks. And the professor is old and ill and he does need somebody."

"So, you're going to start all over again, nursing a sick man!"

"Oh, he's not sick like that," my mother said. "It's not the same thing as with your father. This man is a stranger to me. I go in at eight in the morning, tidy up the flat—which is quite small and easy to clean—do the shopping, prepare his meals, and at five I'm off. I don't even have to stay while he eats his supper. He wants to meet you. I told him all about your scholarship."

I found Professor Schmeidig, in his ancient velvet smoking

jacket, perfectly charming. He talked interestingly to me, comparing the English universities with the prewar universities of Germany, and he talked with a warm gallantry about my mother. He said he was lucky to get someone with a sense of humor, someone with whom one could talk about music. "And she's going to play the piano for me. Sit down, Frau Groszmann."

"I wouldn't be so unkind to you," said my mother. "I haven't practiced since the year before Hitler." But she was persuaded to sit down at the small upright and had apologized her way through half a Chopin étude when I noticed that the professor's head had fallen forward onto his chest. In sleep, his old man's nose and chin looked enormous.

My mother got up and put a pillow behind his back. "It's his age," she said as we tiptoed out. "He even falls asleep in the middle of his meals. You go on home, you have to study. I'll just wait till he wakes up and set his supper on a tray."

My mother called me at seven o'clock to say I was not to worry. She was sitting with the professor until his son arrived from the other end of London. The poor professor had awakened feeling far from well, and she didn't like to leave him.

The next night my mother did not come home till almost eleven o'clock. "And you left the house before six this morning," I said bitterly.

"That's only as long as he is feeling so unwell. What do you want me to do? I can't leave him there, sitting alone, feeling ill and frightened."

"He has a son!" I said.

"His son has a wife and three children. He can't be with his father all the time."

"You're too goddam good and nice," I said, almost in tears, "and it drives me up the wall!"

"It's nothing to do with being good," my mother said. "It makes *me* more comfortable to be with him than to be home worrying about him. Besides, Lorle, you have your studying in the evenings. What am I supposed to do?"

"Go out a bit. Try and meet people. Look at Lizzi!"

Lizzi Bauer, our friend from the old Clinton Lodge days, had been to see us. She had come to London to see if she could hurry her son's immigration to England, and to see, she said, after all those lonely years in Allchester, if she couldn't meet someone. She told us how she had gone to Hyde Park and sat on a bench and noticed this very good-looking man, and how he had come and sat beside her and they had talked. He was a Russian—had been a lawyer back home—a fascinating man. He had been quite taken with her. They had walked around the Serpentine and he had held her hand. He had pleaded with her to come to dinner with him, but Lizzi had said that she was not the kind of person who goes to dinner with a man she meets on a park bench.

"So what good did it do Lizzi to meet him?" my mother said.

"It's just that she, at least, *tries!*" I countered. "One of these days I'll be going out . . . with someone," I said, thinking of the young man with the Kings College scarf, whose back I had seen this morning disappearing into his door on the floor below. "And all the time I'm out, I'll be thinking of you sitting here alone! You know that's the one bad thing about you," I explained to my mother. "You don't even *try* to have a life of your own."

"Yes, I have that from my poor father," my mother said. "We are both very dull. We're no good at anything except doing our duty. But you don't have to worry about my sitting alone. Lizzi has asked me to go to the Viennese Club with her the next time she comes to London. Just let me wait till the professor is feeling better."

The next day my mother was home by five-thirty. The professor was much better. "He wanted to give me his dead wife's gold watch," my mother said.

"Where? Let me see!" I said.

"Of course I couldn't accept such a valuable present. It belongs to his son, and to his grandchildren. He says he wants to marry me," my mother said, blushing and laughing self-consciously.

"So?"

"Lorle! You wouldn't want me to marry a sick old man! Besides, he doesn't really want *me*. He feels grateful that I stayed with him while he was ill. He is afraid to be alone."

"And why can't you consider the possibility that he actually likes you for yourself?" I lectured my mother.

"Anyway," said my mother, "we want to go to the Dominican Republic as soon as you're through with your studies."

"Mummy," I said, "do we really want to go to the Dominican Republic?"

"But don't you want to see Paul and the grandparents again?"

"Yes, but not in the Dominican Republic. Do you know I was asking around among my friends at college and no one except an American girl there has ever even *heard* of the place?"

"But we're not going to stay there. We're going to wait there till our American quota comes through."

"Mummy," I said. "Do we really want to go to America?"

I had found a paragraph in Joyce Cary's *To Be a Pilgrim* about England:

On summer days like this, in Harvest, the rich essence of the ground seems charged upon the air so that even the blue of the sky is tainted like the water of a cow pond, enriched but no longer pure. It is as if a thousand years of cultivation had brought to all, trees, grass, crops, even the sky and sun, a special quality belonging only to very old countries. . . . The shape of a field, the turn of a lane have had the power to move me as if they were my children.

It seemed to me that by the power this had to move me I was, at least by adoption, English. I copied it out, and what Cary wrote about "the new lands where the weather is as stupid as the trees, chance dropped, are meaningless," and showed it to Monique. "My trouble is that I can't apply for British nationality till I'm twenty-one and by that time I may be in America!" I complained.

"You may like America better than you intend," Monique said.

"But I *don't want* to like it," I said. I kept bringing Monique examples of the naïveté of American politics and the crudity of its commercialism; I came across an American article about the Soviet

Union illustrated with the kind of brutal line drawing that made every Russian into a monster.

Monique said, "Ah, but I don't think America need stand or fall by a weekly picture magazine, do you?"

"No, but . . ." I said, outargued and amazed that an American should prove superior to me in sophistication.

The Kings College student and I finally met at the corner of our block and walked home together. He said he had just this afternoon finished the last of his exams and now he couldn't think what to do with himself. He was a Canadian, he said, on a year's scholarship, and had spent all his time with his nose in a book. He wondered if I would show him around London, before he left for home, but the suggestion seemed to me to come too abruptly, out of too short an acquaintance; it didn't seem a proper invitation. So I said, "Actually, now I have my exams coming up and should put my nose in a book. I've done nothing all year except walk around London."

Nevertheless, next day we went to the Tower. He said, wouldn't London be nice if it didn't rain all the time.

"Well, I like London so much I even like the rain. I must have an affinity for damp and fog," I said. I was afraid that I might be sounding too intelligent and he wouldn't like me and would go away, and at the same time I was afraid that if I didn't think of something intelligent to say he would get bored and go away. I wished I had stayed quietly at home.

The following week we did Buckingham Palace and the Houses of Parliament. Each time he came to pick me up I stalled, saying I ought to stay home and do some work, so as not to appear over-eager.

On Sunday it stopped raining and we took a walk along the Embankment. He was leaving for home at the end of the week. "Soon you'll be going to the Dominican Republic," he said. "With all this traveling, who knows, we might meet again." He turned me around so that we stood face to face and put his hand on my shoulder, which embarrassed me. I said, snippily, "And if not in this life, we're sure to meet in the next." After a moment he dropped his hand. We walked on.

"I've been wanting to ask you," he said. "What nom de plume are you going to use, so I can look out for your first book?"

I looked at him as if he had been clairvoyant. "But how fascinating you should say that!" I cried. "How did you know I was going to be a writer?"

"Why, you kept telling me and telling me!" he said.

The next evening the Canadian student knocked at my door and asked if he might come in. I said, "Of course," feeling awfully urbane, for I was alone—my mother was staying late with Professor Schmeidig, who was having another of his sick spells. "You'll have to excuse me if I go on with my work. Exams start Wednesday."

"That's all right. I'm dead-tired myself," he said, flopping down on one of our brownish sofa beds. "I was packing all morning and running around London all afternoon, picking up my ticket, dispatching my luggage . . . Tomorrow morning I leave. Bring your book over here. Sit down by me."

I said no, I had to sit at the table where the light was better.

He laid his head back against the pillow. I got out my book and writing things with a deal of fuss. When I turned around next time, the Canadian student was asleep. I was deeply offended and when he left, later, I said good-by offhandedly and would not look at him.

Then I was in the middle of the end-of-year exams. Professor Milsom, who handed me back my papers, asked me if I had happened, in the course of my reading, to have come across the word "asyntaxis." I had not.

"Ah! No. Well, 'asyntaxis' describes a pathological condition which prevents the sufferer from organizing ideas into sentences."

"Yes, yes," I cried excitedly, "I know just what you mean. I've been aware for some years of a progressive softening of my mind so that now, when I would *like* to pull myself together, there's nothing to get hold of in the general consistency of much, except my own bootstraps." I was delighted at my own description of my predicament, but Professor Milsom continued, with his head bent noddingly over my papers. "Well, well, well, interesting concept, 'asyntaxis'! You might look it up in the dictionary. I do recommend to your notice, Miss Groszmann, the dictionary! I wouldn't say that your paper is altogether without merit. I feel there might be interesting ideas here, if I could read them, and if they were expressed between periods with a full complement of verbs. Do let me recommend to your attention, Miss Groszmann, the full stop and the verb."

Toward the end of 1946 my grandfather had a heart attack. Paul wrote that it was not serious, my grandfather was recovering well, but my mother decided to go to the Dominican Republic without waiting for me. I was to follow in two years, after my finals.

"You see how little good and nice I am," my mother said. "Professor Schmeidig is feeling so miserably sick these days and I'm preparing to leave him without a second thought."

"That's because you're in such a hurry to get to the Dominican Republic to nurse your sick father."

"Talking of sick fathers," my mother said, "yesterday, for the first time, the professor complained to me about his son. Do you know he hasn't been to see the poor old man in three weeks? How alone he will be after I'm gone!"

The evening of the day my mother left Professor Schmeidig's employ, the professor called on the telephone. He had some funny, vulgar things to say about the new housekeeper his son had taken for him. Then he wept. He asked my mother to reconsider and stay in England and marry him. My mother said she could not do that, but she had another idea. Her friend Lizzi Bauer was coming up from Allchester tomorrow, and we would all come over and my mother would cook dinner at his flat.

The evening was a huge success. Lizzi was an ugly, worldly woman of enormous charm. She had a large mouth with large, tobacco-stained teeth, vital, very black hair, and intelligent green eyes. She invariably dressed in navy blue sparked with something crisply white, a collar, or chiffon scarf, or piqué flower, at once chic and feminine. Her figure was small with a high plump back that was almost a hunch; she wore her breasts flattened in the fashion of her own well-to-do and successful twenties in the Vienna of the twenties of the century.

While my mother was getting dinner ready, Lizzi sat at the piano and entertained her host with the naughty cabaret songs of their pre-Hitler days. "Johnny, on your birthday, I'll stay with you the whole night through . . ." she sang, undeterred by her complete lack of voice. She rocked her shoulders, looking toward the professor through the smoke that rose from the cigarette in the ash tray by her hand. She laid her head back laughingly, without releasing the old gentleman's eyes. "Ach, Johnny, if only you had a birthday every day. . . . Johnny, I dream of you so much," Lizzi half sang, half spoke. "Come to my door some afternoon at half-past four." (I thought I would never dare to look into any man's eyes with such an intimate look; it embarrassed me. Maybe there was something wrong with me!) The professor's shoulders were rocking faintly inside his old smoking jacket and his eyes were fixed fulsomely on Lizzi's face. Later, the professor insisted on our all taking Frau Bauer to her train. As the taxi drew up in front of Waterloo Station I thought I saw something: I thought I saw the professor's right hand letting go of Lizzi's left; I would have put it down to some trick of my vision if Lizzi had not intercepted my glance and smiled and raised her shoulders as much as to say, "What do you want me to do—he's an old man." The professor drove my mother and me home to our lodgings and came upstairs to have a cup of coffee. After that he came every evening and stayed to eat whatever my mother had prepared for us. Once he asked if we weren't expecting our charming friend to pay a good-by visit.

"All the way from Allchester!" my mother said. "That's an expensive visit, you know."

"Call her up and say good-by on the phone. I want to pay for it," the professor said very kindly. "And tell her to come and see me when she happens to be in London again. Do you think she **would?**"

"Thank you, but Lizzi and I have said good-by," my mother said. "But *you* can ask her to come and see you. I will leave you her number."

That was the day before my mother's departure. The professor wept so bitterly it left him weak and ill, and we had to take him home. On the way back my mother made me promise to go and see him once in a while. "For me," she said. "He will be so miserably alone!"

Going to see Professor Schmeidig became, like studying, something I was always going to do tomorrow. Then my mother wrote me that she had had a letter from the professor in which he said he was so lonely he lay down nights praying he would not wake again, and the next day I rang his bell. The door was opened by Lizzi Bauer. "I was going to call you later," she said. "I happened to be in London."

"And she came to see me," the professor said from the kitchen door. He was dressed smartly in his best gray suit. He seemed so healthy he looked positively gay, and I felt angry for my mother's sake. I said, "Mummy wrote me that you were not well and I just happened to be in the neighborhood. . . ."

"Come in, come in. And how is my good Frau Groszmann? Come into the kitchen with us. It's my horrid housekeeper's day off, very fortunately. I was just boasting to Frau Lizzi that I make a famous cup of Viennese coffee."

Lizzi leaned in the doorway, ankles crossed, her elegant left hand with its outsize agate ring holding her cigarette. Her intimate, teasing eyes followed the professor on his bumbling way around the kitchen, and once in a while I caught her naughty glance directed toward me.

After coffee Professor Schmeidig led her to the piano and she sang to him. When I got up to leave, she rose as well. The old gentleman fetched her coat and held it for her. As we were going out of the door I saw him put some pound notes into her hand.

"He can afford it," Lizzi said to me in the elevator going down, "and I can't keep coming into town for nothing. I've got an hour till train time. Stay with me and talk."

At the little table in the corner teashop, Lizzi said, "Today I really had him up to here. This afternoon he made me sit on his bed and pulled the drawer out of his night table and emptied the whole thing into my lap! He wanted to give me *every*thing in it, though I don't know what he expected me to do with his old silk handkerchiefs, his bone shoehorn, his old key chain! Finally he came up with this," and Lizzi pulled her white cuff back from her wrist to show me a handsome, old-fashioned gold watch. "It used to belong to his wife," she said.

"I know," I said. "He wanted to give it to Mummy once, but she wouldn't take it. He wanted to marry Mummy, did you know?"

"So he told me," Lizzi said. "He's chock-full of promises."

"No, but he meant it, I know. He asked her for months, and the last week before she left he spent every single evening with us."

"He told me," Lizzi said. "He says he kept expecting me to turn up. He says when my boy gets to London he is going to take an apartment in his building for us, but, for all I know, he may be only a senile old man! We'll see what all the promises come to! And now how about you, Lorle? How is the boy-friend situation?" she asked, watching me with her warm, intelligent eyes.

"Nonexistent," I said. "I never see a man, year in, year out. And if I did, he probably wouldn't notice me. Except a year ago there was this Canadian student."

Lizzi Bauer sat with her cigarette between her long fingers and, under the spell of her intimate attention, I heard myself telling her more about the episode of the student than I myself had been aware of. My answers to her close questioning made it clear to me for the first time that the Canadian student had been in a fair way to fall in love with me; I was stunned. "But what use is that?" I said. "I didn't really like him. Maybe there's something wrong with me. Maybe I'm one of those persons who never really . . . like anybody."

"No, but you may be one of those women who take a long time to grow up," Lizzi said. "And living all those years with two old ladies and going to a girls' high school did not help."

"That's right," I said, very much encouraged, "and now I'm going to an all-women college. Just imagine. A couple of thousand English women in mackintoshes and flat-heeled oxfords."

"I have an idea, Lorle," Lizzi said. "Next time I come to town I'll leave the old man early, and you and I will go and buy you a new dress."

"A dress! Where would I ever wear a dress? And besides, I've just used up my money and my clothing coupons on this suit. . . . It looks much better with a white blouse," I said, upset because I could tell Lizzi did not like my brown herringbone wool of classic cut, though it had taken me three agonizing weeks to choose it, and I could never put down on my scholarship statement how much it had cost me.

The next time I met Lizzi in the teashop at the corner of the professor's apartment building, she told me she had almost had to put me off; Professor Schmeidig had wanted to take her to the bank vault. "But then the son turned up," Lizzi said, "and we all had to sit and have our tea together, like good children."

"I'm glad to hear the son is taking some notice of his father," I said. "So long as Mummy was there he didn't stop by for weeks on end."

"Oh, he comes all the time, now," Lizzi said. "He keeps his eye on me, though, of course, he's all politeness and gratitude because I'm keeping his father company. What he doesn't know is what the old man slipped into my bag at the door." She took out a small pearl-studded brooch. "Not that this is worth much these days. He says the good stuff is all in the vault." And then Lizzi asked me if I still had the little blue dress I used to wear at Clinton Lodge. She had brought me a collar of white piqué, edged with exquisite cotton crochet. It was still in the pink tissue paper in which she had wrapped it in Vienna in 1938.

I wore the blue dress with the white collar the day of the English Society's tea in the student common room. Monique came into the washroom where I was putting on some lipstick; that is to say, I was rubbing rouge onto the cushioned tip of my forefinger, which I then drew across my lips. Meanwhile, Monique, at the next mirror, outlined her mouth with a full, curved stroke of scarlet. I put more color on my own mouth, in short staccato dabs. It looked pretty.

"Ready?" asked Monique.

"One moment," I said and quickly wiped the color off my lips. "Ready," I said.

Everyone in the common room was wearing the uniform tweed suit. I felt silly in my blue dress and Viennese collar, so I kept my mackintosh buttoned.

The guest speaker was a young poet rising into first prominence. He was a tall man in a crumpled suit and amazing sky-blue socks. He had an ugly, charming, witty face and was so nervous he looked sick. He talked about the metaphysical poets, all religion and learning and love and just my cup of tea—but I could not listen because I was preparing the very clever question that I meant to put to him. Question time came and went and I was still waiting for my breathing to calm enough for speech. Tea was announced. In a moment the rare young man was surrounded by a cluster of girls as if he were the center of a many-petaled flower growing in our common room. I saw Monique laughing, holding a plate, feeding the poet chocolate biscuits.

I collected my books. This time I really meant to go to the library to study, but I was waylaid by a bench under the largest of the plane trees and, sitting there, I presently saw walking along the path side by side, in casual conversation, the American girl and the poet. Monique waved to me. I watched them walk through the iron gate, over the little bridge that crossed the lake, and out together into Baker Street.

Professor Schmeidig was so much in love, Lizzi said, that he was becoming a nuisance, always begging her to stay the night, though she had made it quite clear she was not that kind of woman, and, as she said to him, what would they do if the son suddenly decided to turn up?

Toward the end of the month Lizzi called again and asked me to meet her at the Viennese Club. I said I really should work, I had my finals coming up, but Lizzi said to come for just half an hour. Something had happened.

We sat at a small table, and my *Torte* with *Schlagobers* tasted like all the cakes I had eaten on all those Sunday afternoons in Vienna when my grandmother was in town and we went to the *Kaffeehaus* to meet all the aunts and uncles. I looked around me now, and the elderly man with the hooked nose sitting behind me, and the two women talking over their coffee cups, looked and sounded as if I had known them forever.

Lizzi was upset. She had come to London especially early, and she and the professor had slipped away to the bank when who should burst in, as they sat at a table with the strongbox open, but that incredible son. He must have figured out where they had gone or, more likely, had them followed. And he had made the *most* unspeakable scene right in front of the bank guard. He said if he ever caught Lizzi anywhere near his father again, he would have the old man declared mentally incompetent and put away in a home.

"How horrible!" I cried, and blushed, imagining the confrontation. "What can you do! I mean you can't go and see him and you can't leave him now!"

"Why can't I leave him?" Lizzi asked. "I'll not be spoken to like that ever again, I assure you. So that is that! Let's talk about you, Lorle. Any boy friends?"

I was about to open my mouth to tell her what was uppermost in my mind—the poet at the English tea and Monique who had walked away with him—when I noticed something odd, almost like a squint, in Lizzi's eyes. She was looking straight at me but without appearing to see me.

"And how is Franzi? What does she write?" Lizzi asked, and her voice seemed pitched into the near distance, over my shoulder. I turned. The elderly man with the noble hooked nose stood holding his coffee with whipped cream, smiling. He said, "You two ladies are talking so animatedly, it makes a lonely man quite jealous."

"Then why doesn't the lonely man bring up a chair and join the animated ladies?" Lizzi said, looking up with her charming, naughty green eyes.

I rose. "Don't worry about the chair," I said. "I have to get home and do some studying. . . ."

Then the exams were upon me. I have to this day a recurring nightmare in which I am not opening a book that is only one book on one of many shelves of bookcases beyond bookcases unfolding into eternity: and all the while I feel time drawing dizzyingly away like a receding wave drawing the sand away underfoot. Then I awake and know that I am not, that I will not in any future be, cramming for any imminent examinations, and I feel life good and sweet around me.

In my college finals I did as badly as one can without actually failing.

I think I had always expected that something would occur to prevent my having to really leave England and go to the Dominican Republic, but my mother's letters kept coming, full of love and the sure expectation of being reunited with me before the end of the summer, and would I please be sure, she wrote, to go and visit poor Professor Schmeidig and say good-by.

When I rang the Professor's bell there was no answer. I was going to leave a message with the doorman but he said the professor had been taken away to the hospital almost a month ago, though it wasn't until yesterday that the son had come and taken away the furniture and everything and closed the flat. The old man was dead.

When I came out into the street there was a soft summer drizzle and London was suddenly nostalgic. All my English friends had gone home. Monique had left for a short hop to France before returning to New York.

I took the underground to Piccadilly and walked over to Old Bond Street and up and down the sidewalk looking for a new dress. *The* new dress. I knew it in a world of speculation only—at once sexy and austere, elegant and gorgeous. What I ended up with was a navy silk I could not afford, with a potentially daring décolletage that tended to emphasize my thin long neck and my long sharp nose.

"It has a drawstring, Madam," said the exquisite salesperson, pulling the neckline close around my throat the way I saw I would have to wear it until the moment of my blooming, which I expected daily. My oxfords stood on the deep plum-colored carpet and my eyes, in the tilted full-length oval of the rococo mirror, looked back with a haggard eagerness and anxiety from behind my round spectacles. I remember I looked the saleswoman in the face, woman to woman, and said, "What do *you* think . . ." but she had written me off as "no sale" and was rubbing her left eye with a scarlet-tipped forefinger. She said, "It's pure genuine silk, Madam."

On board ship there was a whole crew of Greek ship's officers into whose glamorous company I was drawn through Paula, my cabinmate, a handsome, experienced Polish girl on her way to Trinidad to join a husband she did not love. I wore my pure silk low at the neck and thought, this is me, lying in a deck chair listening to the midnight guitar—smoking and drinking champagne into the small hours—and wished I didn't keep falling asleep. Once I opened my eyes to see the young, beautiful, olive-skinned officer taking off Paula's shoes. She was saying, "Now stop it. Don't be silly." "Come on!" I said to Paula, "Aren't we going to bed?" because they were walking away together along the darkness of the long deck. "Hey!" I cried. "Where are you going?"

There was a Lithuanian student whom I discovered for myself. We talked about the aesthetics of light and about comparative religion. Once, standing at the rail as the sun was setting, his radiant face turned toward me, he said he had something he wanted to tell me, but there was such a pounding of blood in my ears and light exploding that I could not stand it and I said, "What's that book you're reading?"

During the night the boat put in at Guadeloupe, where the Lithuanian student got off, and three days later I myself disembarked in the New World.

Part 2

CHAPTER NINE

Sosua: Paul and Ilse

In 1948, when I arrived in the Dominican Republic, it was ten years since I had seen my Uncle Paul or my grandparents.

Shortly after my parents left Vienna, Paul had gone to one of the training farms that were being established in the outskirts of Vienna by Adolf Eichmann, in co-operation with the Jewish community. On these *Hachscharahs,* young Jews wanting to emigrate to Palestine were to be trained in farm work.

Paul wrote me to England. He enclosed a photograph of a plump young woman in working pants and a bandanna standing between a tall, pretty young man, who is pressing her left hand, and my bespectacled Uncle Paul, whose left hand she is pressing. Paul's far arm is characteristically bandaged in an immense sling. The three young faces look laughingly out of that bitter time.

I suspected nothing; I recalled the day when Paul had come to say good-by to me and how he had told my grandmother to figure the odds against a woman he wanted to marry wanting to marry him, and when, two weeks after the first letter, Paul wrote again to say that he had married this girl, Ilse, I refused, at first, to believe it. When I got used to the idea, I fell in love with the account of the marriage, so much more gallant than my parents' formal wedding in that other world of 1927, in the presence of relatives from Vienna, Budapest, and Presburg, with a dowry including three dozen each of handkerchiefs, petticoats, nightgowns, pillow cases, all hand-monogrammed by the village girls and ready in the young people's Vienna flat when they returned from their Italian honeymoon. Paul and Ilse were married outside the cowshed on the *Hachscharah* by a visiting rabbi, and caught the morning truck bringing eggs into the city. Paul and Ilse moved in with my grandparents, who were still living in Aunt Ibolya's flat. Paul has told me that he and Ilse laughed so much carrying their combined and total belongings in a washbasket up the stairs that they had to stop and sit down on every landing.

My grandmother wrote to my mother on a high note of complaint against this girl whom Paul had brought into the family, who put black stockings in with her white wash though my grandmother had specifically warned her not to. My grandmother said she had begged Paul with raised hands not to marry this spoiled, uneducated child, whom he had known only six weeks, and who was engaged to someone else, but when this Paul, whom everybody thought such a sweet-natured son, really wanted anything, it was no good even talking to him; he took the girl's part in everything.

In September, my grandmother wrote that Paul and Ilse had got a farm-labor visa to England. "Your father and I, of course, have to stay behind. If I had it in me to envy my own children, I would envy Paul and Ilse, who are getting away from Hitler and a nagging mother all in one."

"The children have left," she wrote in October, "and just in time. Two S.S. men came today while we were having breakfast, and we have to vacate by noon tomorrow. When we have a new address, I will write to you."

It was 1939. I was living with the Hoopers. It puzzled me that Paul did not come straight to see me. I used to lie in bed and wonder about it. His first job was on a farm in Wiltshire. Ilse looked after their one-room cottage, and they got themselves a dog. Paul says he had little truck with his fellow workers. The English language was unwieldy to him; he needed all his energies to keep up his work among these professional farm hands. The six weeks' *Hachscharah* training had left everything to be desired, and at the end of the season he was let go. Because of the wartime labor shortage, however, he soon found another place. Our news of Paul and Ilse consisted mainly of the announcements of their changes of address.

I have questioned Paul about this period in his life when I did not know him, and in a letter he described himself for me—using the third person—as a young man "recently cut off from home, *'welt-fremd'* [unworldly], who at twenty-eight had never had to work for a living and whose ideas about life were formed through a rather unsystematic reading of books . . . offered the role of father-lover by his new child-wife. They were madly in love. Though she was younger by some eight years, it was he who became her pupil in love, while she, who was quite uneducated, had a vast longing to be led by him into the world of culture."

I did not meet Ilse till after Paul's internment. Ilse wrote that she was coming to see us on her way to London to get Paul back. I remember her walking into my field of vision, which was blurred with excitement; not tall and suave, as I had imagined her, but, like my mother, plump, with brown hair drawn into the simplest back roll—a mere person like the rest of us, looking, in fact, much like her photograph.

All afternoon, I studied this Ilse who slept nights in my Uncle Paul's bed. Her eyes were perfectly green in a brown face with a warm down, like a summer berry. I went and sat on the bench close beside her, and she pulled me into the crook of her arm. I remember that the skin on the inside of her arm was delicate and dry and softer than anything I had ever known, and I caressed my cheek against it.

From London, Ilse wrote my mother that she had been to the Home Office to get Paul released, but the man there had kept saying that Paul was an alien of hostile origin, even though she had explained that he was Jewish and therefore could not be a spy. She wished her English were better, because she couldn't seem to get the man to understand her.

From the Home Office, Ilse went to Bloomsbury House and was in the waiting room when an American came in to sign up people willing to settle in Sosua, a farming colony for refugees being established in the Dominican Republic. Ilse asked him what about a man who was interned, and the American said he could arrange for anybody willing to go to Sosua to be released. And Ilse signed up for Paul and herself.

Sosua was one of those Jewish dreams of an agricultural haven in the New World. In 1938, Franklin Roosevelt had asked Latin-American countries to accept refugees. Trujillo of the Dominican Republic was the only head of government who welcomed the proposal. (It has been so disagreeable to think of the dictator's doing a goodhearted thing that the Sosuans have been trying ever since to think up some self-serving motive for his action.) Stipulating merely that no settler should become a financial burden on the state, he donated from his own vast holdings the twenty-five thousand acres on the northern coast called Sosua. Here, a group of American Jewish philanthropists established the Dominican Republic Settlement Association, which came to be known as DORSA.

Paul and Ilse left England with twelve other refugees, eleven men and one woman, and disembarked in Ciudad Trujillo on a tropical morning in February, 1941. A Mr. Langley, the DORSA husbandry expert, was waiting for them at the pier and loaded them and their baggage into the canvas-covered DORSA truck for the eight-hour trip from the capital in the south via Santiago to Sosua, in the northernmost part of the island. Paul has told me that he found it beautiful and interesting. He pointed out to Ilse the wild green parrots in the cocoa trees. In the course of the morning, they kept noticing how the palm trees called royal palms, which lined the road, extended their smooth gray stems beyond their crowns like umbrella tips and that on the apex of each there sat one bird.

By noon, the temperature inside the truck had become monstrous. The immigrants fidgeted and drowsed through the long afternoon. It was almost evening when they heard a shouting and clattering of hoofs, like the approach of Indian hordes in American Westerns. They looked out, and there, coming toward them along the shallow valley, was a troop of young, sunburned riders, their open-necked shirts flapping against their bodies, shouting, *"Wie geht's? Grausliche Reise, nicht wahr?"* in familiar Austrian-

and Polish-Jewish accents. The riders fell in with the slowing truck, surrounding it like a convoy.

"Horrible trip, isn't it?" said a curly-haired young man, keeping his horse's nose just inside the truck. "I'm Otto Becker. I suppose you are married to him?" he said to Ilse, who was holding Paul's hand. "Oi-yoi. Didn't you bring any girls?"

"There's Renate in the corner sleeping," Ilse said.

Otto was an extremely good-looking, fair young man around twenty-five, with a flat stomach and strong arms covered with shiny reddish-gold hair. He peered with frank lechery into the darkness of the truck. "So that's Renate, is it. She's no use. She's engaged to Michel Brauner. He's been frantic for her. He's the only one of the Germans not married."

"Germans!" said Paul and Ilse.

"From Germany—like you are the 'English' from England. You're from Vienna, aren't you? So am I. Those Germans—I can't stand them—they were settled out by Laguna eight months ago, but they still come to DORSA for handouts. I work in the office. Three pesos pocket money and nothing to spend it on. Do you know the joke about the canaries? There are two canaries sitting in their cage. One says to the other, 'Where are *you* going to-night?' Ha, ha, ha. God, how I wish you had brought some girls."

The truck had stopped on a green cliff. Otto said, "That's the administration building over there with the white fence around it; there's the machine barn. Those are the barracks—one for us bachelors and one they're just putting up for you married couples." Paul and Ilse saw two Dominican workmen struggling to get a mattress in through the narrow door of a low building of new white wood. Otto lifted the girl, Renate, down from the truck and stood her, newly awakened, on the ground. "Otto Becker is the name," he said.

"Ilselein, look! Our new cage!" Paul said. The green cliff dipped down to white sand lying like a pair of arms around the blue water of the bay.

Sosua fed its two to three hundred immigrants living in the Batey (an Indian word, Paul thinks, meaning "the place from which the settlement started") in two communal kitchens. "Any news?" the diners at the long tables called out to the newcomers. "Is Hitler dead yet?"

"Not dead yet."

"Then there's no news."

Otto Becker brought his plate and sat by them. Afterward, the new refugees stayed for a briefing by Mr. Langley, who spoke in German with a prominent American accent. He explained the DORSA plan: Newcomers were put through an intensive training in agricultural procedures, after which they formed groups of as few as two families or as many as a dozen, to set up co-operative homesteads. For these homesteads DORSA supplied land, tools, seed, livestock, and one house per family. Each settler was debited with his share of the cost, which was to be repaid on time after the farms became self-supporting. Until homesteads could be built and everybody settled, they would be living in the barracks. If anybody had any questions, he should not hesitate to bring them to the DORSA office in the administration building—agricultural questions to him, questions of policy and so on to Mr. Sommerfeld, the director, who would very soon welcome them personally. Mr. Langley said he would meet the men in the field tomorrow, after breakfast. The two women should report for duty in the kitchen.

They came out into bright dusk. Ilse took Paul's hand and drew it through her arm. "Pauli, could we go for a walk and look around?"

"Oh, do let's!" cried Renate, keeping close to Ilse, because the impertinent Otto had taken her arm. This left little Michel Brauner, her fiancé, walking next to Paul.

Michel said, "Renate tells me you have farm experience. Maybe, after Renate and I are married, we could form a group and apply for a homestead?"

"I don't have enough experience to run a farm," Paul said, "but enough to know I don't. As Socrates said, 'I know that I know nothing; others don't know even so much,'" and, hearing his professorial tone, he laughed apologetically.

Michel said, "Nobody in Sosua knows anything. You just start applying for a place."

Otto asked Renate and Ilse to come swimming on the beach the next afternoon.

"Won't we be busy in the kitchen?" Ilse asked.

Otto said, "Nobody in Sosua is busy." He and Renate were pulling ahead because of the extreme slowness with which Paul and Ilse seemed to be moving. After a moment's hesitation, Michel went to take Renate's free arm, and soon the three of them were lost in the rapidly descending darkness.

Paul and Ilse walked on until they reached the edge of the cliff. They lay down together in the night grass. "Pauli," she asked, "that Michel Brauner, is he a good person to run our farm with?"

"Michel Brauner's capacities don't worry me nearly as much as Paul Steiner's. You realize, Ilselein, that in England, between October, 1939, and August, 1940, I was thrown out of three jobs?"

"The last job you didn't get thrown out of. You were interned, and you said yourself how much you learned that year."

"That's true," Paul said. "In that last job I was beginning to feel on firmer ground. I know more than most of these people here. Do you know, Ilselein, I'm raring to get down to work? I want to provide, for you and our children, a house and food, and have something over to begin to pay off the debt we are going to owe DORSA. Poor Mutti!" Paul said in a voice that was suddenly very gay. "At thirty, with the assistance of Hitler, her boy has grown up. So I'm not a poet; I won't lead any revolutions—did I ever tell you about the time in the Dolfuss days a policeman stopped me on the way to my Socialist cell? I was carrying a bunch of pamphlets, but I got out my wallet full of pictures of my little niece, Lore; then he showed me pictures of his two boys, and we parted great friends. A lot of cloak-and-dagger nonsense in the name of an honest new Austria! Now all I want is to get my parents out of Vienna and be quit of the whole European mess." In the darkness below them, the ocean swished and heaved. The black air was warm and very soft. Paul's wife made herself comfortable in the crook of his arm, and Paul said, "Ah, Ilselein, one might almost be happy here!" And it turned out that the future Paul had pictured for them was precisely what Ilse wanted for *her* happiness.

Inside, the barracks had a long, narrow corridor, with washrooms at either end and rooms leading off it, rather like the compartments in continental trains. Each room was furnished with an iron bedstead, a washstand, and two wooden chairs, and was separated from its neighbors by wooden partitions. Paul named their room the *"Badekabine"* for its resemblance to a swimming-pool *cabaña*. Ilse said the whole of Sosua felt like a summer-holiday place; you got out of bed in the morning and pulled a dress over your head and off you went.

On the way to the kitchen for breakfast, Paul told Ilse that he expected no holiday in the fields. The intellectual, he said, had a disadvantage as a farmer. Nothing came to him directly, by instinct. He was a man looking at the world through spectacles; he must have everything explained so he could understand the theory of what to do in practice. But there was this advantage—he could master in years what took the peasant generations.

Mr. Langley met his new trainees in a field that had been cleared of rocks and tree stumps by two native employees of DORSA. There was a plow to which a mule was hitched, and a barrel of yam plant—a long green tangle of stalk and leaves, which Mr. Langley told them to cut into foot lengths and lay in furrows in the ground. Mr. Langley asked if anyone had plowed before, and Paul said he had, but never with a mule. The older, blacker of the Dominicans, called Jesús, demonstrated how to guide the animal with one hand while steadying the plow with the other. "It needs practice," Mr. Langley said. "I will be back presently to see how you are doing."

They watched him ride away down the sea road toward the Batey. "I bet he's rich," said Farber, who had been a traveling salesman in Poland. "I asked him how he knew German, and he said he studied to be a veterinarian in Frankfurt, but now he breeds cattle in America. He must be a millionaire."

"America, America. Land of Opportunity," said Max Godlinger, a man with a bald head and a pointed, old man's stomach.

The two Dominicans in the far corner of the training field were cutting down the tall grass. They sang rhythmically as they walked, swinging their machetes.

Paul, who had been experimenting with the plow, said, "Someone come and hold onto this animal. The plow is going every which way. Hold still, you."

In the Batey, Ilse sat beside Renate in the sun behind the kitchen. They were peeling yams, which DORSA imported by the truckload from the market of Puerto Plata, on the far side of the bay. They could see the white beach below, and three young men running down toward the water. The Atlantic spread before them, so still it might have been made out of solid blue, except that, way out, the sun glimmered and seesawed on little waves.

By noon, the sun stood directly over the square of the training field, and where it glanced off the waves it pierced the men's eyes like motes of dust. To the right, the mountains quivered behind a haze of heat. Paul walked after the mule, lifting his boots to a rhythm that had come uncalled into his mind:

> *Mensch, was du liebst,*
> *In das wirst du verwandelt werden:*
> *Gott wirst du, liebst du Gott,*
> *Und Erde, liebst du Erden.*

Pools of sweat had collected at the back of his knees and made little runnels down his calves.

"Hey, Steiner, look behind you!" Farber called to Paul, and Paul turned and saw how the furrows, which started out parallel, ran indistinguishably into one another across the field.

"Who needs yams," said bald Godlinger. He came from Vienna and was a furrier by trade. "We did perfectly well all these years without yams."

"I'd like to remind you that we did by no means perfectly well in Vienna," said Paul out of dusty lips. He picked up a hoe.

"What are you doing?" wailed Godlinger. "You're not going to straighten them by hand?"

"It might make up for lost time," Paul said, "if some of us would start cutting up the yams."

"Godlinger, roll up your sleeves," said Farber. Godlinger obediently rolled his sleeves up over his pink and hairless arms.

The green tangle out of the barrel seemed to have no beginning or end. They called Paul over, and Paul said they might begin by stripping the mess of leaves and blossoms off the stalks.

The two Dominicans had packed up their tools and stood awhile watching the field full of working white folk before they took the road toward the native village, which lay in the direction opposite from that in which Mr. Langley had disappeared in the early morning.

Mr. Langley had not returned by late afternoon, when the trainees had all the neat, finger-thick stems laid in the makeshift furrows, so they collected their hoes and walked the mule back to the Batey.

After the white-hot road, the inside of the barracks felt like a cave—dark and damply cool. Paul found Ilse sitting on the bed, her hair wet. She had spent the afternoon on the beach with Renate and Otto and what seemed like dozens of young men at loose ends. She fetched Paul cold water and a clean shirt. Paul told her about the ruined yam field, and the poem by the seventeenth-century mystic, Angelus Silesius, that had gone around in his head. Ilse sat on her haunches on the bed, looking up at Paul, who stood in his underwear and raised his chin, like a singer, to recite:

> "Man, you will be transformed
> To that which you hold worth;
> God, if you love God,
> Earth, if you love earth."

He was both delighted and surprised that Ilse had no difficulty whatsoever with the concept of becoming the thing loved, and he told her how, on the road walking back, he had found the last line for a poem he had been carrying around in his head for years.

"I even remember where the first line came to me. Down by the Danube, in Fischamend, there is a footpath. . . ."

["*Ich denke und du düngst. . . .*"]

"I think thoughts, you grow things.
And if my thought in your mind's night
May seem no matter—"

Paul grimaced. "A very Karl Kraus sort of pun," he said.

". . . yet my mind brings
To light the seed that you manure."

Then comes this nineteenth-century sort of idea. Paul suddenly longed for Dolf, who would have recognized each derivation and applauded each happy stroke. Marking his rhythms like a conductor, Paul went on:

"And when our shadows which we cast shall rest,
That in life's flick'ring light had wildly swung,"

Paul raised his chin.

"I shall be turned to thought, you into dung."

["*Alsdann wirst du zum Dung, ich zum Gedanken.*"]

After supper, Paul and Ilse gave the slip to Renate, who was bickering with Michel. They walked up the road to see the yam field, and Paul talked to Ilse about Angelus Silesius, and Karl Kraus, about Heine, and his poet friend Dolf. Ilse said, "Renate says you won't be happy living in Sosua, because you are an intellectual."

"Much she knows about *that*," Paul said.

Ilse said, "I was trying to tell her what you said this morning, how being an intellectual was like looking through spectacles. It's funny—I understood everything while you were explaining it to me, but I couldn't explain it to her. She says you've known Vienna and you'll never be able to live without music and everything—no culture and no books."

"You can tell Renate from me that I have indeed known Vienna, and that we're the victims of its culture and its books." When Paul was excited, the muscles of his mouth seemed to become paralyzed so that the effort of speaking bared his irregular teeth, giving him a look that was almost cruel. Ilse clung to his arm, and he held on to her. Through his painful, tight lips he said, "It was my Vienna that turned on me. It was my books."

In the weeks that followed, the trainees weeded and waited for the yams to sprout.

"Godlinger, you should cover your head. You'll get sunstroke," Paul said.

Godlinger took out a handkerchief and put it on his bald head, which was turning a dangerously red color, as he walked beside Paul, making conversation, using his hoe like a walking stick. "When my American quota comes through, my brother and I are opening a fur store in Chicago—quite small, just the family. My wife always says, 'Strangers don't work for you; they work against you.' You can leave some of the weeds," he said impatiently, waiting for Paul, who had stooped to tear at a tough root with his hands. "A very smart businesswoman, my wife. She stayed in Vienna to wind up the business and will come straight to America."

In March, a group of twenty arrived from Switzerland. It included Michel's huge, fat mother and his brother Robert with his wife and little daughter.

"Any news? Hitler dead yet?" the Sosuans asked.

"No news," the "Swiss" answered.

"If you happen to need any yams," Farber said to Mr. Langley, who had brought his new trainees to the field that Jesús and his partner were clearing for them, "I have a bushel—pink, very good quality—I could let DORSA have cheap."

Mr. Langley's face, under its tough outer skin, seemed to have fallen into a chaos of bewilderment. "Yams . . . I don't know that we need any more yams." Then he found firm ground. "Very enterprising of you, though, Farber. Very enterprising, indeed. If you go over to the office, I'll tell Mr. Sommerfeld to settle up with you."

"Farber, Farber," said Paul, "where did you get yams?"

"From a yam farmer, Paul," Farber said. "I tell you, Paul, there's no product for which a good salesman can't find a market, and no market for which a good salesman can't find a product. Paul, look at Godlinger weeding."

Paul looked, and saw Godlinger, with his sleeves rolled up over his pink arms and a handkerchief tied under his chin, leaning on his hoe talking to Mr. Langley. As they came closer, they heard Godlinger saying, "My brother is in Chicago working in a big fur company, by name of Silverman—maybe you know it?" and Mr. Langley answering, "I'm from Texas myself," in a pure Frankfurt accent.

"Mr. Langley, one moment," Paul said as Mr. Langley was swinging himself onto his horse. "Although I have had some farm training both in Vienna and England, my knowledge is necessarily limited, and in any case inapplicable to this new crop and unknown soil and season." He spoke with the circuitous courtesy he had used in speaking to his professors at the Vienna University. "I would like to mention, sir, that we would all benefit from more formal instruction. How long, for instance, does it take the yam to sprout after planting?"

Mr. Langley was shielding his eyes against the sun, looking toward Jesús and his partner, who were clearing the next field for a new group expected from Italy. He said, "How long it takes the yam plant to sprout, of course, depends, as you say, on the soil . . . the season. . . . I will talk to you about it when I come back from Puerto Plata. Two of my bulls are arriving from the States today."

"Mr. Langley, one other thing, sir," Paul said, talking very fast as he felt Mr. Langley's anxiety to get away from him. "What are the chances of bringing my parents to Sosua?"

"Talk to Sommerfeld about a visa," said Langley, as he set his horse in motion. "That's his problem."

"*Was singt der Schwarze?*" Farber asked Paul. "Come, Professor, you and Ilse always have your heads in your Spanish grammar. What's that black singing?"

Paul listened to Jesús, who stepped rhythmically behind his machete, singing,

> "*¿Dónde está Pedro?*
> *Ya no le veo.*
> *Ya me parece*
> *Que me tiene miedo.*"

Paul translated,

> "Where is Pedro?
> I don't see him.
> It seems to me
> He's afraid of me."

"Ask him—maybe he knows how long it takes yams to sprout," Farber said.

Paul spoke to the Dominican in the next field, and reported to Farber, "He says they would have come up two weeks ago if we hadn't ripped off the leaves and shoots. But he saw us do it—I remember him standing and watching from the road. Why didn't he say anything?"

Jesús said, "They will come up a week sooner, a week later."

"Why doesn't Langley tell us these things?" Paul cried, in a fury.

"*El Señor* Langley *no sabe nada,*" Jesús said. "He doesn't know anything. About bulls and cows he knows."

They returned to their work. Walking behind his machete, Jesús sang:

> "*El Señor* Langley
> *El no sabe nada.*
> *Ya me parece*
> *Que él tiene miedo.*"

Mr. Langley's two magnificent prize bulls arrived and were corralled. One never recovered from the seasickness of the crossing and died, but the other was put to work to improve the Sosua stock.

The "Swiss" had planted Farber's yams, and began weeding.

The "English" continued to weed their yams, which had sprouted according to Jesús' prediction, until Jesús spoke to them from the roadside. *"No se necesita.* The yam plant is hardy and kills its own weeds after the first weeks."

"Hey, Paul, let's not tell the 'Swiss,' " Farber said. "It might be bad for their morale to have nothing to do with themselves."

Meanwhile, the "English" joined the holidaying Batey people. Paul and Ilse spent the hot afternoons down on the beach; they studied their Spanish; they swam. Renate, Michel, Otto, and the young men at loose ends roughnecked in the mild breakers, or sat in the sun telling jokes and singing old student songs with new rude lyrics, or groused.

"Sosua, *ech,"* they said. "I wish the American quota would start moving."

"That Langley," they said, "with his phoney American accent. A Frankfurter is what he is."

They said, "That Sommerfeld, who does he think he is, making us paint the barracks? Doesn't he have enough *Schwarze* to do it?"

"Sommerfeld knows what he is doing. It took him less than a month to settle the 'Germans' in Laguna, to show the rich Americans and his bigwig Dominican friends what a high-powered administrator he is, but in the last eight months, not one single person has got settled."

"As soon as everyone is settled, Sommerfeld is out of a job. He's not such a fool."

"Sommerfeld is certainly no fool," Paul said, "though he does enjoy maneuvering and disposing of people. But think, what a job—settling three hundred urban Jews on virgin soil on a tropical island!"

"You think too much, Professor," someone said.

"Paul, you want to be our representative in the settlers' council?" Otto asked.

"Thanks, but no. No politics for me."

"It's hot," someone said. "Let's go for a ride."

Paul and Ilse watched the young people scramble up the rocky cliff path on which, presently, Godlinger came slithering down. Godlinger said, "I've been waiting at the administration building since morning, but Sommerfeld didn't have time for me today. I should try him tomorrow. Did you hear what the 'Italians' said about the new pogroms in Vienna? They said they are taking women now. I want Sommerfeld to bring my wife here."

"I went to see him last week about my parents," Paul said. "He showed me a list two pages long of settlers who want visas for their relatives."

"He said I should try him tomorrow," Godlinger said. He fell silent, sitting with his head on a pillow of sand, his handkerchief tied under his chin. His mouth fell open, and the corners of his lips drooped in a lonely way; he slept peacefully under the sun.

The yam field was covered with a mass of green leaves and pinkish blossoms. Paul took Ilse to see the swelling tubers cracking the earth, and, because the evening was sweet, they walked on in the direction of the native village. Presently Ilse began to tremble. "There's someone walking behind us."

Paul looked around. "It's Jesús, Ilselein. Jesús, *cómo está?* I've taken my wife to see the yams pushing up." Paul fell into step with the Dominican, wanting to practice his Spanish. "How long does it take for the yams to achieve their full size?"

"Five months, they get very, very big," Jesús said. "But if I were the *señor,* I would harvest them now. Once they show above the ground they are apt to be stolen. Good night to you and to the *señora.*" Jesús raised his hat to them, and pulled ahead so that they could see his back outlined against the dying brightness from the sea. His pockets bulged, unmistakably yam-shaped.

In May, Erich Marchfeld, a Viennese doctor for whom DORSA had furnished a makeshift hospital, pronounced Ilse pregnant. She was happy and nervous. Paul was very tender with her. He procured an extra pillow for her feet from the DORSA office; he drew diagrams for her on a piece of paper, to explain the growing of her womb and why it was making her feel ill.

The prospect of the infant in the *"Badekabine"* and the realization that there was no effective training program in Sosua persuaded Paul to begin application for a homestead. Michel and Otto came in with him. Michel was especially eager, for Renate had promised to marry him as soon as he was settled, saying, "What's the use of moving into the barracks and then moving again!" Otto kept making up hilarious lists of what they would need, and Paul found himself both chairman of the group and advocate for the realities. In the second week of June, the "Steiner Group," as they came to be known, carried their requisitions to the DORSA office. They were asking for five cows and one horse per family, one mule for the group, plus chickens, pigs and a two-wheeled cart, a tool shed for equipment, a place to store fertilizers, seeds, and crops, a milking shed, and three houses.

"And a thoroughly workmanlike list," said Director Sommerfeld. He was an elderly American of Polish extraction, a small, ugly man with a large head, furrowed like a bloodhound's, with moist little eyes and moist drooping lips. The three men stood before his desk in the carpeted front office. It was very sunny and still. Paul watched the director check the items one by one with his pencil. When Sommerfeld looked up, he said, "We're putting up a couple of houses in Bella Vista," and Paul felt ill with excitement and misgiving to think that he might be about to farm his own farm. "But I see," continued the director, "that you are asking for a three-house homestead."

"We have talked this over, sir," Paul said. "Michel has the care of his mother, but Otto could live with my wife and me for the present."

Director Sommerfeld nodded his great head and made a note in the margin. "And then who says we can't build a third house, eh?" he said, and raised his face, transformed by a smile of very great charm.

Paul said, "Sir, I would also like to mention that I have some farm experience—six weeks' training on a *Hachscharah* in Vienna and almost a year's farm work in England—though I'm very much aware that this is a mere beginning."

"A beginning—very well put. That's what we are all trying to accomplish here, my friends," the director said. "A bitter, bitter beginning. Let me talk this over with Mr. Langley, see what the situation is as regards livestock, and I will let you know. Good-by, gentlemen."

The three men made him little bows and turned toward the door, which had been opened from the outside to admit a burro carrying a man called Halsmann, from the Laguna settlement. He rode up to the director's desk, upon which he upturned a basket of tomatoes, shouting, "A present from me to DORSA! It has taken me five months to raise a tomato crop, which the DORSA kitchen won't buy because it gets tomatoes from the DORSA *colmado,* which gets tomatoes from Puerto Plata." He pulled his burro's head around as if he were setting an Arab stallion into a gallop and trotted the little animal out through the lobby and the front door. The Steiner Group had got to its knees after the rolling tomatoes, but Paul says he looked up surreptitiously and saw Director Sommerfeld, not at all discomfited, looking out of the window after the burro and rider with the open-mouthed interest of a child.

In July, Paul decided to remind Sommerfeld about the visa for his parents—afraid equally of making a nuisance of himself and of letting himself be forgotten. He went to the administration building, where he found Godlinger already sitting in the lobby. Shortly, Sommerfeld came through on his way to his office, and he said, "Godlinger, you are becoming a fixture here. I have no time for you today. I'm expecting Señor Rodriguez, the representative of our so-called benefactor, from Ciudad Trujillo. Paul Steiner, my friend!" he cried in the pleasantest fashion to my astonished uncle. "And how is our little mother-to-be? We must see about that homestead for you people, before the arrival of the son and heir!"

"If you would be so good, sir," Paul said. "But what I've come about today is to ask if there is any further opening for bringing my parents out of Austria."

"And my wife," said Godlinger.

"Tell me, Godlinger, you were a furrier in Vienna, were you not?"

"Yes, Director—'Godlinger Furs.' Maybe you have heard the name. On the Ringstrasse. I manufactured; my wife was in the shop. I have a brother in the business in Chicago."

"And you would like to join him there, would you not?"

Godlinger's face opened up with joy. "Oh, Mr. Sommerfeld, if that could be made possible . . ."

"And I suppose, Godlinger, you consider that for a furrier it is a waste of his time training to be a farmer! I suppose, with your mind on your fortunes in the U.S.A., you have no interest in Sosua. I would like to know, Godlinger, why you suppose that DORSA should take any interest in anything about you? If I had it in my power—which, however, I have not—to bring over anybody's relatives, I should bring over Steiner's here, who puts in a day's work in the field instead of sitting in the DORSA lobby. Rodriguez! My good friend!" cried Sommerfeld. He turned his charming smile on the tall, elegant Dominican who stood in the front door. "Walk in, walk in, and welcome to Sosua. I want you to meet two of our settlers, Godlinger and Steiner, who have been talking to me about getting visas for their relatives who are still in Germany—one of the subjects I want to persuade you to take up with the President, our good and great benefactor." He took his visitor by the elbow and propelled him into his office.

In the evening, the two men, nursing a magnum of champagne, were seen driving in the DORSA jeep to Puerto Plata, where they spent the night. Within the week after Señor Rodriguez' return to the capital, came letters from the President's office, granting certain privileges, including the return of two truckloads of lumber that had been extorted from the construction department, and thirty visas for the relatives of Sosua settlers. These Director Sommerfeld distributed according to a system known only to himself. None was given to either Godlinger or Paul, and only one to Halsmann of the Laguna Settlement, though he had both his own and his wife's parents to provide for. The Laguna people told of the hysterical weeping that came nightly from Halsmann's clapboard house.

In the second week of August, a batch of Red Cross letters

arrived. Farber saw Paul reading the familiar twenty-five-word form and asked, "Hitler dead yet?"

"No, but my parents were alive as of May twenty-eighth," Paul said. They were sitting at Bockmann's. Bockmann had started selling coffee and his wife's cake on the grass behind his house.

Dr. Marchfeld came over and said, "I've got Max Godlinger in my hospital. He's had news that his wife has been deported, and he's cracked up completely. He keeps saying he didn't put in enough work in the fields."

"Lieber Gott," Paul said, "I think I can explain that. . . ."

That week Sosua had its first suicide; one of the young men hanged himself in his room in the bachelor barracks and started the Sosua cemetery on the hill behind Bella Vista.

On the first of September, Michel Brauner heard through his brother Robert's little daughter, Susi, who had it from Hansi Neumann at school, that the Neumanns were to get the Bella Vista homestead. The Steiner Group went to the office to see Director Sommerfeld.

"What do you want from me?" Sommerfeld said. "You asked for a three-house homestead. Bella Vista has only two houses."

"But we talked about that, sir," Paul said. "You remember, we said we could do with two houses? You made a note."

"What note? Where? I don't see any note! Here on your list it says three houses. You can see for yourself. You are too big a group for the Bella Vista homestead."

"Sir, how about those houses going up in Barosa?"

"You're too small a group for the Barosa homestead. I'm settling the whole Swiss group as a unit."

"But they came after us," said Michel. "That's not fair!"

Sommerfeld was studying their list again. "I have a note here that Steiner trained for six weeks in Vienna," he said.

"On a *Hachscharah,* sir."

"And that makes you an expert, I suppose."

"And a year he worked in England," Otto said, aghast.

"I said it was a mere beginning," Paul said at the same time.

"Because you spent six weeks on a *Hachscharah,* I suppose you think it is unnecessary to avail yourself of our training program here. I spoke to Mr. Langley, and he says you have planted yams. You came in February. Now it is September, and you have planted yams. Go away, my friends, and train yourselves. Train, train, train! When you are ready, *then* come back and we will talk about a homestead."

It was November. The rainy season had set in. Ilse stayed in the *"Badekabine,"* "nesting," as Paul said, while he put on his mackintosh and went to the settlers' council. He had, after all, been chosen as one of three representatives to act as liaison between settlers and administration.

The meeting was a plenary session, held in the mess hall of one of the kitchens, and the mood was one of general complaint. Halsmann had lost two cows from overgrazing his pasture in the drought that had preceded the rain. He complained that Mr. Langley had been riding around the country buying up cattle for the huge Swiss settlement, so that when the Laguna people came with their hard-earned pennies, the *Schwarze* were asking fancy prices. "They say, 'That's what the Americano is paying,' but when *we* go to DORSA for three miserable cows, there are no more funds. Meanwhile, our respected representatives, whose job it is supposed to be to look out for our interests, are busy negotiating with Sommerfeld about chairs and tables for Bockmann, here, to open himself a little café in the Batey—"

"Listen, Halsmann, you loudmouth," said Bockmann, rising so that he appeared to be thrusting his large bland face into the other man's red, irate face across the width of the room. "I owned the best café on the Prater Allee, and the Nazis confiscated it, sent me to Theresienstadt, and took my oldest son to Poland, and I'd like to know if I shouldn't be entitled to five tables and twenty chairs to put up in the grass back of my house."

"They took away my slaughterhouse," said Halsmann, "which supplied half of Frankfurt, and I'd like to know what it would hurt DORSA to give me three miserable cows."

"You've had three cows, Halsmann. You've had six cows. Nine

cows," said Otto Becker. "Listen, I worked in the office. I know exactly how many cows you have had."

"Let me tell you," Bockmann said, "that when I get my tables and chairs I won't keep coming back for handouts. *I* happen to know how to run a café."

"So that the people in the Batey can sit more comfortably on their fat behinds," said Neumann, who had recently moved to the Bella Vista homestead and looked sick with worry and overwork.

"And they, if you please, get *their* mothers and *their* brothers brought over here!" Halsmann shouted, looking at little Michel Brauner, who flushed scarlet. "While I, who have been working for thirty hours a day for two years, can't get a visa for my wife's parents!"

Dr. Marchfeld spoke in a chilly, still voice, without rising from his chair. "And you would encourage Sommerfeld's method for punishing those who are so unfortunate as not to have been settled yet by refusing them the salvation of their nearest relatives. I'd like to remind you, it's a method that has driven Godlinger out of his mind."

Paul, who had been looking from one to the other, stood up. "Gentlemen, if I might have the floor," he said.

"*Ja, ja,* Steiner," Halsmann said. "You are going to explain the whole thing to us." Paul felt his mind deliciously clear and his words so easy that he laughed. "Halsmann," he said, "rest awhile. Let me talk. If I'm not mistaken, we were considering whether DORSA, which has driven the price of cattle out of the range of Halsmann's pocket (which may or may not be empty as a result of his own mismanagement), should or should not supply Halsmann with three more miserable cows. However, through inattention, I suppose, I lost the thread of the discussion. We seem now to be considering the question of Halsmann's responsibility for the deportation of Max Godlinger's wife. . . ." Looking around him, Paul saw that he had the attention of the assembly. Afterward, Otto Becker put his arm around Paul as they walked out together into the rain, which was still coming down with a steady intensity. "That was telling them, Professor."

"Old loudmouth Steiner, eh?" Paul said and laughed. He was

looking forward to telling Ilse how he had taken over the meeting, for here at last he had found something he was good at.

In the barracks, Ilse was lying on the bed.

"Are you ill?" Paul asked.

"Oh, no, it's just that when you're not doing anything in particular in this *'Badekabine'* the only thing to do is get into bed—especially when it's raining outside. Renate was here all afternoon. She has left Michel."

"Poor old Michel," Paul said. "He's been getting it from all sides today. Halsmann gave him a hard time at the meeting. What excuses did Renate have?"

"She says that in Berlin Michel was going to be a doctor, but now he'll never do anything, and she can't remember why she ever said she would marry him. She's sorry for him. She cried."

"Well, when she dries her eyes," Paul said, "she can marry Otto."

"She says Otto isn't an intellectual."

"Poor Renate, she has swallowed culture and doesn't know how to digest it."

"It's you she likes, you know," Ilse said.

"Me!"

"I was terrible to her," Ilse said. "I used to just love to talk about quarrels and boy friends, but all afternoon while she sat here talking I kept wishing she would get off the bed, because I needed the space to put your shirts. Look, I put all the long sleeves together and all the short sleeves, and I rearranged the suitcase to make a space for the baby's things. And don't you notice anything? I've moved the furniture. The washstand is where the chair used to be and the chair is where the washstand used to be. Don't you think it makes the room look bigger?"

That year, the seasons behaved unnaturally. In December, the rain stopped and there was an intense wave of heat. Mr. Langley started a program of instruction in animal husbandry. Paul came back from the sun-struck fields and found Ilse lying on the bed, crying with fright. She said she had been bleeding. "Poor Pauli," she said, "you look so exhausted, and now I'm worrying you."

"Ilselein, I'm just tired, and you're not worrying me. Where's the diagram I drew you? You remember what I told you about the baby descending?"

Ilse said, "Tell me about the first time you saw a baby born."

"All right, you lie back." He told her once again about the first delivery he had attended as a medical student. There had been the laboring woman, the doctor, the nurse, and Paul Steiner the student—four people in the room. And in an instant the baby had come out and there were five people.

The next day Paul stopped off at the hospital. Dr. Marchfeld said, "Paul, you're looking green."

"You, too! Ilse keeps feeling sorry for me. I'm just tired. Have you ever tried to corral six calves that would rather stay with their mothers? I thought I was going to get used to the heat, but I'm minding it even more this year. Also, we didn't sleep last night. That's what I've come to ask you about. Erich, why is Ilse bleeding?"

"All right, old colleague. What does bleeding in the last month of pregnancy suggest to you?"

"*Placenta previa,*" Paul said, with the tiny satisfaction of someone producing his credentials in good order; at the same time, a slow terror started hot between his shoulder blades. "Do you think it would be better to get her to the hospital in Puerto Plata?"

"Certainly, it would be better, but under the circumstances I'm not going to risk her starting labor on that infernal road. We'll keep our eye on her here."

In their room, Paul found Ilse whimpering in panic. He ran for the doctor, but by the time they arrived back at the barracks Ilse's blood was gushing in fantastic quantities, and the baby, deprived of the oxygen that the ruptured placenta had carried away, had suffocated. "Poor Pauli," Ilse said.

"Poor nobody," the doctor said. "Paul, sit on that chair, and Ilse, put your head down." He spoke so briskly that Paul looked up with a wild leap of hope, but the doctor's face was a dark red. Beads of sweat stood along his hairline.

All night Paul sat by Ilse's head. He massaged her hand. Her face was a blotchy dough color, with great bruised eyes. She said, "I wish, Pauli, you could lie down for a bit."

"I wish you would stop worrying about me, because that's more tiring than anything!"

She looked startled, but she was quiet after that, and he must have closed his eyes, because he awoke to see Dr. Marchfeld folding up a towel.

The doctor said, "She is dead, Paul. You go and get cleaned up."

Paul said, "I shouted at her. I just wanted to speak with her once more."

The doctor said, "I'll have her taken over to the hospital. Get yourself a clean shirt. Come."

"I just wanted to speak with her," Paul said.

Dr. Marchfeld pointed him toward the washroom.

In the shower, Paul came totally awake. His head was very clear. He even felt the pleasantness of the clean cotton shirt on his freshly dried skin, and already he saw how he would live in the future—perfectly normal in his actions and perceptions, and perfectly unfeeling within.

Paul was putting things away in the suitcase when Otto came in. "That goddam quack doctor!" Otto said, and began to cry.

Paul took a piece of paper and drew a line on an imaginary graph. "It's more complicated than a wrong diagnosis, or wrong treatment," Paul said. "I know. I was a medical student. I've heard doctors say, 'If only this happens' " (Paul crossed his time line), " 'before this happens' " (he crossed it farther along), " 'in this five minutes I can save a life.' "

"Don't *defend* him!" Otto said. "I've brought you some coffee."

"No, thank you," Paul said.

"Just have a little coffee," Otto said, and looked so desperate that Paul said, "We'll both have some. There are two tooth glasses on the washstand."

Otto stayed with Paul for a week, going about his business by day and returning at night full of Sosua news. Frau Halsmann had left her husband and moved to the Batey. Among the new group from Luxembourg was a woman called Sarah Hankel, who had almost been left behind because where the emigration form said "Profession," she had written "prostitute," and the emigration officer had made her tear it up and start over. Two of the men were escapees from concentration camps, and Otto told Paul the stories they were telling, which were still new in those days. The next morning Paul went to see Sommerfeld about visas for his parents, not hesitating to use the blackmail of his recent tragedy.

The news of the death of Paul's young wife came to us in England. It struck home at my unsatisfied youth, my dream of love. I was in such awe of this Paul who had had love and lost it that it was years before I dared write to him.

Paul answered with an extraordinary letter in which he wrote— still as if he were speaking of some third persons—about "two people spun in their cocoon of passion and pioneer dreams, in a world in explosion, too fantastic to be believed while it had lasted. When that chapter of tenderness was over, Paul was left numb and sober. He knew he must not die, because his parents were still in Vienna and would be lost if he did not help them, and that meant incessant begging and badgering at the DORSA office, perhaps for a long time. He knew this with a clear head and a dead heart."

My grandparents did not, in fact, get to Sosua until September of the following year. My grandmother, at the time a sick woman, was brought off the boat on a stretcher. Paul procured a three-cornered pillow from the DORSA office so my grandmother could sit upright through her sleepless nights. He massaged her feet and brought her three meals a day from the communal kitchen, which my grandmother, herself a beautiful and fastidious cook, was unable to eat. She was convinced that Paul's recent stomach upsets had been caused by the oil used in the kitchen. Paul saw the necessity of getting a house of their own, and, rousing himself out of the lethargy in which he had lived the last year, reorganized the defunct Steiner Group. After the marriage of Renate and Otto, Michel had withdrawn, but Michel's older brother, Robert, wanted to get out of the large "Swiss" group, and came in with them.

My grandmother was dead against the idea. "What kind of a farmer is Paul going to be? He was never any good with his hands. Besides, look at him—he isn't strong enough."

"It's my nature to look starved, Muttilein. I'm feeling much better."

"We should move to town and open a little shop like our shop in Fischamend," said my grandmother.

"No," said Paul. "No, no, no. No little shop."

The group returned hopelessly from their talk with Sommerfeld. Building in Sosua had virtually stopped since America's entry into the war. There was a shortage of money and building materials of every kind. Paul and my grandfather went to work in the DORSA storeroom. My grandmother, who had recovered her health, quarreled with Renate and refused to speak with Frau Halsmann, who was having an affair with one of the boys from the bachelor barracks, eleven years her junior. It was not till the spring of 1944 that the homestead at Ferrocarril was completed and offered to the Steiner Group.

During the middle years of the war, Sosua's economy became integrated into that of the rest of the country. Its harvests were considerable, and Sosua cattle—the offspring of Mr. Langley's prize bull—brought good prices in a market already driven high by the wartime shortage. There was a boom in tortoise-shell Mogen Davids after Farber had stocked the general store (of which he was now the manager) and given his new Dominican wife one to wear around her neck when she visited home. His onetime partner in the tortoise-shell business was left with an oversupply of crosses, which he had intended for the native market; for a while, the two men did not speak to one another. The experimental dairy cooperative was showing profits for everyone except my grandmother, who had been forbidden to sell the butter and cottage cheese she made in her own kitchen, and when she went to Bockmann's café—which now served hot Viennese dinners and had a one-lane bowling alley—she sat at a corner table and would not speak to *anyone*.

In the midst of the general prosperity, the new Steiner home-

stead was having its first hard years. Paul's eggplant harvest had
failed, each fruit rotting at the point of contact with the earth.
"It may be just my two left hands," Paul said, "but next time I'm
going to try planting a month earlier and harvesting before the
rain sets in—with one corner planted the same as this year, for
a control. That should eliminate the wet-ground factor, unless the
rains start a month early or half a dozen unknown factors get in
the way. Oi! I'll do it on my own time."

"On your own time, you should sit a little," my grandmother
said.

"I'm afraid to sit. I may not want to get up again," Paul joked.

But his strength was seeping out of him. He felt the heat as a
persecution that never let up. Every job he did seemed to him in-
adequately done and needing to be done over more carefully, and
he forced himself to do it again.

The second harvest was not as bad a failure as the first, but the
homestead needed a substantial additional loan from DORSA,
and Paul's health had broken. My grandmother nursed him and
cooked for him and talked to him about starting a shop in town.

The war was over. Hitler was dead. Renate persuaded Otto to
move back to the Batey and take over the Sosua trucking conces-
sion to carry the produce of the dairy co-operative and the new
privately owned sausage factory to the town markets. Robert
Brauner, wanting to have the entire homestead under his control,
bought out Paul's share, and Paul opened the little shop in Santiago.

I remember once, when Paul and I were walking in Santiago
together, we talked about Ilse. Neither of us mentioned her name.
I had asked Paul if a person in the first throes of loss wants to be
left alone or to be nursed along, and Paul said the person wants to
be left alone but that he had been helped by Otto's presence. "The
very irritation of having him there acted as a distraction. In the
moments I had to be talking to him, I could not concentrate on
the pain." Paul said that he had recently found three lines of a
poem in his head. "And I know they are about my poor wife:

"You are like the moonlight in the day,
Invisible—yet perceived
By the heedless heart no longer grieved.

It's just like me to have the first three lines of a poem that I don't know what to do with," he said.

"Pauli," I said, "what are you going to do with yourself?"

"Try and make a go of the shop until our quotas come. In America, I'll try and get a job—perhaps in a laboratory, where my medical training might be useful."

"I don't mean just that," I said. "You never go anywhere."

"Don't worry about me, Lorle."

"But I do," I said, and I felt like crying. "Omama didn't even want you to go for a walk this evening, for goodness' sake."

"I'm afraid your Omama cares more for my being home than I care for going out."

"But you have to make a stand, Pauli."

"No, I don't," Paul said. "I'm too old to make a stand on principle. If I should ever find anything I want to do enough to make a stand, I will, I promise you. But there's nothing, Lorle, that I want."

CHAPTER TEN

Santiago de los Caballeros:
Omama and Opapa

It was in hot, late summer that I arrived in Ciudad Trujillo. My
mother met me at the pier, and we took a chartered taxi, which,
in the absence of a railroad, carried the better class of passengers
across country.

My mother, who had not seen me in two years, sat looking at
me while I looked out of the window not liking this new country
where I was going to live. The mountainous areas seemed brash
and new, lacking in composition; the plains were sunburned and
monotonous except for the miserable palm-leaf shacks and occasional bursts of gross, oversized vegetation. Over all stood the
unrelieved, unlovely white heat of the sky. At every crossroads,
we stopped at the little inspection posts. The soldiers joked with the
driver and the three chatty Dominicans in the back seat, who were
putting up good-naturedly with the heat, the noisy *merengue* on
the car radio, and the road rattling beneath us.

I was feeling sick and I leaned out of the window, but even the
breeze raised by our motion felt secondhand and warmed-over.
I thought there would be relief when we stopped for lunch in one
of the small, hot, towns, but the taxi-driver led us into a flyblown
restaurant where a crippled Chinaman served us hot fried chicken,
rice, and warm Coca-Cola.

When we got back into the car, which was now the temperature of a greenhouse, the driver turned the *merengue* on the radio to full volume. By midafternoon, we arrived in Santiago.

Santiago de los Caballeros is a dusty native town lying inland and low between mountains. It has narrow streets and painted wooden houses. Across the first floor of each house runs a narrow *galería*, where people rock in rocking chairs or stand leaning on the painted, turned-wood balustrades.

"That's ours, the yellow house," said my mother, and there on the veranda stood my family, smiling and smiling. I could tell that they were fantastically pleased to have me there. They had last seen me when I was ten years old, and now I was twenty. I saw that my grandmother was wearing the same kind of hairnet and striped-calico apron she had worn in Fischamend, and I remembered how bald and frail my grandfather was. But Paul, bespectacled, skinny, and hook-nosed, was different from the person I had been remembering all these years. They all escorted me along the *galería* into the front room, which had been converted into a little grocery shop, with neat, well-stocked shelves, scales, meat slicer, and cash register. The adjoining living room had bare wooden walls and a wooden floor and strange windows that had no glass, Paul explained, so that what little air came in might circulate.

"Lorle, look! Pauli had this piano here for me the day I arrived," my mother said.

"Would you like to sit in my rocking chair?" my grandfather asked me in his thick Hungarian accent.

"She would like to sit at the table and have coffee and cake," my grandmother said, aping him, as I remembered her doing in my childhood.

"*Ja so,*" said my grandfather.

I was excited. "This is all so strange and familiar! *Sacher Torte* with *Schlagobers* in San Domingo, and eating in a room next to the shop so that someone can watch the door, the way we always did in Fischamend."

"Do you remember, Lorle, how much we used to laugh?" my mother asked.

"Do you remember," my grandmother said, "once your parents were on a holiday and you stayed with us. You badgered me to let you sell something, so I showed you where the shoelaces were kept and said you could wait on the next person who asked for shoelaces, and the next person who came in asked for shoelaces and you laughed so much you had to run to the bathroom?"

A customer came into the grocery, and Paul and my mother and my grandfather all rose. Each said, "You sit. I'll go."

"Franzi will go," said my grandmother. "Sit down, Joszi."

My mother returned and reported, "That was Mercedes. Five cents' worth of butter for Señora Molinas' boy friend."

"Hey," I said, "do you think you would have recognized me if you had seen me in the street?"

Paul said he would not, but my grandmother said that I had a certain look of Ibolya, her eldest sister. "Around the eyes. Your Great-aunt Sari had light eyes like that; the boys all had dark eyes like me."

"Take off your glasses, Omama," I said. "You didn't always wear glasses, did you? You have real black eyes."

"I remember once in the Kaffee Norstadt, in Vienna," said my grandmother, "I was waiting for Joszi and I looked up and in the door stood Miklos Gottlieb, staring at me. He came over and said, 'Frau Rosa, you haven't changed. Your eyes are as black as ever.' That was years after I had married Joszi."

"Your Omama always had beautiful eyes—black eyes, like a gypsy," said my grandfather.

"Eat up, Joszi," my grandmother said, "and go upstairs and get ready for the doctor."

"*Ja so,* the doctor," said my grandfather.

"I'll do the dishes. You sit, Muttilein," my mother said, but my grandmother said, "You stay in the shop with Paul. I don't like him to be alone."

"Why can't Paul be alone in the shop?" I asked as I helped my grandmother carry the dishes into the kitchen. "There are no customers now."

"You never know who will come in. This is not Europe. These people go around with knives."

"All of them? Every single one of them, Omama?" I asked, and my grandmother and I would have had our first argument there and then if my mother had not called me from the living room. "Come, Lorle, here are some friends to meet you. This is my Lore. Herr and Frau Freiberg have come to say hello and good-by. They're going back to Vienna the day after tomorrow. Please sit down. I will get coffee."

"Aber bitte, don't make yourself any work for us. We did not come to eat."

The Freibergs were a middle-aged couple and completely uninteresting, I thought. "Are you going back for good?" I asked Frau Freiberg.

"You know how it is here—this heat," said Frau Freiberg. "No good for our people." She turned down the corners of her mouth at the Dominican Republic. "Look at your Uncle Paul. Herr Paul, you're not looking well. You should come back to Vienna and finish your medical studies."

Paul said, "Vienna threw me out of the university. I prefer to broil in a Santiago grocery."

"I have a sister there," said Frau Freiberg, "and her boy Edi, who was like my own. I haven't seen him since he was three—imagine; now he's fourteen. You should see the letters he writes. Sigi, you have Edi's last letter? They were hiding out in Holland all through the war. Terrible! I lost my brother in Poland, but Elli and the boy are back in their own flat on the Ringstrasse."

"Ah, Vienna! *'Wien, Wien, Nur Du Allein,'* " sang Herr Freiberg. "The music, the food, the women—eh, Paul?"

His wife said, *"Ja, ja,* I'd like to know what you think you can do about the women!"

"What are you going to do professionally?" I asked.

They both turned down the corners of their mouths and shrugged their shoulders.

"Sigi has connections. Have you got the letter here, Sigi, from

Karl Haber—that's a friend of Sigi's from his old glee club, the
Wiener Gesangverein. Aha, Frau Steiner!" They both rose and
shook hands with my grandmother, who had come in from the
kitchen. "How is poor Herr Steiner? And how is it to have your
big granddaughter?"

My grandmother nodded her head sidewise with a strange smile
and sat down a little back and sidewise, and when the Freibergs
had gone she said to my mother, "How is it that when people come
you don't call me? Lore you call, but not me."

"I called you," said my mother, dumfounded.

"I heard you clearly. You said, 'Lore, here are friends to see
you.' Not a word about me."

"*Aber* Mutti," my mother began, just as Paul came to the
door, saying, "Lorle, this is Herr and Frau Grüner, Rudi Grüner.
My niece Lore."

My grandmother got up and went back to the kitchen.

The Grüners were younger but no less vulgar, I thought, than
the Freibergs. They had brought me a piece of the jewelry that
they manufactured and sold—a dreadful tortoise-shell brooch
stuck with imitation pearls. Their great white fat son Rudi sat down
in the rocking chair and said not a word.

I chatted with Mrs. Grüner. "You and your mother must come
over and have tea with us Sundays," she said. "We just love your
mother, and we wish we could see more of her."

Paul came in with a dapper little man in a white suit, carrying
a boater. "This is Doctor Perez, Opapa's doctor."

Dr. Perez had a pleasant, mobile face that frowned and wrinkled
to illustrate what he was saying. He shook my hand with both
of his, saying, "You are very—how you say? *Muy linda*—very
beau-ti-ful," and he leered at me in the friendliest way, as if he
liked me a lot. He said, "We are—*cómo se dice?* Neighbors. You
know it?"

"Doctor Perez has a very lovely daughter. Juanita is eighteen,
isn't she?" my mother asked, looking unhappy all the while, because she had inadvertently hurt my grandmother's feelings.

"Maybe you tich English?" Dr. Perez suggested.

"First, I better learn Spanish," I said, and before Herr and Frau Grüner left, they forced Rudi into offering to come and give me Spanish lessons.

Afterward, my mother went to fetch my grandmother out of the kitchen, but my grandmother said, "I heard Frau Grüner ask you and Lore to visit, but I notice she didn't ask me."

"Mutti," said my mother, "it's just because Lorle and I were in the room and you were not. I know she wants you to come."

But my grandmother could not forgive my mother. She said, "Ibolya and Sari were going to a *Kranzerlball* once, the year I turned sixteen—so Ibolya must have been nineteen, and Sari eighteen—and there were a lot of young people. I remember Miklos Gottlieb was there, and my mother said, 'Why don't you take Rosa along?' but then, of course, I wouldn't go." And it was clear my grandmother had not forgiven her sisters in a lifetime.

Upstairs, the three areas—where my grandmother and grandfather slept, where Paul slept, and where my mother and I slept—were separated from one another only by swinging gates like the barroom doors in Western movies. When I awoke next morning, my watch said eight. Everyone was already downstairs, and the room was bright as noon. A *merengue* was blasting from a radio across the street. I leaned out of the window. The street was a walking market, with peddlers in straw hats calling out their vegetables and girls in shredded rags of dresses carrying baskets classically on their heads. A donkey loaded down with sacks of pineapple had come to a standstill at the corner. On its bare back a woman sat sidewise, smoking a cigar, suckling a baby, and curling her toes to keep hold of her flopping slippers while she kicked the animal in the stomach and beat it with a cactus across the ears. A man wrapped in a feather coat stopped under my window and I saw that the coat was made up of a couple of dozen chickens strung together by the legs and hanging from the pole he carried across his shoulders; more chickens were draped around his neck and tied to his belt. I thought the birds were dead, until my grandmother appeared on the *galería* and poked them under the feathers so that they flapped their wings and squawked as if she were tickling them.

"*Cuánto?*" asked my grandmother in the irate voice of someone expecting to be cheated. "*Cómo?* Forty centavos? You think you can take advantage of me, because I don't speak Spanish!" she said very loudly in German. "You think I don't know you charge Señora Molinas only twenty-five centavos! I'll give you twenty-five centavos. No? *Adiós*," and she turned away.

"Señora! *Qué venga!* Thirty centavos," the chicken man called. My grandmother came back and counted the pennies one by one into the cup of his huge dusty black hand. The chicken man raised his face to my window, showing the gap where his front teeth should have been, and started a loud Spanish wailing, which I took to be a justified indictment of my grandmother.

When I came downstairs, she was quarreling with Pastora, the maid. Pastora was a little hideous black woman who gave the impression of being misshapen. Over her petticoat she wore a piece of black gauze torn along the bottom and sewed together down the back with large loose stitches. I could tell that Pastora was dressed up, but my grandmother was taking off her own ankle-length calico apron, saying, "Wrap yourself in this. Tell her, Paul."

My grandmother's great eyes were popping, her nose an angry beak. Her hairline was hidden by the elastic of the net under which her hair was flattened—not unlike the *schaitel*, or wig, that separates Orthodox Jewish wives from freewheeling womanhood. "No shame!" my grandmother was saying. "Coming out like that on the *galería* in front of the chicken man. Go upstairs. Go! Make the beds. And no shoes. Disgusting. You can see her toes. Children, breakfast! Lore! Joszi! Pauli!" called my grandmother, not mentioning my mother.

"Franzi," Paul said when everybody was sitting down, "I wish you wouldn't come down at six every morning. Let me have half an hour by myself to do my exercises."

"If Franzi doesn't want to come down, I will," said my grandmother, without looking at my mother. "I don't want you to be alone in the shop, Pauli."

"I want to get up, Muttilein," said my mother, stroking her hand over my grandmother's arm. "You don't have to come down."

"I don't open the shop till half past six," Paul said. "I'm physically in bad shape these days. By lunchtime I'm good for nothing, and I find that if I do half an hour of exercises every morning, in the nude, I feel better all day."

"But you, Vater," my mother said to my grandfather, "you needn't come down so early. The doctor wants you to take it very easy."

"But I have always come down after I am awake," my grandfather said. "And I have to tidy the shelves and have everything in good order before the shop opens. Mutter, you could take an extra hour of sleep. Paul and I can get our own breakfast."

"Typical," Paul said to me. "Have you noticed how the members of Jewish families can't bear to see each other work?"

(The following morning, at six o'clock, my mother heard Paul downstairs and leaped out of bed to go and help him. After that, Paul tried being down by five-thirty, but my mother always heard him.)

When breakfast was over, I carried the dishes into the kitchen and found my grandmother already at the sink, whipping on her toes like a tennis player waiting for service, plucking the chicken.

"Omama, why are you starting lunch at half past eight?" I asked.

"The soup," my grandmother said. "I'm already late. Thirty cents for this skinny bird. This will never make a soup like our Fischamend hens—and look at these miserable carrots."

"Would you like me to clean them for you?"

"If you like. Not with that knife—with this, and beautifully. Don't peel. Scrape."

"What difference does it make so long as they are clean?"

"All the difference if you work beautifully or not."

"Omama, how come you don't use some of those wonderful local vegetables they were selling in the street?"

"They're no good for us," said my grandmother, and as my

mother appeared in the doorway she said, "Franzi, you do the
carrots. Use this knife, and scrape." Which was the first time my
grandmother had addressed my mother directly since my mother
had forgotten to call her when the Freibergs had come to see me
last night. My mother's face broke in relief, and she went and
embraced my grandmother and kissed her.

I walked away. For the rest of the morning I hung around the
shop. The shop was called *Productos de Sosua,* because it sold
the specialty cheeses and sausages made in the settlement, but its
main business was a brisk traffic of our poor neighbors coming
all morning for infinitesimal quantities of staples.

At twelve o'clock, we sat down around a table covered with
the same kind of ugly, shiny oilcloth my grandmother had had
on the table in Fischamend. My grandmother stood lightly on her
toes, ladling out the beautiful burnished soup. She filled each plate
only two-thirds full, and the smallness of the amount was in
direct proportion to the undiluted strength of its taste; it was the
nature of my grandmother's soup that it was all gone before the
surprise of its delicate, strong essences, as varied on the tongue
as wine.

"A wonderful soup, Mutter," said my grandfather from under
his mustache. "As long as I have been married to your grandmother, every meal was a surprise and a pleasure," he said.

"Eat, don't talk," said my grandmother. "Eat, Paul. Eat, Lore."

After lunch, my grandparents went to rest upstairs, just as they
had always done in Fischamend. I said I was going to stay with
Paul.

"Paul will want to rest, too," my mother warned me on her way
to her room.

Paul said, "Well, my grown-up niece Lore!" He sat down on
the rocking chair. From there he could watch the shop. "Not that
anybody comes during the siesta hour."

The street was silent. The noon brightness seemed trapped inside
the room despite closed shutters; the heat was intense. Paul had
laid out his account books, but his head began to drop, nod by
nod, until it hit his chest and he snapped awake, setting the rocker

in motion as he leaped to the door of the shop, which stood empty except for an excess of light. He came back and sat down, saying, "This rocking chair is a mistake. Tomorrow is Thursday. The Sosua truck will be here and I don't have my order ready." He drew the account books determinedly toward him and fell asleep. Where his head came to rest upon his shoulder, a pool of sweat formed on his shirt. Little by little, he lost that hold with which sleepers in public places still keep themselves erect, slipping forward on the hard wooden seat until his legs buckled at the knees.

When my grandparents came downstairs at half past two, my grandmother stood in the door looking with pity and something of her habitual anger at her sleeping son. Then she laughed. Paul opened one eye. My grandmother said, "I wish you would come over here and look how uncomfortable you look sleeping over there."

Paul laughed and sat up.

The heat had imperceptibly lessened. One could forget to think about it. The *merengue* had started up outside. The street was coming awake—not commercially, as in the morning, but socially, like an outdoor drawing room. Little Señora Molinas, a child-sized, gray-faced woman, came out and rocked on her pink *galería* next door, watching Mercedes, the little seven-year-old servant girl, feed a plate of rice and beans to Señora Molinas' baby, América Columbina.

"You see that skinny woman all in black on the *galería* across the street, talking to Doctor Perez?" Paul asked me. "They are nodding to us. —*Cómo está?*— She is known as 'La Viuda,' 'The Widow,' though she has never been married. She lived in that house with a younger brother, an anti-Trujilloist, who talked too much and was fetched away, the story goes, seven years ago and is in jail in the city. She's been wearing mourning, in protest, ever since. On the veranda next to her, rocking in the chair, is Señora Perez, the doctor's wife, with her daughter Juanita."

"Did you notice the Molinas baby's crooked foot?" Paul asked me over our coffee. "There's so much of that here, and they've never heard about remedial exercises. I have thought of applying for a correspondence course that one of the Southern universities in the United States is giving. With a diploma and my medical background, I could make myself a small clientele here, and later, perhaps, give up the shop and move to Ciudad Trujillo."

"We're not going to move to Ciudad Trujillo," my grandmother said. "And you don't need any diploma."

"Don't, Omama!" I whispered.

"What 'Don't, Omama! Don't, Omama!' "

"Don't discourage Paul when he wants to do something."

"Paul has always wanted to do everything except what he was supposed to do. He never passed his exams in medical school, because he was writing poetry and messing with politics. Now it's remedial exercises."

"Well, what is he supposed to do here?" I said, enraged.

"Concentrate on the shop, which is going into the ground, just as every business his father ever started went into the ground," said my grandmother. "When we had our stationery shop in Vienna after we were married, I said to him, 'Joszi, if you don't have the courage to borrow capital and stock up properly, you may as well close down.' Of course, we went bankrupt and had to move to Fischamend, where we were the only Jews and I had to send my children away to Vienna to school. In Fischamend, I said to Joszi, 'If you keep giving credit upon credit to these anti-Semites, the shop will go into the ground.' But the Nazis repaid him—they took the whole shop away before it could go bankrupt."

I had gone to my grandfather's chair. From behind, I clasped my hands around his thin chest to shield him from my grandmother's words, but he said, "Your Omama is perfectly right. She was always a better businesswoman than I."

"Ah, you think I am being cruel to your grandfather," my grandmother said, with her bright black eyes on me. "Many people have thought so, but they have not been married to him."

Later in the afternoon, Señora Rodriguez came to take a piano lesson from my mother. She was a German woman, married to the Dominican diplomat. They had a large summer home just outside

Santiago. The señora carried herself very straight and wore her hair in a complex and perfect coiffure of interwoven braids. Her eyes were bright blue and her lips looked thin, as if she were feeding inwardly on them. While my mother was out of the room, Señora Rodriguez told me how much she valued her. "She is a wonderful human being. When you have lived in this country awhile, you will understand how necessary it is to have someone with whom you can really talk and make music. I've been trying to persuade her to come to the capital. I could get her piano pupils. I was telling your daughter, Frau Franzi, how you could come to town and stay with us till you got settled."

My mother made Señora Rodriguez play Czerny, and outside the window the neighbors gathered to listen. She played a Bach prelude and fugue, and the neighbors took one another by the hands and danced.

Before she left, Señora Rodriguez invited all of us to come to tea on Sunday, but my grandfather begged off on account of his health, and Paul on account of my grandfather. Afterward, Paul told me the Rodriguezes were Nazis.

"Are all Germans Nazis? Are there no exceptions?" I asked.

"All Germans have the tendency, and, yes, there are exceptions," Paul said. "But Rodriguez was made consul-general in Frankfurt in his twenties and fell in love with Germany and married it and brought it back here intact."

I was ready to argue, but the shop was filling with the afternoon rush of business.

After supper, when there was only a trickle of customers, I said, "Let me sell something."

Paul showed me where the butter was kept, and presently came little Mercedes from next door. She looked, from her gray bare feet and washed-out rag dress to her laughing gray-black face, as if she were covered with a layer of dust, out of which her two eyes shone with an unnatural brightness. She curled herself up on the floor under the counter, giggling and making faces at me behind her spread fingers.

"All right, Mercedes," Paul said, leaning over the counter to pat her on the head. "No time to play. *Que quieres, tú?* What do you want?"

"*Cinco centavos de mantequilla.*"

"Mercedes wants five cents' worth of butter for Señora Molinas' boy friend, Lore!" I weighed out the pat of butter under Paul's direction, and my grandmother came and checked it and found it overweight and shaved off the hair's breadth that made it exact.

"Omama!"

"With these small quantities," my grandmother explained, "always weigh correctly, because our profit gets eaten up with waste and work and wrapping. The people who buy a lot have to get extra weight."

"But that's not fair!" I cried.

"When I was a boy, my father has had an inn," my grandfather said from the door in his slow Hungarian voice. (I remember that it was always a surprise to me to hear my grandfather speak and that his speaking lips were always turned up in the faintest smile. My mother says he once told her that he sometimes thought of things to say, but when he thought of saying them it seemed too much trouble trying to say them in German.) "Every market day the farmers come back from town and they get drunk. My father said, 'Körmöczi, you had nine slivovitzes,' when he had only eight."

"But that's robbery!" I cried.

"Yes," said my grandfather. "Have I ever told you when I was a boy the chieftain of the robbers took me to school? There was a robber band in the forest between our village and the town, and in spring and autumn my father left a barrel of Tokay at the edge of the forest, and in return Betyár Bácsi—Uncle Robber, I used to call him—fetched me and put me in front of him on his horse and took me to school. In the evening, he brought me back."

In my mind's eye the shop in Santiago with its counter and cash register had faded into a deep-green forest out of the Brothers Grimm, with a dozen robbers in green hunting suits.

"All right, Joszi, go inside. You don't have to stand," said my grandmother.

"*Ja so,*" said my grandfather and went and sat down inside.

The rest of us moved out on the *galería* together, leaning on the balustrade, talking.

"What did your father do, Omama?" I asked my grandmother.

"Produce children," my grandmother said. My grandmother had a goiter, and whenever she was angry it swelled, setting her head back with a handsome look of pride.

"He was a wine merchant, wasn't he?" Paul asked.

"Later. When we came to Vienna, he was nothing and he had nothing—a wife and five children. Ibolya must have been seven, and there was Sari and I and Kari and poor Ferri, who was only a baby. Him we had to leave in Hungary with the grandparents, and Mother cried all the way to Vienna. Three weeks later, she had Wetterl, who is in Paraguay now. We had two rooms and a kitchen, and every year Mother lay down in the big bed in the back room and had another baby and gave it to us girls to look after. After Wetterl there was Pista and then Hilde, who is in Canada now—" and my grandmother went down the gallery of her thirteen brothers and sisters. "There were little children everywhere," said my grandmother. "The night before Mother died, I dreamed about a child in a white gown, and so I knew what was going to happen. At forty-five she had to die. Poor Ferri and I were the only ones who grieved for her. I remember he stood at the foot of the bed and cried and cried. He was always a skinny little boy," my grandmother said. Then she added, "Mother was bad to him."

"What do you mean, bad? Bad how?"

"She shouted at him. He used to hang around her all the time, and she shoved him. Father told me once that even in the train when they brought him to Vienna when he was five, Mother didn't like him to touch her. Once he had chilblains," said my grandmother, and stopped as if she were not going to tell the story after all. However, in a minute, she said, "Mother said she was going to bathe his feet—only she used boiling water. After that, the older children wouldn't speak to her. Once I took the little children to the park, and Mother ran after us without a coat. She had a scarf, and she put it on Ferri and she knelt and she hugged him and kissed him and called him pet names in Hungarian, and then she ran back into the house. But in the evening poor Ferri splashed his spoon in the soup, and she sent him to bed."

"You loved her, didn't you, Mutti?" my mother asked.

"To me she was kind," said my grandmother. "She always told Ibolya and Sari to take me along where they were going. They used to say I was her pet. They never liked me, and they were angry with Mother because of all those babies. I asked her once, after I was married and pregnant with my first baby and she was carrying Heini and already so ill, I asked her, *'Warum haben Sie so viele Kinder gehabt?'* ['Why have you had so many children?']—we never said 'thou' to our parents—and she said she was afraid if she didn't, Father would go to other women. Everything was always for Father. He was the only one who had meat for supper, and he would take one of the children on his lap and feed him from his plate."

"I remember Grandfather after he came to live with us in Fischamend," my mother said. "He was a beautiful old man—always clean." (The German word my mother used was *"appetitlich."*)

"And a woman's man to the last," said Paul. "When he was eighty-seven and bedridden, I once saw him pinching the maid."

"Every man pinches the maid," said my grandmother.

"Not Opapa, I bet," I said.

"What do you know about your Opapa!" said my grandmother. "I'm going up. Come, Joszi. Paul, don't forget to lock the cash register, and the shop and the back door. When are you coming up?"

"As soon as I've done the Sosua order for tomorrow," Paul said.

"But Omama, it's only half past nine."

"Paul is tired," said my grandmother. "He needs his rest. Don't forget to turn out the lights."

After noon, on Thursday, came the red Sosua truck, driven by Otto Becker, who put his arm around Paul's shoulder and said, "Well, Professor?"

"Well, Otto?" Paul said, and put his arm at an awkward angle around his friend, who was two heads taller and twice his diameter.

"You're getting fat, Otto," my grandmother said.

"I like to eat," said Otto. "Not like Professor Skin-and-Bones here."

"I like to eat," Paul said, "but every time I let myself go I get a stomach upset and end up thinner than ever."

"And I like to sit," Otto said.

"I would be a great sitter myself, if I had the opportunity," Paul said. "How did Churchill put it? 'Never has so much work been done by such a lazy man, with so little success.' "

When Otto had unloaded and sat down for his cup of coffee, my grandmother questioned him about everyone in Sosua. "How's that Frau Halsmann? Is she living with her husband again? I said to her once, 'Frau Halsmann, imagine if you had an extra pair of eyes—one in each ear—how you could flirt with three men at the same time!' And how's your wife, Otto? Does she still spend all her evenings with that Dr. Marchfeld who has been dying these last five years? She reminds me of my sister Sari. Whenever I came to visit in Vienna, she was washing a sick neighbor's floor or doing a neighbor's shopping while her children got their own dinner. Ibolya didn't marry till later, but Wetterl was like me—all for the family. Hilde would have liked to eat her dinners in the restaurant, and her breakfast and supper, too."

My grandmother would have gone down the gallery of her seven sisters, discussing each with regard to her household habits, but Otto had another five hours' drive to the city markets. When he had gone, my grandmother still sat at the table with a charming and malicious smile. "Pauli, can you think of anyone in Sosua whom I didn't insult?"

At supper, I argued with my grandmother and had a run-in with Paul. My grandmother sent me to turn out the kitchen light, and I said, "But we'll be going out with the dishes in ten minutes."

"We can always put it on again," said my grandmother. "Why should we make the electric company rich?"

234 *Other People's Houses*

I said, "Just how much do you think it costs to burn one seventy-five-watt bulb for ten minutes?" and found myself confronted by Paul, rearing up.

"Go out into the kitchen and turn off the light!" he said, with a snarling mouth, and I went and turned out the light.

My mother came out after me and said, "Lorle, try not to quarrel with Omama."

"Me quarrel with Omama! It's Omama who quarrels with everybody! It's all right for us to be stingy with our butter, but when the chicken man puts a price on his chickens, *he*'s taking advantage! When Pastora makes herself a new dress, she's a slut! Omama has no sense at all of other people's points of view!"

My mother was shocked and hurt and said, "But Omama has always been good to people. During the First World War, we used to get food parcels from the relatives in Hungary, and Omama cooked hot meals for all the Fischamend children."

When Paul had closed up the shop, he invited me to come for a walk. He said *"Buenas noches"* to Señora Molinas, rocking to the rhythm of a *merengue* with her policeman boy friend, and made a little bow to La Viuda, and to Dr. Perez and young Juanita, leaning on the balustrade of their *galería*. Paul walked me along a street of good-sized shops, past the cinema and post office to the little square formal park, where we stood for the flag-lowering ceremony that took place daily at sundown. We had an ice at the Chinese restaurant on the corner. There was a freshness in the darkening air. We started back.

"Mummy says I shouldn't quarrel with Omama," I said. "But Omama is impossible. She can order everyone around, but you say one word to her and she is insulted for the next twenty-four hours."

Paul said, "Your Omama has a tendency toward paranoia. From her childhood, she seems to have felt that her sisters were in a conspiracy to neglect and insult her."

"Her sisters! Her children! The whole world! I remember once, in Vienna, we met Omama in a *Kaffeehaus*. She had just come back from a holiday in Baden, or somewhere—I remember how she was dressed, in a light-gray silk suit with tiny woven black dots, and a hat over one eye. She looked marvelous, and not at all like the Omama from Fischamend in the apron and hairnet. And there was Tante Ibolya, and Sari, and Onkel Pista—a whole bunch of relations—and Omama was telling us about her holiday, how Fräulein So-and-So had bored her with all her conquests, and Frau What's-Her-Name had worn a décolletage down to here, and there was an anti-Semitic man who had never said so much as good morning. All of a sudden Omama smiled and said, 'And then there were *mount*ains and *trees*.' All the aunts and uncles laughed and laughed. No, but Pauli, she does think everyone outside the family is at least carrying a knife with the intention of robbing and murdering us."

"A notion not altogether fantastical if you remember that she lived under the Nazis until six years ago, and now, Lorle, in her old age, she finds herself surrounded by people talking a language she doesn't understand. There she is now."

We had turned the corner into our street and could see my grandmother on our *galería,* looking this way and that. Her eyes in her peaked white face looked terrified. "I didn't know where you had gone," she said. "I thought something had happened."

"What is Pastora doing on the *galería?*" my grandmother asked the next morning. "She has been sweeping it for half an hour."

"She's leaning on the balustrade talking to the chicken man," Paul reported. "She has red ribbons in her hair."

"Disgusting," said my grandmother.

"Why is it? I'm glad somebody is having fun," I said. I tried to catch Pastora's eye as she went sulkily past me upstairs, but she did not notice. When she came back downstairs, she was smiling, wearing the tortoise-shell brooch the Grüners had brought for me.

"Thief! Robber!" cried my grandmother.

"Maybe it's not mine," I said. "I mean, she's got it pinned right to the front of her blouse."

Pastora raised her arms and shouted in Spanish.

"She says she's an honest woman," Paul translated. "She says she found it in the wastebasket."

"Tell her she's a liar," said my grandmother.

"Omama! I don't even want the ugly brooch," I said. But the next day my watch was missing.

"Paul, call the police," said my grandmother, and she made Pastora turn her pocketbook upside down on the table.

"You see," Pastora kept saying. "Nothing. I am an honest woman."

"You stole it yesterday," said my grandmother. "You took it home."

"You come to my home! You search me!" said Pastora.

"Let's go then," said my grandmother. "Come, Lore."

People stared at my grandmother and me walking in the wake of Pastora, who hurried on, bent forward and limping, I noticed for the first time.

"Let's go home, Omama," I said. We were leaving the familiar streets and coming into a different country, where the road was a gash of dried rutted mud, and the shacks looked like dog huts constructed of pieces of wood and corrugated iron. Naked babies and little long-legged pigs played in a ditch that carried sewage downhill. A *merengue* blared.

Pastora threw open the door of one of the shacks—a single room the size of a closet. It had a littered mud floor and no windows, though light seeped in between the wooden slats on which Pastora had pinned an over-life-size face of Betty Hutton. I remembered it from a copy of *Life* that had lain around our bathroom for weeks. Pastora's bed was a wooden chest without a lid, which seemed to double as a wardrobe, for it was filled—like the counter of a bargain basement—with pieces of stuff. I recognized my grandmother's calico apron.

I said, "This is silly. I can't begin to look for anything in this mess." We stepped outside, into what must have been Pastora's kitchen, because there were three charred bricks supporting one of our old coffee tins, full of rusty water.

"Where have you hidden the watch?" my grandmother shouted at Pastora, pointing to my wrist. "Do you want me to go to the police? *Policía? Sí? Policía?*"

"*Sí, sí, la policía,*" said the chicken man, who was suddenly standing there, too. "*Hay justicia aquí. Ella*" (he pointed at my grandmother) "*le hace acusación a esta señora*" (he pointed to Pastora) "*de robar. Son testigos ustedes!*" He pointed his forefinger around the group of little children and pigs who had gathered. "*Es testigo usted!*" ("There is justice here. She has accused this lady of being a thief. You are witnesses! *You* are a witness!") He jabbed his finger at me. "*La policía, sí, sí, sí!*" he yapped, with his face so close to mine that I was staring down the black hole of his toothless mouth.

"Let's go, Omama."

"We'll see you at the police station. *Policía! Adiós,*" said my grandmother.

In the evening, Paul took a quarter pound of butter over to Señora Molinas' *galería* to ask the advice of her policeman friend, and it seemed the police knew all about the chicken man with a monomania about slander laws. "*Es un loco.*" The policeman made a moron face and tapped himself on the forehead. It was always the same story, he said. First, this man would hang out with the maid; then the maid was caught stealing some worthless object; then something else was missing, and when the maid was accused, suddenly there was the chicken man, threatening slander. "But he always fouls it up somehow. Take you, now—the only witnesses he has are from that street over there, and your own mother and niece. Don't you worry, I'll take care of everything for you, my good friend, and for your charming family."

We never saw Pastora again. Every morning now, a boy with a tender new goatee came up our street, hung with chickens and singing, "*Llego las gallinas! Llego las gallinas hermosas!*"

Sunday, after lunch, the shop was closed. Señora Rodriguez was to send her chauffeur for us. My mother dressed my grandmother's fine gray hair. My grandmother wore her best dress of

pewter-colored silk, which made her old woman's face gleam a
rare, pale gold. She had taken off her glasses.

"Omama, you look beautiful with your hair loose—and without
your glasses."

My grandmother waved the compliment away with a rejecting
right hand, but she was pleased. She said, "Now that I think back,
I must have been a pretty girl, but then I only knew I had a big
nose. Ibolya was the beauty; she had a little nose. Sari had a little
nose, too, but too thick. Pista had a nice strong nose for a man—"
and my grandmother went down the gallery of her brothers and
sisters as to noses. "I'll never forget the time I was waiting for
Joszi in the Kaffee Norstadt, and Miklos Gottlieb came up and
said, 'Frau Rosa, you haven't changed.' For years, I thought he
meant my nose. However, now I remember what he said was,
'Your eyes are as black as ever.' I'll never forget how he stared
at me."

Señora Rodriguez seemed devoted to her house and to her
garden, which flourished in a green profusion in the middle of the
dusty, burnt-out landscape; her cabbages grew large; her hens
laid eggs; her geese cleaned themselves with their beaks till they
were immaculately white. Her cook was black and wore a decent
blue linen dress. The señora showed us around the house. She
herself had widened the handsomely tiled *galería* that surrounded it
on three sides. We sat in the shade, in large cushioned chairs,
where plants in copper pots spread huge tropical leaves. Rodriguez,
a slim, very handsome man who looked a good many years younger
than his wife, came out to join us. He had a fine military carriage
and wore his hair cropped so close to his skull as to give the
effect of baldness. Señor Rodriguez sat down between my mother
and my grandmother. The cook came with a tea trolley, followed
by a delicate Negro girl in a childish dress, whom Señora Rodriguez
introduced as Teresa.

Teresa carried the cups and plates of thin buttered bread from
guest to guest with a pinched little smile of extraordinary sweetness, saying, *"Bitte, Sie wollen?"* to each in turn.

"Teresa, you can sit beside Señorita Groszmann." (I looked

up surprised—that was me.) "Practice your German. I'm taking Teresa to Germany next year, when I visit my parents. She is going to become a Protestant this Sunday."

"What do you do to become a Protestant?" I asked Therese, making conversation.

"I wear white dress. I sing hymns," said Teresa, sitting very straight and smiling her ingénue smile.

My mother and Señor and Señora Rodriguez were talking about music. I saw my grandmother holding her teacup. She had an embarrassed smile on her golden face. She was not wearing her glasses, but below her silvery dress her old woman's lace-up shoes stood a little sidewise to the party.

On Monday afternoon, Rudi Grüner came to give me my first Spanish lesson. The family tiptoed behind us. When we were finished, my grandmother brought coffee and cake and asked Rudi if he didn't think I would soon be speaking perfect Spanish. Rudi sat stolidly, with his head drawn into his shoulders like a boy in the presence of his parents' friends, and said I was doing brilliantly.

When he had gone, my mother asked me how I liked him, and I said, "Very much. He looks like a steamed suet pudding without the treacle."

My grandmother said, "Lore is like my sister Ibolya—too choosy."

Rudi came back on Wednesday, and I did brilliantly again except that I had a little difficulty with my first irregular verb. Over coffee I asked Rudi questions about life in Santiago, where he had lived since he was nine years old, but he had little to say and he asked me no questions at all.

Afterward, we saw him stop outside the Perez *galería,* chatting to Juanita and illustrating his conversation with an animation of face and hands that made him look like a Dominican boy.

In the evening came the Grüners with a letter from the Freibergs, who had arrived in Vienna. The fellows of Sigi's old glee club had met them at the airport with songs, and, except for the omnipresence of the Russians, they wrote, Vienna was—well, Vienna. Imagine, on Sunday they were going for a picnic on the Kahlenberg!

On Thursday came the Sosua truck.

On Friday, Rudi gave me my third lesson, and I had the same difficulty with the first verb that I had had in my second lesson. And afterward, Rudi leaned over the railing of the Perez *galería* and kidded with Juanita.

I stood around the shop. I said, "I want to sell something." But my grandmother said that I gave overweight. I should let my grandfather do it; and later, in the kitchen, she said I didn't wash the green peppers beautifully enough, I should let my mother do it.

When Paul put on his straw hat to go to the post office for our mail, I said I would go along—hoping I hardly knew for what.

While we were gone, my grandfather happened to be alone in the shop when two boys came in. One asked for a box of Chiclets, and the other for half a pound of cheese, and while my grandfather was weighing out the cheese the first boy ran away with the Chiclets, leaping over the *galería* railing, and the second boy leaped after him, and Grandfather ran around the counter and down the *galería,* and he stood in the street shouting. That evening, he had another heart attack.

"He's not doing badly at all," said Dr. Perez, "but we must keep him in bed. *No* walking up and down stairs."

"You hear, Joszi?" said my grandmother.

My grandfather stroked his mustache and said, *"Ja so,* but now I feel much better."

"I'll tell you when you feel better," Dr. Perez said and winked at me with the leer he seemed to feel my due as a woman.

My mother asked me to stay with my grandfather when the afternoon rush started.

"Is it very busy now in the shop?" asked my grandfather.

"That's not your problem, Opapa," I said. "Paul and Omama and Mutti can manage without you, you know, perfectly well."

"Ja so," said my grandfather.

We sat looking at one another. I wished I had a book. I said, "Tell me a story. Did you really go to school with the robber chief?"

"Until I was thirteen years. Then my father sent me to Vienna to be an apprentice in a draper's shop. The owner was called Benedick, a cousin of your Omama. He arranged the marriage, but that was many, many years later."

"What does an apprentice do?"

"Tidy the shelves and put everything in good order before the shop is opened. He waits on customers and makes deliveries. We were three boys—Pista, from my village, and Karl, from Vienna and older. Every morning, he and Pista pulled the blankets away at five o'clock in the morning to make me light the stove." My grandfather smiled mildly at the jokes of his youth.

I saw in my inner eye the back room of a shop and furnished it with shelves of boxes and bales of fabric, arranged precisely like the storeroom behind my grandfather's shop in Fischamend, except that there were three beds in it; it was winter, dark, at five A.M., the stove unlit—and my mother came in, wearing a sleeveless cotton dress and bringing my grandfather's supper tray. "I should come down, if you are too busy," said my grandfather. "I'm feeling much better."

"You heard the doctor, Vati!" my mother said.

But the next morning when Paul came into the shop to open up, my grandfather, fully dressed, was standing on a ladder arranging the coffee tins in a tidy pyramid.

Paul was very angry. He helped my grandfather down and led him upstairs, saying, "Now I want you to walk very, very slowly, please."

After that, we never left my grandfather alone. My mother sat with him in the mornings. She taught him Spanish words out of a grammar book. When my grandmother finished cooking, she would go up. I remember I stood at the bottom of the steps, listening, because I could not imagine what they might have to say to one another. I heard my grandmother say, *"Setz dich.* Sit up, Joszi. I will plump your pillow." In the afternoon, when my grandmother was needed downstairs in the shop, I went to sit with my grandfather.

"Tell me a story," I said. "Why did you need a third person to arrange your marriage?"

"Because I was busy working in the shop, saving my money so I could open a shop of my own, so I could get married," said my grandfather.

"Opapa, do you remember the first time you saw Omama?"

"Oh, yes," said my grandfather. "I remember the day Benedick took me up to the flat. Your Omama was sitting by a window with one of the babies on her lap. And all the time she kept watching me with her big black eyes. She had black hair, like a gypsy. Your Omama was always a good wife. She is a good businesswoman in the shop."

"Hey, Opapa!" I cried. "Why are you getting out of bed? Where do your think you are going?"

"I just thought I would open the shutters."

"Then why don't you ask me to do it? That's the Molinas' yard, isn't it?" From the window, I could see the neighbors I knew only from their public *galería* life in the intimacy of their back yard. The yard was square and had a mud floor, with scarlet flowerpots all around the pink walls, and a lemon tree growing in the middle. Under this lovely tree sat Señora Molinas, brushing América Columbina's hair. Mercedes was sweeping with an outsize broom and doing a silly head-wagging dance to distract the squirming baby.

"Do you remember, Lorle, our yard in Fischamend?" my grandfather asked.

At supper, I asked my grandmother if she remembered the first time she saw Opapa.

"Yes," said my grandmother. "My father had asked Cousin Benedick to find a husband for me, because I was already twenty-four. I could have married Miklos Gottlieb." My grandmother pulled her shoulders up and dipped her head, in something between a shrug and a sidewise nod. "He dressed very well. He was very handsome, always with some girl. Once he said to me, 'Fräulein Rosa, I am a man who cannot be without a woman, but you see I always come back to you.' But I wouldn't speak to him. He didn't marry till four years after I married Joszi. Her name was Rosa, like mine."

"Do you remember Opapa in those days?"

"Yes. He had a bad temper."

"Opapa had a bad temper?"

"Yes. The week after we were married, I told him to borrow some money and stock up properly. He threw an ink bottle at me. *Aber ich hab' ihm's Wilde abig'räumt,"* my grandmother said in pure Austrian, meaning, "I stripped the wildness off of him."

"But Muttilein," said my mother, "he took poor Ferri in after your mother died, and Ibolya when she got divorced, and he was good to Grandfather when he came to live with us."

My grandmother acknowledged her husband's virtues with her shrugging nod. "He didn't drink and he didn't gamble. Miklos Gottlieb, you know, drank. Once I went to see my father in the shop, and he and Miklos were drinking wine together in the back. His wife—that Rosa Frankel—she wasn't good for him. But then, I wasn't good for Joszi," my grandmother said. "I wouldn't have been good for any man," and she made a gesture with the right hand, like the downward half of a wave, that had the effect of someone pushing away a plate of food or an unpalatable condition.

On Wednesday, Señora Rodriguez came for her last piano lesson. They were moving back to the city and would return to Santiago at Christmas. She brought a jar of marmalade made from her own oranges, for "poor Herr Steiner."

In the evening, the Grüners came to sit with my grandfather. "What are these bad things we hear of you?" they said to him.

"Ja so," said my grandfather.

"We had a letter from the Freibergs," said Frau Grüner. "Imagine—poor Erna has broken a leg and Sigi has to nurse her. She says her sister is always busy with the boy, and he is cheeky in return. Sigi wants us to send him some tortoise-shell pins, to start an import-export business. Sigi has talked to his friends in the glee club about the Nazis, but all they want to talk about is the Russians."

"And how is Rudi?" asked my grandmother. "He didn't come with you?"

"He was going to come, but you know young people," said Frau Grüner. "They don't like illness."

"He hasn't been to see us for weeks," said my grandmother, "though we see him all the time on the *galería* with that Juanita Perez, climbing all over one another. He's become a real native, hasn't he?"

Frau Grüner rose, bristling. She bent over my grandfather, saying, "Now, we want you to get better soon. You are a good man. We are all very fond of *you*," and she led her husband downstairs without saying good-by.

My grandmother sat grinning. She said, "Well, children, on to Ciudad Trujillo. I've insulted everyone in Sosua and I'm halfway through Santiago."

My grandfather seemed to have accepted the fact of his illness and to be actually looking frailer. The fingers that stroked his mustache looked transparent and trembled a little. He no longer asked questions about the shop, but spent the day propped against his pillows, watching the workday life in the Molinas' back yard. One day he said to me, "So she is opening a shop next door, just as I always thought."

"Who? Señora Molinas? Whatever makes you think so? I mean, I know she's not."

"Look," said my grandfather. "They are folding up the linens."

"Opapa! That's only Mercedes shaking out the tablecloth."

My grandfather said, "We always used to display the linens—tablecloths, dish towels, and handkerchiefs—in the window facing the Fischamend Square, do you remember?"

That weekend the rainy season set in. I had never seen such a furious, inexhaustible descent of water. América Columbina and

all the children came out and played in the flooded gutters, but
the grownups went inside and closed their doors.

When Paul came downstairs in the morning, he found Manuela,
our new maid, sleeping on the floor. She explained that she couldn't
go home in the rain. She would get her hair wet, and if one got
one's hair wet, one got pneumonia and died.

"She can't go home in the rain, but she can sleep on the floor,"
said my grandmother. "They're not our kind of people."

I said, "What's so great about our people? All *you* ever do is
quarrel with them."

This was rude. My grandmother went out into the kitchen and
didn't talk to me the rest of the day.

And day after day it rained, at times in a fantastic downpour—
as if an immense bucket was being upturned over Santiago—until
the water rushed turbulently down the gutters. Then the rain settled
back to a steady, muted rustling, without hope of any end. I woke
up in the mornings to hear my grandmother in the next room
setting my grandfather's tray across his bed, saying, "Sit up, Joszi,"
and then my mother called us to breakfast.

The shop remained empty. Paul sat in the rocking chair, studying his course in remedial exercises. "This is near criminal," he
said. "The information is laughable, and they propose to teach by
correspondence exercises impossible to understand except in practice. But I know all this. What I need from them is a diploma, so
I can get work. Then maybe we can all move to the city."

The Freibergs wrote my mother. They were so sorry to hear
about poor Herr Steiner's illness. They were coming back to
Santiago; Vienna was nothing for our people any more. What
with the Russians everywhere and business so poor and stoves
having to be lit now that autumn had come and maids not four
dollars a month as in the Dominican Republic but three times that
a week—ridiculous! They would be back before the end of the
year. They sent their best to everyone in sunny Santiago.

From the bed where my grandfather sat propped against his
pillows, he looked across the muddy yard. "Look! Señora Molinas

is talking to a salesman in the back room—you see, where the light is on," said my grandfather. "He has his sample case with him."

"But Opapa, that's Señora Molinas' policeman friend—don't you remember?—who always sits on the *galería* and sends Mercedes for five cents' worth of butter. He brought his suitcase. I suppose he is moving in."

"*Ja so,*" said my grandfather. "He always likes his butter every evening. You see now he is showing her his tie, shirt, his undershirt, his drawers . . ."

It was December; the rain had stopped. In the mornings, I woke to the sound of the chicken boy with the goatee singing out his wares and the birds flapping and gurgling as my grandmother tickled them under the wings.

Then it was Christmas. Every house in our street had its papier-mâché tree imported from the United States, decorated with glass tubes filled with a colored liquid that bubbled when plugged into the electric outlet.

The Rodriguezes were in Santiago for the holidays, and my mother, my grandmother, and I went there for the Christmas Eve celebration. Señora Rodriguez had ordered a yew tree from the mountains. It smelled of the forest and was decorated in German fashion with brown tallow candles smelling of honey, and hung with silver chains and golden glass balls, and chocolates, candy, and cookies wrapped in colored foil. There was an elderly German gentleman staying in the house. "He is leaving for Germany as soon as he can get his passport," Señora Rodriguez whispered. "He's just come out of prison, poor man. He was arrested for spying for Germany near the end of the war—though my husband tried to get him out of the country. Germany was doing so badly already, you know; one had to do every little thing one could." Señora Rodriguez asked my mother to play "Silent Night, Holy Night." She said she could never get used to celebrating Christmas with the sun high, in eighty-nine-degree weather. It didn't seem right.

That week La Viuda's brother was pardoned and sent home. He was a little brown man who stood embarrassedly on the *galería* next to his sister. La Viuda wore a flowered gown as if she were going to a garden party, accepting the congratulations of the neighbors.

Frau Grüner seemed to have forgiven my grandmother and came to the shop. She invited us all to her house on Sunday to welcome the returning Freibergs. My grandmother said she wasn't going. "It's you she wants, and Lore," she said to my mother. "She doesn't want me."

"She asked for you especially," said my mother. "Frau Freiberg has always been fond of you, Mutti. I'll do your hair. Go and fetch Omama's silk dress, Lorle. I'll stay with Vater, and you and Paul and Lore go, even if it's just for an hour."

At the Grüners', I watched my grandmother sitting with Frau Freiberg, who was saying, "Vienna is nothing any more for our people," pulling down the corners of her mouth and shaking her head in dismissal of the Old World.

"But here is no good, either," said my grandmother. "The climate . . . Paul has not been well a day since he came to Santo Domingo."

"He wouldn't like the cold in Vienna any more," Frau Freiberg said. "And everyone so—I don't know—I used to say to my sister-in-law, 'What would it hurt you to put on a little lipstick? Why don't you go out somewhere?' You wouldn't recognize the old Vienna. No culture. You remember the opera, the theater, the music. Everybody who is anybody has gone to America."

"We never used to go anywhere," my grandmother said. "I lived, from the time I was twenty-six till Hitler came, in a village outside Vienna. We were the only Jews. There was nowhere to go, no one to see. Once a month, I came into Vienna to visit the children."

"Sigi's old friends at the glee club kept saying they would invite us, but they never did. Karl Haber was very funny about it. Once he said what did *we* know, living on a tropical island all these years while they had been through hell—first the Germans, then the English and Americans, now the Russians. But the Americans weren't so bad. I was saying to Herr Paul just now he should wait till he gets to America and finish his studies."

"Paul will never finish anything," said my grandmother, throwing her right hand out in her half wave of resignation and rejection. "He never finished his medical studies. Now he has got his diploma for remedial exercises, and it turns out that a United States diploma doesn't count in the Dominican Republic."

"But it's all different in America," said Frau Freiberg. "Sigi's sister and brother-in-law live in Queens. That's near New York. He works in a zipper factory—fifty-five dollars a week and the apartment cleans itself, she says. Next year, they are going to get television."

"America!" said my grandmother. "A friend I know, a certain Miklos Gottlieb, went to America—New York. I will never see America. I will go into the ground in Santiago," and my grandmother nodded her body from the waist, like a man praying in the synagogue.

Frau Grüner brought coffee and *Sacher Torte*. My grandmother whispered to Paul not to eat it; it was heavy and would upset his stomach. After that, Paul and I were ready to depart, but my grandmother didn't want to go home.

In the Dominican Republic, children get their presents from the Three Kings on the Feast of Epiphany. The street was gay with balls and hoops and new dolls. Mercedes came to the shop for a quarter pound of rice and laid her arm along the counter and put her head on it and rubbed her left ankle with her right instep and said, *"No me dejaron nada,"* which means "They didn't leave anything for me."

All morning La Viuda's brother went up and down the street asking everyone if he had heard of the accident on the road to Ciudad Trujillo. It was not an accident, he said, but an anti-Trujilloist friend of his, whose car had been forced over the cliff by Trujillo agents.

The following day, two policemen came walking down the

center of the road and fetched away La Viuda's brother, and she came out on the *galería* and wept in grief and fury.

That night, my grandmother dreamed about a little child in a black shift leading a baby and beckoning, and so she knew that some calamity would befall us. We said it was only because Mercedes was always in and out with little América Columbina and we were seeing La Viuda in her black weeds again, but one afternoon that week, in agony, my grandfather died. My mother leaned her arms against the wall and put her head in them and cried with deep, painful sobs.

Paul closed up the shop. Herr and Frau Grüner and Rudi and the Freibergs came bringing food, according to Jewish tradition. They said what a good man my grandfather had been. When they were gone, my grandmother said, "I know what they think. Everyone always thought I mistreated Joszi."

"No, no, no, no," said my mother.

"I never told you what he did to me on our wedding day. He carried the stair carpet my father had given us, so we would save the carrier's fee. On our wedding day, he took me home carrying a stair carpet! A woman can't forgive that kind of thing," said my grandmother, with her angry eyes and her nose standing large and bleak in her white face.

There was no Jewish cemetery nearer than the one in Sosua, so my grandfather's body was buried in the Catholic graveyard in Santiago de los Caballeros.

Afterward, the neighbors came to sit with my grandmother—Dr. Perez and his wife and daughter, La Viuda, and Señora Molinas with América Columbina. On the third day, Paul reopened the shop.

One Sunday afternoon, when Paul and I were walking up and down the street, he said, "I sent away for a course in bookkeeping, in which I am getting a certain amount of practice through the shop, and I might perfect myself and maybe get a job in the city until our American quota comes. Your Omama would be so much happier."

"In town or in America? You mean she needs more people to quarrel with?"

Paul said, "I wonder if you remember, Lorle, how you used to love coming out to Fischamend for visits."

"It was lovely," I said.

"When Franzi and I went to school in Vienna, there was nothing more wonderful for us than to come home weekends, to fill up the house with our friends. Omama always made a perfect feast of food, and Franzi played the piano, and there were stories. Omama loved to laugh. Opapa used to keep asking what the joke was. It is curious that a woman who is so little capable of happiness herself should have been able to fill her house with such an immense amount of fun!"

There is a triangular traffic island at Broadway and 157th Street. It has benches, six dusty trees, and pigeons. Every time one of the Fifth Avenue buses lumbers past, the pigeons rise into the air—spreading disease and germs over everyone, my grandmother used to say. Here, in summer, at evening time, the elderly German-speaking population of Washington Heights comes together; and one day in 1951, my grandmother happened to mention her old friend Miklos Gottlieb to one Hilde Hohemberg, who had a cousin who happened to live in the same house as Herr Gottlieb and knew him and knew that Rosa Gottlieb had died a year ago after a long illness. And Miklos, hearing that my grandmother was in New York, asked to be allowed to pay his respects.

I looked forward to this meeting that promised to be the very cliché of romance. My grandmother put on her pewter-colored silk dress. She let my mother arrange her hair, but under protest—like a very young girl who doesn't want to acknowledge wanting to make an impression.

"It was me, you know, he wanted to marry," my grandmother said.

"Did he ask you, Omama?"

"He spoke to my father. He asked my father what he would

give me for a dowry. But even if he had asked me, I would not have married him. He was flighty."

The old man to whom I opened the front door did not fill the role of decrepit, doddering, has-been manhood in which I had cast him. He was a very old but dapper little person, in a well-fitting suit with matching vest, and he carried a walking stick. His mustache was of the First World War Viennese style and suited the style of his face. He turned his tiny, very blue eyes appreciatively on me, with a frank tribute to youth and womanhood not unlike the more vulgar leer that Dr. Perez in Santiago had thought my daily due.

My grandmother came out into the hall.

Miklos Gottlieb hooked the crook of his walking stick over his wrist so as to have both his hands free to take my grandmother's right. "*Ja,* Frau Rosa!" he said. "Still those beautiful black eyes!"

My grandmother acknowledged the compliment by pulling her head a little forward and down into her shoulders. My mother said, "Muttilein, take Herr Gottlieb inside. I'm coming with the coffee."

My grandmother sat down in a chair over by the window while Miklos Gottlieb complimented the room, the persons in it, and, presently, what he was given to eat and drink, ending with a neat observation on the smallness of the world and the water that had passed under the bridge. "But you, *liebe* Frau Rosa, you have your children here with you. I have lost two sons—my Johann in the First World War fighting the Allies in Caporetto, and my younger one, Franzl, in the second war, in London, in a German raid." He looked around to have us appreciate the irony.

"I have lost, too. I have lost," my grandmother said, nodding the upper part of her body. "My Franzi lost her husband. My Paul lost his wife—twenty years old. I was still in Vienna. The night before I heard, I had my dream about a little child."

"If you dreamed it the night before you heard," I said, "it could hardly count as an omen of the event, as she must have died weeks before you had the news." I wanted the old people to stop keening over their dead.

"We follow one another across the world, and we leave our dead behind," my mother said. "My Igo in a huge graveyard in a Jewish slum in London, Paul's Ilse on a hill in Sosua, and my father in a Catholic graveyard in Santiago."

"And Ibolya in Auschwitz," said my grandmother.

"Ah, the lovely Ibolya with the charming nose," said Herr Gottlieb.

"And Sari God knows where in Hungary," said my grandmother. "And Ferri and Kari taken away in Poland." And my grandmother went down the gallery of her eleven dead brothers and sisters, naming the places where they had been murdered. "And of the three of us alive, Wetterl is in Paraguay, and Hilde in Canada, and I will go into the ground in New York."

"And my Roserl," said Miklos Gottlieb, closing his eyes so that they looked like little trembling pebbles set deep in their sockets. Tears pressed out between the lids. "My poor good wife, my golden Roserl—five years she was ill; the last two she couldn't move out of her chair, and she had to die, and what am I without her?"

"*Ein bisserl Kaffee,*" my mother said and filled up his cup, but my grandmother got up and walked out of the room. When Herr Gottlieb was leaving, my mother had to fetch her out of the kitchen.

Miklos Gottlieb had perked up and recovered his sprightly gallantry. There was a tear, a shining, perfect sphere, still poised on the ruddy crest of his cheek. He held my grandmother's hand, saying, "You see, dear Frau Rosa, I told you I would always come back to you." But my grandmother would not answer him.

CHAPTER ELEVEN

Ciudad Trujillo:
Don Indalecio Nuñez Aguirre and I

After Opapa's death, and with the "American quota" still off in some indefinite future, I began to wilt. The white sky burned unremittingly over Santiago. Inside the house, I roamed from the shop into the kitchen and upstairs to look out of the window. It is incomprehensible to me, now, that I never acquired any regular duties. I seem to have fed on great expectations of coming, presently, into some fate worthy of my talents, a faith encouraged by the family, whose eyes I could feel following me around with doting concern. Only my grandmother said, "Lore will never get married."

"In Santiago I certainly won't," I said. "Who is there in Santiago?"

"What's wrong with Rudi?" asked my grandmother. "Lore is like my sister Ibolya. No man was ever good enough; this one was not tall enough, that one was not smart enough . . ."

"But she got married!" I said anxiously.

"At twenty-nine she married the butcher, who was a great brute. She left him after six weeks."

I was relieved that Ibolya had got married at twenty-nine. It gave me a definite year on which to fix those expectations. However much I quarreled with my grandmother, I believed in the wisdom of her black predictions. The more they went against my best hopes, the more likely they seemed.

Paul said, "Lorle should go ahead to live in Ciudad Trujillo, where she can meet people and can get an interesting job—drawing, perhaps. There's nothing for her here," and he wrote to the Hotel Parisienne, which belonged to a Viennese acquaintance from Sosua, and arranged for me to travel into town with Otto, but I said I was going by bus. "If I'm going to live in a refugee hotel, I will at least travel like a Dominican. That's the trouble with us," I said. "We stick so close together, we never see the country and we never meet the people."

"What people! You don't want to meet these people," said my grandmother. "You remember, Paul; the first maid we had, who borrowed my good little vegetable knife because she said she had quarreled with a neighbor and the neighbor had a knife and she did not."

"She brought it back the next morning," Paul said, "saying she had made up with the neighbor."

"You see," I cried, "an honest, peaceable woman." But my grandmother's páranoia had infected me, and when I went to the bus stop I saw in a panic moment the dozen black peasant faces turned on me with a single gap-toothed nightmare smile.

The bus must once have been painted bright blue and orange, but it was so scratched and banged up that it looked like a child's toy left from some previous Christmas. On the roof was a pyramid of tin suitcases, market baskets, and livestock. A turkey tied by the legs hung over the side of the bus.

I climbed up the rickety steps and sat down beside the only other woman traveler, an old grandmother in a clean, faded cotton dress, who said to me, *"Qué me pica el pavo!"* I lifted my shoulder in a practiced gesture of nonunderstanding and regret. The old woman giggled and leaned up against me, and when I looked where she pointed I saw the naked, scarlet head of the turkey looking in the open window. The bird had corrected its upside-down situation by bending its neck into a U, and was regarding the grandmother's fat black arm with a most human expression of suspicious irascibility before taking another peck.

The bus driver asked the owner of the turkey, *"Este pavo, amigo, es macho o hembra?"* ("This turkey, my friend, is it a male or a female?")

"Que va," said the owner—to the best of my understanding— "I want you to take one look at this splendid bird. Can you doubt it is a male?"

"It is a male turkey," the driver explained to the old grandmother, and he took his seat at the wheel.

The old woman smiled shyly at me and shrugged her shoulders. The driver started up, his foot full on the gas, so that we all fell back in our seats and the gamecocks belonging to a stout man in a loud houndstooth jacket awoke and began to croak in excited pebbly voices inside their canvas sacks, which lifted for a moment like helium balloons into the air, and settled for the journey, only giving out, once in a while, low pebbly noises, like creatures distressed in their sleep.

The bus rattled on the road—Dominican roads are so cheaply made that every rainy season washes them away—and the heat was intolerable. The stout man in the houndstooth jacket brought out a bottle of whisky, which he passed among the men. He was organizing a game: Bets were laid, and the first person to catch sight of an oncoming car received the pot. The bottle made the rounds.

We were soon climbing into the mountainous region. The driver turned and said, *"Mira! Accidente por allá abajo!"* ("See the accident down there!") I could see, far below us in the bottom of the ravine, the wreck of a navy-blue car. While everyone's attention was thus diverted, the driver called out, *"Un carro!"* Everyone laughed and clapped him on the back. They passed him the bottle. By now the men were standing up, hands on the seat in front, spurring the driver to go faster to see what was coming around the next hairpin turn, which the vehicle took on two wheels, skipping the water-filled holes like a Mickey Mouse bus, sending

pebbles rolling down the cliffs on our left. The grandmother
crossed herself, crying out aloud to Jesus and Mary to have mercy
on us, but every time the road straightened below her and she
found herself alive she turned her happy face to me with a shy,
apologetic smile. But I could neither cry out nor smile back, for
I had my teeth clenched, holding on to myself. By late afternoon,
as we descended into the southern plain, within sight of the tall
modern buildings of the city's main street, my jaw and shoulders
ached.

Ciudad Trujillo (now renamed Santo Domingo) is the chief port
and capital of the Republic. Around its Spanish cathedral of ancient brown stone the houses are painted the same white, pink,
and earth-yellow as the houses in Santiago, with the same wooden
galería with painted balustrades, and patios with scarlet flowerpots. I gave the driver the address of the Hotel Parisienne and
asked him to let me off at the nearest stop, but the community of
the bus decided on a small detour to take me to the very door. The
gamecock owner, now completely crocked, helped me carry my
suitcase up the steps, his jacket wings flying, and handed me with
a profound and unsteady bow to the care of the proprietress.

Frau Bader, a juicy Viennese blonde, showed me to a tiny
room opening onto the back yard. She was giving me special rates,
in the hope, she said, that having a young girl about would keep
the place jumping. The Parisienne was the stopping-off place for
visitors from Sosua, and the regulars, too, were Central European
Jews, all waiting for their American quotas. Janos Kraus, the
young Hungarian painter who had the room next to mine, wore
his hair in cliché curls behind the ears, which immediately decided
me against him. "Doctor" and "Madame" Levy were Viennese,
too. He was not a real doctor, said Frau Bader, who sat with me
while I ate my first dinner, but had taken a course in pedicure
after the Nazis confiscated his restaurant. They had hidden out in
Paris all through the war. "Madame" Levy gave French lessons
and would speak German only with a French accent. Frau Bergel
was from Frankfurt and taught the piano. Frau Bader asked me
what I was going to do. She said she used to have a lovely girl,

Magda Fischer, living in the Parisienne who had done very well for herself working in the Hotel Jaragua, and it might be worth my while to apply. There were lots of Americans in and out.

And so my first job was at the Jaragua, at that time the only hotel of chic and size in town. I stood behind a glass counter next to a potted palm in the beige-and-scarlet, glass-and-metal lobby, selling cigarettes and waiting for romance.

In the mornings, taxis brought the daily Americans from their Caribbean cruises. They hung around the cool of the lobby. A sunburned middle-aged man in a sport shirt came and stood at my counter, talking. He said he could tell I was Jewish, too. An elegant young man asked me where the golf course was, and three old ladies wanted to know where there was something wild that they could go and see, but I looked past them all to the exquisite elderly woman in lilac tweeds, with bored arrogant eyebrows, who sat talking with no one, drinking cups of espresso. In the evenings, the taxis came to take them back to the boats on their way home to America.

My free afternoons I spent walking on the main shopping street, called El Conde. It had tall office buildings like the one that housed the American Consulate, where one day—at this very moment, perhaps—my American papers might be processed. Next door was a small, pink, one-story house with little shops like the small-town shops of Santiago. There was the chic Magda's Dress Salon, and the Café Madrid that opened like a stage onto the street, where I walked up and down pretending not to be looking in at the front center table occupied by the English colony. Mr. and Mrs. Darcy had sat there every afternoon for the last fifteen years and sit there, I understand, to this day. Darcy was quite an old man with a pale, long face and aristocratic mustache, who looked out in silent benevolence over his beer and pipe. The talking was done by his wife, who was many years younger, fat and plain like a peasant, a loving, sensible, useful woman. The British Embassy people, the English officers from the shipyard, and English business people and their families simply stepped in from the sidewalk. Mrs. Darcy would call the waiter to bring up a chair and iced tea if it was a lady, beer for a gentleman. No one came who did not belong, except myself, and I cannot remember doing it. I recall the weeks in which the English table was the center of my consciousness, but oblivion covers the moment, the excuse or blind determination with which I stepped over my shyness into the Café Madrid. I remember sitting beside Mrs. Darcy, talking. I said I had lived in England from the time I was ten, which was precisely half my life, and that I had a B.A. in English from Bedford College in London. "Do you happen to know it? On the Inner Circle, in Regents Park. If you got tired of Beowulf you could watch the geese from the lake walking across the lawn. I adore London! All I want is to get back. . . ."

A lady at the table who worked for the British Consulate said, "That shouldn't be hard, under the circumstances," and she sent me a notification, within the month, to come and pick up my visa.

I was horrified: Behind the memory of white geese under the great plane trees on the jewel-green lawn appeared, like a double exposure, my bespectacled self, in mackintosh and oxfords, on a cold drizzling English June day, coming across the bridge into Baker Street in such an agony of loneliness that I can recall it in my memory like an event; I remember I stood a moment to diagnose the cause and felt my feet wet and knew I hadn't a sixpence left for my gas meter.

"A visa! To England!" I cried. "How marvelous . . . only I won't have money for a while. . . ."

"The visa is renewable," said the lady from the consulate.

"And my mother depends on me to go with her to America," I said, and blushed. I walked home thinking the English were through with me forever. But the very next week, Mrs. Darcy waved me in from the sidewalk, ordered my tea, and said she had been speaking about me to the ambassador of X, who was looking for an English teacher. In the next months, her patronage provided me with a sizable clientele wanting to learn English with a British accent—even one that came via Vienna. I soon gave up my job as a cigarette girl in the Jaragua.

The ambassador was my best customer. His chauffeur fetched me five times a week, before breakfast, and at the end of every lesson the ambassador propositioned me.

The chauffeur, seeing us emerge onto the front steps, threw down his wet swab and snapped to attention at the door of the huge black Lincoln Continental that dripped and gleamed and sparkled wetly on the gravel drive. The ambassador had stopped with his forefinger raised to command attention.

"You." He pointed to me and contracted his brows in concentration. "Mit?" he appealed to me.

"Meeet?" I suggested.

"Meeet," the ambassador corrected himself, "me," he pointed to himself and leered archly, "at 'otel Jaragua this night?" he finished triumphantly and cocked his head for approval. He was small and stocky and hardly taller than I.

I shook my head. "Will you meeet me at the Hhhotel tonight," I pronounced.

The ambassador giggled and slapped his thigh. "I mit you! I mit you!"

"That's right," I would reply, "I'll meet you tomorrow morning, seven as usual. And will you please review chapter six, about the interrogative in English."

The ambassador looked crestfallen and threw his hands out. "You not love me!" he said.

Janos Kraus, coming up the drive with his palette and box of oils to do the ambassador's portrait, raised his panama in confusion, not knowing whether to bow first to the gentleman who was an ambassador, or to a fellow refugee who was a lady; the ambassador handed me into the car, and, looking back, I saw the Hungarian bowing from the waist and the ambassador kissing his fingers to me by the veranda steps.

"How are you doing, Ticher," asked Jaime, the chauffeur.

"Teeecher."

"Teeecher," Jaime corrected himself. He got his lesson free every morning while he drove me to and from the ambassador's house.

He surprised me with the idiomatic, slapdash English I seemed to
have taught him in the six months in which the ambassador had
not learned one new rule or unlearned one old mistake. It seemed
to me that those who learned English caught it out of the air and
those who did not catch it were never going to learn it. The road
from ignorance to knowledge was a mystery to me.

"Isn't it a fine day? Is right, 'fine day'?"

" 'Is *it* right?' Yes, it's a very fine day." We were driving along
the handsome Malecon that runs along the Caribbean, which lay
very still and blue to our right. On our left were the fanciful villas
of the rich, set back in their great gardens. On the lawns sprouted
the small black boys holding water hoses so that they seemed to
be urinating splendid, sparkling arcs of water, keeping the grass
green under the intense brightness.

The blonde Frau Bader brought my breakfast to the table on
the *galería* and sat down opposite. She was in her forties, good-
looking despite her bad teeth, and was about to marry a fourth
husband. Her wit was gross; her walk, her gestures, her whole person was so vivid that in her presence my bones felt fragile. I liked
her, and I was sorry that I was being a disappointment to her—
for men were by no means pouring into her hotel on my account—
so I had mentioned to her the ambassador's advances, and now she
was on at me to bring him to the Parisienne. "We'll cook you a
Viennese dinner the like of which that man has never eaten."

"I'm sure you would," I said, "but I don't want to encourage
him."

"Why not?" asked Frau Bader.

"He's married," I said.

"So?" said Frau Bader. "You should have been here the year
Magda Fischer lived here. The place was jumping. Of course, she
was a big red-headed girl, eighteen and what a beauty! You know
her dress salon on the Conde! They used to live here, she and
her mother and Eva—that was her little sister—when they first
came from Hungary. One day President Trujillo saw her—imagine!—and he drove up to this very gate and sent his chauffeur,

a lieutenant, in a uniform, walking up these stairs for Magda to come for a drive. She said she couldn't, alone, just like a Dominican girl, but the lieutenant said she could bring her mother, so what could they do? It seems the three of them sat in the back, the President between Magda and her mother, and all the time he kept talking with Mrs. Fischer, he kept holding Magda's hand. Mrs. Fischer told me afterward, she said, what could she do? And a week later he sent the lieutenant to fetch Magda to a party, and Magda said she couldn't go because her mother was ill, poor thing, but the lieutenant said she could bring her little sister—Eva must have been, what, thirteen—and a pretty little thing already. It seems there were all these V.I.P.'s, a whole motorcade, and they drove out to one of the President's estates and there was a *fiesta* in the garden, with lanterns, and Magda sat next to him and little Eva sat next to the lieutenant. They gave her some wine and she fell asleep on his lap. I remember I sat up with Mrs. Fischer till the morning waiting for the girls to come home, but let me tell you, the President paid for Mrs. Fischer's operations, and the nurses, and the funeral. That girl could have had anything she wanted—a house, an estate, anything—but she always had her head screwed on the right way. She told him, she said, she needed to earn her living and she made him furnish the shop on the Conde. And little Eva used to bring the lieutenant up here for my dinners. Why don't you bring this ambassador?"

I shook my head. I said, "It's nothing like that with the ambassador and me. I mean, when he invites me he isn't serious. He just thinks he's paying me a compliment. It's his way of being polite to girls." I waited for Frau Bader to say, why shouldn't he mean it? but she said, "So? If you can't get him, why don't you invite some of your English friends?"

"I don't know them that well."

"What do you mean? Every time I walk down the Conde I see you sitting at that table."

"Yes, but I'm not on the kind of footing where *I* could invite *them,*" I said.

"Why not?" asked Frau Bader.

"Here's my next pupil," I said.

This pupil who came to the hotel for her lessons was one Doña Piri, a Dominican, a woman close to fifty, very small and dried up, with a pronouncedly heart-shaped face that must once have been charming but was now wrinkled and furrowed over and yellow like the face of an octogenarian. She wore her hair orange and frizzled to stand away from her head. Her nails were long and blood red, and at the beginning of each lesson she sharpened her pencil to a needle point on the sole of her shoe.

"Doña Piri," I said, "I was wondering if three lessons a week isn't more, perhaps, than you need. . . ." (I wanted to say, "Doña Piri, your English is as good as one of your limited intelligence can make it, and I don't know what to do with you for a whole hour.") "I mean, your English is quite fluent . . ." I said.

"But my accent," cried Doña Piri. "It is terrible. I love your accent, Señorita. You speak such an educated English."

"Well, thank you."

"And you dress so well. You always dress, how do you say it, like ladies."

"Ladylike? Thank you, Doña Piri, but . . ."

"I think you have beautiful taste. I have been moving yesterday. I would like that you should come and help me arrange my room."

"I should like you *to* come," I said. I never took seriously Doña Piri's bids for intimacy. I could not believe that she liked me any better than I liked her.

"I should like you to come to dinner, maybe tonight? I want to invite some friends . . . a friend . . . there is a gentleman . . ."

The invitation took on a new aspect, and I began to consider going to dinner with Doña Piri.

"I have his picture here. It happens he was in the newspaper." Doña Piri dipped into her outsize red plastic pocketbook and handed me a newsprint picture of two men in laughing conversation, of whom I recognized one as President Trujillo. Doña Piri pointed to the caption with a sharp blood-red fingernail. "This here, you see, it says, *'Don Indalecio Nuñez Aguirre habla con el Generalissimo Dr. Rafael Leonidas Trujillo Molina, Presidente de la Republica y Benefactor de la Patria.'*" I was surprised that Doña Piri had a friend so evidently a man of the world, and I saw, too, that he was by no means the man for whom my life was held in abeyance. He was fat and quite elderly.

"Is President of United Picture, old friend of my family." Doña Piri was watching my face so anxiously that I thought I saw how the land lay, and I smiled and said knowingly, "I'd be very glad, Doña Piri, to have dinner with you and your friend. This evening will be fine." I was sincerely glad that old Doña Piri should have a man of her own.

"Hello Ticher," said the three pretty girls in chorus. They were sisters, one aged seventeen and twins of fifteen.

" 'Hello teeecher,' " I said. "Good morning. Please sit down."

A *merengue* came from inside the house. The rocking chairs and table for the lesson had been set up on the *galería,* which was beautifully tiled and ran around four sides of a very old patio with flowerpots and climbing plants that filtered and dappled the brightness. It looked cool, but it was, in fact, extremely hot. The young girls wore loose house dresses and had their hair in curlers, and they rocked and giggled and poked each other. The older sister, whom I thought the prettiest even though she wore glasses like me, said, "Ticher, why you have no boy friend?"

"How do you know I don't?" I asked, blushing under their six black eyes.

"We saw you. Yesterday—*con los Ingleses*. In Café Madrid."

" 'With the English. In *the* Café Madrid,' " I said. "I saw you, too, walking by with your mother." I would have asked them to stop rocking, but their mother, who chaperoned the class at a small distance, sat in a rocking chair, and she was rocking, too.

"Emanuela," the mother called into the house, "turn off the music and get the front door. Hot, isn't it?" she said to me, fanning her armpits with a palm leaf.

The maid showed in "Doctor" Levy. We greeted one another, and when Doña Maria was well insulated from the lesson, with her feet in water and with the *merengue* continuing into its hundredth chorus, I said to the young girls, "Today we will have English conversation. We will talk about boy friends. If a boy friend asked you to come for a walk on the Conde, would you go?"

The girls looked prettily at me. They said, "Yes, and Mama would come with us."

I said, "Supposing a lady you knew asked you to come to dinner, would you go with her?"

"Mama would go also," they said.

"English girls go everywhere alone," I said. "Don't you ever wish you could go out alone?"

"Oh yes, we do wish it," they said out of politeness, but I could tell from the pretty roundness of their throats and cheeks and their bright giggling eyes that they dared more under their mother's wing than I in the pride of independence.

I said, "Now we will have English dictation."

"There's a gentleman on the *galería* asking for you," said Frau Bader at my door that evening.

"A gentleman!" I said, and wished I had my mother here to go with me. I wished I were staying at home.

"Why don't you ask him to dinner? You know I make a special price for you!"

The man standing at the head of the steps was small, fat, and old. He wore a very light, buff-colored suit open over his large stomach, upon which waved a loose, brightly patterned tie. He gave me a remarkably delicate hand and said he was Indalecio Aguirre and that Doña Piri had asked him to give me a lift because it was difficult to find her house. He spoke English well. He appeared to be so nervous that I wanted to put him at his ease, and I said, "That's kind of you, though I'm quite used to getting around by myself."

"Wonderful," said this Don Indalecio, and he took my elbow

to lead me down the steps to where an immense chauffeur-driven car stood at the curb. I was gratified to know that both Frau Bader and Julia, the hotel maid, were watching my man-accompanied departure. Don Indalecio got in after me and settled, I was relieved to see, well over to his side of the back seat as we drove off into the tropical sunset that turned the day into total darkness within seconds.

"Is it a very long way?" I asked.

"Quite a way, the other side of town." Don Indalecio told the chauffeur, in Spanish, to drive by way of the Boulevard Benefactor de la Patria. To me, he said, "I've not seen it since it was reopened last month. There, look: all widened, macadamized, planted with noble palms. As splendid a thoroughfare as you're likely to see, leading to absolutely nothing."

I laughed appreciatively. Don Indalecio was pointing to the end of the thoroughfare, where two dilapidated huts stood, one closed permanently, the other housing a little ramshackle grocery lit inside with spirit lamps. Beyond lay open country.

"Those buildings on the right are army barracks," Don Indalecio explained, "and over there you see the lights of the airport."

"I've never been here before," I said. "I like to see new parts of the town."

A slight shift in the gentleman's position alarmed me, but Don Indalecio had merely turned his head and seemed to be studying me. I found myself telling him about myself, that I was Jewish, came from Vienna, that my uncle had a grocery in Santiago, that I had a degree from the University of London and taught English. Don Indalecio listened with a mannerly and benevolent interest, nodding his head and saying, "Very good. Aha!" from time to time, as if confirming what he heard. And it occurred to me that Doña Piri must have told him about me.

"I seem to be teaching mostly diplomats and their families," I boasted.

"Ah yes, our local foreign corps! Have you noticed what a dog-eared lot of humanity they send us out here? Do you happen to know the ambassador of X?"

"Oh, I teach him five mornings a week," I said.

"Then you know he's a near moron."

"You're so right! He is!"

"And the minister of Y, a good man, who had his insides shot up in the First World War. As for the consul of Z, he might have gone far if he hadn't married his mistress."

"What's wrong with marrying your mistress?" I asked, to show how broadminded I was, and noticed that Don Indalecio looked at me with increased satisfaction.

The car had begun to bump over the baked surface of a mud road. The headlights picked out a cactus hedge with clothes hung out to dry upon it and houses of slats and corrugated iron like the houses where Pastora lived in Santiago. Women with large bellies stood in their black door holes watching the great car go by.

We passed into a new section, slithering and lifting across newly churned land, no longer field and not yet road. On either side stood little, new, modernistic stucco bungalows. On the veranda of one I could see Doña Piri looking out for us.

Doña Piri bustled around me, like a puppydog. "How you like?" she kept asking, as we walked inside the little house. The colors were pastel and harsh; everything looked painfully new. Don Indalecio whispered, "Doesn't it look like a stage setting? Look at the little window curtains, the sofa, the table set for three."

It had already occurred to me that Doña Piri had indeed arranged this little scene for Don Indalecio and me, and I laughed, frowned, and shook my head at him. But Don Indalecio continued unabashed. "I feel, my dear Piri, that as soon as the señorita and I have gone, this whole room will be carried away again."

"Come now," I whispered, as Doña Piri excused herself and went out to her kitchen, "she means *so* well."

"Do you think so?" asked Don Indalecio, turning to look into my face as if for information.

"You know, she only moved into this house a few days ago."

"Aha! That explains it." He put out a furtive finger to poke the pink wall. "It looks as if it's hardly set in its mold."

"Doesn't it!" I laughed.

Don Indalecio was tapping the sofa for me to come and sit beside him, and he offered me a cigarette. He sat with one fat leg crossed easily over the other, cigarette held between the fore and middle fingers of his elegant right hand, and entertained me. Don Indalecio was a Spaniard, but he, too, had lived in England; he had read books, even confessed deprecatingly to having written one. He spoke English with wit and grace. I crossed my legs and held my cigarette elegantly between fore and middle finger.

During dinner Don Indalecio continued to give me his attention, to the exclusion of our hostess. His shoulder seemed turned against her, and I kept wanting to redress the balance by turning the conversation toward her. "I think this is going to be a very pretty place once it gets the feeling of being lived in," I said to her.

"Of course, we don't know yet," said Don Indalecio, "whether it's going to *be* lived in."

"You're not going to stay here?" I asked Doña Piri, puzzled.

She said, "Did you know that I owe this house to Don Indalecio?"

"You do?" I asked. There seemed to be something in the air that I had not understood or had misunderstood.

"As I recall, my dear Piri, this was all your great idea," Don Indalecio said, with such an edge in his voice that I thought they were quarreling, but as I looked from one to the other, they were both smiling at me.

Doña Piri said, "The señorita has beautiful taste, and she is going to help me arrange the furniture."

"I don't know why Doña Piri thinks I know anything about arranging furniture. I live in a hotel room, you know."

"Some day soon, you shall have a house of your own," said Don Indalecio, "and not a stage setting!" He smiled meaningfully at me. I frowned at him and glanced at Doña Piri, but her eyes were on me as if to make sure I was enjoying myself.

"Of course," went on Don Indalecio gaily, "I was speaking only of the décor. The cast," he said, looking gallantly at me, "is delightful."

Doña Piri beamed. She suggested that I might enjoy sitting out on the *galería*, but first I went to the bathroom, where I put on some more lipstick.

When I came outside, Doña Piri and Don Indalecio were sitting on two chairs close together and talking, but stopped politely when I joined them.

I said, "How nice it is to see two old friends in conversation together." The parallel smiles with which they were looking at me made me blush as if I had said something silly. I shivered and Doña Piri jumped up to fetch me a shawl.

It was a mean little wool shawl. It was a mean little *galería*, looking across the mutilated earth of the road to the constant blinking of the many-colored airfield lights. There was the untidy clutter of a large unfinished building going up on a rise in the ground at the end of the road. I said I thought I must be going home.

Don Indalecio rose at once and signaled to his chauffeur, whom I saw, as I said good-by to Doña Piri, leaning over the back of the car as if he were adjusting the number plate.

Don Indalecio settled himself beside me in the back seat and said, "I was wondering if you would mind my just stopping off for a moment at a cottage I have near here. I have to pick up some papers."

"Fine," I said.

I kept glancing sidewise at the bulk of his shoulder and the expanse of his soft, pendulous cheek, which seemed, in the half darkness, to be very close to my eye. He was breathing in an odd way, with sharp, quick heaves. I wondered if it was asthma, and when he bent forward to speak to the chauffeur and his arm inside his jacket became pressed against mine inside the shawl Doña Piri had insisted on my taking, I would not move away for fear of offending him, but sat rigid, hardly breathing, with every nerve withdrawn from the contact and waiting deep inside myself for the arm to be removed.

The car turned into a side road that soon became nothing more than a thickly wooded mud drive. We stopped. In the darkness outside was a house. Don Indalecio did not immediately get out.

"You'll excuse me, won't you? I shan't be a minute. Or would you like to come in and have a drink before we go on? Come and see my bachelor's retreat."

I could not think, under the stress of the moment, of a way to refuse the invitation without the immodesty of seeming to presume that this man wanted what he had not even hinted at. And I wanted to be brave about life. I said, "I'd love to."

The chauffeur held the car door. There was gravel underfoot. It was dark. Don Indalecio had gone ahead and seemed, by the sound of falling and creaking objects, to be making his way across a cluttered *galería,* groping for the light switch. The light came on inside what appeared to be a quite small, ramshackle bungalow. Don Indalecio threw open the door, and in the sudden illumination I caught a glimpse of the chauffeur's face, which appeared to me in that moment horribly, evilly awry, before I realized that he was grinning at me.

I walked into the lion's den and then refused to sit down in it. "No, thank you. I don't feel like sitting."

"Let me take the shawl."

"Thank you, no. I'm a little chilly," I said and shivered.

Don Indalecio excused himself and left the room, and I heard the lavatory chain pulled. It seemed to me that during the twenty minutes we were inside the cottage, Don Indalecio went out three times, while I kept walking around with my handbag held over my bosom and my arms wrapped around my handbag, remembering to hold my shoulders straight the way my mother was always telling me.

The room was a crude, simple one, a bachelor's country quarters. There was a big modern refrigerator right next to the front door, a shabby, comfortable armchair, and a handsome mahogany table cluttered with male objects: a pair of flannels, a gun, an old airmail edition of the New York *Times.* On the wall over a simple fireplace hung a landscape painted with a fresh, loose stroke. When Don Indalecio came back in, I said, "Who did this? It's good."

"You think so?" He came and stood beside me. "It was done by a young friend of mine. Juanita Rivera. She exhibits in the

Galería des Bellas Artes. I'm glad to have your opinion of it. I want to buy some more paintings, and I was hoping for your advice. My own taste is quite rudimentary." He grinned down at his terrible tie.

At that moment I liked him enormously. "Well, this is quite, quite good," I said. "I like it."

"I have another one of hers inside that I should like you to see." Don Indalecio led the way into a smaller room with a bed, from which I averted my eyes, fixing them on the portrait that hung above it. It was Don Indalecio's profile as I had seen it beside me in the car when he had thought himself unobserved, self-absorbed, with the great cheek relaxed and loose. What the little portrait revealed with the impact of immediate conviction was that Don Indalecio looked like nothing so much as a sad, subtle, indecent old woman.

"It's very good. A very sensitive portrait, but I think I like the landscape better still," I said and turned on my heel and marched back out into the front room. "This is somehow a bigger picture. It's *her* advice you should get in buying paintings. Compared with her, I'm an amateur."

"Yes. Well, yes, but that young lady, you see, is a little angry with me. She doesn't give me her advice any more. Well," he said, "let's go."

Don Indalecio picked up a roll of papers, took me by the elbow and walked me out, locked the door, put out the light, and handed me back into the car, where he sat silently hunched into his corner of the back seat.

"By the way," I said, "if you're really interested in pictures, maybe you would like to come up to the hotel where I live."

Don Indalecio seemed to rally at this.

"There's a Hungarian painter called Janos Kraus, who's not bad. I could arrange for you to have dinner with him. Frau Bader's dinners, as a matter of fact, aren't bad either."

"Fine, fine," said Don Indalecio and jerked his head so sharply away that I looked sidewise to see his profile with lips turned down, the fat, womanish old cheeks drooping sadly.

I kept talking about Janos—that he was talented, though derivative—until we arrived in front of the hotel.

Don Indalecio got out to say good-by. He held my hand a moment. "Perhaps you and I could have dinner sometime. Maybe we can visit the Galería des Bellas Artes together and you can teach me about modern art. Then we could go to the Jaragua, or to your hotel, for dinner."

"I should like that very much," I said sincerely.

"You would?" said Don Indalecio, and he looked quite pleased.

By the time I returned from the ambassador's lesson next morning, the maid, Julia, had a message for me from Doña Piri, who had called on the telephone. She was prevented from coming to her class, but would I have dinner with her and Don Indalecio tonight, or the night after. I wished the good woman would let up and let things take their course. Before I left I said, "Julia, if that lady calls again, tell her I will return her shawl when I see her."

But as I walked up the Malecon toward the house of Señora Ferrati, my next pupil, it occurred to me that Don Indalecio might have asked Doña Piri to arrange another meeting. He must really have liked me. I began to wonder if I might be more charming than I had any idea of. I began to smile. I smiled at the sleek black diplomatic cars gliding past and at the skinny black children watering the cosseted lawns. Even the Ferratis' silly, pastel-green castle with its stucco battlements looked engaging in this holiday world, this perpetual summer light.

The Ferratis were refugees, too, but they were Spanish and rich. I was shown up to the señora's cool, shuttered bedroom, where she was busy with herself in front of the dressing mirror. "Ah, the señorita! Would you mind if we only had half an hour this morning? I have Doctor Levy coming to do my feet. And let's just have conversation."

"Then speak English, please."

"Oh, I forget. I go to canasta (is right?) to Señora Ambassador of X. Is awful bore. This night we go to 'otel Jaragua. Is too much. Makes me nervous."

The señora did not look at all nervous to me. With her ample body and warm skin color, dressed in a beautiful, elegant suit of white piqué, on the way to some party, Señora Ferrati was living my daydream, except that I had met her husband on the stairs, a dull, dapper little man with a precise military mustache. Yet the señora had about her a look of enjoyment. I used to study her.

"I will ask you a question, and you answer in English. Do you happen to know someone called Indalecio Nuñez Aguirre?"

Señora Ferrati looked up from her nails, which she was painting a hot pink color. "You have new boy friend, is it?"

"No. No, no! He is a gentleman I met at the house of a mutual acquaintance. He is Spanish, too, and I just thought you might have met him. I think he is the president of some big movie distributor."

Señora Ferrati furrowed her brow and thought she recalled having met such a person once, and she looked at me with such a pleased, nosy expression that I told her all about last night.

"Dear Señorita, he is interested in you," she kept saying. "He must be immensely rich, and he is interested."

"But he is an old man," I said. We had both forgotten about speaking English.

"How old?"

"Fifty, or sixty, maybe."

"So? How old are you?"

"Twenty-one."

"Oh. Well anyway, then what happened?"

"Nothing. We had dinner. We sat on the veranda. He's quite a cultured man. He has some good pictures by a girl, a painter called Juanita Rivera, in his cottage in the country."

"You went inside his cottage?"

"Why not? There were some papers he had to pick up," I said, and colored.

"Well, *then,*" asked the señora, "what happened?"

"Then he took me home to the Parisienne."

"Oh, my dear. Yes. And then?"

"He went home."

"My dear Señorita, you have made a conquest! Do you know a man like that can make your fortune?"

I shook my head fastidiously, but I saw a house of my own on the Malecon, a salon consisting of all the prettiest and brightest people on the island. In a mental letter to my English friends, I described my husband, a businessman, it was true, but witty and cultured. And all the time I knew that this was not for me.

The señora was flapping her hands to dry her nails.

"I was saying to my husband only yesterday, I said the Señorita would be one of the best catches in town: She is white, and she is pretty, and she is educated. If the señorita had a fortune she could get anybody."

I pushed my glasses up on my nose and said, "I am not pretty."

"I think you are pretty!" the señora said in a sincere tone. "As I said to my husband, the señorita is so spiritual-looking."

"Oh, that," I said, and my heart dropped.

"I often wish I looked more spiritual," said Señora Ferrati, putting a handsome cross on a heavy silver chain around her throat.

"Besides," I said, remembering the things in the air yesterday that I had not understood, which still vibrated like false notes in my mind, "he might be married for all I know. He looks sort of settled."

The señora folded a square of hot pink silk between the white of her suit and her olive skin. It gave her a sudden brilliancy. "Oh my dear Señorita! Don't talk to me about married men!" She rose. The lesson was over. "You know what I shall do at the canasta party?" I thought for a moment that she was about to invite me along, but she said, "There's sure to be someone there who knows your Don Indalecio. I'm going to find out all about him. I'm going to be your detective."

On the stairs I met "Doctor" Levy, who would have passed me with a bow, but I stopped to ask him how he did. He thanked me for the recommendation which had introduced him to Señora Ferrati. It was a pleasure, I said. I asked him if he had ever come across a Don Indalecio Nuñez Aguirre. He said, no, the gentleman he had never met, but he did the señora's feet regularly.

"You mean Señora Aguirre? The wife of Don Indalecio?"

Indeed yes, and sometimes he was called to do the feet of her older, married daughter who had two little girls, and he would be glad to recommend me as an English teacher next time he was there.

The hotel was deserted after lunch. The guests, even Frau Bader herself, had crept into their rooms to hide from the full blast of the midday heat. A turkey screamed in the next yard. Of course I had known all along! Had I not told Señora Ferrati that Don Indalecio was probably married?

The maid knocked at my door.

"Señorita, that lady called again."

"Oh, she did, did she. You gave her my message?"

"Yes, Señorita. She said, 'Damn and blast the goddam shawl, what I want to know is when she's coming to dinner again!' "

"Oh. Thank you, Julia."

Julia still stood in the doorway on her splayed feet, her skimpy dress pulled tight over her swollen stomach like the women I had seen yesterday in the doors of their shacks.

Julia said, "Señorita, you remember you said you would teach me how to write?"

"So I did. You mean *now?* Oh! All right. Sit down here."

I gave her a pencil and the notebook I had bought (thinking I was going to write a story I had in mind about a girl in a refugee hotel on a tropical island) and I said, "All right. Open it. No, no! Why in the middle? On the first page. Here: I will draw you a line of loops, like small e's. Now you copy them here. No, Julia! Start on the *left*-hand side. I will lie down on my bed and you call me when you have finished."

It was beastly hot. The turkey was crying and Julia sat with her nose within three inches of the pencil, which she held painfully in a cramped fist.

"Why are you turning over, Julia? You can't have finished the page. Let me see."

Julia had done three loops where I had shown her, and she had done a giant loop in the middle and two more and now she was turning over. I stood and looked at her: I was trying to empty my mind of the concepts "page" and "book"; to imagine what it was like not knowing pictures, not having lived in England—it was as difficult as trying to imagine knowing what I did not know—the passionate life that Julia must know, behind those black doorholes of her home. I said, "Julia, where do you live?"

"Way out, Señorita, in the country."

"The other side of town, near the airfield, isn't it?"

"Oh no, Señorita. Near the airfield is where the bad women live."

"No, I mean beyond the army barracks."

"Beyond the army barracks, this side of the airfield, is where they live."

"No, no. Where there is a new road, and buildings going up."

"That's where they are building a sporting house and houses for the girls, and a new road for the gentlemen's cars."

"Ah, I see . . ."

I saw in one of those backward revelations—as if I were watching the replay of a movie I had seen before—Don Indalecio's chauffeur bending over the back of the car; only this time I saw that he was removing a small blank shield that had hung over the number plate.

"There goes the telephone again, Señorita."

It was Señora Ferrati, for me, calling from the middle of her canasta party. "My dear, I have such a thing to tell you, you have no idea. I must see you. It's so terrible I can't tell you over the telephone!" Señora Ferrati sounded happy.

"Wait," I said. "You are going to be at the Jaragua tonight? I can come and meet you there."

"Oh, dear Señorita, meet me there! I have to fly back to my table. What an absolutely awful thing! Good-by."

"Good night, Señorita," said Julia out of the darkness as I left my hotel that evening. I looked around and could just make out her cotton dress a shade lighter than the night bushes. Julia was leaning over the hedge, watching the people go by; and I knew with a shock that black Julia's Saturday evenings were as lonely and her poor nights as innocent even as my own.

The new girl behind the glass counter of the cigarette stand wore a deep décolletage and shoulder-length hair. On Saturday nights, the lobby was full of well-to-do Dominicans who came to dance in the open-air patio, skinny men in light, loose-fitting suits with padded shoulders, and their well-fleshed women, in tight skirts and draped bosoms, wearing flowers in their hair.

I stood in embarrassed solitariness, wearing the mask of one who watches life tumbling about her, and was so glad to catch sight of my ambassador standing at no great distance that I waved enthusiastically. He came over to shake hands, smiling horribly with his teeth only. "Ah, you come here! You say you not come!" Now Señora Ferrati, in a gay, grand, flowered gown, was coming toward us. The ambassador bowed over her hand. He kept saying, "My wife is somewhere around. Ah, you know the Señorita! She is my English teacher. Won't you and Señor Ferrati join my wife and me in the patio."

The señora promised to join him, but first she walked me away to the ladies' room, and under pink neon lights, sitting on beige leather stools, surrounded by walls of mirror, we put our heads together.

"Dear Señorita, you will never guess. This Señora Lopez at the canasta party has known the Aguirres forever and, my dear, he has a wife and two grown-up daughters."

"I know. I even told you this morning I thought he must be married. You remember I told you that?"

"Wait! It seems there is this woman, Pilar Cruz, who was his mistress, my dear, for fifteen years! Can you imagine?"

"You know something! That's what I thought at first, that Don Indalecio and Doña Piri were lovers, but now I am *sure* she planned for him to meet me. . . . I mean, you don't mean *my* Doña Piri?"

"Doña Piri. Piri Cruz. Everybody knows her. It seems he kept her for fifteen years," said Señora Ferrati with her happy greedy eyes.

"Maybe they were in love!" I said.

"Oh, Señorita! Anyway, it seems since she has got too old she makes a living getting girls for him. Señora Lopez told me her husband told her that Don Indalecio told him that the girl he had now was getting difficult, crying all the time and demanding . . ."

"I know," I said, "a painter and a very sensitive one. You remember I told you about the painter."

"Well, anyway, Don Indalecio promised this Doña Piri this house, or she asked him for a house, I forget which, if she got him a new girl. Isn't that just awful? I mean, can you imagine? I have to run. My husband will be looking for me."

"Are you going to sit with the ambassador?" I asked, hoping she might ask me to join them.

"Yes, and I want to look for Señora Lopez. She said she might be here this evening and she was going to try and find out more from her husband. So? What kind of a detective do I make?"

I went and stood in the door of the patio. The *merengue* band was playing at the far end of the dance floor. Waiters in white coats passed among the tables, under the colored lanterns. A group of English people I knew from the Café Madrid sat at a table so near me I could see the whisky glasses between their elbows and hear the clipped, precise accents just like my own.

"Hello Ticher," said the three young girls in chorus.

"Why, hello! How do you do?" I said to their stout mother, hovering and smiling behind them. In the semidarkness their sweet, pale dresses gleamed and rustled, and their six black eyes watched me.

"Good-by, Ticher," they said.

"Hey, hello!" called Janos, the painter. "Come and join us." He was sitting with "Doctor" and "Madame" Levy, Frau Bergel, the piano teacher, and her daughter Lilli, lately come from New York, who had begun to give English lessons like me, but with an American accent. I saw them for a dreary group of foreigners, professionals, like latter-day courtiers living off the city's dog-eared aristocracy.

"Sit down," they said. "Stay with us."

After that, Janos and I began to go about together. He was very much like me—self-involved, unhappy, and arrogant—and I could not stand him. He complained a lot about his talents wasted in this uncivilized outpost of the world, but I thought his talents rather minor. It was my social talent, I thought, that was going curiously undiscovered: Doña Piri had seen how I would do for Don Indalecio and Don Indalecio had thought me entertaining enough. I could never figure out why the English colony, or the Dominicans, or the diplomatic set failed to "take me up."

Soon even Doña Piri stopped calling me. She never came for another lesson. A month after the dinner party, I met her in the street and started toward her. I was ashamed of the trouble she had taken to set a trap for me, that there had never been the slightest chance I should fall into it. I thought I had made a fool of her. "I'm sorry," I said, "I still have that shawl of yours," and found myself smiling, for a split second, into a look of pure, straight hatred, before she averted her eyes and passed by as if she had not seen me. During the next two years, I ran across her frequently. She must have moved back into town. From the progressive shabbiness of her dress, I judged that she had fallen upon bad times. I'm sure she blamed me, for she never again gave evidence of our acquaintance.

Don Indalecio's picture appeared in the papers again. The caption said that Indalecio Nuñez Aguirre, President of United Pictures Cia., was going on an extended business trip, and Señora Ferrati asked if we might have just English conversation. "I have such a thing to tell you. Remember that Don Indalecio and his girl friend? Well, it seems he went back to her and things went from bad to worse. It seems he has this cottage in the country . . ."

"I know," I said.

"And there was a fight and his gun went off, my dear Señorita! And the girl is in the hospital and Don Indalecio has to go away to the United States until it all blows over, can you imagine? Isn't that terrible? I wouldn't speak to that man for the world. Do you mind if we just have half an hour? I have to run. The Lopezes are giving him a good-by dinner. I'll tell you all about it tomorrow. You remember how I told you not to get involved!"

"I remember," I said. I saw in my mind's eye the violent scene in that place, among the objects where I myself had stood holding my handbag over my bosom and my arms around my handbag, so that nothing had been able to happen to me. It frightened me that I had not been tempted. I began to fear that I might be incorruptible forever.

CHAPTER TWELVE

New York: My Own House

In 1938, when Austrian Jews understood the meaning of Hitler's coming, we ran to the American Consulate. Each one was given a number, as customers are in some New York bakeries, to insure their being served in the strict order of arrival. But the "American quota"—as the system was familiarly known—resembled a bakery system gone awry, and issuing a separate series of numbers to people who came from different streets.

My grandparents' numbers, on the quota allowed to persons born in Hungary, came through first, in 1949, nearly a year after my grandfather's death. My grandmother, who was then seventy-five years old, went on to New York alone. She wrote that America was no good. The Jewish Committee had found her lodgings with one Amalie Kruger, an old witch who couldn't even cook a proper soup, and when my grandmother had wanted to show her, she had told my grandmother to get out of her kitchen, and my grandmother was never going to speak to her again. God alone knew if she would live to see the day of our coming to America, for she was ill with longing.

Paul's number came through in 1950, and he followed my grandmother to New York. One evening, as he was taking her for a walk on Riverside Drive, they happened to run into the Freibergs, who had been in America for over a year and were about to return to Vienna. "The New York summer is nothing for us people. Worse than Santiago. You wait and see! And there is no culture in America," they said, and they turned down the corners of their mouths in unison and shook their heads. They offered Paul the remaining lease on their apartment on West 157th Street. It consisted of a narrow hallway leading to a kitchen, with a room for my grandmother on the left side and a room for Paul on the right. When my mother and I arrived in May of 1951, Paul moved his bed into my grandmother's room and bought two couches for us and a piano for my mother, and the right-hand room became a sitting-dining room, with a plastic-topped kitchen table for the four of us to eat on. The place was shabbily furnished with a number of large rickety chests of drawers from the Salvation Army, but I was on the whole gratefully surprised—the rooms were of decent size, the ceilings high. In my mind's eye, I redisposed the furniture, painted it; I could see the couches covered in some rich fabric. The place had possibilities. Paul promised that some day he would help me rearrange it.

The first evening, Paul walked me one block down to Riverside Drive.

"Why, it's pretty!" I said. "It's as pretty as the Thames Embankment. Prettier—if it weren't for all that horrible advertising." I pointed beyond the highway with the twin white lights coming, red taillights going in both directions. Road without end, I thought. (I was pleased with the thought—must remember to put it in a letter to my university friends in London.) The New Jersey shore threw its commercial neon messages in shivering paths of prime color across the water. "So garish," I said. "The sky is positively purple with it. Look!"

The next morning, my mother and I set out for the employment agencies. My grandmother stood in the hall door, saying, "Have you your handkerchief? Money? Keys? Have you got your lunch bag?" she asked Paul, who was leaving for work. "Come back soon!" she said to each one.

The sun was shining straight up 157th Street as we walked down, shielding our eyes against the flashing windows of the Republican Club over the Rexall's at the corner. The sleazy Broadway small-town shops and the green-and-yellow taxis gleamed, freshly washed by the early May morning sun. We went down into the subway and climbed out at Forty-second Street. I came bringing my London University B.A. Eng. (Hons.), a prize in a short-story contest, and my talent in drawing, "looking," I told the interviewers, "for an interesting job." They asked me to fill out a card, and when they had looked it over they told me to go and learn shorthand and typing, get a year or two of American experience, and to come back again. As Paul put it that evening, "America, the land of unlimited opportunity for people who can work the I.B.M. machine."

Paul was working in a well-known New York research foundation. He had applied for a laboratory job, where his medical training might be useful, but his degree from the University of Vienna was not recognized in the U.S. However, the personnel department had expressed interest in his experience with livestock in Sosua, and he got a job as animal attendant. He had asked if there was any chance of being promoted to the laboratory, and they said you could never tell what opportunity might turn up.

My mother found work in the kitchen underneath the Fifth Avenue branch of a famous restaurant chain, helping prepare hors d'oeuvres. My mother says she did not know most of the house specialties, and even after she had learned how to make them she did not recognize their American names coming distorted down the speaking tube, and the angry Negro woman at the next worktable would not tell her. My mother was afraid she was going to lose her job and came home evenings crying from nervousness and exhaustion.

I got a job as a file clerk in a shoe factory in Queens at forty dollars a week. I sat with the girls at a long table, transferring incoming orders onto pink cardboard sheets. On my left sat an obese pimply blonde named Charlene. I told her that I had just arrived from the Dominican Republic, where I had taught English, that I was Austrian but had lived ten years in England. Charlene leveled unblinking blue eyes insultingly at me and said something to her friend about people with accents going back where they came from. It was Charlene's job to make up the list of lunch orders, which it was my job to fetch from the luncheonette downstairs. She waited till precisely twelve so that I was bound to lose ten minutes of my lunch hour, till I discovered that by dawdling a little I ran into the crowds from the other floors at the pickup counter and could waste fully twenty minutes of hers. I remember the thrill of my victory, which was short-lived, for she retaliated. We got cleverer each day in mutual meanness.

In my dreams at night, Charlene and I embraced and explained ourselves to one another, but mornings, before I went to work, I vomited. At lunch time, to avoid the sight of her obscene back turned toward me, I went out. I walked around the factory district, stepping over abandoned railway lines, seeing no one for minutes on end. Then two workmen in blue overalls, sitting on the steps of a rusty railway wagon drinking coffee out of Thermos flasks, waved to me. I felt happy. Presently I found myself at the edge of water, on the far side of which the huge slab of the United Nations building stood on its reflection. I ran back to the factory writing a mental letter to my London friends.

In the evening, as I came up the street, I saw my grandmother at the kitchen window, and when I stepped off the elevator she was holding the hall door open. I kissed her and said, "Why do you have to stand around waiting for us? You could sit down."

"Your mother is late!"

"How late? Eleven minutes!"

"What could have happened to her!" my grandmother said in distress.

"Well, let's see." I held up my hand and counted the possibilities on my fingers. "Maybe she got into conversation with her supervisor; maybe she walked up Fifth Avenue to look in the shop windows; maybe the subway got stuck between stations—"

"You think something happened on the subway?" my grandmother asked and went back to the kitchen window. "There she is!" she said. "And there's Pauli, too," and she waved to them until they disappeared into the house door below her. Then she went to stand in the hall door to watch the red light of the ascending elevator bringing her children home.

"I made some poppy-seed strudel," my grandmother said. "The table is all set."

But Paul said he was going to shower and change and go over to have dinner with Dolf. One of the first things Paul had done when he arrived in New York was to look for Dolf in the Manhattan telephone book. He found him, too. Dolf had married. He was still writing poetry—in German—with no one to read it. Paul went to see him once in a while, to take great draughts of friendship and conversation, and each time my grandmother was unhappy and tried to dissuade him.

"Your wonderful friend Dolf, thoughtless as ever, making you go out again after a day's work. You look exhausted."

"I feel fine, Muttilein."

"Why don't you eat here and go afterward? What does his wife know about your delicate stomach?"

"She's a fine cook. Very good."

My grandmother took him to the door to see that he had his handkerchief and everything. "Come back soon," she said.

"I don't understand Paul," my grandmother said when we three women sat down to supper. "How he can keep going to the house of a friend who doesn't think of inviting his mother, his sister, and his niece."

"Omama," I said, "what would you and Dolf have to talk about?"

"Lorle!" my mother said, with a pleading look to me not to be rude to my grandmother. And she proposed that we should go down and sit in the triangle, the *Dreieck'*, as my grandmother had come to call the traffic island at the corner.

Frau Hohemberg, who lived in the house where my grandmother had had her first lodgings, sat by my grandmother. "So this is the daughter and granddaughter? Why aren't you out with a boy friend?" she asked me.

"She doesn't have one," said my grandmother. "She is too choosey."

"I'll go out. Don't you worry about me," I said.

But *I* was worried. There was a picture printed permanently in the back of my mind—I had seen it through a door in the moment it had taken someone to open it and pass inside—a woman sitting on a high stool, swinging a leg; a man supporting himself on an elbow stood leaning toward her. Maybe I had only read about it in a book. On Saturday evenings, especially, I thought about finding such a door, but some bars, I knew from the movies, did not admit single women, and I didn't know the names of drinks; no one might come and lean on the bar toward me. I looked at my ankle and doubted if it was the shape for swinging. My mother invited my grandmother and me to come to the triangle.

I said, "Not me! I'm going out."

"Where are you going?" asked my grandmother, when she came to the hall door to see me off.

"I don't know," I said.

"When will you be back?"

"Since I don't know where I'm going, it's hard to say how long it will take."

"Lorle!" my mother pleaded.

"Why don't you want to tell me where you are going?" my grandmother asked, very much surprised.

"Because I'm twenty-three years old, Omama, and might want to go somewhere you wouldn't approve," I said, though I think her interest in my affairs would have irritated me less if there had been an affair to scrutinize.

"Thank you," said my grandmother, her eyes starting angrily out of their sockets. "That will be a good thought with which to lie in bed at night waiting for you to come home."

"Don't think about me. I don't need you to wait for me."

"I will never ask where you are going again, I promise you," said my grandmother. "The best thing I could do would be to die," she said, and went into the living room.

"Go quick and kiss her," my mother whispered, but my grandmother was laying out a game of solitaire and would not look at me.

I took the subway to Times Square and walked among the lights of the advertisements that blinked and ran and jumped, changed colors, and started over. Yah, I thought, yah, "TIMES SQUARE, CROSSROADS OF THE WORLD," indeed! It reminded me of the Viennese fair to which our maid, Poldi, used to take me around Christmas time, where the country people set up their gaudy booths. I walked, self-consciously philosophizing, describing in an imaginary letter to London the fifteen-cent turtles with "Greetings from New York" in red paint on their tiny backs, the Texan hats on which a woman at a rattling sewing machine would put your initials in rickrack for thirty cents. A fat girl in blue satin, wearing a flowered hat, pointed to the window next to the shooting gallery, where a crowd stood watching a Negro in an outsize chef's hat broiling frankfurters.

There was a bookshop. I went inside. Under the shrill lights, I saw titles I was ashamed to appear to be looking at, but I found a fascinating book called "Writers' Yearbook," and inside there was a list of writers' clubs—one in Antioch, three in California, and one in Manhattan. I copied out the Manhattan address and went home and wrote a witty letter to the club. (For weeks, I tasted the delicious phrases in my recollection.)

"Frau Hohemberg has a nephew, a very nice young man. She has told him all about Lore," my grandmother said the next day, not addressing me directly, because she had not forgiven me.

"He must have been thrilled," I said.

"He wants to get married," my grandmother told my mother.

"Good luck to him," I said.

"Lorle," my mother said, "why don't you at least see this young man? You might like him."

"Who said I wouldn't see him?" I asked, and began to wait.

Toni Lustig came on Friday to take me to the local movie. He had a very pleasant face with Jewish brown eyes, exactly like the eyes of all my grandmother's brothers. Out of the sleeves of his navy-blue suit his wrists emerged nakedly, without cuffs. I cannot recall what film we saw, but I remember coming up the aisle afterward. Just as I was going to say, "What a nothing picture *that* was!" Toni said, "Wasn't that a lovely movie?" I told myself to keep silent. We had come out into midsummer-night Broadway. I asked him what he did.

"When I first came I was a *Packerlschupfer,*" Toni said in Viennese dialect, which means literally "one who chucks little packages around," that is to say, a shipping clerk. "Then I was a bus boy. Now, I'm working as a waiter and going to hotel school at night. What about you?"

"Well, in the Dominican Republic I taught English. I went to college in London," I replied. And, thinking I might be sounding intellectual again, I said, "Now I'm just a file clerk and a bad one. But," I added, "I'm going to be a writer."

"Oh," Toni said. "You are a writer! What are you writing about?"

"About a girl who saves all her money to buy the dress that's going to make her nose small and round."

"But a dress doesn't change a nose," Toni said.

"That's right," I said, "because it's never the right dress. So she starts saving all over again, and meanwhile she is getting older, but she says, 'It's just the touch of rheumatism I had this morning that's making me look badly. Tomorrow I will be pink and smooth, and my nose will be round—and my glasses will fall off.' "

"So in the end what happens?"

"She dies."

"Oh! Don't you ever write about happy people?"

"I don't believe in the species. When did you ever see a happy person?"

"I'm happy," Toni said.

"A beautiful young man," my grandmother commented next morning, with a question in her voice.

"A very nice young man, nicer than I," I said. "But just the littlest bit stupid."

"Poor old snobbish Lorle!" Paul said.

"Lore will never get married," said my grandmother.

"Lorle, you criticize too quickly," my mother said. "How can you know anyone after a single evening? Even if he is not the right person, he might introduce you to people. You have to start somewhere, you know."

"Yes, I know, Mummy."

"Meaning, 'shut up, Mummy'?"

"Meaning, I wish you would pay me the compliment of letting me make my own life at my own time. Just please don't worry about me."

"You're quite right," said my mother, looking anxiously at my grandmother, who, however, failed to be insulted and laughed gaily. "I've just this minute stopped worrying," she said, and folded her hands in her lap with the air of one who is not going to lift a finger.

That Saturday evening, I reminded Paul of his promise to help me rearrange the furniture. After we had moved everything around, my grandmother said she didn't see that the room looked any better than the way she had arranged it before we arrived.

I said, "The trouble is that it's impossible to see the space relations and planes till you've actually moved the pieces. Pauli, maybe the piano here and the couches parallel and then the table can go under the window." But this change still failed to produce the elegant order, the sense of space, for which I yearned. "How about the couches forming a corner under the window?" I said, and ran head on into the end of Paul's patience.

"Omama has a headache, your mother looks exhausted, and so am I. I'll give you a choice. You can leave it as it is."

"But it's not right this way," I said.

"Then we will put it back the way it was."

"But it was *ugly* the way it was," I said.

Horrified, I saw that even this word had not the power to move Paul. He loomed larger than life, with an angry mouth, saying, "This is your Omama's house, and you are only one of the four persons living it it. We must choose between your sensibilities and everybody else's comfort."

I went into the bathroom and cried, because I would have to go on living in an ugly apartment and because Paul had spoken to me in irritation.

When I came into the kitchen the next morning, he was studying the Sunday *Times* help-wanted columns. He told me that he had looked in at the laboratory on his lunch hour to ask if he could do anything, and they had asked him to wash some test tubes and he had dropped the bucket—a horrible mess. Paul said, "I'm going to put in an ad for myself. 'Wanted: situation with excellent pay for man no longer young, no experience, two left hands, talent for sitting down.' "

"Lend me the 'Help Wanted—Female,' " I said. "I keep looking where it says 'Wrtg.' or 'Coll. Grads.' I keep thinking somewhere there is this fascinating job surrounded by a set of handsome, kind, and interesting people."

Paul said he had been thinking about me. He very much regretted that he had no hand skills, and this might be the time for me to acquire some.

"Yes, I have been thinking, myself, of taking some evening courses. Maybe comparative religion."

No, no, Paul said, he had meant something more like shorthand and typing. "Only I think it should be something adjacent to your talents and interests—commercial art, perhaps."

"Ech, commercial art!" I said, and then I said, "Pauli, am I getting horribly on your nerves?"

"Horribly," Paul said. "Your mother and I were talking about you and saying that we're sorry for the man who takes you on, but that you are well worth the trouble."

"What man?" I said.

Toni never called again. For weeks, I tried to recall the words Paul had said about my being a lot of trouble to a man but worth his while, and I could never make out in my mind's ear if he had said, "the man who *will* take you on," or "the man who *would* take you on."

It was hardly three weeks later that my grandmother came

home from the triangle with the news of Toni Lustig's engagement. She had seen the girl, and she had buck teeth and was older than he.

One day, I opened our mailbox and found my witty letter to the writers' club, stamped "Address Unknown." I put my hand inside the mailbox and felt all around it; there was nothing else. The box next to ours had its door hanging open, and I felt inside it, too, and stood a moment, frightened that I was losing my good sense.

That winter, I took evening courses in shorthand and typing, and by the spring of my second year in New York I got a job with a public relations firm on Madison Avenue. They liked my British accent, and at first clearly thought that at fifty dollars a week I was a bargain. The firm was a new undertaking by two men, one of whom was nervous and one good-natured. The good-natured one did his own letters, and so did the nervous one after he found how badly I typed. Their clients—Danish Whale Meat, A Refresher Course in Male Magnetism, and A Proposal for Sending the Liberty Bell to the Philippine World's Fair—made little work for anyone. The nervous boss told me to keep looking busy. I asked if it would be all right for me to write my own stories, and he said that would be just fine.

On my lunch hour, I walked alternate pavements north and south, peering hungrily into the shop windows of high-class dress houses and aristocratic antique shops. At home, I undertook to paint the furniture. "If I could think of exactly the right color," I said.

"Brown," said my grandmother.

"Brown! Like imitation wood? Never! Paint should be paint. Red and blue aren't very elegant. Green is impossible. Gray, maybe."

"Nobody in America has gray furniture," said my grandmother.

"How would *you* know?"

"I know," said my grandmother. "I hear what people say."

"Where? In the triangle? What Frau Hohemberg says?"

"I've been in homes."

"In Frau Amalie Kruger's home. Just stop and think, Omama—when have you ever been inside an American home?"

"I have been, I have been," said my grandmother.

"Let me do it in gray, Omama. You'll see it will look so much nicer," I said, and my grandmother raised her right hand, palm out, and made a motion of throwing it away—of giving up.

I agonized a week over the precise shade, and presently the apartment was full of large rickety chests of drawers painted gray, and my grandmother went to bed ill from the commotion and the smell of turpentine mixing with the heat of August.

In the fall, Paul married Dolf's sister Suse, with whom he had gone to school in Vienna, and they moved into an apartment of their own in the Bronx. My mother moved into the bedroom with my grandmother and left me the sitting room, in which I moved furniture around like mad. I made what I thought a handsome corner of the two couches, and sewed Chinese-red burlap covers for them, which, my grandmother complained, were too scratchy to sit on. Nor could she make friends with the Danish teakwood coffee table I had got on sale; it was too low for playing solitaire. So my mother moved the old kitchen table into the bedroom, and there, from that time on, my grandmother mostly lived.

When my mother took a job in a bakery on Broadway and began to work late hours, she bought my grandmother an immense square black television set for the long evenings ahead.

"That nice Liberace; he's Jewish, isn't he?" asked my grandmother.

"Oh Omama! He's not! That's an Italian name," I said.

"I think he is Jewish," said my grandmother. "But this man—" She pointed to the screen. A master of ceremonies was introducing a little dog which wore a ballet skirt and stood on its hind legs. "I don't like *him*. He is an anti-Semite," my grandmother said.

"He uses Jews on his show all the time," I said. "What makes you think he is anti-Semitic?"

"I can always tell," said my grandmother.

"But you don't understand a word he is saying. What are you judging by?"

"I can always feel it," my grandmother said, patting the air with her right hand in a gesture that was proof against the arguments of mere logic.

On Saturday, my grandmother said, "Frau Hohemberg says there's a nice young woman who used to work on the machine next to hers, who goes to a club on Broadway with a lot of nice young Jewish people. They have lectures and do interesting things. They go to artists' studios and to the stockyards, and in summer they have picnics. She's going to give me the address for Lore."

"I don't want to go to the stockyards or to picnics with any nice young Jewish people," I said. "But you, Mummy! You should go out once in a while."

"I go out," said my mother. "Last Sunday, Omama and I went to tea with Frau Hohemberg."

"Yes," said my grandmother, "and Frau Hohemberg had specially invited her brother, who is a widower, for you, and all you did all afternoon was play with Toni Lustig's baby."

"But Muttilein, the baby was so much more charming than Frau Hohemberg's brother. He has a very high voice and a smelly cigar."

"But Mummy, maybe he would be interesting once you got to know him," I said. "Or he might know some other people. You have to start somewhere. Omama has her television."

"You don't have to bother about Omama, because Omama will soon be dead anyway," said my grandmother and went into her bedroom.

"Mutti! Lorle! I wouldn't even know where to go," my mother said.

"There are clubs!" I said impatiently. It was a long time after my mother had learned to keep out of my affairs that I stopped advising her on hers.

Then my grandmother took to going out by herself. In the fall, Paul had a son, Peter, and every week my grandmother undertook the trip, involving two changes of subway and one bus, to the Bronx.

I got fired from the public relations office—the nicest job I ever had—when the nervous boss put a name and phone number on my desk and asked me to put a call through, and I said, "One minute; as soon as I finish this paragraph."

I branched into commercial art. I was hired in the capacity of apprentice-saleswoman-receptionist-bottle-washer in a small, sixth-rate studio at thirty dollars a week. The boss said, "You stick with me. I'll make a designer out of you."

"You think I have talent, then?"

"Don't worry about talent. You keep your eyes open. I'll tell you what's selling. You'll be a designer."

I think he must have had high blood pressure. He was a huge, red-faced Pole called Polacek, who believed that the more you yelled the more you got out of people. "You've got to yell at them!" he yelled after hearing my embarrassed tone with a customer on the telephone. "Now sit down and paint."

"I thought you wanted me to—"

"Don't think. Paint."

A tall, handsome girl called Margery helped me mix my colors when the boss wasn't looking, and Mrs. Shapiro, the head designer, whispered that he really had a heart of gold—it was just his voice was loud. Mrs. Shapiro was built small and round, rather like my mother, and had the clear skin and happy eyes of a young girl. Sometimes her husband came to pick her up, and he, too, was small and round, with clear pink cheeks and the same charming air of happiness. Mrs. Shapiro talked with a modest tenderness of her two teen-age children and the senile mother-in-law who lived with them in their little house in Queens. Once, after work, I followed her downstairs and invited her for a cup of coffee.

"I'm studying you," I said. "You look like a happy woman and I've always contended there was no such thing."

Mrs. Shapiro said she was going to bring me last month's *Woman's Own*. They had an article in there how you must give and give, and happiness would come back to you. She said it had always worked for her.

The studio was at Broadway and Fortieth Street, in the middle of the garment district, which is within a block of the Crossroads of the world. During my lunch hour that autumn I walked systematically northward, and south, first along Broadway, then Seventh Avenue, and then east and west, and I was beginning to love New York. I had given up describing everything in letters to London. England had never replied.

One day, Margery asked me to come to a Jewish Youth dance with her on Saturday. "I wish you would come," she said. "I want to go, but I don't want to go my myself."

When I met her on the sidewalk outside one of the dowdy Broadway hotels in the Seventies, I could see that she was frightened, and she told me she always threw up before she went dancing.

"So do I! I throw up in the morning before work!" I cried, drawn to her by the coincidence. "I'm scared all the time that I'm going to paint something wrong and ruin Polacek's designs."

"Me," said Margery, "I only throw up before I go dancing. Grab those two chairs, quick! So we don't have to stand around if nobody asks us."

The hall was large and badly lit. On the far side stood a grim stag line backed against the wall, from which we saw a man suddenly part and drift like a falling star toward us across the dance floor. I looked at my feet. But it was Margery he was coming for, and as he led her away she turned and gave me a desperate shrug. She was a head taller than he—a splendid woman beside that ferret-faced runt hiding his sad back and narrow shoulders in a loose-hanging, jazzy jacket three sizes too big.

A man with a purple chin under a day's growth of beard took me by the wrist and swung me around as if I were a gate he was closing upon himself. With an absent look, he pursed his mouth as if he were about to whistle a little song, and hooked his chin like Alice's Duchess over my shoulder. We danced. I thought there ought to be conversation, and I told him that this was my first dance in America—that I had been brought up in England and had taught English in the Dominican Republic. I asked him what he did.

"Electrician," he said. I was trying to think up something more to say when the music stopped and he walked away.

Ferret-face brought Margery back and sat beside her, and they seemed to be talking animatedly. They danced the second dance together. The electrician reappeared and claimed me without a word, closing me upon himself. He was breathing hard, and his hardening body crowded me so that I pulled back, but I thought, That's what I oughtn't always to do, and I tried to soften myself in his arms. My partner noticed neither my withdrawal nor my attempt at surrender, but I seemed to have given satisfaction, for when the dance was over he said I was a peach and walked off clicking his tongue.

At the studio on Monday, Margery told me that her dancing partner had taken her home and got grabby in the subway. She said there was another dance uptown on Saturday—a much nicer crowd, attached to a temple—but when, the next Saturday, we met on the sidewalk outside the hall, we saw Ferret-face in the doorway, and out of the ground sprang the electrician, who yanked me around by the wrist, saying, "Peach! Where did you get to last Saturday? Peachy-peach."

I refused to dance with him a second time, which put it out of my power, as I said, quoting Jane Austen to Margery, to dance with anybody else.

"Why does it?" Margery asked. "Why can't you dance if some-one else asks you?" Margery said she was going to Grossinger's next summer. "I'm going to be twenty-nine next week!" she said.

"What's Grossinger's?" I asked.

On Christmas day, I had a phone call from a man who said he was Donald. I did not recognize either the name or the voice, which was thick as if he had a cold. The only man I could think of was the electrician, and I felt scared.

"What's your name?" he asked.

"How could you call me if you didn't know my name?" I asked.

"I just dialed," the man said. "It's Christmas and I'm a little drunk. Not drunk exactly. High. You don't have to tell my your name if you don't want. But would you talk to me a minute?"

"I suppose so," I said.

"You have a charming accent. You are not American?"

"I'm from Vienna," I said with a frightened sense that I was giving something away. "But I was brought up in England," I added.

"I'm a refugee, too," the man said. "From San Francisco. Would you allow me to call and talk with you once in a while? Say once every two weeks?"

"I think better not," I said. "But I wish you a happy Christmas. Good-by."

"Good-by," he said. "Carry on."

I was still listening when the receiver at the other end was placed in its cradle.

I had an image that year of a city made up of badly lighted single rooms like the one in which I imagined my drunk sitting by his telephone, like the bedroom in which my grandmother sat by her television during the long winter evenings; of innumerable ballrooms lined with men, their backs to the wall, and girls like Margery, who threw up before she went to meet them. These days, I threw up, not only before going to work in the mornings, but Saturday evenings when I was not going anywhere, and one day when I finally got a letter from England, and frequently for no reason at all.

With little Mrs. Shapiro I had a running argument. I tried to persuade her that she was not *basically* happy. "You just have moments, even hours, when you seem to *feel* happy." Mrs. Shapiro said she had thought about what I said, but she could not discover that she was basically miserable.

In May, I had a most enjoyable quarrel with Mr. Polacek and quit the studio for a new job, where I got sixty dollars a week.

In July, I met Claire. As the number five bus on which we were both riding uptown bent into Seventy-second Street toward the river, she turned to me and said she was an actress. She said she had just arrived from Rome, where they had wanted her to do the main part in *Bitter Rice,* but her cousin Vittorio de Sica had explained the advantage of her working in Hollywood and so she had come over. She had a suitcase beside her, and a mackintosh over her arm. She wore her hair like a little girl, open and shoulder length, and her face, without a trace of make-up, was nothing less than beautiful. "I'm originally English," she said, and I was very pleased, for I had feared I detected under the British accent a guttural Middle-European "r" very like my own.

I said, "I haven't spoken to a real English person in three years! I spent half my life in England."

"Come up to my digs. They must be around the corner here somewhere." As we walked to West End Avenue, Claire told me that a painter friend of hers had offered her his room. "We happened to get talking at the airport in Rome as he was taking off for Greece, and when he heard I was coming to New York he gave me his keys."

The room smelled of heat and rancid oil. It was bare, except for a refrigerator, a couch covered with scarlet terry cloth, on which Claire, despite a certain dumpiness, disposed herself with a heartbreaking grace, and a telephone, which she picked up. She asked to speak to Elia Kazan.

"Look in the freezer," she said to me, covering the mouthpiece. "He said there was some ice cream."

Elia Kazan was out, and Claire left her name and number. "You must meet him," she said. "I'm going to give a party as soon as I have a bit of money."

"Where did you meet Elia Kazan?" I asked.

"I haven't yet," Clair said. "I want him to get me a part in something so I can get enough money to go to Hollywood. Vittorio won't be there till the autumn."

The telephone rang. From Claire's end of the conversation, I understood the caller to be a friend of the room's owner. "In

Greece," Claire said. "He won't be back till September. But why
shouldn't you come and sleep here anyway. And maybe you could
pick up some food on the way? I've got a friend here, and we're
finishing the last of the ice cream. . . . I don't think he has any
money for a hotel room," she said when she had hung up. "And
anyway I believe in free love, don't you?"

"Oh, of course," I said, entranced by this free and world-wide
intercourse in keys and beds and food, in which, however, I could
not see myself included. I stood up.

"Where are you going? You might like him. Or maybe he knows
other men around town," Claire said, getting shamelessly to the
heart of my misery. "You have to go? Give me a ring."

It was on Saturday evening, quite three days before I had
figured I might properly call Claire and invite her to an English
tea, that she called to invite me to a party being given by two
Pakistani students on her floor. I might like them, she said.

"It's after nine," my grandmother said. She never asked me any
more where I was going. "I wonder when your mother will be
back?"

"Quarter past eleven, Omama. The same as always."

"You have your money? Keys?"

"Omama, I'm twenty-six years old. I've been getting out of the
house and back, all by myself, since I was ten."

"Wait till I am dead," she said. "I won't bother you much
longer," and she returned to her room and closed the door. After
that she never came to the door to see me off and check that I had
my necessities, and I remember that I missed it.

A very dark, very young man with eyes unnaturally long and
large, and long languid limbs, wearing a pink plastic apron, opened
the door and said that Claire was helping with the curry. He led me
through a room full of chatting young people into the kitchen,
which had a jungle temperature.

Claire was standing on the drainboard, peering into the top
shelf of the cupboard; her lovely head seemed to be floating just
below the ceiling behind a cloud of steam that was rising from
the sink. She said, "This is my friend Lore. She's English, too.

And this is Abdullah Shah." She pointed to a second man, less dark, less beautifully tall, and less young, who was stirring a pot. "These poor lads have no dishes. Tomorrow, Muhammad," she said to the young man who had let me in, "you and I go to Woolworth's," and so I knew that the beautiful young man was hers and that I had been invited to meet the other, who raised his eyes to look at me and said, "How are you?" in an accent straight from Oxford.

Later, when I was sitting on the floor with an Israeli student and his Hungarian girl, eating the furiously spiced curry and drawing air into my burning throat, Abdullah came with his plate and sat in a chair just behind me. He ate intently in silence, but I had a sense that he was listening, so I launched upon an eloquent indictment of the American textile industry. "It is totally commercial," I said. "This is the year of the 'conversation' print, with Roman theme. If the gladiators with the aqueduct in the background—aqua, pink, and black—sold last week, so this week everybody paints chariots with the Colosseum in the background, in pink, black, and aqua." Out of the corner of my eye, I saw Abdullah yawn, rise, and carry his plate into the kitchen.

But he returned presently, stood behind me, and said, "Let's go."

At the door, we were intercepted by a fat young Indian, who said, "Where are you going? We were supposed to talk business."

"Come with us then," Abdullah said without enthusiasm. "It's too hot in here."

"I wanted to tell you about those washing machines," the fat Indian said as we walked up Riverside Drive between the black trees and the night-populated benches. Couples were kissing in patches of darkness; an old man slept stretched out neatly; a student was reading a book under a street lamp. A middle-aged couple walking two little dogs passed by, the woman saying *"Grauslich heiss"* ("miserably hot") with an Austrian intonation strangely familiar to me as I walked between my two Orientals. The fat young Indian was saying, "There's a chap I know who has a friend who has one of these washing-machine places that nets him two hundred forty a week."

"That sounds good," said Abdullah.

"This chap must have money immediately. So he's letting it go cheap, for five thousand dollars—two thousand down."

We walked in silence.

"So what we need is three thousand dollars."

"Pink sky," Abdullah said, looking up.

"Pink-purple. That's one of the first things I noticed," I said excitedly.

Abdullah breathed deeply and said, "We must have put too much curry in that chicken."

The fat young man became genial. "Well, I'll be getting back to your party. I think we have something here. Think about it and call me."

"Right, I will. Good night."

"Spry for frying, Spry for baking," I said. "All those ghastly advertisements."

"That's what makes the charming purple sky," Abdullah said. He yawned and begged my pardon. "I can't remember when I slept the last time. Ever since I came to New York, I've been living this frustrating life—I work at the Voice of America all day without making any money; I give parties all night without making any friends. Every year I get another degree I don't want. I've got a B.A. in English from Oxford, and then I came over here and got an M.A. in Geology from Michigan, and here I am at Columbia taking a Ph.D. in Political Science—"

"All right, I'll ask! Why are you?"

"Because I'm in the U.S. on a student visa, and if I stop studying for half an hour they'll send me home."

"And would that be so very bad?"

"Terrible. I've been away for eleven years. I'm a westernized Oriental. If I talked to my people at home the way I'm talking to you, they wouldn't know what I meant. Then there's my family. Pakistani women are impossible."

"And American women?"

"They are very charming," Abdullah said, with the inward smile of a man looking back to many a tender history.

Abdullah telephoned the following evening to ask if he could come up after his last lecture.

"What, now he is coming up? At ten o'clock?" my grandmother asked. (She never got to approve of Abdullah and his strange hours.)

He came bringing a book he had to read for a term paper, already two weeks overdue, and asked me if I would make a précis of it for him. He knew what he was doing: the more work I invested in him, the more attached I became.

Claire had become a part of the Pakistani students' household, filling their shelves with crockery and their icebox with food that she cooked, and ate with them. Then "Elia" took her to dinner at Sardi's, where she met "Harold," who lived in Stratford and was immensely rich. 'He adores me, and his son-in-law is a V.I.P. in the Shakespeare company," she told us.

"And you think this Harold can do something for you?"

"At eighty-three? Precious little, poor sweetheart, as you can imagine, but I adore him and he's going to get me into the company next season. And I can live with him over the winter."

Claire packed her suitcase and took her mackintosh and borrowed traveling money from Abdullah—Muhammad was studying film making at the time and had no job—and we all took her to the Port Authority Terminal.

"What does your cousin think of the new plan?" I asked.

"What cousin? I don't have any relatives."

"I thought you said Vittorio de Sica . . ." I said, and blushed scarlet as a sudden sophistication tied into one neat answer the many loose ends of Claire's adventures.

"Vittorio de Sica!" Claire said. "He's in Hollywood." And she stared in surprise at the name I had pulled out of last week's dream when she was already in the full flow of today's. She kissed Muhammad and Abdullah and me, and, waving and weeping warm tears, she rolled out of my life as she had come into it, by bus.

About this time, I came to the conclusion that not only was American design terrible, but I was a terrible designer. My austere and fastidious eye watched my very own hand drip lines and figures of helpless vulgarity that were not even commercially successful because my interior quarrel kept me from developing an honest

professional touch. I gave up "originating" and began to perfect
myself in the skill of "repeating," the technical part of textile design. It means the reworking of the designer's painting in such a
way that its top will meet its bottom without a break when en-
graved on the rollers that print it onto the lengths of fabric. Though
I never became good enough not to be frightened of every new
design, I began to free-lance so that I could make room for a few
hours of writing.

In the fall, I enrolled in a course in creative writing at the New
School. The people sitting around the long table were none of them
particularly bright-looking, but in the course of the first class they
spoke with individual voices, and, as the term proceeded, turned
into persons. There was a couple called Herb and Louise, both
very tall and both blond, who sat side by side, looking not so much
at one another as out together, and they looked very kindly at me.
After a story of mine had been read, they asked me to have dinner
with them before class the following Thursday. We ate at a Mexican
restaurant in the Village, and I talked a great deal. I said, "Do
you know you are the first honest-to-goodness Americans I've ever
sat down to dinner with?"

Louise said she had come all the way to New York from a
small town in Indiana to avoid having to eat dinner every day
with honest-to-goodness Americans.

Herb, who came from the same town, said, "If Lore wants to
meet Americans, you should take her home to visit your family
next year."

"Oh, I wish you would. I'm serious. All I've ever met in New
York are Pakistanis, Indians, and Hungarians, and Israeli, German,
and Austrian Jews."

"Pakistanis, Indians, and Jews!" Herb and Louise said with
increased respect. "You must give a party and introduce us."

In class, before the instructor arrived, I paraded this interesting
inability I had discovered—the inability to penetrate America—
for the benefit of the oldest of the students, a middle-aged Negro
called Carter Bayoux, who dominated the class with his powerful
presence and silence. He invited me to dinner for the following

week, after class. "We will go to a jazz place and give you an introductory course in Americana. I'm a great teacher," Carter said.

He called the following day. "We made our date for next Thursday. We both forgot that it's Thanksgiving and there won't be any class."

"I didn't forget. I never knew."

"You won't be celebrating with your family?"

"We don't celebrate anything any more. No Christmas because we're Jewish, and no Jewish holidays because we were assimilated Austrians, and no Austrian holidays because we got thrown out for being Jewish, and we haven't acquired the American holidays yet."

There was a silence, and then Carter said, "And I don't have anybody to celebrate with, so you and I will put on the dog together."

"This lady and I are going to put on the dog because it's Thanksgiving," Carter Bayoux said to the waiter at the restaurant. "What will you have?"

"I didn't think we had a choice. I thought it was turkey?"

"You may have the turkey. I'll take *Tournedos de Boeuf*."

"I'll have that, too, whatever it is."

"Two *Tournedos de Boeuf,* and bring us a Chambertin '49," Carter said.

"Have you noticed that brutal poster of a red-faced turkey running in terror from a greedy-looking Puritan with a raised hatchet?" I asked Carter. "That's American Thanksgiving for you."

Carter was looking at me with very bright brown eyes opened so wide that the irises stood free of upper and lower lid. He seemed to be waiting for me to continue.

I said, "I've been too shy to tell you, but I did awfully like your story about the Negro journalist who marries the white psychiatrist. I thought it was quite powerful."

"And you also thought that because I'm a Negro and write bitter stories, you and I were going to sit here and make snide remarks about Thanksgiving together. I'm an American, you know. At any rate, there's nothing else I am," Carter said, keeping me

impaled on his bright stare and staying with me through the rise
of my blood to a full flush and its fading, so that we seemed to
come out together at the far end of my first lesson. "I may order
a French dinner and wine, but I do it affectionately and with a
bit of bravado, like an American. And I'm a sentimental about
Christmas and Thanksgiving, too, and if I celebrate by getting a
little drunk it's because I'm alone. I left the Negro world when I
married a white wife, but I never married the white world. And
then I divorced my wife."

"That's like a Pakistani friend of mine," I said. "He's lived in
America for eleven years and he's no longer an Oriental, and yet
he's not an Occidental, either."

"No," Carter said. "It's not like that at all. I have not, like
your friend, lost my culture, nor, like you, my country. My iso-
lation is peculiarly American. When you told me that you didn't
have any holidays to celebrate, I was moved for you."

I looked at him amazed. I had been boasting when I spoke of
our emancipation from public celebrations. Now, I was suddenly
moved myself. "It *is* rather sad. There's my mother working in
the bakery because it's one of their busiest nights, and my grandmother watching television of which she doesn't understand a
single word."

"Then we will take your grandmother some flowers," Carter
said.

"I'm afraid she'll only think they're an extravagance."

"But that's why we are taking them to her," Carter said.

I had my fears about my grandmother's reception of this large,
portly, elderly brown man, but she rose from her chair and took
Carter's bunch of yellow pompons, and made him a small bow of
politeness belonging to another style of manners. She even made
a try at conversation, pointing to the television and saying, "Liberace. *Spielt wunderbar.*"

Carter looked at me.

I said, "She listens to that horror every week. She says, heaven
help us, that he plays wonderfully."

Carter turned to my grandmother and said, "Beautiful, wonderful!" and played the air with his fingers, nodding his head up and down.

My grandmother had discovered someone she could talk to. "Liberace *ist ein nobler Mann*" [literally, a noble man—a gentleman]. "He is always polite—not like the young people who dance in the afternoon. I watch them, but they have bad manners," my grandmother told Carter in German.

Carter kept nodding and smiling. My grandmother nodded back with a bright, shy smile. After he had gone, she said he was a noble man.

The following week, I gave a party, pleased to find that I knew enough people in New York to fill my sitting room. My grandmother insisted on staying in the bedroom, but she had put on her best pewter-colored silk dress and looked out of her door every time the bell rang. When Carter arrived, she came and stood outside her door, making him a little smiling bow, but Carter seemed nervous and upset and walked straight into the room already full of people and voices and did not notice her.

When I was a child, I used to sit on the blue-on-blue carpet in our *Herrenzimmer* in Vienna, trying to catch the small hand on our mahogany clock in the act of moving from one hour to the next, and I never could. Once in a while, and always by accident, I have caught that visual click of time advancing. One day, I looked in the mirror and saw that though my nose was still long and sharp, it was newly accommodated by a softened cheek. The eyes behind my spectacles had lost their eager anxiety spelling hopelessness, thanks to Abdullah and to time. Simultaneously, I noticed my grandmother take a leap forward into old age. "It's just that she's been ill," I said to my mother, when I saw by the way she looked at my grandmother that she had noticed too. "You wait a week and she'll be just the same."

However, my grandmother remained visibly shrunken, with a new economy in all her motions. "Your mother is going to make the supper when she comes home," my grandmother said.

"Are you going to the Bronx?" I asked. Paul had had a second

son, called John. My grandmother said maybe next week she would
go.

"Then why have you got your silk dress on?"

"It's time for Liberace."

"So?"

"He always wears a tuxedo," my grandmother said, and turned
the knob and sat down facing the box and smiled as Liberace
appeared, playing himself his own theme song. The camera panned
onto that face cursed with a perpetual smile. With horror I saw
my grandmother lift her hand and wave delicately with her fingers.

"Omama, do you know where Liberace is? In California. Do
you know California is a thousand miles from New York?"

"But I can see him," my grandmother said.

"You've been to the movies, Omama. You've seen figures moving on a screen."

"But he is smiling at me," said my grandmother.

"He's smiling at the camera, Omama. Can't you imagine a man
standing in front of the camera and smiling into it?"

"Where is the camera?"

"Nowhere. In California."

"Come here, Lore! Stand behind me. You see, he is looking
right at me," and my grandmother smiled at Liberace and nodded
her head.

"Omama, do me a favor? Come over here just for a moment.
Please."

"I'm too tired."

"All right, I'll turn the television around. Look! How could
there be a man inside this box? Omama! Imagine a piano!"

My grandmother said, "Aren't you going out with Abdullah
tonight?"

"I haven't seen Abdullah in a year. Where's your *TV Guide?*
Here, 'Liberace.' Look—in parentheses it says 'film.' That means
he isn't even live in California. This program was filmed days
ago—maybe months."

In the following days, I noticed that my grandmother was not watching television. "Do you want me to turn it on, Omama? It's time for Liberace."

She raised her right hand and then threw it away. It didn't matter.

"Don't you like him any more?"

"He's on film," said my grandmother.

"Omama, would you like to go down to the triangle?"

"I don't want to get dressed. Maybe tomorrow," said my grandmother.

"Come on, Omama. You have to get out sometimes. Would you like to go and see Paul and the little boys? Do you want me to go with you? I'll get your silk dress for you. Come on, Omama."

My grandmother rose slowly. She said, "I'm going to die soon. What am I waiting for?"

"So am I going to die. So is everybody," I said, for I considered this a malicious line on my grandmother's part. If it was anything besides, I didn't want to know. And I noted how in the street she waited for the lights to turn green more carefully than I, who had my whole life to lose, and how cautiously she stepped off the sidewalk into the dangerous road.

We took a taxi. My grandmother said, "I've been thinking about God."

"What have you been thinking? Do you believe in God, Omama?"

"God . . ." said my grandmother, and was silent, and in a moment she threw him away with the downward wave of her right hand.

Paul was looking skinny and tired. Earlier that year, he had left his job as animal attendant at the research foundation and got one in the sales office of a numismatist, sorting coins. He was bad at the meticulous and uninteresting work, and got shouted at. At home were his two energetic little sons, aged four and three. Peter kept switching the television on and off and little John turned round and round. My grandmother, who could not understand a word of the children's English chatter, looked glad when it was time to go home.

When we left, Paul was sitting on a chair between the boys' beds. He was playing a toy mandolin from Macy's fifth floor and singing the children's song that he had translated and transplanted from the German for them:

> On the Hudson River
> Swims a crocodile,
> With his tail aquiver,
> On his face a smile.
>
> Do not use your gun.
> Do not spoil his fun.
> Catch him with a broomstick
> Baited with a bun.

From time to time he laid down the instrument and, with no can opener, pressed two triangular holes into a nonexistent beer can and out of the larger opening fetched himself great refreshing draughts of the imagination.

One evening, I brought home a new job and carried it straight to the drawing table, which was permanently set up in the sitting room. I unrolled the painting and studied the intricate blue and purple roses, of which I would have to forge a dozen more, with such nervous distaste that when I realized my grandmother had followed me in, I said, "Hi, Omama," without turning around, though I felt the strangeness of her standing there behind me. It was months since she had even come into the hall to meet me. Presently I knew that she had gone away. I followed her into the bedroom. She was sitting on the chair facing the silent television. "Did you make supper, Omama, or do you want me to make it? Mummy is going to be late."

"You make it," my grandmother said.

When I brought in the plates, my grandmother was sitting in the same position, and I said, "Omama, don't you want to turn your chair around? Omama?"

She put her right hand on the table edge as if to help herself up, but still she sat.

"Omama!"

My grandmother rose slowly, but remained standing.

"Turn around, Omama." I moved her chair for her, and she sat down on it. "Aren't you going to eat?"

She picked up her fork but did not raise it to her mouth.

"Don't you feel well, Omama?" I asked her.

My grandmother's right hand twitched, as if in memory of the old wave of rejection and resignation. I asked her if she would like to go to bed and she said she would. She leaned on my arm, moving so slowly across the room she seemed to be forgetting how to put one foot before the other. I took off her shoes, but she had not the strength to lift her legs onto the bed. I called my mother, and by the time she arrived my grandmother had lost her speech. My mother called the doctor.

My mother stayed home from work and nursed my grandmother. Her power of speech returned, but she seemed to find nothing worth the trouble of saying, nor anything to eat that tempted her to chew. Yet soon she was sitting up, and in another week she could stand, though she never regained more than the merest shuffle of a walk.

"You won't be able to stay home from work permanently," I said to my mother.

"I know," she said.

"Besides, it isn't right for you to spend all your life nursing sick people—Daddy, and Professor Schmeidig, and then Opapa, and now Omama . . ."

"I know," said my mother. Her face was flushed. The tears that dilated her eyes began to roll down her cheeks.

"Of course, I'm at home most of the time, but how would I go downtown to collect and deliver work? I mean, she can't be left even for a moment."

"No, no," said my mother. "You can't live like that. We will have to put her in an old-age home."

"Mummy, it won't be so bad," I said. "They have trained personnel, and there will be other old people. She'll never have to be alone again."

"That's right," said my mother, and all the time she was crying and crying.

Once a week, I went to visit my grandmother in the nursing home in a converted brownstone around the corner from Central Park West. My grandmother sat in a chair next to her bed. I sat next to my grandmother and studied the gray wallpaper with the green and yellow chrysanthemums and worm-like leaves, looking for the repeat.

"So? Warm enough for you?" said an obese Negro nurse to Mrs. Kelly, who sat, on an August dog day, in two sweaters with a coat wrapped about her legs, guarding the closed window. The nurse stuck the last spoonful of applesauce into the baby-pink face on the pillow in the bed next to my grandmother's and said, "Good as gold. Never any trouble out of her. Not like you, Mrs. Mankjewicz. Now you cover up—aren't you a terror!" the nurse said to Mrs. Mankjewicz, who was dying of diabetes, and tucked the sheet around her. "And how are you today?" the nurse asked, and stroked her hand over my grandmother's hair.

When she had turned her back, my grandmother made a face at her and said, "She doesn't understand a word I say. But the night nurse is German. America!" said my grandmother, looking all around the room until she came to Mrs. Mankjewicz, who had thrown her covers off again and was waving her two skinny stumps, amputated at the knee, in the air. "America is no good."

"Good-by, Omama," I said. "I have to meet a friend on Riverside Drive." And because my grandmother asked me no questions, I said, "His name is David."

"Come back soon," she said.

That corner of Seventy-fourth Street still has the power to move me to a dry sort of tears, like sinuses aching behind the eyes. I walked out of the nursing home with a gasp of joy into the city lying in the exhaustion of the late-afternoon heat. Behind me, lovely Central Park was green, and the young girl crossing at Columbus Avenue swung her meager shoulders and swished her gay skirt, printed with orange, black, and turquoise galleys. It had pyramids in the background, which hit me familiarly so that I followed her a block uptown to get a closer look—and yes, no hand but mine could have painted that awkward curl of the prow. It was a "conversation" print of the Egyptian period, which preceded the Roman era and placed the fabric squarely in my year at the Polacek studio.

I turned down Amsterdam Avenue, assailed suddenly by a complexity of misery in which I tasted the familiar ingredients of loneliness and shame and the beginnings of nausea, and, stopping for the light at the corner of Broadway, I looked inward, wondering what was the matter *now*. Out of the corner of my eye, I saw the marquee of the Hotel X and recalled intact the dimly lit dance hall, and myself softening experimentally in the arms of the sad and beastly electrician. New York is as full of my past as of my old textile designs walking about its streets; on Fifty-seventh Street, for instance, there is a car dealer of the same name as the editor who turned down my first story, and every time the Fifth Avenue bus carries me past his sign, I feel an embarrassment grown so faint by now I hardly bother to diagnose its cause. It is, I think, the way our histories become charged thus upon the air, the streets, the very houses of New York, that makes the alien into a citizen.

The traffic lights had changed, and I crossed Broadway. At West End Avenue, I caught the warm wind stirring from the river, and saw David waving from a bench under the heavy summer trees.

My grandmother died the night of her eighty-first birthday and was buried in a huge graveyard in New Jersey. My mother lives alone on 157th Street. David and I were married, and moved to an apartment in midtown. Like the little dog who turns and turns around himself to shape a place in the earth to fit his own proportions, I hunted the antique shops until I found our dining table —drop-leaf, eighteenth-century, and English. David said, "You don't think Queen Anne might be misplaced on West Seventy-second Street?" I said, "Yes, but, please, I need it." And so we made ourselves a home.

I keep looking around me: The war is still cold, and overseas;

no one of my people, this moment, is ill; every day there are hours when I can write, and we have our friends. My husband is Jewish too, but he was born in America and accepts without alarm this normal season of our lives; but I, now that I have children and am about the age my mother was when Hitler came, walk gingerly and in astonishment upon this island of my comforts, knowing that it is surrounded on all sides by calamity.